YESTERDAY'S PAPER

THE KNOCKNASHEE STORY - BOOK 2

JEAN GRAINGER

History, despite its wrenching pain, cannot be unlived, but if faced with courage, need not be lived again.

Maya Angelou

THE STORY SO FAR...

Ireland, 1938

In the Irish village of Knocknashee, nestled in County Kerry, Ireland, twenty-year-old Grace Fitzgerald gazes out at the vast Atlantic Ocean. Her delicate beauty belies the strength she's cultivated living with polio in a world that often overlooks those with disabilities. One fateful day, overwhelmed by frustration with her circumstances and her overbearing sister Agnes, Grace pens a heartfelt letter, seals it in a bottle, and casts it into the sea.

Across the ocean, on St. Simon's Island off the coast of Georgia, USA, Richard Lewis – heir to a prominent Savannah banking family – stumbles upon Grace's message in a bottle. Intrigued by the raw emotion and eloquence in the letter, Richard feels compelled to respond, initiating a correspondence that will change both their lives.

As letters traverse the Atlantic, Grace and Richard forge a deep connection, sharing thoughts and dreams they've never dared express to those around them. For Grace, Richard becomes a confidant, someone who sees beyond her physical limitations to the vibrant spirit within. For Richard, Grace represents understanding and encouragement as he grapples with his desire to break free from the expectations of his family's banking dynasty and pursue his passion for writing.

While their bond grows stronger, both Grace and Richard face challenges in their respective worlds. Grace makes a shocking discovery: her sister Agnes, entrusted with Grace's care since their parents' death, has been embezzling her money. The betrayal cuts deep, made worse by the revelation that the local parish priest is complicit in the deception.

Meanwhile, Richard's announcement that he intends to become a writer instead of a banker sends shockwaves through his family. His parents are aghast, unable to comprehend why he would forsake the secure and prestigious path laid out for him. Even Miranda, the woman everyone expects Richard to marry, fails to understand or support his dreams.

As war looms over Europe, Richard extends an invitation to Grace, offering her the chance to come to America for better medical treatment. Grace, seeing an opportunity for both healing and a chance to meet her kindred spirit, eagerly accepts. However, fate intervenes cruelly when Agnes suffers a stroke just before Grace is set to depart, forcing her to cancel her plans.

With conflict escalating in Europe and America's role in the war uncertain, Grace and Richard find themselves caught in a tangle of duty, desire, and global events beyond their control. Despite the growing obstacles, they cling to the hope of one day meeting, sustained by the understanding and acceptance they've found in each other's words.

CHAPTER 1

KNOCKNASHEE, CO KERRY, IRELAND

*J*anuary 1940
Grace Fitzgerald opened the gate that led from the schoolyard into her own garden and smiled to see several clusters of snowdrops poking their heads up through the frosty ground. She'd planted the bulbs last autumn, and the sight of them lifted her heart, though her right leg ached badly as she limped to the front door.

Her day spent teaching her class of four- to eight-year-olds had been great fun as usual but also exhausting, and she longed to set down her heavy basket of books and rest for five minutes in her kitchen with a cup of tea.

The morning had involved arithmetic and spelling, followed by another two chapters of *The Turf-Cutter's Donkey*, illustrated by Jack B. Yeats, brother of the famous poet; the older ones had taken turns to read aloud. Then after lunch, to everyone's delight, she got out the brand-new powder paints she'd bought yesterday from Mr Delaney, their travelling supplier.

It was wonderful to see the little boys and girls being creative, but hard work clearing up after them, especially on days like today when her leg hurt.

The children helped by washing their brushes under the outdoor tap, but forty-three pictures of donkeys and mountains needed to be pegged up to dry on a line strung across the classroom, and the floor had to be mopped because somehow the powder paint got everywhere, and the old newspapers she'd used to cover the tables had to be bundled up and burnt in the stove before the turf fire was tamped down.

Grace's work gave her no end of joy, but it was a lot to cope with at the same time. Especially as there were so many more children now. People who never came near Knocknashee National School before had started sending their sons and daughters, and while Grace loved to see them all bounce fearlessly in the door – and she welcomed each new child with a big smile and a lemon sherbet – it meant there were now eighty-two pupils to manage instead of sixty-five.

Thank God for Declan.

Grace had given him the eight- to twelve-year-olds to teach, keeping the younger ones herself. More and more children were staying past twelve now as well which was gratifying. It would have been easier for her to take the older children, as they were more manageable, and if she needed to deal with something in her role as headmistress – a worried parent or a school inspector – she could have left the class on their honour to behave and they would. But she did really love teaching the little ones the best, even though they couldn't be relied upon not to set the school on fire or get a pencil stuck up someone's nose if she turned her back for an instant.

Father Iggy was a great help to Declan too. He came in for an hour a day to do lessons with the weaker groups. There were boys and girls starting school for the first time in the older class who should have been reading and writing long ago but couldn't because their parents had refused to send them to Agnes.

Father Iggy had once confided to Grace that he would have loved to have been a teacher, but as the second son, the farm at home going to his older brother, he was bundled off to the seminary aged twelve. He spoke of his time in the seminary sometimes, and Grace felt sorry for him; it sounded like a lonely childhood. Even so, he made a lovely priest, and life was so much easier now that he'd taken over from Canon Rafferty as head of the school board.

No one was quite sure why the bishop had taken a notion to move the canon to some tiny parish up in County Tipperary, but rumour had it that Knocknashee's former priest had been caught with his hand in the collection plate. Whatever the truth of it, the whole place seemed to exhale when the news came through that the move was happening; everyone had had some kind of a run-in with him at one time or another.

Only two people were unhappy to see him go. One was Kit Gallagher, his sour housekeeper, who thought very highly of the canon and baked him no end of sweet cakes. And the other was Agnes.

Poor Agnes. When she heard the news of the canon's relocation, a long, sad trickle of tears leaked out of her drooping left eye and down her thin, lopsided face, and Grace couldn't help feeling sorry for her sister, even after everything that had happened. Poor, foolish, deluded Agnes, thinking Canon Rafferty was her friend. Since she'd had her devastating stroke last year at the age of thirty-three, the canon had not visited her once, and now he was gone without even saying goodbye.

Agnes was the reason Grace couldn't go straight down the hall to the kitchen and put the kettle on. Before she could relax with a cup of tea, she needed to pop into the front sitting room, which she'd converted into a bedroom for Agnes, and say good afternoon and share the news of her day. It was a ritual she liked to stick to even though she wasn't sure if her sister appreciated it.

As she opened the front door into the hall, Dymphna O'Connell came out of the sitting room carrying an untouched bowl of custard. Seeing Grace, the slight, careworn woman put her finger to her lips. 'She's asleep, Grace,' she whispered.

3

'And how was she today?' murmured Grace as the older woman closed the door softly behind her.

'She's hardly said two words since this morning, nor eaten more than a spoonful or two, though I made her some carrot soup for lunch with no lumps or a bit and normally she likes that.'

All of Agnes's food had to be mashed, as she couldn't swallow large pieces. Since the stroke, she'd existed on scrambled eggs, soup and custard. Her left hand was paralysed and her right hand very weak and shaky, so Dymphna or Grace had to spoon-feed her.

Dymphna O'Connell was yet another person Grace couldn't have done without.

When Teresa, Agnes's previous carer, had left to get married, Grace put a card up in the post office advertising the position of carer for Agnes. But the tyrannical reputation her sister had built up for herself in the village meant Grace was not exactly inundated with people desperate to replace Teresa. Despite the dire financial need of many in Knocknashee, they weren't *that* desperate.

But Dymphna, a widow with two small children, was badly in need of a job, and for Grace, she was a godsend.

'Now come on through to the kitchen, let you, and I'll make you a cuppa. I baked a few queen cakes this morning – they're in the tin,' added Dymphna as she carried the custard away down the hall.

It sounded like a blissful idea, but the poor woman looked even more worn out than usual.

'No, you get on home,' said Grace as she followed Dymphna to the kitchen, walking slowly because of the pain in her leg. Polio was like that. Sometimes she would hardly feel it; other times the ache was enough to bring tears to her eyes. 'I sent Paudie and Kate on before you with instructions they were to have their lessons finished by the time you get back.'

Dymphna smiled at the mention of her seven-year-old son and five-year-old daughter. 'And you know as well as I do, I'll go home to find them up on that new donkey of Bill Shannon's and not a copy-book opened,' she said softly as she set the tray on the counter.

'Probably,' Grace conceded with a chuckle. 'So you'd better go and get them off the donkey, and I'll bring that custard to Agnes when she wakes up.'

'Yerra, they'll be grand for half an hour. Let you sit down there, and I'll put the kettle on.'

'I can make tea for myself, Dymphna, honestly...'

'I know you can, but 'twon't take me a minute, and you look like if you don't sit down, you'll fall down, you poor *craythur.*'

'Well, if you're sure.' Grace sank onto her chair as Dymphna lit the gas under the kettle.

Progress was a wonderful thing. A Cornishman called Ritchie Gill had brought the idea for bottled gas back from America in 1934, and it was beginning to catch on in many rural areas of Ireland. Grace had felt guilty buying it, knowing it was an extravagance Agnes would never have allowed if she was in the fullness of her health, but it made Dymphna's life so much easier as well as her own.

The older woman made a pot of tea and opened the tin, offering Grace an iced bun, which she took. It was only as she bit into the soft sweetness that she remembered she'd not eaten since breakfast.

'These are delicious, Dymphna. Will you have a cuppa with me before you go?'

'I will so.' The other woman sank into the chair opposite to Grace, poured out two mugs and took a bun for herself. 'Tommy, God rest him, was a divil for cakes and sweets. He had a wicked sweet tooth altogether.' She sighed. 'He never got a treat in the orphanage, so he always said he had plenty of making up to do.'

'He married the right woman so,' said Grace. It was good that Dymphna spoke of Tommy. Most people would never mention his name again due to the circumstances of his death.

Dymphna nodded sadly. 'I hope so.'

The young widow was only thirty-seven, but the loss of her husband had carved deep lines of grief on her face. Her hair was grey at the temples, and her deep-set brown eyes were filled with sorrow. She was a soft person, kind and gentle, and when her beloved Tommy had walked into the sea one night, it had shattered her heart.

Nobody really knew what drove poor Tommy, a man who was

utterly devoted to his wife and children, to take his own life, but he did, and to heap more pain on the already distraught family, the canon hadn't allowed him to be buried in consecrated ground.

Tommy O'Connell was laid to rest in the *cillín*, an unofficial grave-yard that had served for centuries as the final resting place for unbaptised infants, new mothers who died before being churched, beggars, the mentally disabled, strange bodies washed up from shipwrecks – all manner of reasons the Church deemed the person unworthy of a Catholic burial.

Canon Rafferty had insisted it was beyond his authority, that the laws of the Church clearly stated those who were to be afforded an ecclesiastical funeral rite and those who were to be denied.

Tommy wasn't the first person to take his own life that Grace had heard of, but usually the family said it was an accident to avoid the scandal, and nobody would contradict it even if they knew it wasn't true. But poor Dymphna had no such option, because Tommy had left a note to say how much he loved her and his children and how sorry he was for all the trouble this would cause.

The poor man wasn't in his right mind obviously.

He'd been raised in an orphanage, being a foundling with no family, and maybe his childhood had eaten away at him, in the same way Declan McKenna still got dreadful flashbacks to his time in the reformatory at Letterfrack, after the canon took him and his baby sister away from their widowed father.

Grace took a refreshing sip of her tea. 'How are things, Dymphna?'

Dymphna responded with a wan smile, and the lines of tiredness and loss seemed to deepen. 'Not too bad. Better since I got this job – you were a lifesaver. I don't know what would have become of us if you hadn't given me this, really and truly I don't.'

Tommy had been a fisherman, like most of the men around, and he and Dymphna and the children had existed hand-to-mouth. Dymphna's family never approved of her husband. They owned a shop in Dingle, and the Tommy O'Connell out of the orphanage was beneath them to their way of thinking, so they cut Dymphna off when she married. When he died, her mother did come to Knocknashee, but because she spoke so unkindly of Tommy and was so critical of what he'd done, calling him selfish and useless, Dymphna put the run on her and so was entirely alone.

'Well, 'tisn't everyone could do it,' Grace said, glancing in the direction of the sitting room. Dymphna was so good-hearted and trying her very best. God knew Agnes had been next door to impossible with Teresa, but Grace was sure Agnes was being ten times more difficult with Dymphna due to the poor woman being Tommy's widow.

Yet as always, Dymphna was unfailingly considerate. 'Poor Mistress Fitzgerald got a right bad knockout with the turn she took, God love her. Sure which of us wouldn't be a bit out of sorts if it happened to us?'

This was one of the many reasons Grace thanked her lucky stars she'd hired this woman. Only a truly kind-hearted person like Dymphna could call the carry-on of her sister a 'bit out of sorts'. It wasn't as if Agnes had been an easy person to contend with before the stroke. Grace was fifteen years younger than her sister and could never remember her laughing or having fun.

She did, though, remember overhearing her parents discussing how Agnes had been such a happy, sunny child. 'Just like our Gracie,' Kathleen had sighed to her husband. 'And then she turned sixteen... Well, Eddie, I thought it was just the way girls can get at that age, moody and strange, and she'd grow out of it in a year or two, but she never did. I wish I knew why she's so angry and bitter.'

Her parents had been in the sitting room with the door ajar – they thought they were alone in the house – and nine-year-old Grace, who had slipped home to get her favourite toy, a rag doll called Nellie, knew she shouldn't be eavesdropping, even by acci-dent, and tip-toed upstairs. But not before she heard her father reply, 'I wonder, where did our Agnes go at all, Kathleen? Even doing a line with young Cyril Clifford doesn't seem to make her happy.'

Kathleen and Eddie Fitzgerald had both been very wise, caring people, and Grace tried to run the school now as they had, with kindness and a love of learning. But clearly even they had no idea why one of their daughters had turned out so miserable and cold.

Grace finished her tea and walked Dymphna to the door. 'Thank you for everything, Dymphna. I couldn't manage without you.'

'I'll see you after the weekend, Grace. Oh, and Charlie dropped this off for you.' She handed Grace an envelope that was perched on the hall table.

Grace felt a surge of happiness as she took it. It was a letter from Richard. The sight of the American stamps never failed to thrill her.

With a last word of farewell, she closed the front door after Dymphna, then slipped Richard's latest letter into her pocket. She longed to rip it open on the spot, but first she had to see if Agnes was awake. If she was, then Grace would try to get her to eat her custard and have a chat, then persuade her to do her exercises. After that she'd have her daily hot bath and do her own exercises, and then the copybooks needed to be marked. Finally, if Agnes was still awake, she'd read her another chapter of *The Last September* by Elizabeth Bowen or play her some music, and only then would she retire to her own room with a hot water bottle and a mug of cocoa, tuck herself up in bed and read Richard's letter.

Having his letter to look forward to would get her through the long evening.

She opened the door into the sitting room, which was in darkness. Every morning before leaving for school, Grace would open the heavy curtains so Agnes could watch the world go by – or as much of the world as ever passed through Knocknashee. But it clearly gave Grace's sister no pleasure, because she almost always ordered Dymphna to close them again.

Not that it mattered now; the sun was going down over the bay, the last of the daylight fading.

'Are you awake?' Grace whispered, and a small movement and a grunt came from the barely visible figure in the bed.

She lit the tilly lamp and moved closer. Agnes was thrown awkwardly against the pillows. Both Grace and Dymphna tried over and over to straighten her, make her more comfortable, but she always seemed to find this position. Despite all her sister had done to hurt her in the past, Grace hated this cruel existence for her; it was humiliating. 'How are you feeling, Agnes? Will you eat a little custard now?'

This time Agnes didn't even try to answer. The stroke had paralysed her left arm entirely, and she could no longer walk unaided. The left side of her face drooped, and when she spoke, her speech slurred a bit. It was hard to believe her once formidable sister, the scourge of Knocknashee, was reduced to this, lying here day after day, stuck inside a body that wouldn't do as it was bid, reliant on people for everything. Nobody deserved that fate.

'Well, I'll fetch it anyway, and we'll see.' Grace limped back to the kitchen and warmed the custard in a little milk pan on the gas stove before turning it into a clean bowl and adding a few drops of the herbal remedy Tilly O'Hare's mother, Mary, sent down every week to improve Agnes's appetite. Mrs O'Hare was often called on to tend the sick; many trusted her more than they did Dr Ryan. Mary was a Bean Feasa, a wise woman, a *seanchaí*, a storyteller and a font of all wisdom, but Agnes didn't like or trust her.

She never mentioned the remedy to Agnes. If her sister knew it came from Mary O'Hare, she'd think it was poison. Agnes didn't understand the concept of forgiveness. It would never strike her that people whose lives she had made a misery when she was a great power in the town might later turn around and be kind to her out of goodness and pity.

Grace returned to the sitting room, carrying the warm bowl, and set it on the bedside table next to the small brass bell she'd bought for Agnes to ring if she needed anything. She did her best to straighten Agnes against the pillows, then sat down in the chair beside the bed. 'Now I've brought you some nice custard that Dymphna made you earlier.'

Her older sister turned her face away, sliding a little down the pillows again. She could speak, albeit a bit slurred sometimes, but more often than not, she chose not to.

'But you have to eat, to keep your strength up. Dymphna says you only took two spoonfuls of the carrot soup she made you for lunch?'

Agnes grunted, a sour little sound.

'Well, she thought you would like it. Oh, and she baked some lovely queen cakes just now. What if I crumbled one into this custard for you to make it sweeter?'

This time Agnes remained silent. Grace decided to take that as a yes and returned to the kitchen for the cake. When she crumbled it into the custard and stirred it around, Agnes finally opened her mouth. Grace spooned in a little bit, then gave her sister time to hold it in her mouth before slowly swallowing.

As she waited until Agnes was ready for the next mouthful, she talked about her day. 'The children painted some lovely pictures this afternoon. I was reading them *The Turf-Cutter's Donkey* and they love it, so there were lots of donkeys and mountains and families having tea on the bog...'

Agnes, who had never allowed art lessons because of the mess, grimaced and choked slightly on the cake crumbs. A glass of water sat beside the bed, covered with a linen cloth, and Grace uncovered it and held it to Agnes's lips so she could take a sip to help swallow.

'Declan was teaching weights and measures today,' she continued. 'He lifted over the weighing scales from the post office, and the children really enjoyed guessing weights of different things – a rock, a pot of jam, a book – and then using the scales to see how close they were. The children really love him. He was wasted as a junior postman. Not that there's anything wrong with being a postman, but he's a natural-born teacher.'

Grace was very proud of Declan. After all those awful years in borstal, for him then to come home and turn his life around had been a huge achievement.

'He's not suitable,' was all Agnes had to say as she pulled a sour face.

'Ah, Agnes, I know you weren't keen at the start, but if you saw how well the children are doing with Declan, you'd have to admit he is doing a great job. Now, another mouthful?'

Grace did keep a few small secrets from her sister, like Mary O'Hare's remedy and the letters from America, but most things she was open about, even if she knew Agnes wouldn't approve. Like buying the gas stove, and Declan teaching the older children, and the art lessons. And the canon having been sent to Tipperary. Keeping her sister in the dark about everything felt too much like lying; it didn't seem right. And supposing Agnes one day had a change of heart and asked for Father Iggy, or anyone at all, to come in and see her and she found things in Knocknashee had changed entirely and she'd never been told?

'Now Dr Ryan is coming tomorrow to check you over,' Grace continued after Agnes refused to eat any more. She'd eaten most of the bowl, though, so Mrs O'Hare's remedy must have worked. 'He wasn't happy with your progress last time, so why don't I help you with the exercises he prescribed you? Or maybe we could give you a hot bath and then I could show you the different exercises I use for my leg? If they can work for me, maybe they could work for you. It's amazing how much better my leg is now.'

It wasn't the first time she'd offered to do this for Agnes, it was more like the hundredth time, but as usual Agnes turned her face away, ignoring both suggestions completely.

'Well, what about this. I think maybe I've saved up enough money to buy a wheelchair for you, and I could push you around Knocknashee to get a little fresh air?'

A long time ago, Dr Warrington, the kindly polio consultant who had looked after her during her long four years in a Cork hospital, had gifted Grace a wheelchair. But Agnes had immediately consigned it to the spare room, saying it would make her little sister lazy, and later, after throwing Grace out of the house, she'd burnt it, along with Grace's old rag doll Nellie and all their parents' possessions and letters. It was a shocking act of viciousness, and Grace still didn't understand how Agnes was capable of such irrational rage. All that was left of Nellie were the two blue glass buttons she'd had for eyes. Grace kept them in an old matchbox in her bedside drawer upstairs.

'Don't you think that would be nice, Agnes? I could push you down to the beach one day, and you could see the sea? I'm a good swimmer now. It's wonderful if your body doesn't work so well – it makes you feel like a normal person almost because you can float. That's how Tilly taught me. She held me until I learnt how to float. All you have to do is face the sky and let your head fall back. Me and Tilly could both help you? It's a lovely feeling...'

'Go away, Grace,' said Agnes wearily. 'Just. Go.'

So Grace gave up and went to run her daily bath.

CHAPTER 2

The little whitewashed bath house that Declan had built for her was an oasis of calm and peace. Apart from the fact that the hot bath gave her respite for her leg, it was her sanctuary, especially on days when she'd spent a lot of time on her feet. Today was one of those, and she'd been kept going by the thought of sinking into the deep water, which was heated by the contraption Declan had made – a copper tank with a combustion chamber, wrapped in sheep's wool to keep it from cooling too fast.

After leaving the steaming water to run – it took a good half hour to fill the enormous bathtub, which was once a cattle trough – she went back into the house and painfully climbed the stairs to her bedroom, one at a time.

There were four rooms upstairs. The largest one at the front of the house was vacant now that Agnes, who had taken it over when their parents died, had gone downstairs. Their brother's room was also empty except for the neatly made bed, because Father Maurice had not been home since Grace was a child. Two years older than Agnes, he was a priest and on the missions in the Philippines, and even when Grace had written to him about Agnes's stroke, all she'd got was a

Mass card in return and a few lines to say he was praying for her and her sister.

The third was the room where her wheelchair and all her parents' belongings had been stored until Agnes burnt everything in a fit of rage after Grace refused to hand over any more of her wages.

The fourth bedroom belonged to Grace, and even though it was the smallest, she still preferred it. The bed was the same one that she'd had as a child, but at four foot eleven, she didn't need a larger one. It was covered with a bedspread that she'd crocheted in all different colours, using wool unravelled from old jumpers. The red rug that brightened the dark wood floor had come from her *mamó's* house, Daddy's mother. Nellie, her precious rag doll, was gone, burnt to ashes by Agnes, but her mother's watercolour landscapes were still on the walls. As a teacher, Kathleen Fitzgerald had regarded art at least as important as arithmetic.

There was a fireplace in her room, but lighting it would take too long. Shivering in the cold air leaking through the old wooden window frame, Grace took off her good 'headmistress' clothes – a long black skirt and white blouse, brightened by a lavender cardigan from Peggy Donnelly's drapers, her favourite colour – and folded them on the bed; she would wash and dry them over the weekend. Then she changed into a soft crimson dressing gown and tartan slippers, presents sent to her at Christmas by Lizzie and her husband, Dr Hugh Warrington, which had accompanied their usual invitation to come and stay. She would love to go if she could leave Agnes overnight, but Dymphna had children to look after and Agnes would make anyone else's life even more of a misery.

Downstairs in the bath house, the tub was filled as high as it could go, and as she climbed in, some spilled on the wooden floor. A divine scent enveloped her. She had added one of the bath salts Richard had sent over for her at Christmas. She didn't use one every time, as she was trying to make them last, but she felt she deserved one today. The scent was something called sandalwood and pine, and she closed her eyes as she inhaled and allowed the warmth of the water to permeate her cold body. She knew she felt the chill even more than other

14

people; Dr Warrington said it was common for polio survivors because of poor circulation in their damaged limbs.

As she lay there, she thought dreamily about her plans for the school. Declan worked so hard, but he was only getting a teaching assistant's wage, which she knew from her own experience was very little. It was topped up by a few pounds from parish funds, thanks to Father Iggy, but he deserved more and she needed to talk to the Department of Education about that. If she could earn a head-mistress's salary without a diploma in education, then surely Declan deserved to be paid a bit better too. Besides, he was twenty-one now, and if he decided to get married, he would need a decent salary to keep his wife and children.

Not that Declan showed any sign of courting. He was very shy outside of the classroom. He was such a good-looking young man, though, slender and tall, with a strong jaw and long-lashed indigo-blue eyes under arched eyebrows. He wore his silky dark hair longer than most men, and it gave him a slightly raffish look. He'd confided in Grace how much he hated having his head shaved at school every two months, winter and summer, and swore that when he was older, he'd let his hair grow, and he was sticking to it.

Anyway, it suited him. Half the unmarried girls in the village were after setting their cap at him, and one was bound to catch his eye eventually. Probably Sally O'Sullivan, a tall, graceful beauty who turned heads when she went up to receive at Mass, or else maybe Teresa's cousin Maura Keohane, who was so light on her feet, she could dance like a butterfly.

Grace pulled her mind back to thinking about the school.

She had plans for a monitor as well, an older student who could help her teach the youngest ones and keep order on the playground. There was a girl in the senior class, Janie O'Shea, and she was bright as a button. There was no way her parents could afford for her to go past the primary school, but if Grace could get her a position as a monitor, she would receive an annual gratuity from the state that could be a small wage for the girl, and she would be a tremendous help. She was fourteen, and the law stated she needed to be fifteen to

15

be a monitor. But her birthday was in June, so she would be fifteen by September, so she could start then. Her mother would jump at the idea, Grace knew; Mrs O'Shea wanted a better life than she'd had for her daughters. Mr O'Shea might be a harder hurdle to get around, as he'd probably want Janie for the farm till she married. What a waste of a fine brain that would be, to relegate the girl to milking cows and feeding hens until some dull young farmer came courting and took her away with him to milk *his* cows and feed *his* hens.

She would love to save Janie from such a fate. And with all the extra pupils in the school, the more teachers she had, the better. If she could get Janie to start off the infants, and if Father Iggy could continue to manage an hour a day with the older children who needed extra help, she would be able to achieve so much more. And if the numbers continued to rise, then they might be cleared to hire another teacher.

Grace felt the hand of her father on her shoulder as she made her plans. Like her mother, he was a huge believer in education setting people free. The law said children up to the age of fourteen must attend school at least seventy days per year, but rural areas such as theirs were exempt, as the children were needed on farms. As headmaster, he'd had to rely on his powers of persuasion to get them in the door, and he'd been successful for the most part. But after Eddie and Kathleen Fitzgerald drowned and Agnes took over the school, suddenly children were needed on the farms again. If her parents were looking down from heaven now, Grace hoped they were delighted to see those numbers reversed...though they must be very sad to see Agnes brought so low.

The water was beginning to cool, and she had to do her exercises yet. The Warringtons had shown her how to use heat to soften the muscles of her leg, followed by special stretches to help the limb start moving again. The treatment had been devised by an Australian nurse called Sister Kenny, and while the medical profession was still suspicious of it – the official policy was to immobilise the affected limb – it helped Grace a lot. Her right leg still ached, but it was far more flexible and strong than ever before. She really must persuade Agnes to try it; she was sure it would help her sister's paralysed left arm and leg.

She got out of the deep bath and did her stretches by the light of the tilly lamp she'd brought with her. Tilly had bought her a rubber mat to put in the bottom of the bath to make sure she didn't slip, which was invaluable. She wrapped herself again in her dressing gown, took the lamp and stepped out into the yard, shivering in the bitter January cold after the steamy warmth of the bath house. She walked back through the kitchen and up to her room. She had no steel on, so progress was slow, but her leg still felt easier than before.

In her bedroom she opened the wardrobe and took out her favourite old dress for warmth and a hand-knit jumper. She had a very thick pair of stockings too. They had been darned so many times, she couldn't wear them to school, but now she pulled them on, over her good leg first and then over the bad one, and then slipped her feet back into the tartan slippers.

Looking in the mirror on the inside of the wardrobe door, she had to laugh.

Like the bedspread, she had knit the jumper herself from wool ripped from other garments, so it had one brown sleeve, one dark red, a green and blue–striped front and a yellow and red and green–striped back. The dress was one Lizzie gave to her the last time she was there; the doctor's wife had grown too fat for it. But Lizzie was much taller than Grace, so it hung nearly to her ankles. The grey woollen stockings and the brown tartan slippers completed the scarecrow look.

Grace didn't care, though. She was warm and comfortable, and sure, who'd be looking at her?

Her thick auburn hair was mad curly, just like her daddy's, and sometimes she thought she looked like one of those china dolls, with her upturned nose, the exaggerated curve of her lips and huge green eyes flecked with gold that caught the light.

'I'm right quare looking,' she often told herself. Agnes could no longer bully her physically, but her sister's constant refrain that no one would ever want to marry a cripple had sunk deep into her heart.

That had been her sister's excuse for taking all of Grace's wages – that she was saving the money in the post office for Grace's future, when Grace would be alone and would need to pay someone to mind her. Of course, the money went into the canon's belly and not her savings fund, but she tried not to dwell on that.

She'd come to accept her husbandless, childless fate. Sure, didn't she have all the children she could ever want in the students of Knocknashee?

Hugh and Lizzie Warrington had no children of their own either, and they too dedicated their lives to the care of other people's children. Like her, maybe if the couple had a family of their own to mind, they wouldn't be able to do such a good job of helping others. Perhaps God had made things this way for a reason.

Before closing the wardrobe door, she ran her hand across a row of several lovely light summer dresses she'd never worn. These were the ones that Lizzie had insisted she buy before her trip to America, the trip that never happened.

Imagine, she thought, *if I'd have been able to go to America...*

She stopped. Thinking this way was pointless. The trip didn't happen and it never would now; that was the reality, and she had to accept it.

America was not to be for her, any more than marriage or children of her own.

Now when she bathed every evening, using her toes to top up the water, she sometimes tried to imagine what it would be like to languish in the warm water of the hot springs in Georgia in the United States. She wondered if President Roosevelt still went there. Probably not. He had more on his mind these days than his bad legs. War, war, war – it was all anyone could talk about, she thought with a sigh.

Closing the door on all those pretty dresses, she slipped out of her childhood bedroom and made her way back down to the kitchen.

Dymphna had left two plates under a cloth on the side, one for Grace, with potatoes, carrots and a baked pork chop with apple sauce ready to heat up, and another for Agnes, the vegetables mashed with milk and butter and the pork finely minced into the smooth stewed apple.

Grace warmed her own plate over a saucepan of boiling water on the stove, covered with the lid, and heated Agnes's portion in the milk pan. Then she put their two dinners on a tray, upturning a bowl over Agnes's plate to keep it warm.

The temperature outside the house must have dropped, as even moving a few feet from the kitchen range made her shiver. She carried the tray down the arctic hallway and opened the door to the sitting room. In there it was toasty, and she quickly closed the door behind her with her elbow to keep the heat in.

A fire burned steadily in the grate. Coal was very hard to come by now that this war had started, so they only used turf, but this year's store was good and black and dry, so it burnt hot without too much smoke. The house faced the ocean, so the wind was relentless, but this room was cosy, especially with the stuffed patchwork draught excluder that lay along the foot of the door, keeping out the cold air from the hall.

Last term Grace had used the arts and crafts lesson to show her older boys and girls how to make draught excluders, using a big bag of remnants Peggy Donnelly had given her from the drapery shop. The children filled the long fabric 'sausages', as they called them, with sand from the beach that Grace had dried out in the kitchen range at home, and stitched on eyes from a big tin of old buttons donated by Tilly's mam – she'd been collecting them for years – and even some long forked tongues made from old trimmings of leather that Pádraig O Sé, the cobbler, had given her in an unprecedented act of generosity. The end result was a very funny collection of multicoloured snakes.

Her students had given them as Christmas presents to their parents, who were delighted their children had made something so clever and useful – draughts were a big part of life in Knocknashee – and she'd taken home the one she'd made herself to keep the sitting room warm. Agnes had rolled her eyes. She didn't approve of snakes, no more than St Patrick, who had driven them all out of Ireland fifteen hundred years ago.

'Are you hungry, Agnes?' Grace asked now, bringing the tray over to the bedside table.

In the bed, her sister was glassy eyed, leaning to one side again.

'Let's get you upright for your dinner.'

She readjusted Agnes on the pillow to make her more comfortable – her sister, always thin, weighed next to nothing now – and laid a white napkin on her flat chest as a sort of bib.

'Agnes? Will you have a bit of mashed potato and carrot? And pork minced very fine with apple?'

'Sounds disgusting,' Agnes said.

'Will you not even try a little? I've brought in mine, so we can eat together, like we used to do in the kitchen, remember? Just you and me together?'

Agnes made a sound, but it wasn't anything recognisable as a word, more an expression of disgust. And Grace had to admit, her sister was right – there was nothing good about those times to look back on. There'd been no chatter and laughter, none of the usual companiable stuff between sisters. Agnes had been as miserable and bitter then as she was now. The happy, sunny child their parents remembered had disappeared years ago, when Grace was still a baby.

'Don't you think you should eat, Agnes?' Grace asked, but her sister made no response. The more annoyed Agnes was, the less she bothered to speak.

'Well, maybe you're not hungry right now. I'm just going to bring my own dinner over to sit beside the fire, and I'll ask you again in a while. You just rest now.' She took the napkin away, straightened the patchwork quilt and gave her sister's limp left hand a gentle squeeze. Agnes had never encouraged any physical affection, but since the stroke, Grace had taken to giving her an odd touch. And though Agnes couldn't squeeze back, she didn't glare at Grace or withdraw her hand, so maybe she was getting used to it.

Grace hoped she might even like it. Life would be so much easier for them both if her sister would soften towards her, though how much time there was left for that to happen was anyone's guess.

Dr Ryan, the local GP, had said that Agnes's condition would deteriorate if she made no effort to eat or move. Any chance of a full recovery from a stroke was more or less gone in the days afterwards. It was possible to get some movement back, but only if you were prepared to put in the effort, like Grace did with her leg. He also didn't rule out another stroke; apparently it was common for people to have more than one. On the other hand, he said he knew of people who had one stroke and who lingered for years. It was impossible to know.

Leaving Agnes's plate on the bedside table, still covered by the upturned bowl, Grace carried her own over to beside the fire, where she placed it on the side of the stone hearth while she threw another sod of turf into the grate. When she'd run the house, Agnes hardly ever lit a fire, but Grace knew her sister needed warmth, and it was good for her own leg as well. She still couldn't believe Agnes had preferred to spend her stolen wages on pampering the canon rather than on heating their own house.

There was a big old armchair by the hearth, a bit battered but so large and comfortable, Grace could curl up in it comfortably, even with her bad leg. It came from the Warringtons' house in Cork. Hugh and Lizzie had seen how much she loved it, and one day last October, they'd arrived with it in their car. She sat down in it now with the tray on her lap. It was so cosy here by the fire. It reminded her of when her parents were alive, when the sitting room was properly lived in, a bit messy but warm and welcoming.

After Eddie and Kathleen Fitzgerald died, Agnes turned this room into a cold, impersonal place. Now it was brighter and softer again, with rugs Grace had crocheted herself and quilted cushions on the chairs and sofa that she'd stuffed with goose down. The dust covers had been taken off the piano and gramophone, and later, if Agnes was too tired to concentrate on listening to a chapter of *The Last September*, she'd play some music. Something light.

Her sister used to favour hymns or nothing at all, but since the canon left Knocknashee without a word of goodbye, she'd twist up the one side of her mouth that worked if she heard anything religious. So maybe an Irish air on the piano, like 'The Mullingar Races' or something else that was popular. Or she could play the gramophone record Richard had sent her for Christmas, which had arrived in a flat wooden box, wrapped up in a huge amount of brown paper and string.

The song on the record was 'Over the Rainbow', sung by a girl called Judy Garland, who Richard said in his Christmas card was still only seventeen. Listening to it reminded Grace of being that age herself, and longing for a better, different life. She'd been seventeen when she threw an old bottle into the ocean containing a message to St Jude. And months later, like an answer to her prayers, Richard had written back from the far side of the Atlantic.

Agnes had been very suspicious about who sent the record, and Grace, put on the spot, told a panicky lie, that it came from Tilly, who had bought it from a travelling salesman in Dingle with the money she'd made from selling turkeys. Well, the bit about the turkeys was true. Grace's best friend, Tilly, managed her widowed mother's farm, a few acres on a stony hillside overlooking Knocknashee. She kept bees for honey and hens for eggs, and tended one cow and a flock of mountainy sheep, and last autumn she'd bought a load of turkey chicks and fattened them up for Christmas.

Grace felt terrible for involving Tilly in her lie. 'I'm so sorry. I was so pleased to get it, I unwrapped it and put it on Mammy's old gramophone straight away, and of course Agnes wanted to know where it was from, and I couldn't think what to say. I know I should tell her about Richard but...'

'Grace, you don't owe your lying, thieving sister anything,' said Tilly firmly. They'd met at Bríd Butler's sweetshop in the town and were walking up main street sharing a paper bag of warm toffee while catching up on each other's news. 'And you can tell her anything you like about me. She hates me enough as it is, so you can tell her I've sprouted horns for all I care. In fact, do tell her that. I'm sure she'll believe you, and I'm dying to know what she'll say.'

Tilly still hadn't forgiven Agnes for all the years she'd treated Grace so badly.

But Judy Garland wouldn't sing tonight, because by the time Grace had eaten her baked pork chop with apple sauce, Agnes was fast asleep.

Deciding not to wake her, Grace brought both plates back to the kitchen, washing hers and leaving Agnes's covered in the freezing-cold larder. She picked up the basket of copybooks from the corner where she'd left it, went back to the sitting room and took her seat in the armchair by the turf fire again, where she corrected sums and spellings and wrote encouraging notes by the children's little stories.

Last November, after being headmistress since September, she'd jokingly told Richard that her hand ached from all the correcting of books on top of the other things she had to do, and he'd sent her an inkpad and a rubber stamp that said 'Good Work!' and another of some smiling little creature, a beaver according to Richard, with its thumb up. He'd explained it was a gesture to say 'all is good', and the children especially loved seeing that on their work. There seemed to be nothing that wasn't available in America.

As the fire died down to a soft, comfortable glow, she stamped and stamped and left nice comments to encourage her pupils, all the while looking forward to reading Richard's latest letter.

Outside in the street, everything was quiet, no raised voices from those coming home from O'Connor's pub, everyone staying in by their fires, driven in by the unusual cold. The sea normally kept the town above the freezing point, but not tonight. January was usually a time of frugality anyway, after the expense of Christmas.

In the stillness of the room, Agnes's slow rhythmic breathing, sometimes a bit ragged, was the only sound that kept her company.

At last Grace placed her pen down, rose from the armchair and crossed again to the bed. Still her sister slept, her mouth slack, her thin frame barely registering on the mattress. Agnes had always been 'careful with her figure', for some reason never wanting to fill out into womanhood from her angular teenage self. But now the stroke had ravaged her to the point of emaciation. Her pale hair fanned out on the pillow, and Grace straightened a strand of it and thought how it was a pity Agnes had never let it hang loose before the stroke. Her sister could have been as pretty as their mother. But the old Agnes had never allowed anyone to see her with her hair unpinned, and the only person she'd ever smiled at was the canon.

Leaving her, Grace stood and opened the heavy curtains a little. The cooler air behind the curtains was unpleasant, but she needed to see out, beyond this room, this village.

The night was still, no breeze off the inky-black sea. There had been a storm for the last two days that had blown itself out. The trees were bare; whatever few leaves had lingered through December had been ripped off by the recent wind. The frost would fall later, and Grace suspected the place would be sparkling white in the morning.

A few dim lights shone from some of the houses. Nobody had electricity, but paraffin tilly lamps and gas lamps were common. Killarney got electricity last year, and several of the other big towns had it too, but as Charlie said, it might not be a good idea to hold your breath waiting for the Rural Electrification Scheme to come to Knocknashee.

She had never thought it was much use herself till she went to stay with the Warringtons in Cork, and they had it in their house. Being able to just flick on a light switch and flick it off again when you were finished was amazing.

She looked back to the bed. It seemed like Agnes was going to sleep the night.

After banking down the fire, she limped out of the room and into the kitchen. There she filled a stoneware hot water bottle from the kettle on the range and made herself a cup of hot cocoa, then carried them, one step at a time, up the icy staircase into her room. By the light of the moon pouring through a gap in her curtains, she pushed the hot water bottle between the freezing sheets and set the mug of cocoa down on the little table beside the bed. Then she lit the tilly lamp and changed her dress for a thick flannel nightie and bed socks, put her colourful jumper back on again, fetched Richard's letter from where she'd left it on the dresser and got in under the heavy feather eiderdown.

The tip of her nose still tingled with cold, but her heart filled with warmth as she finally slit the envelope.

CHAPTER 3

*D*ear Grace...
> Grace smiled to herself, snuggling down against her down-filled pillows, stuffed with feathers from the few geese Tilly kept for a while before deciding they were too much, always fighting and arguing and breaking into the vegetable garden and eating the cabbages. Hens and turkeys were a lot less trouble.

Dear Grace...

Again she lingered over those first two words. It gave her such pleasure, the way she and Richard had finally dispensed with calling each other 'Miss Fitzgerald' and 'Mr Lewis'. It was Richard who had suggested it; she wouldn't have dared.

What a day. I've just come back from the wedding of the century, where 237 (but who's counting? My mother was, actually...) of the richest people in Savannah, Georgia, turned out to witness my former intended, Miranda Logan, getting married to my sister's ex-fiancé, Algernon Smythe.

"All the right sort of people" were there—that's another direct quote from my mother. She hissed at my father through clenched teeth all through the ceremony while glaring daggers at Sarah and myself. Our whole family was stuck at the same table for the reception, which made things horribly awkward. Father sat staring moodily at his plate, not helping at all; he hates

weddings. Nathan did his best to keep the conversation going. Our older brother is good at that sort of thing—bedside manner and all that. And his wife, Rebecca, did her best too. My sister-in-law is sweet, and to make conversation more than anything, she was just talking about how exhausting it was to look after children and she was glad of the break, while our own mother nodded, as if she knew anything about it. Rebecca and Nathan's two delightful little girls were in Detroit with their nanny; it was the first time they've ever left them. Our parents, on the other hand, were never there. Nathan and Sarah and I got all our affection from Esme.

Esme was the coloured housekeeper who had raised all the Lewis children. Richard always spoke of her with real love and affection, far more than he did of his actual parents.

Of course, Algernon and Miranda are both from long lines of "the right sort of people," which is what makes poor Mother so furious that Sarah and I let them slip through our fingers. You'd think it would be enough for her that Father owns his own bank, but there's no end to her desire to climb to the very pinnacle of Savannah society. As far as Caroline Lewis is concerned, there's nowhere in the world more important, not Washington or New York or anywhere. In fact, especially not Washington or New York! My parents despise the Yankees. Bad enough Nathan lives in Detroit and is a doctor instead of a banker. Just as well he married a Southern belle, or they wouldn't be talking to him either, any more than they are to Sarah and me. I'm the worst son in the world for deciding to be a writer instead of going into Father's bank, and Sarah's not far behind for turning down Algy's offer of marriage. People like my parents do not understand doing anything but the exact same thing as the generation before. If they knew Sarah was dating Jacob Nunez, well, I don't know what they'd do. Mother would probably faint on the spot.

Smiling, Grace paused to take a sip of her delicious cocoa. She knew Jacob Nunez was the exact opposite of what Richard's parents would want in a son-in-law. He was a newspaper photographer, which she thought sounded very glamorous but apparently was disreputable if you were Mr and Mrs Lewis. He also supported Roosevelt's New Deal, which was very, very disreputable, and on top of everything else, he was a Jew, which made him so disreputable that the word 'disreputable' didn't even begin to cover it. Richard had been against the relationship at first, but he'd come to like Jacob a lot, and they'd even started working on news features together, with Jacob taking the pictures and Richard writing the articles. Their first, about the American Coast Guard, was published in the *Capital,* an important New York paper, and several others had made it into the *Savannah Morning News,* which didn't pay so well, but still, it was something. Not that Richard needed money anyway, unlike Jacob. Even though Richard's parents had cut off his allowance, he still had a trust fund from his grandmother. The wealthy old lady had also left her three grandchildren a beautiful 'summer cottage' on St Simons Island off the Georgia coast. It made Grace laugh that Richard referred to it as a summer cottage. She'd seen a photo, and it was in fact a huge solid house, bigger even than Dr Ryan's large Victorian place just outside Knocknashee.

Sometimes she thought her American pen friend really did live in that magical land 'somewhere over the rainbow', even if he didn't know it.

Grace went back to reading.

Theobald and Arabella Logan are enchanted with their new son-in-law. Mama Logan was determined to make a match for her daughter that would elevate the whole family and ensure her daughter is kept in furs and pearls for the rest of her days, and she's certainly succeeded with Algernon Smythe.

And Algy's parents looked delighted with themselves all day, like they couldn't believe their luck. The Smythes are fabulously wealthy, but they are not a good-looking family. Algernon in particular has a face like a fish, so— as Sarah murmured in my ear—the injection of the fine features of Miranda into the breeding pool of the Smythes can only be a good thing for the future grandchildren. Miranda has brains as well, and a good sense of humor when she's in the mood—two more qualities that Algy severely lacks. To be honest, I don't know how Miranda's going to stand being married to him, but hopefully she'll think it's worth it for the pearls and furs.

Her father clearly thinks it's a great commercial deal anyway; his father-of-the-bride speech was all about joining two Savannah dynasties, and it contained not one word about love or compatibility or friendship or fun.

Then came Algernon's speech, which was a long, extended metaphor about—you guessed it—yachts.

Grace chuckled. Algy Smythe was the heir to his father's luxury yacht business, and the way Richard told it, he always had boats on the brain.

Miranda had to sit there with an admiring smile while he talked about how he was ready to "batten down the hatches" with her for his wife, how she was in "ship-shape" condition, how he had spent so long before "coming safely into port," once or twice "sailing too close to the wind" (by which I suppose he meant proposing to my sister) before realizing he liked the "cut of Miranda's jib."

By this stage Sarah was winking at me every time he used a nautical phrase and I was struggling not to laugh. On and on he went, while poor Miranda's smile became more and more fixed.

He was destined to never again be "in the doldrums" and was determined to "toe the line" now that he was "safely at anchor." He was giving a "shot across the bow" that he was a married man now, and was ready to "lower the boom" on his old bachelor days. It might take some time to "know the ropes," but he was looking forward to learning to "fathom" married life.

At this point Sarah murmured to me, "Do you think he's going to crack a bottle of champagne off her head next?" which sent me into a fit of laughter that I had to muffle with my napkin. When I'd calmed down, I looked up, and Mrs Logan was gazing down at me from the top table with a very smug smile. She clearly thought I was in tears and that I must be kicking myself for not being a good boy and going into the bank, in which case she would have handed me her daughter on a plate, garnished with rubies and all sorts. Ha! Little does she know, I think of myself as having had a lucky escape.

Anyway, I've enclosed a picture of my family with the bride and groom. Miranda and Algy insisted on having their picture taken with every table, and they mailed the photographs out afterward. All in color, no expense spared. It was a nice idea, but my mother opened it and had to go to bed for two days, so distressed was she at the technicolor proof of her children's ineptitude. Jacob too got quite gloomy when Sarah showed him her copy—he'd love to work in color but can't afford it, and anyway, there's no point, as newspapers are printed in black and white and that's never going to change.

Grace looked into the envelope and there was the picture, which she'd missed in her hurry to pull out his letter. She took it out and studied it closely. It was printed on thick card, the colours bright and glossy.

Four of the people she recognised straight away, from two photos Richard had sent her before. There was Richard himself, as handsome as ever, his blond hair slightly longer than in the last photo, his skin tanned gold. His brother, Nathan, had the same hair, only very short, and the same square jaw and dark-blue eyes, but somehow he was not as handsome – how was it the same features came together perfectly on some people and not on others? Their sister, Sarah, didn't look anything like her brothers. Her hair, cropped into a bob, was dark and curly and her skin pale; she had a narrow, willowy figure, and her azure dress hugged her tightly and finished at the knee.

The older man must be their father, Arthur Lewis, a tall and imposing man with an intimidating moustache. His beautifully tailored suit exuded money, as if it were lined with gold. Though he had the same physique as the boys, it was Sarah who had his colouring; he was pale-skinned, with a stiff wave in his dark hair.

The second smiling young woman – an elegant, pretty brunette – must be Nathan's wife, Rebecca, Grace thought. And the older woman beside her had to be Richard's mother.

Caroline Lewis wore a beautiful crimson dress and a necklace and earrings of glittering rubies, but her angular face was drawn in a look of undisguised martyrdom and her smile for the photographer was more of a snarl. Like a bulldog chewing a wasp, as Pádraig O Sé might say. The reason for her simmering fury was crystal clear. Her daughter and youngest son had turned down their chance to marry two of Savannah's most eligible young people – Miranda and Algernon had married each other instead – and it was sticking in her craw.

At last Grace focussed on the bride. She already knew that Miranda was a rare beauty, as she'd seen her picture before. But in her wedding dress...well, she would take one's breath away. The low-cut tight-fitting bodice embroidered with silver flowers showed off her perfect breasts and narrow waist, and the dress fell to her ankles like liquid silk. Her perfectly coiffed sleek blond hair was threaded with pearls; more large pearls adorned her ears and throat.

Thinking of what Richard had said about the marriage being more of a commercial arrangement, Grace studied the bride's upturned face for signs of regret. But Miranda was smiling, her cupid's bow lips slightly parted, her clear blue eyes gazing up coquettishly from under golden lashes.

So she must really have been in love with Algernon, even though her new husband genuinely did resemble a fish, with his soft body, slack and slightly gormless grin and round eyes...

A moment later, though, Grace realised that it wasn't Algernon that Miranda was gazing at with that adoring expression. It was Richard.

With a shiver of shock, she looked from the bride's face to Algernon's. The groom didn't seem to have noticed the direction of his wife's gaze; he looked perfectly happy and content. Richard hadn't noticed either; he had eyes on the photographer, his arm flung around his sister's shoulders, smiling like he hadn't a care in the world.

Maybe she was reading it wrong. But she stuffed the photo back into the envelope so she didn't have to see it and went back to the letter with a worried feeling.

Anyway, that's it. The wedding of the season is over and done with, thank goodness.

Either Richard was putting a very brave face on it or he really didn't mind that Miranda had married someone else.

On more important matters, I'm afraid there's still no movement on my and Jacob's plans to go to Europe. His foreign editor at the Capital *has lost interest for now as there's nothing much going on over there, just the Russians trying to invade Finland and making a hash of it.*

On this side of the world, Canada has sent a division of men to England, though apparently they don't have any modern armaments, so I don't know how much use they will be. And a German "pocket battleship" popped up, firing at merchant ships off the coast of South America, can you believe it?

Some British cruisers forced it into port in Uruguay, and the German captain panicked and scuttled his own ship. What a coward.

Here in Savannah, people are still going on about Gone with the Wind *—some people have been to see it multiple times. Have you seen it yourself yet? Is there a movie theater in Knocknashee? The film's set right here in Georgia, and most people I know are more excited about Scarlett O'Hara and Rhett Butler than they are about whatever's happening in Europe.*

Except Jacob, of course. He's more worked up about Hitler than most. He's very focused on what's happening to the Jews in Germany, though he's having a hard time getting a newspaper interested. I did try to help him get something into the Savannah Morning News, *which I'll tell you about now if you don't mind this letter getting a bit long.*

Last week I took him out for a feed of fried green tomatoes, grits, shrimp and fried chicken in the Crystal Beer Parlor. Sarah told me he needed it because he lives mostly on Rice Krispies. He says he loves the "snap, crackle and pop!" But I think it's more that they're cheap.

Grace wondered what on earth Rice Krispies were, and how they snapped, crackled and popped.

So we went out, and he was starving and bolted his food down. I bought us a beer, but he wouldn't relax—he was like a cat on a hot tin roof, said he couldn't stay as he needed to be at the Mikve Israel synagogue by eight. Some Jewish man who had escaped from Germany was going to speak about what it was like there now.

I had nothing else to do, so I said I'd go with him and take some notes for a possible article. It's only a ten-minute stroll to East Gordon Street, so we drained our beers and left.

I didn't know what to expect. I had never been inside a synagogue before, but it's not as different from a normal church as you might think. I mean, there were pews and arches and an altar and stained glass in the windows, and nobody seemed to mind me being there.

The rabbi, which is what Jews call their preachers—in Ireland you say priests, don't you?—introduced our speaker. He was a very small man, academic looking, balding with heavy round glasses. Apparently he'd learned English as a boy but hadn't spoken it for years, so he was a bit hard to follow at first. His accent was very heavy, and I had to focus hard to catch every word, but soon, like everyone else—the place was full—I was rapt in the story.

Grace, I'll try to tell it to you in the way he told it. As I said, I was taking notes because I thought it might make a feature for the newspaper.

He started off like this. "My name is Henry Schlisser, and I used to own four bookshops in Hamburg. We supplied almost all the schoolbooks in the city, some university textbooks too, as well as everything else. Business was good. I was doing well, we had a beautiful apartment, my daughters wanted for nothing. My wife shopped in the best places. My two daughters played piano and violin. When Hitler and the National Socialists came to power, they made rules and laws to exclude Jews from civil life. Education, medicine, business, the law, the press—these things were forbidden to us. But I kept my bookshops. The Jews had been persecuted many times, in many countries, and I told my family this too would pass, that Hitler was a joke, that everyone knew he was a madman. Truly, that's what I thought."

He shook his head then, as if at his own naiveté.

"But I was wrong. The German people, all of them, they love this madman and they follow him. On Kristallnacht, over a year ago, they turned on the Jewish businesses, and everything I had was destroyed. My shops were vandalized and looted beyond repair. Our customers, our neighbors, people we thought were our friends—not one of them stretched out their hand to save us.

"So we used what we had left, some jewels of my wife, family heirlooms, and some cash I had saved, to get passage on board the St. Louis, *a ship bound for Cuba. It was not easy to obtain the necessary documentation, but I did it, but only for us four. I had to leave my parents. My wife had to leave her older sister. We were so upset, so heartbroken..."*

Here Schlisser stopped to wipe his face with a large handkerchief he pulled from his pocket. When he continued, his voice was hoarse.

"Under a Nazi flag, we sailed to Cuba. It took two weeks. Everyone on board was Jewish. Almost a thousand people. Though we were sad, we were glad too. My wife and I knew we were doing the right thing for our daughters, that they would be safe now."

He wiped his face again and took a sip from the glass of water on the table beside him.

"But at Havana, they say no. Our visas are no good now, we cannot disembark. We tried to ask, to beg, to bribe even, but nothing would work. We had to sail away. Then we tried to land in Florida. The same story. Not allowed to disembark. We sent telegrams to your president, to people in power, everyone, anyone. We were desperate. But the answer always was no. The last resort was Canada. We tried to land there too, the same response. No. We were sent back where we came from."

Grace, I'll be honest with you, I found it hard to believe. My country turned that ship away? Knowing what the people aboard were fleeing from? It seemed inconceivable that I hadn't read about it or heard about it if it was true... And I could see it was news to everyone there, including Jacob.

Schlisser went on. "Eventually we were all disembarked in Antwerp, and I tried again to get a visa with the last of the money I had saved. I had some business contacts in the publishing world, and this time I was lucky. My wife and children and I made it to the USA because a dear friend here, an American man I used to have as a customer in my shop when he lived in Hamburg, had connections. We stayed in touch, and he helped me. We are grateful, and we feel so very lucky."

There was a smattering of applause and some broad smiles, and the rabbi stood up and held out his hand. "You're welcome here in Savannah, Mr. Schlisser, you and your family. We welcome you and open our hearts to you."

Schlisser nodded at the rabbi, but instead of taking his hand, he turned back to the podium and went on speaking. "I thank you for your friendship, but we are only one family. So I ask myself, what about all the others? The ones without influential friends or jewels to sell? What about our people who don't know anyone to vouch for them? What will become of them? Because"—and he paused here and seemed to make eye contact with every single person in the room—"and you must be sure of this, Hitler will not stop. This is why I have come here this evening, to explain. He will not stop. He wants every Jew —man, woman, child, every one of us—gone. He wants us gone from Germany, Austria, Europe, maybe from everywhere. He wants Jews gone from the face of the earth."

He paused so that what he'd just said could sink in, looking slowly around the room, meeting everyone's horrified eyes.

"It seems fantastical, I know, and maybe you sit there and think I exag-

gerate, or I am too pessimistic, and that sense will prevail. I thought that way myself, but now I know it will not. I have seen it with my own eyes. Unless the whole world sees the truth, and acts, it is Hitler who will prevail."

This time Schlisser did turn and shake the rabbi's hand, then went to sit down with a woman and two girls who were obviously his wife and daughters. The silence that followed was deafening. The rabbi waited a few moments before going to the podium to speak. When he did, he opened his mouth and closed it again. Like everyone else, he seemed stunned.

Eventually he managed, "Thank you, Mr. Schlisser. We are all...well..." Then his voice dried up. He led a small round of applause, but it was very muted compared to before; everyone looked shaken and frightened. We all believed Schlisser now.

After the meeting Jacob took some pictures of Mr. Schlisser with his wife and daughters. They just looked like any normal family, nothing remarkable at all, which made his prognostication even more chilling for some reason. Then I drove Jacob back to his apartment, an awful, squalid dump on the edge of town that he shares with some crazy anarchist types who never do the dishes, and as I drove, I talked to him about the article I was going to write.

"We really need to get this out there, Jacob," I said. "People need to know this stuff."

The weird thing is, Jacob just shrugged. His usual passion, his burning determination to show the world what's happening seemed dimmed, diminished. Replaced with a resignation, and a deep pain.

"People won't want to hear it," he said quietly.

I was astounded. "Well, they'll have to. We'll show them, in pictures and words. This is an eyewitness account—no one can deny it's true. Maybe then they'll stop thinking Gone with the Wind is more important than what's happening over there in Europe..."

But I couldn't shake him.

"I'm telling you, Richard," he said, "there's no point. Roosevelt knows that America won't go to war to protect Jews, and the newspaper editors know that too. If congress or the electorate thought for a second that this was about saving the Jews, they'd never allow America to get involved. It's not just here—in England it's the same. A Jewish guy I know, born and raised in London, works for the Jewish Chronicle over *there, says Churchill's telling the newspapers to downplay the Jewish side of it, that it doesn't help to rally people to the cause, quite the opposite."*

Anyway, the long and short of it is I did persuade him to send our photo-feature to his foreign editor at the Capital, *and the editor turned it down as "old news," although I'm pretty sure he didn't report it when it was "new news." Then I tried the* Savannah Morning News *and the* Savannah Evening Press *as well, and it got turned down there as well. In the end we got it published in the* American Jewish World. *We didn't get much money for it, but we sent what we did get to the Red Cross. It felt like the best thing to do.*

Anyway, that's enough about that. I better sign off now, as I need to be up bright and early to cover the Savannah Ladies' Glee Club's dress rehearsal of their upcoming show, Isn't It Romantic?, *not exactly cutting-edge journalism, but I'm afraid stuff like that is the bread and butter of a cub reporter's life.*

Write back as soon as you have the time, Grace, and tell me what people in Ireland think about the war and everything. But most of all, tell me about you.

Your long-winded American pen pal,

Richard Lewis.

PS Here I am again! Did you think you'd gotten rid of me? It's morning now on St. Simons Island, and I have to tell you, I had a dream last night that I went on a trip to Ireland to visit you and met Father Iggy, who was as round as a barrel and had ENORMOUS glasses like telescopes, and we bought a bag of toffee in Bríd's candy store and took turns riding on Tilly's pony, Ned, who was wearing his American cowboy saddle. When I woke up, I was quite annoyed to realize it was just a dream! I hope if Jacob and I ever do get posted to Europe, we'll be able to swing by. It doesn't look very far on the map?

A rush of emotions crowded Grace's brain. Richard had dreamt about Knocknashee? And seemed to think Europe was such a small place, he could just 'swing by'? It was funny and endearing, but also terrifying. The thought of her larger-than-life American friend turning up in her home town... He would find the place so small and

35

backward. No, she didn't think it would work, someone like Richard crossing over to her side of the rainbow.

PPS Didn't you once tell me you had a rag doll named Nellie, which your mother made for you and named after Dame Nellie Melba, her favorite singer? Well, here's something I found out from the menu at the Crystal Beer Parlor. Peach Melba—I'm sure you know this already, but in case you don't, it's a dessert of peaches and raspberry sauce with vanilla ice cream—was invented in 1892 by the French chef Auguste Escoffier at the Savoy hotel, London, to honor the Australian soprano Nellie Melba! So now you know.

And that's it from me,

Your even more long-winded American pen pal,

Richard

With a sigh – she was always sorry when his letters came to an end – Grace folded the pages back into their envelope with the unsettling photograph and cuddled down into her bed, now toasty warm thanks to her hot water bottle. His last paragraph about Dame Nellie Melba was so interesting, but it had also made her a little sad. She'd never said it to Richard about Agnes throwing Nellie on the fire; it was too awful. Grace would be twenty this June, and far too old for childish things, but she still missed the feel of that little cloth body, pressed comfortingly against her cheek at night.

Closing her eyes, she pulled the crocheted quilt up to her chin and thought about Richard's letter. She hoped she would dream about being in the Crystal Beer Parlor and eating shrimp and drinking beer with him and his fiery sister, Sarah, and the mysterious Jacob.

Instead she dreamt about Nellie, her constant childhood companion.

CHAPTER 4

The first light of dawn crept reluctantly over the mountains behind Knocknashee, tinging the heavy grey sky with an eerie yellow. Grace yawned and turned her head to look at her little green bedside clock. Half past eight in the morning. Agnes had usually rung her brass bell by now. Being a Saturday, there was no school, but she still had to get up to look after her sister.

Shivering, she rolled out of bed and went to the window, which was covered in ice. She breathed on the pane until she'd melted a little hole through which she could see out. Her prediction had been right. Everything was under a blanket of glittering white frost. Despite her flannel nightie, thick woollen jumper and bed socks, she could feel the cold in her bones, and her right leg ached fiercely.

She longed to climb back into her warm bed, but she needed to get up; Agnes had to be washed and fed and helped to the toilet if she needed it.

It would take too long to light a fire, so she undressed and dressed again as quickly as she could. Her knitted lambswool winter underwear – long johns and a long-sleeved vest, a home-made Christmas gift from Mary O'Hare – was a godsend. She dragged on her thick darned stockings, fixed her calliper over her wasted leg, pulled on the woollen dress and multi-coloured jumper, then shoved her feet into her boots, one of which had a built-up heel and room to slot in the rods of her steel.

Limping downstairs, she opened the door to Agnes's room and was relieved to find the embers of the fire still glowing and the room warm.

Agnes was still asleep, her jaw slack, her eyes shut. It was quarter to nine, and the church bells were calling the town to the daily Mass, loud and clear in the still, cold air. Agnes was usually awake by now, but the day was long enough for the poor woman, lying there helpless, hour after weary hour, Grace thought she might as well sleep on. When she woke she would ring the bell, and then Grace would bring her tea and some porridge with sugar and cream.

Grace coaxed the fire back to life and added a few bits of turf, then left, closing the door behind her, and went back to the kitchen, which was also still warm thanks to the banked-down range. Outside in the yard, a robin was perched on the bare cherry blossom tree her mother had planted in the back garden, feathers fluffed against the cold. Its little feet must have been freezing, as every twig of the tree was covered in ice. Looking at it now, it was hard for Grace to imagine how in the spring it would be in full, glorious bloom.

Grace had a sudden memory – her father teasing her mother about the futility of planting a cherry blossom. Its period of flowering was so short, just a few weeks, and the ever-present winds on the peninsula often made it shorter, so sometimes the garden was covered in pink petals within days. He'd joked that Kathleen should have planted an ash or an oak.

Mammy said the cherry blossom was her tree and she loved it, then told him that *maireann an chrann ach ní maireann an lámh a chuir é* – that the tree would survive long after the hand that planted it did.

Mammy was a great one for the *nathanna cainte*. She had so many sayings, and Grace smiled at the memory. The little robin perched on the branch fluttered suddenly down, landed on the frost-whitened windowsill and stared in at her, its little dark eyes fixed.

'Hello, Mammy,' Grace whispered, crooking her little finger at it, a tiny wave. Her mother had been convinced robins were the souls of the dead, come to watch over the living, and maybe they were. Grace would like to believe it anyway. She missed her father and mother every single day, even though they'd been dead now for eight years. The little bird looked cold and hungry, so she fetched one of the sweet cakes Dymphna had baked yesterday, opened the window a fraction and crumbled it on the sill. The robin flew back into the tree until she'd closed the window again but then drifted back for the soft, sweet crumbs.

Grace opened the door of the range and gave the turf a poke to bring it to life, then used the gas stove to boil the kettle. She made a saucepan of smooth creamy porridge and ate a bowlful with honey from Tilly's farm, then went back to check on Agnes, who hadn't yet rung her bell. Her sister was still asleep.

Grace climbed the stairs to fetch Richard's letter, some fresh notepaper, her fountain pen and a bottle of lilac ink and brought them back down to the kitchen, where she could sit by the warm range and drink more tea while she thought of what to write.

It was her third bottle of lilac ink since she'd begun writing to Richard, and it was already down to the dregs; she'd have to write to the stationery shop in Cork for more.

Dear Richard, she began, having dated the letter as she always did, enjoying the use of his first name. But then she stopped and sucked on the top of her pen.

What should she say about the wedding? He was so funny about it, but did he really not mind losing a girl as beautiful as Miranda Logan – *and she has brains as well*, Richard had written, *and a good sense of humor when she's in the mood* – to a man with a face like a fish?

Grace took out the photo he'd sent with his letter and studied it again, hoping she'd been wrong about the way Miranda was trying to flirt with Richard instead of with her new husband, Algernon Smythe.

But she wasn't wrong. How sad for Miranda. It was obvious she should never have broken it off with Richard just because he'd decided to be a writer instead of a banker.

At the same time, Grace couldn't help being shamefully relieved that the stunning heiress had married someone else. It was ridiculous, she knew. Richard would find another girl soon, of course he would; every young woman in Savannah must be throwing herself at him. But it was so nice to think of him being alone for a while.

Grace flushed scarlet, though she was alone. *For goodness's sake*, she admonished, *would you ever have a hair of sense?* This was the real world, not a fairy tale. Richard Lewis might live somewhere over the rainbow, but Grace Fitzgerald lived here, in Knocknashee.

Shaking her head, she filled her fountain pen with what was left of her ink and began to write.

Thank you so much for your wonderful letter. It sounds like you had fun at the wedding even if your parents are still a bit upset at you. I do hope Miranda will be happy. Maybe she will come to love yachts as much as Algernon does.

And that was all she was going to say on *that* subject.

You asked me what Ireland thinks of the war. Well, Mr de Valera, our leader, is very keen that we have nothing to do with it. He doesn't call it a war, he calls it 'the Emergency', and it doesn't get much coverage in the press – any bit of news we get about it is very limited.

Lizzie Warrington wrote to me a few days ago that she was in the ladies' reading room in the Cork City Library and looked at the international and some of the English newspapers too and was shocked at what they were reporting. It made her realise we're not being told the whole story over here at all.

I didn't know, for example, that all Jewish people in the areas controlled by the Germans are forced to wear a yellow star on their clothing to mark them as Jews. That seems horrific, and if people are behaving badly towards them, it must be so frightening to be so easily identifiable. God love them all.

Mr Schlisser's story about the refugee boat was very moving, even if hard to believe everyone turned them away – but of course I believe him if you do, and why would anyone make that up? I'm glad you found a newspaper to take the story, even if the American Jewish World *didn't pay very well. I think you are an excellent writer, by the way. The way you wrote Mr Schlisser's story, I felt like I was there in the synagogue with you.*

Surely the world will have to do something to stop Hitler as more and more stories like that emerge? I hope so.

The Irish envoy to Berlin up to last year was a man called Charles Bewley, and he told the papers here that Jews in Germany were perfectly safe, and anyway that they were the bad ones because they were involved in 'the international white slave trade' and we shouldn't give them visas. De Valera dismissed him last year when he found out what an awful liar he was. To think Mr Bewley comes from such a respected family; his cousins or something own a very famous café in Dublin – we've even heard of it in Knocknashee.

De Valera isn't against the Jews, quite the opposite – you can tell Mr Nunez that. He made sure they are protected by our new constitution, which he wrote a couple of years ago. Some people, the Catholic Church mainly, weren't keen, but at least most of the Church here is against Hitler even if they're not madly in favour of helping the Jews. The Bishop of Galway wrote a pastoral letter to be read in all churches in the diocese calling for an end to the disgusting behaviour of Hitler's followers over there, and the German attaché to Dublin got very upset about it. Big pity about him!

You say people in America are more excited about Gone with the Wind *than the war. I'd love to see a film set in Georgia. There's no cinema in Knocknashee, but maybe it will come to the cinema in Cork, and if it does, I will try to get to see it. I owe the Warringtons a visit. They're always inviting me; it's just so hard to get away for a night with Agnes the way she is. Did I tell you Tilly has a ram called Clark Gable? She bought him for next to nothing because he had a gammy leg, but Tilly said she knew not to judge by appearances because of me having a gammy leg as well, and in Clark Gable's case anyway, she was right; he's made sure every one of her ewes has a lamb every spring.*

That was very interesting about Dame Nellie Melba and the dessert.

She paused, thinking she might tell him the truth about Nellie the rag doll, but decided against it. It wasn't like they kept secrets from each other. Why would they? They were never going to meet. It was just that it still made her too sad to think about it, those two blue glass eyes, cloudy with smoke, left in the matchbox upstairs.

It's so funny how you dreamt about being in Knocknashee and meeting

Father Iggy, round as a barrel and with spectacles like telescopes. He's not very round any more, by the way. Kit Gallagher, the housekeeper at the rectory, has him and the new curate, a quiet nervy young priest called Father Donnchadh Lehane, on starvation rations. She worshipped Canon Rafferty to bits, and now that he's gone, she won't bake cakes or any kind of dessert, and so Father Iggy especially is after losing loads of weight – even Pádraig O Sé says his shoes will last a bit longer now.

As for Ned the pony, well, he lives in the field at the back of the school now. He's too old for farmwork and pulling heavy carts of turf. The field belongs to the Church, but Father Iggy lets the school use it so the children can play football – that's something the canon would never have allowed – and he suggested Tilly put Ned in there now that he's retired. He keeps the grass down, which saves cutting it, and it saves her having to use her own grass, as she has little enough. The field faces the sea and gets a lot of wind and rain, but Declan built Ned a shelter so he can stay out of the worst of it. He doesn't seem to mind the children running around at breaktime, and they all love him and jump up on his back while he just stands there looking perfectly content.

Tilly bought a very skittish young pony to replace Ned. She calls him Aonbharr, after the horse that belonged to Manannán mac Lir, the Irish god of the sea, who the stories say was 'as swift as the naked cold wind of spring'. She rides him bareback down from the farm every Sunday afternoon, and when the weather is good, she saddles up Ned and brings me on a ride to the beach. She says I'm as light as a child so it's no bother for Ned, and I'm more confident of staying on now, as the cowboy saddle is so easy to sit into, and I love the freedom of having four working legs under me.

You asked me to tell you about myself, but apart from small things like this, nothing much has changed in my life since I wrote last.

I'm still busy with the school – there are eighty-two children now – and caring for Agnes, though Dymphna, the lady who took over from Teresa, is proving to be a godsend. Between her, Declan and Father Iggy, my life is made easy. There's a girl called Janie O'Shea who I'm hoping to recruit as a monitor, and if I can get that agreed to by the Department of Education, I'll begin to feel I am managing –

There was a tap on the back door, and Grace looked up in surprise, putting down her pen. There was no side entrance from the road into the back yard, only a gate that led into Ned's field behind the school, so the only person who ever came to the back door was Tilly – but as she'd just written to Richard, that was always on a Sunday afternoon, and today was a Saturday.

CHAPTER 5

Tilly's high cheekbones were flushed crimson with cold and her full lips chapped with ice. She was dressed in a man's overcoat, heavy boots and tweed cap, and she had strands of hay in her short dark-brown hair and stuck to her woollen scarf.

'It's brutal cold out there. I brought Ned down a bag of hay,' she explained, as she stood shivering with her hands over the range, soaking up the warmth. 'Aonbharr hates going at anything slower than a canter, but I had to rein him in to a walk, the ice was so slippery. I had to come today because I'm taking the train from Dingle to Dublin to visit Marion tomorrow to see the new baby, though if it's like this, I doubt Bobby the Bus will be driving to Dingle – that man loves any excuse to stay in his bed, so we'll have to see. Who are you writing to? That rich boy in America again? You'll have to give him up when you and Declan are married...'

'Oh, stop that.' Grace laughed as she lit the gas under the kettle. It was already hot from sitting on the range, so it wouldn't take a second to come to a boil. 'You know Declan's got his eye on Sally O'Sullivan.'

'He has not, or if he has, it's only so he knows where she is so he can keep away from her. She's a sharp tongue, that one, like her mam.'

'Well, Maura Keohane then.' She swilled out the teapot and added more tea leaves.

'Ugh, she's too sweet to be wholesome.'

Grace laughed at the old insult. 'Just because you're a sour old lemon.' She got down an extra mug from the dresser.

'At least you know where you stand with me...'

The sound of Agnes's brass bell rang through the house, and Grace, who was filling the teapot, gave such a start, she splashed hot water over the rim. She'd almost forgotten her sister was in the house, she'd been so happy chatting to Tilly. She hoped her sister hadn't heard her laughing with her best friend in the kitchen. Agnes hated Tilly and her mother like poison, worse than she hated... Well, worse than all the other people she hated.

The ringing was followed by a thud, then the bell tinkled a few more times and stopped. Agnes must have dropped it and it had rolled across the floor. With her finger to her lips, warning her old friend not to let Agnes know she was in the house, Grace handed Tilly the kettle to finish filling the teapot and limped down the hallway to the sitting room.

The room was still in darkness apart from the low orange glow of the fire. She drew the curtains to let in the daylight. Sure enough, when she looked, the brass bell had rolled away across the floor, almost as far as the piano. Grace stooped to pick it up and brought it back to the bedside table.

'Are you ready for your porridge, Agnes? It won't take me a minute to heat it up.'

A low groan came from the bed, and for the first time, Grace looked properly at her sister...and realised something was very wrong. Agnes's always pale skin was corpse white, the left side of her face drooping even more. Her left eyelid was closed, and the right hand with which she'd reached for the bell hung over the side of the bed, its fingers clutching feebly at the air.

'Agnes, what's happened? Are you in pain?' Her heart in her mouth, she hastened to prop her sister up higher against the pillows, praying this wasn't the dreaded second stroke that Dr Ryan had said might happen.

Agnes gave another groan, nothing articulate.

'Try to stay sitting up, Agnes. I'll go to get Dr Ryan…' She lifted her sister's right hand and laid it back on the covers. Agnes gripped Grace's fingers in return with surprising strength, and her one open eye strained with terror, like a frightened horse.

'No…no…stay…' gasped the stricken woman. 'Stay…Grace…'

'I can't stay. I'll be quick – you won't know I'm gone,' begged Grace, trying to extract her hand. 'I'll be back before you know it.'

'No…no…stay…'

Grace made an impossible decision. She picked up the brass bell in her free hand and rang it furiously until the sitting room door opened and Tilly appeared, looking extremely reluctant to be summoned into the presence of her nemesis.

'What's the matter?' Tilly whispered from the doorway.

Agnes groaned even louder, and anger as well as fear came into that one pale-blue eye.

'You have to go for the doctor. Agnes doesn't want me to leave her, and anyway, you'll be so much quicker than me.'

'Dr Ryan isn't in town, Grace, remember? He's gone to his aunt's funeral in Limerick.'

'God help us, how did I forget? What are we going to do?' Grace fought back a surge of panic. The last thing Agnes needed was to see her fall apart. She forced herself to breathe. 'There must be someone…'

Tilly threw a hesitant glance towards the bed and asked in a low voice, 'Will I get Mam? She might know what to do?'

'Naa…naa…naa…naa…' Agnes shook her head, turning it from side to side on the pillow, her voice getting stronger in her rage.

But Grace felt a rush of relief. Of course, Mary O'Hare. Grace knew her sister didn't like Tilly's mother any more than she liked Tilly, but Mary was a Bean Feasa, a wise woman, good at herbs and all sorts of natural remedies, like the one she sent down every week to help Agnes eat. Besides, she was the only option they had. 'Do, but be quick, Tilly. Please be as fast as you can.'

'Naa…naa…' groaned Agnes, but Tilly was already gone, running back down the hall through the kitchen to the field behind, where she'd left her new pony with Ned.

'It's all right, Agnes.' Grace soothed her sister, patting the hand that still gripped her own. 'Mrs O'Hare will help you. Lots of people think she's as good as any doctor, or better even. She'll know what to do, and she's a good person. Please, she doesn't hold any bad feeling towards you if that's what you're worried about…' When her sister was head-mistress, and Grace and Tilly still children, Agnes had slapped Tilly so hard with the leather strap that Tilly's palm bled. Mary O'Hare had come to the school and threatened Agnes and called her a *cailleach*, the first time anyone had ever called Agnes a witch to her face. It was a day nobody present would ever forget. But after Agnes had her stroke, the good woman had been nothing but kind, sending down the weekly remedy and also eggs and honey and a knitted cardigan to keep Agnes warm, all of which Grace had to pretend came from someone else.

The curtains were open and the winter light streamed in, and as Grace tried to soothe and comfort her sister and help her again into a more comfortable position, Tilly's tall, strong figure flew by. She had ridden Aonbharr down from the field through the schoolyard and now rode him bareback as he galloped along the icy cobbled street, with the pony doing his reckless best to hurry.

At once she regretted telling Tilly to make haste. If the horse slipped and fell, her best friend would surely break her neck. She said a frantic prayer half to God and half to her parents to be with Tilly now, to keep her safe.

Leaning against the pillows, Agnes calmed and suddenly fell into a restless sleep while still clinging to Grace's hand.

Time passed. Outside in the freezing world, snow began to fall, settling on the ice-covered ground and roofs. The clock on the mantel ticked away the minutes loudly in the silence. *Is it always that loud?* Each minute since Tilly had disappeared felt like an hour…

The church bells rang again, calling all the lazybones like Bobby the Bus to eleven o'clock Mass, and a few shivering figures appeared on the street, the women wrapped in shawls and the men with their caps pulled down and collars up, clinging to each other to keep from falling as they made their way to church over the treacherous snow-covered ice.

Almost an hour gone…where was Tilly? Lying by the side of the road, and the horse with its leg broken?

And then she heard it, the clattering of hooves and rumble of wheels over the cobbles. There were the O'Hares, mother and daughter, pulling up in the horse and cart outside, Mary muffled to her eyes in a huge thick shawl and Tilly in her big man's coat, jumping down to tie the reins to the snowy fence.

Grace eased her hand out of Agnes's and hurried as fast as she could to the door, admitting them, pale and shivering. Mary was stooped with arthritis, her shawl crusted with snow, and her dark hair had come loose of its pins in the wild ride and hung in melting ropes against her reddened cheeks. Grace noticed the dark shadow of moustache on her upper lip.

'Let me get you something to warm you, some tea, some cocoa – I have a drop of brandy…' Grace gasped.

'Never mind that, let me go into her,' Mary O'Hare said firmly, stripping off her snowy shawl and handing it to Grace, then repinning her long dark hair. 'But bring me a jug of hot water and a small glass. I have a remedy with me that might help ease her for a short while.'

Grace limped hastily to the kitchen, where she threw the shawl over the clothes line that crossed a corner of the room. Tilly followed and draped her coat over a chair near the range; underneath she wore a man's shirt and trousers that did nothing to disguise her perfect upright figure.

Grace poured a jug of hot water from the kettle on the range and Tilly fetched a whiskey glass, and the two of them returned to the sitting room to find Mary O'Hare sitting hunched beside the bed and Agnes awake but with her head turned mulishly away.

Mary took the glass from her daughter and tipped in some dried crushed herbs from a blue paper bag, the sort sugar was kept in, and topped it up with hot water. 'Now you take this, Agnes, it will ease your mind,' she said, in her deep, gravelly voice.

Agnes shook her head, saying nothing. If her mouth hadn't been so slack, Grace thought, she would have pressed her lips together.

'Ah, now do, Agnes,' murmured Grace, bending over her. 'Let me sit you up. I promise if Mary O'Hare says it will work, it will work – don't you know when you decide to eat your food it's because I've put in a remedy that Mrs O'Hare has sent down to you out of the kindness of her heart?'

Agnes's one open eye swivelled to look at her, with a flash of anger or hurt pride or both, but she must have accepted Mary O'Hare meant her no harm, because when the wise woman put the glass to her lips, she drank in slurping, dribbling sips.

As she did, a little colour came back into her cheeks, her left eye opened and her mouth lifted so it barely drooped. Grace felt a huge rush of astonished relief. 'Are you feeling better, Agnes? You look so much better...'

Her sister inclined her head and did something she hardly ever did, something she hadn't been able to do since the stroke – she smiled. And Grace was reminded yet again how much her older sister looked like their mother, and how pretty she could have been if she'd been happy in her life instead of looking always so grim and sad.

'Mary, what a wonderful remedy, thank you,' Grace said.

But Mary O'Hare frowned, shaking her head. ''Tis a powerful remedy but a short-lived one. It helps to bring a person back but never for long. Only enough for them to make their peace.' Then she turned to her daughter. 'Tilly, go for Father Iggy. There's no time to waste.'

'Father Iggy?' Tilly's eyes opened wide. A priest was only ever called urgently to the house when a person was dying and needed to be anointed. 'But Mam, the Mass has only just started – maybe I should wait?'

'And I don't know if Agnes wants to see him?' Grace threw a questioning look at her sister. Ever since the canon had abandoned Agnes, she'd refused to see any priest at all, not even Father Iggy or the shy new curate, Father Lehane.

Agnes looked back at her and then at Tilly. 'Go,' she said, in a strange, calm voice, not slurring at all.

Tilly glanced at Grace, who gave her a short nod, then fled. Grace felt the tears rise in her throat, and her legs went weak; she had to rest her hand on the corner of the bed to steady herself. 'Agnes, don't give up hope, please don't.'

Agnes smiled again, then turned her head towards the wise woman hunched beside the bed. 'How long?' she asked, in that calm, steady voice.

''Tis time, Agnes, time to make your peace,' Mary answered gently. 'Will you say an act of contrition with me?'

Agnes nodded. Grace stood there shaking and trying not to cry.

Together, Agnes and Mary said the prayer, their voices soft and hoarse in the sun-filled room, quiet but for the ticking of the clock.

'Oh, my God. I am heartily sorry for having offended Thee, and I detest all my sins because I dread the loss of heaven and the pains of hell, but most of all because I have offended Thee, my God, who art all good and deserving of all my love. I firmly resolve, with the help of thy grace, to confess my sins, to do penance, and to amend my life. Amen.'

When they finished, Mary blessed herself and then made the sign of the cross on Agnes's forehead. Agnes closed her pale-blue eyes and breathed long and deep, as if part – but not all – of a weight was lifted from her heart. Then she opened them again. 'Father Iggy?' she asked.

Grace went to press her face to the freezing pane, her breath clouding the glass until she rubbed it away, but the street was empty, only whirling flakes of snow making everything ghostly. 'I can't see him, Agnes. I'm sure he'll be here soon.'

For the first time since she'd taken the remedy, a note of agitation crept back into Agnes's voice. 'I need to see him. Important.'

Grace longed to comfort her. She moved to be closer, but Mary

O'Hare held her hand up to stop her and leant in to say softly to Agnes, 'You can tell Grace what is in your heart, *a chroí*. You can take this chance to repent of your sins, to be truly sorry for all you have done in this life. You'll soon see the face of Jesus, and if you speak the truth to Grace, you can meet Him with a clear heart and mind.'

'Father Iggy...' Agnes was getting frightened.

'Father Iggy will come, I promise. But still, time is short. So tell everything now, for once and for all, and make what is wrong, right, and help your sister understand everything that has happened.'

Agnes shuddered from head to toe, and Grace's heart missed a beat, fearing yet another stroke. 'Mary, please, don't make her do this. It's too much for her. I forgive her everything. There's no need for her to go through this –'

'No,' Agnes interrupted, and her voice was stronger again, like a guttering candle that flames up before it dies. 'I need to say it.' The words were slow, deliberate and slightly slurred, but they were clear enough to understand.

Grace pulled up a stool Declan had made for her for Christmas; she used it sometimes with a cushion to rest her bad leg when she was sitting in the armchair. Now she brought it to the side of Agnes's bed and sat, her eyes on a level with her sister's face. 'There's no need to tell me anything. I forgive you, Agnes...'

But her sister said in a fierce whisper, 'Listen.'

So Grace sat in silence and listened. The dying woman shut her eyes, as if composing her thoughts, and then opened them again and spoke. It was as if she was summoning her strength one last time. Her voice when she spoke was steady, slow and deliberate, but she enunciated and Grace could understand each word.

'I'm a sinner. Our parents raised me a happy child, they taught me religion, and I knew right from wrong. But when I was sixteen, I tempted a man.' She paused, breathed and went on. 'Canon Rafferty – he saw the sin in my eyes, he saw it more clearly than me, and he was tempted. And it was my fault.' Her voice, weak but clear, was all they could hear.

'He brought me into the sacristy after Mass. He told me I was

51

wrong to tempt him, that he was a man of God, that I had to stop. But I...I couldn't stop, I didn't know how. The devil was in me, looking out of my eyes. He made me pray with him. We knelt, we held hands, but the devil in my eyes forced him to kiss me, and...and other things. I am a sinner, Grace. A terrible sinner.'

Grace was shocked, not only at the revelation but also because Agnes had not spoken at length like this since her stroke. Grace had assumed she was no longer able to, but clearly that wasn't the case; she just had chosen not to communicate.

'The devil was in Canon Rafferty, not in you,' Grace exclaimed. 'You were only a child. 'Twasn't right, but you were only a child.'

'I was to blame,' Agnes said, in a dull, steady voice. 'Sixteen is old enough to know right from wrong. When you were sixteen, Grace, you chose the path of goodness, and you have had your reward. Every child in the town loves you, everyone cares for you. But when I was sixteen, I chose the path of sin. And once I had sinned, I sinned and sinned again, until there was nothing to save me from hell. So I closed my heart to everyone but him and hated everyone, and they hated me.'

Grace's eyes welled with tears. Here was the answer to the question her parents had asked each other when she'd overheard them talking years ago in this very room. 'She was such a happy, sunny child,' their mother, Kathleen, had said. 'And then she turned sixteen... I wish I knew why she's so angry and bitter.' And their father, Eddie, had asked, 'I wonder, where did our Agnes go at all?'

'I wish you had told Mammy and Daddy, Agnes. They would have protected you.'

'I longed to tell them, Grace, but Michael – Canon Rafferty – he told me it was our secret. He said if I betrayed him, if I destroyed him, then God would punish me and my loved ones. So I said nothing. I wanted to spare them. But God punished them for my sins all the same.'

'Oh, Agnes, God didn't punish them, he only took them home...'

'It was my fault they drowned – the canon said so.' It was horrifying, how she came out with it in such a matter-of-fact way.

'How could you believe such evil codswallop?' burst out Mary O'Hare, running her hands through her thick black hair, tangled as a crow's nest by now.

'Evil? Michael was not evil,' explained Agnes in the same matter-of-fact voice. 'He had cleansed himself of sin. He had wrestled with the devil and won. He had learnt to resist me. He had made his peace with God. And he tried to help me. He advised me to take Cyril Clifford as my young man, to put myself beyond temptation. He said Cyril Clifford was God's plan for me. And I would have obeyed God's will, I would have married Cyril, but then you got polio, Grace, and Cyril left me because of it. He said he was frightened of the disease, but it was my fault because I couldn't love him – the polio was just his excuse...'

Grace groaned softly and buried her face in her hands. All those years of Agnes telling her how she could be a married woman now if it wasn't for Grace getting polio and scaring Cyril away. The guilt she had made Grace feel for even existing... And it wasn't even true.

'Then when you came home from the hospital, I burnt your leaving cert results on the fire and told you that you'd failed...'

Mary O'Hare shot Grace an open-mouthed look, but this confession came as no surprise to Grace. Nearly a year ago, she'd found an old letter to her from Dr Warrington, congratulating her on her excellent exam results and offering her a place to stay while she attended the teaching college in Cork. Grace had always regretted not going to college; Father Iggy said she was a natural teacher, and she knew she'd picked up a lot from her parents, but she thought there must be so much more to learn. Agnes's falsehood had robbed her of that chance.

'He...Michael...he said...' Agnes's delivery was slower and more halting now. 'He said it was better...that way. You could stay in... Knocknashee...keep me company. I wouldn't need a husband. You could help...in the school...the house. He and I, we could go on pilgrimages together...' Her breath expelled raggedly, the effort of speaking visibly weakening her. 'I did everything for him. I thought he loved me, but he left me without saying a word.'

Tears flooded down her ashen cheeks, an agony of rejection that was hard to witness. With her right hand, she groped the air, as if to find someone there; Grace took it in her own and kept it. Despite the fire burning high, Agnes's hand was cold as death. Grace kissed and squeezed it in a vain attempt to warm it, her heart breaking for her poor deluded sister.

'Don't be kind to me, Grace,' moaned Agnes feverishly, her voice strengthening again. 'I took the wages you earned as assistant teacher and used them to tempt Canon Rafferty and lead him astray...'

Another disbelieving glance across the bed from Tilly's mother. Grace bit her lip, lowering her eyes. She'd told nobody about her sister's theft of her wages except for Richard, who was safely on the other side of the ocean. She hadn't even told Tilly. Grace's parents were so proud of the Fitzgerald name; they would turn in their graves if it got out their oldest daughter was a thief.

'And when I confessed to him, he said it was not your money because I gave you bed and board and clothed you and everything.'

'I know, Agnes,' Grace said, very quietly. 'Please, I know everything you're saying, about the exam results and everything. Please stop talking now – you're wearing yourself out. Don't say any more about anything.'

'I think let her talk, Grace. She needs to tell it,' Mary said, firmly but not unkindly. 'I won't pass anything on. I was never one for gossip. You can trust me. But she can't go to her maker with such terrible things on her mind.'

Agnes's eyes slid towards Mary O'Hare, and she nodded slightly and inhaled once more. And when she spoke, it was as if summoning the strength from her toes. 'I tempted a priest. Our parents died because of my sins. Michael told me.'

Grace's heart bled for her. What wicked nonsense the canon had fed to her poor vulnerable sister to bend her to his will. 'Agnes, our parents' death was nothing to do with you.'

'It was, Grace, listen to me. When I was twenty years old, the age you almost are now, four years after I first sinned in tempting him,

Michael sent me to New York. I was to ask a man for three thousand dollars and bring the money back to the canon...'

Grace stared at her sister, open-mouthed, unable to believe her ears. Agnes had been to New York, all by herself, and never said a word of it? And she'd asked a man for three thousand dollars? That was an eye-watering amount of money.

'I found the man, and he had the money...' Agnes gasped and stopped. She took a deep, shuddering breath and rested her head back on the pillow. Beads of perspiration formed on her white forehead. Her mouth drooped again, and her left eyelid closed.

'Do you want to stop talking now?' whispered Grace.

But Agnes shook her head and carried on. Though she was fading fast, she was kept going by the same fierce determination she'd always had, the steel at the core of her being. Maybe she could have done great things if life had treated her differently.

'The man agreed, but the man's wife asked if the baby's parents were dead...'

Again Grace could hardly grasp what she was hearing. A baby? What was Agnes talking about now?

'She said she'd heard terrible things about stolen children and she couldn't benefit from someone else's grief, so I promised her the baby's parents were dead, and when she asked how they'd died, I said they drowned in a boating accident coming back from the islands near Knocknashee.'

Grace was confused. Maybe Agnes was raving now, her thoughts a jumble.

'Our parents died that way, Agnes...'

Her sister's pale-blue eyes met hers, weary and resigned. 'I told a wicked lie, and God punished me by drowning our parents that exact same way in a storm, a storm that came out of a clear blue sky.'

'Agnes, no. God isn't cruel that way.' She rubbed her sister's freezing hand in both of hers, desperate to comfort her, to lift this unnecessary burden of guilt. 'Father Iggy will tell you. God is love.'

Agnes shook her head very, very slowly, turning it on the pillow from side to side. 'God is justice. And justice is harsh. Michael told me so. When our parents died, I confessed to him how I'd lied, and he said it was righteous of God to punish me, because to tell such a lie was a terrible thing. I asked if I should tell the father how I'd sold his daughter...'

'The father?' asked Mary O'Hare sharply. 'Agnes, did you bring a baby to America? Is that what you're telling us? And you took money for that child?'

She nodded. 'Three thousand. I took her there, and they gave me the money.'

'And who was this baby, Agnes?' Mary asked gently, moving closer.

'I should never have... It was wrong...and he was so heartbroken, it wasn't fair. But Michael said it was for the best, and I did it. He told me to, but I did it.'

Mary and Grace exchanged a startled glance, and the hairs stood up on the back of Grace's neck. Was Agnes talking about the postman's daughter? When Mrs McKenna died in childbirth, the Church said Charlie couldn't raise his children with no woman to help him and on such a low wage; he wasn't the postman then, only a lowly farm labourer. Declan was six and taken to Letterfrack, but Siobhán was a newborn, and it was whispered the canon had sold her – babies were worth big money in America – but it was only a rumour; nobody ever knew.

'Michael said...never tell...it was God's plan...but I wish...I wish...' Her voice faded to nothing and her head lolled to one side, her right eye closing as well as her left. She was falling asleep.

'What do you wish, Agnes?' Grace pressed her sister's hand, rubbing it, willing her to speak before it was too late. 'Was the little girl Siobhán McKenna? Can you tell us who you sold her to, Agnes, please?'

Agnes didn't answer, but Mary O'Hare took her by the shoulder and gave her a slight shake, and the dying woman's one good eye fluttered open again.

'Please, Agnes, who did you give Siobhán to?' Grace needed to know – Charlie did too, and Declan. Agnes could not die and not tell them.

'Father Noel... Father Noel...Dempsey... New York...'

The front door banged open and then the sitting room door. Father Iggy rushed in, Tilly on his heels, and went straight to the bed.

Mary and Grace stood and moved away, gathering with Tilly in the corner of the room, as the priest sketched the sign of the cross and blessed himself.

'I caught his eye when he was giving the reading,' whispered Tilly, 'and he stopped and came down to me and asked what was wrong and left Father Lehane to do the communion. But the street is pure ice – the snow is freezing solid – and it was slow going. I had to hold him up in case he fell.' Tilly was much taller and stronger than the little priest, who looked like the cold winter wind might blow him away now that he'd lost so much weight.

Standing over the bed, Father Iggy took a small bottle of holy oil from his bag and using his thumb made a sign of the cross on Agnes's forehead, anointing her.

'God, the father of all mercies, through the death and resurrection of His son, has reconciled the world to Himself and sent the Holy Ghost among us for the forgiveness of sins, through the ministry of the Holy Church may God grant you pardon and peace, and I absolve you from your sins, in the name of the Father, the Son and the Holy Ghost.'

Agnes's eyes remained closed, her body unresponsive, her breathing laboured. Father Iggy bent over her, bringing his face very close to hers, wanting her to hear him, his lips moving rapidly as he prayed the prayers of the last rites.

Grace took a step forwards. She was not ready for this.

'I commend the soul of you, Agnes, to almighty God, and entrust you to your Creator. May you return to Him who formed you from the dust of the earth. May Holy Mary, the angels and all the saints come to meet you as you go forth from this life. May Christ who was crucified for you bring you freedom and peace. May Christ who died for you admit you into his garden of paradise. May Christ, the true shepherd, acknowledge you as one of his flock. May He forgive all your sins and set you among those He has chosen. May you see your Redeemer face to face and enjoy the vision of God forever.'

The last rites given, the little priest straightened and, with a kind expression, beckoned Grace over and indicated for her to take her place at Agnes's bedside.

'Talk to her, Grace, and let it be your voice she hears as she leaves this world,' he whispered, his solemn eyes huge behind his thick round spectacles.

Grace sat down on the stool again, and Father Iggy paused to squeeze her shoulder in a gesture more friendly than clerical before he moved away. They had become good friends, the little priest and Grace.

As she wondered what to say to her sister, how to begin, Mary O'Hare came over and whispered in Agnes's ear, 'Eddie and Kathy are coming for you, *a chroí*. You're going home. You were more sinned against than sinning. Jesus will welcome you, all your pain will be left behind...'

Then even Tilly came and laid her hand on Agnes's brow. '*Go n-eirí an bóthar leat, a* Agnes,' she said gruffly, and Grace hoped the old blessing, may the road rise to meet you, meant Tilly had forgiven Agnes too.

Then mother and daughter left the room, taking Father Iggy to the kitchen, where Grace knew they'd take care of him, make him a sandwich and a cup of tea, give him a glass of whiskey and let him get warm by the range.

She was grateful to have the time alone with her sister; there was so much she wanted to say to her. She took Agnes's right hand again, and this time it was as cold and limp as her left hand had been since the stroke.

'Agnes...' she began. But then stopped. The words were so hard to form. She tried again, and this time they came. 'I'm sorry for what happened to you when you were sixteen. It wasn't right. I think I understand you better now. As Mary says, you were more sinned against than sinning. And I know we didn't always get along, but you were all I had for such a long time, and you're my sister and...I love you…' Grace could hardly get the words out. Tears trickled down her cheeks unchecked. She did love Agnes. She had to love Agnes; they were family. 'And I forgive you for anything that might have gone on between us. And I'll tell Charlie about Father Noel Dempsey in New York. I don't know who he is, but maybe he has the answer. Has he the answer, Agnes?'

Agnes sighed then, deeply, and for a moment, Grace thought she was going, but she inhaled slowly a second or two later. Maybe Grace had imagined it, but a flicker of a smile seemed to play on her sister's drooping lips, and her mouth emitted a small rush of air that sounded like a word, sounded like 'Mammy', but maybe not…

And that was the last word Agnes ever spoke, if indeed it had been a word. Peace descended. Her breathing grew shallower, and she seemed very calm, as if whatever she was experiencing was not painful.

Holding her hand, Grace spoke of times when she was a child and their family would have picnics on the strand, or how their father, who hadn't a note in his head, would sing pieces from the light operas as he shaved, the discordant song reverberating around the whole house.

She reminded Agnes about their mother's cherry tree in the yard that Daddy said was a totally unsuitable tree to have where they lived because the blossoming season was so short, but how Mammy said it was short but worth it, and that was how life was – short but worth it.

She told her that she was going to write to Maurice and ask him to come home for a visit, that she would love to get to know her brother.

Sometimes she was silent. Tilly and Mary came in and out, offering cups of tea and slices of brack, but she wasn't hungry. She told them they should go home, but they said they'd wait, that they were fine in the kitchen, dry and warm. Father Iggy was long gone; there were other people in Knocknashee who needed him.

All day long Agnes lay in the warm room, Grace by her side, her breathing shallow but steady and calm.

As the sun sank over the western horizon, bleeding a crimson trail across the ocean, and the gunmetal clouds turned purple and apricot,

Grace startled awake. She must have dozed off, leaning forward on Agnes' bed.

'Agnes, I'm here...'

But no more words were needed. Her sister's shallow breathing had ceased. Her face was unlined, at peace, no trace of pain – physical or emotional – remaining. As beautiful as their mother at last, all anger gone.

Agnes was dead.

CHAPTER 6

ST SIMONS ISLAND, GEORGIA, USA

February 1940

Richard Lewis sat at the table in the kitchen, reading Grace's latest letter while absently eating a plateful of peach and arugula salad that Esme had left out for him before she retired to bed. The housekeeper was an old woman now, and her joints were stiff, so as much as she loved him – and he knew she did; she'd been far more of a mother to him than his own – she didn't wait up for him past nine any more.

Nor did Doodle, the ancient chocolate Labrador. He was fast asleep in his basket and hadn't even twitched when Richard opened the back door.

He and Sarah had been out all day. They'd gone to rescue Jacob Nunez from the filthy hovel in Savannah he shared. They'd picked him up in the Buick, although he'd made Richard park it around the corner so as not to arouse the ire of his roommates, who believed all ownership as theft or some other such garbage, and whisked him off for a long weekend on St Simons Island, where they could feed him something more nutritious than Rice Krispies – which the anarchists kept stealing anyway, as well as drinking his milk.

'Sheer indulgence while half the world starves,' Jacob had grumbled as he climbed into the car, but Sarah rolled her eyes at him.

'Richard and I are going to the King and Prince Resort to eat burgers and ice cream and drink beer, and you can come and I'll pay, or you can stay here in this horrible apartment and eat the wallpaper, anything the cockroaches have left behind, but what you can't do is come and whine about the price of everything when children are starving in Russia.'

'I'll come but I'll pay,' he retorted, triumphantly brandishing a wad of dollar bills at her over his shoulder. He was sitting in the front beside Richard, while she was stretched out on the back seat. 'Spent the most boring afternoon of my life yesterday. I had to shoot the celebrations for a dairy's fiftieth anniversary, three generations of milk producers and farmers. All they wanted to talk about was cows. The world is going to hell in a handbasket, and they only care about cows.'

'And I had Esme make up Nathan's bed,' Sarah continued, ignoring the 'hell in a handbasket' comment, 'so you can sleep on a mattress without bedbugs for once, if that's not too much luxury for you. Otherwise you can sleep with Doodle in his basket in the kitchen. He has plenty of fleas, so you'll feel at home.'

'I'll see how I feel at the time.' Jacob grinned, stuffing his money back in his pocket.

Richard stared ahead as he drove. He didn't think Jacob was really going to sleep in Nathan's bed. He suspected the whole thing of putting on clean sheets and airing the room was for Esme's sake; the sweet old lady would be horrified if she thought her beloved Sarah was a loose woman.

It made Richard a bit uncomfortable himself, if he was honest, as much as he understood the world was changing. Sarah wasn't that bold as to be totally open in front of him, and he wasn't going to ask – she would bite his head off if he did – but it bothered him.

He loved Sarah, she was his sister, but…

Well, in the traditional world in which they'd been raised, if a guy from his social circle convinced a girl to let him go all the way, then as long as it was a girl from a class inferior to his own, as all other classes were, there was almost a sense that it was a good thing. A boy getting his wild oats out of his system before settling down with a respectable girl, the sort you married. But if a girl of their own set…well, if they got a reputation as the kind of girl who did that, they were ruined.

He remembered a heavy petting session with Miranda last summer in his car, before she'd abandoned him for Algernon. He'd placed his hand on her thigh, under her dress, and she'd slapped it away, saying, 'You know how it goes, Richard. You try, I say no.'

'Do you want to say no?' he'd asked, amused and frustrated all at once.

'Doesn't matter, I have to.' She'd said it as if this was set in stone and only a fool would question it.

That was the full extent of his own experience to date, but on the odd occasion he'd spent any time in Jacob's apartment, when they were working on a story together or something, he'd found himself surrounded by young men and women who seemed to have abandoned the rules entirely for a life of hedonism and self-expression.

Spontaneous parties would start up at the drop of a hat, big pots of unrecognisable food made by someone, crates of beer and cheap red wine.

The men were all penniless poets or artists and would sit around all night talking passionately about Karl Marx, the divide between rich and poor, the 'coloured question', and how oppressed women were by men.

The young women drank and smoked as much as the men. They wore trousers when they weren't modelling naked for the would-be artists, in between waiting tables at disreputable bars, because someone had to buy the beer and cheap red wine. And most shocking of all, they didn't seem to care about kissing in public, not just the men but sometimes each other.

The bohemians were kind to Richard because Jacob introduced

him as a fellow journalist and they approved of that; Hemingway was a journalist and he was a bohemian. And in return Richard pretended to be a bit of a bohemian himself, even growing his hair an extra couple of inches. He was an imposter, though. He wasn't living on a shoestring like Jacob; he was safely cushioned by his grandmother's money. And Sarah was the same. As much as his sister pretended money didn't matter, she was never going to marry Jacob Nunez while he was a poverty-stricken photographer. Luckily Jacob had an ace up his sleeve; his uncle was a jeweller in Manhattan who had no children of his own. One day Jacob had the option to enter his uncle's business and settle down. Not yet, though. Not until Hitler was defeated and a new world built on the ruins of the old.

Only stopping to park the car at the summer house and leave Jacob's bag in Nathan's bedroom, the three of them headed off for a burger at the King and Prince Resort overlooking the beach.

Three huge burgers, three towering ice creams and several beers later, Jacob settled the bill as promised. 'Cows are boring, but they sure pay well,' he remarked, then suggested a moonlit stroll on the beach.

He didn't say Richard wasn't welcome, but Richard left him and Sarah to it anyway. For one thing it was only fifty degrees, not especially cold but not warm either. For another he needed to finish an article for the *St Simons Weekly*; he'd been battling for two days straight to inject some interest into the most recent meeting of the Georgia Farm Bureau. He would just have to hope Sarah was as sensible as Miranda and wasn't going to ruin her reputation.

When he entered the house by the back door, the first thing he saw was an envelope with Irish stamps propped against a bottle of Heinz Tomato Ketchup on the kitchen table – Esme must have guessed he'd come in this way – and all thoughts about the benefits of the newfangled fertilisers versus good old-fashioned dung went out the window.

It had been a while since Grace had written last. He'd been expecting a letter earlier, to be honest, and while he wasn't pining away or anything like that, he was pleased to see she hadn't forgotten him. He'd been beginning to wonder if something had happened to distract her. Maybe it had. Maybe she'd met someone.

He opened the letter with a sudden sense of foreboding.

As Grace always did, she'd written the date and her address at the top of the letter.

12th of January 1940, Knocknashee.

Dear Richard,

Thank you so much for your wonderful letter.

He smiled, relieved. So she had written back right away. The letter must have been delayed crossing the Atlantic due to the trouble in Europe.

It sounds like you had fun at the wedding even if your parents are still a bit upset at you. I do hope Miranda will be happy. Maybe she will come to love yachts as much as Algernon does.

Richard chuckled at the idea of Miranda waxing lyrical about anchors and topsails. It wasn't the yachts she'd married Algernon for, it was the lifestyle that came with them – the cocktail parties, the French chefs, the excursions to exclusive island retreats where servants waited on her hand and foot.

Grace didn't say anything more about the wedding, she just left it there, and went straight to answering his question about Ireland and the war. Her country clearly didn't intend to get involved. And then she got to the part he always enjoyed the most, about her day-to-day life in Knocknashee.

He laughed out loud at the story about Tilly having a ram called Clark Gable because of his prowess with the ladies. And at how Father Iggy was getting thin because the housekeeper at the parochial house, Kit Gallagher, had adored Canon Rafferty and was refusing to bake any sweet cakes now that he was gone.

The field faces the sea, wrote Grace, *and gets a lot of wind and rain, but Declan built Ned a shelter so he can stay out of the worst of it.*

Reading this, Richard felt a stab of…what? Annoyance? This man Declan seemed to be able to turn his hand to anything. One minute he was building Grace a special bath house with an immersion boiler for hot water, an act of generosity that had apparently 'transformed her life', the next he was teaching math and geology and all sorts to the older children in her school. Now he had built Ned a stable, probably from a tree he'd cut down and sliced into planks himself.

Meanwhile, what was Richard doing? Playing at being a journalist while living off his trust fund.

OK, he wasn't a total failure. He and Jacob had covered several stories together by now. He still got a kick out of seeing his name in print, and some of the articles were good, even if they ended up mostly in small local papers with circulations of less than five thousand. He'd had a feature published in the *Savannah Evening Press* about the impact the banking collapse had had on the South, which he'd researched and honed to within an inch of its life. That he was the son of Arthur Lewis, well-known banker, might have helped open a few doors, but he didn't use his connections. If he was going to succeed, or fail, he would do it on his own merits, or lack thereof. He also did a lot of sports coverage – he loved baseball, but also football, basketball and hockey – and then there were the bread-and-butter stories like the one he was working on now about the Georgia Farm Bureau.

He was especially pleased with another article he'd been working on for a while, which he planned to send to the features editor of the *Capital* when it was finished.

But he was aware he hadn't found his niche as a writer. He'd tried writing songs and failed. He would love to come up with some poetry, or maybe a novel…that was, if he could think of what to write about. He kept that dream to himself, though. He didn't want to end up like Jacob and Sarah's friends, spending more time talking about what they were going to write than actually doing it.

You asked me to tell you about myself, but apart from small things like this, nothing much has changed in my life since I wrote last.

Richard breathed a sigh of relief. Clearly Declan hadn't proposed or anything like that; she would have told him, the way she told him everything.

I'm still busy with the school – there are eighty-two children now – and caring for Agnes, though Dymphna, the lady who took over from Teresa, is proving to be a godsend. Between her, Declan and Father Iggy, my life is made easy. There's a girl called Janie O'Shea who I'm hoping to recruit as a monitor, and if I can get that agreed to by the Department of Education, I'll begin to feel I am managing –

At this point, without a full stop or anything, the letter broke off. Puzzled, he turned to the next sheet of paper, which was dated three days later.

15th of January 1940, Knocknashee

Dear Richard,

I can't believe I'm saying this, but my sister, Agnes, is dead.

She passed on the day I started this letter. I can't tell you how sad it was.

Before he read any further, he went to the refrigerator and took out a beer. So Agnes Fitzgerald was dead. He flipped the cap off and took a long drink. He wasn't sure if it was an act of celebration or a good-riddance toast. It was a difficult one to fathom. As far as he could see, Grace's sister was a tyrant who continued to bully Grace even after she'd had a stroke. But he supposed she was Grace's only relative, apart from a brother she didn't remember, so he understood that she was upset of course.

Bringing the bottle back to the table, he sat down again.

I was there with her at the end, and on her deathbed she told me a very disturbing story, how Canon Rafferty kissed her and maybe worse when she was only sixteen, and then told her it was her fault for tempting him. She believed him. She thought the devil was in her. It was terrible to hear. Oh, Richard, I know he's a priest and everything, but I've had such hate-filled thoughts about him...

Astonished, Richard read on as Grace described that harrowing deathbed confession.

I'm telling you, Richard, because I have to tell someone. Only Mary O'Hare knows, and she won't say a word, not even to Tilly; she's like the tomb. But I still find it hard to believe. Poor Agnes, she was only a girl, and the canon must have been in his forties then. He was the one who should have stopped it. He was the one who had taken a vow of celibacy.

And more than that, he encouraged her to lie about my leaving results and to steal my wages, and something else so wicked I could hardly believe my ears when she said it. Richard, I think I mentioned Declan McKenna, Charlie's son?

Richard took another long, slightly annoyed drink of his beer. Yes, he remembered Declan. Sometimes he felt he was never allowed to forget him, Grace mentioned him so often.

Anyway, I might have told you this already – I can't remember, we've been writing for so long – but when Declan was six, his mother died in child-birth, and he and his newborn sister were taken away from their father by the canon. Declan was sent to a reformatory even though he'd done nothing wrong, and the new baby girl just disappeared. Everyone thought she'd been adopted but no one knew where, and the canon always said he didn't know anything about it except that Charlie couldn't care for them and they were better off now.

Well, it turns out he did know. He made Agnes take the baby to America and sell her to some couple for three thousand pounds. I'm going to have to tell Charlie and Declan the truth, but I've decided to wait until after the funeral, I don't know why. Out of respect for Agnes, I suppose – I feel she deserves to be buried in peace.

She went on to explain how she was planning to delay the funeral for more than the customary three days because she'd sent a long telegram to her brother, Father Maurice, in the Philippines, telling him his sister was dead and asking for him to write back.

Richard turned over the page.

Saturday, 3rd of February 1940, Knocknashee.

I don't understand my brother, she wrote in her neat, clear hand, and the paper was slightly torn where she'd crossed the T, as if anger had caused her to press extra hard on the nib.

I was so happy when the letter finally arrived from the Philippines, but there was nothing in it but a Mass card, saying he would pray for Agnes's soul. No words of loss, no enquiry about how it happened.

All I wanted were some childhood memories from when our poor sister was happy, before she was sixteen, a time I don't remember at all. And there was no one else in Knocknashee I could ask to stand up and say a kind word for her. Father Iggy did his best at the funeral Mass. He kept telling us how God is very forgiving, but I'm not sure anyone believed him. They are so used to a diet of hellfire from Canon Rafferty, it will take a long time to convince them God is love, especially where my poor unfortunate sister is concerned.

There was a blot on the paper there, like a tear had been rubbed away, and then Grace seemed to recover her natural composure, because she went on more cheerfully.

Apart from that, the funeral went better than could be expected. Our local undertaker, Seán O'Connor, has a way of running things seamlessly, without ever appearing intrusive – it is a gift. He had no time for poor Agnes when she was alive, but he was so gentle and respectful now that she is dead, and I was so grateful for his guidance. People always call him Seán 'the Last Man to Let You Down' O'Connor, and it's a joke of course, but it's true as well – he didn't let me down.

I was so afraid no one would come, but all our friends and neighbours turned up, and all my pupils from the school with their parents, and it was a dry day and not too cold.

Seán and his three brothers – they get called on the very rare occasion when there are no male relatives or friends of the deceased to carry the coffin – lowered the coffin into our parents' grave; she is to lie forever at my mother's left hand. And then Father Iggy said the last decade of the rosary for the repose of her soul, and I threw in a handful of earth and then all the snowdrops I'd picked from our front garden. I planted the bulbs last autumn, and I was so happy when they came up in January. I never dreamed they would be the only flowers I could find to throw into my sister's grave.

After the earth was piled over the coffin, people lined up to sympathise with me, and they did their best to find something nice to say about Agnes.

Nancy from the post office was first. It was her daughter Teresa who was Agnes's first carer after the stroke, and Agnes gave her an awful time. But Nancy said nothing about that. She just said she was sorry for my troubles, and I said to her I was glad so many people came. She told me everyone was very fond of me and didn't want me to be lonely.

It was Nancy O'Flaherty who mentioned last year how Agnes had never put my wages into the post office. I wish I could tell her now that it was all the canon's doing, but I don't know. She might think even less of my poor sister for tempting a priest – women so often get all the blame.

Richard winced when he read that. Only a short while ago, he'd been thinking it was fine for a man of his class to 'sow his wild oats' but that if his sister was caught doing the same, she'd be ruined.

That's why I'm glad it was Mary O'Hare with me when Agnes confessed. Mary has a way of looking at things. She knows what's right and wrong, and she knows it's different from what's respectable and not. For example she knows her daughter in Dublin is a saint for looking after six stepchildren as well as one of her own, though to begin with she thought Marion an awful eejit altogether, while most people would say Marion is not at all respectable because she married a divorced man, though his wife is dead since – she passed away a few months ago. It was an ease to the poor woman and to Colm too, God be good to her.

Dymphna O'Connell, who took over from Teresa, was next, with seven-year-old Paudie and five-year-old Kate. 'We're sorry for your troubles, Miss Fitz,' the little ones chorused. She has them so well brought up.

I'm going to keep her on until she finds another job. She can cook and clean a bit for me, and maybe do the odd half hour in the school as well. It would be nice to have someone to help tidy up after the art classes.

Then came Pádraig O Sé. I dreaded what he might come up with, as he has a notoriously vicious tongue and was one of the few people to always call Agnes a cailleach *to her face. His big rough hand grasped mine while he spent ages trying to think what to say, until he managed, 'Well, you might get a bit of peace now.' It was the best he could do, I suppose.*

Kit Gallagher was up next. She's the housekeeper who is starving poor Father Iggy in revenge for him replacing the canon. She has a face like she is permanently sucking a lemon. 'My condolences on your loss,' was all she could say. She hated my sister more than anyone; she was jealous how Agnes and the canon were together so much. If only she knew the truth. But then she added, looking around, 'How strange that saint of a man Canon Rafferty didn't come to your sister's funeral.' She couldn't just leave it. Why do some people never miss an opportunity to say a mean thing?

For myself, I can't tell you how relieved I was that he didn't come. I'd half expected him to turn up, for appearances' sake if nothing else, and I don't know what I would have done. I couldn't have shaken his hand or even looked at him.

Peggy Donnelly of the draper's shop was there, and she gave me a hug.

'I'm sorry for your loss a pheata. Agnes was... She was...' She was really struggling with what to say and finally came out with, 'Well, she was a very devout woman, God rest her.'

Bríd Butler from the sweetshop whispered in my ear, 'I left a few sweets back at the house for you, Grace. Don't be passing them around at the afters, keep them for yourself, a bit of something sweet to cheer you up. God rest your sister, ar dheis Dé go raibh a anam dílis.'

That means 'may her decent soul be at God's right hand'. I really hope it's true, Richard, I hope that's where Agnes is. In this world she looked for love from a man unable to give it, not just because he was a priest but because he was evil, and she closed her heart to everyone but him. And now I hope she learns the truth of love from God. I know my parents are in heaven and will be so pleased to see her and love her too.

After Bríd the people just kept coming. Packie Keohane, the grave digger, and his wife; John and Catherine O'Shea; Paddy and Eileen O'Flynn with their eleven children; the Ó Gealbháins from the pub in Dingle; Cyril Clifford and his mother; Biddy O'Donoghue from the grocer's and her husband, Tom, stinking of too much cologne as usual. He actually winked at Tilly, who was standing beside me, and kissed her cheek, though she wasn't a mourner or anything to do with Agnes really. That man has no shame, carrying on like that in front of his wife, who has to pretend not to notice.

On and on it went, until my hand was sore and my leg aching from the cold weather, and there were the afters to get through yet...

But then Hugh and Lizzie Warrington arrived from Cork, and I was so pleased to see them, I felt better again. They said they were sorry to miss the church. Their car burst a tyre coming over the gap and went into a ditch, and they had to wait until a farmer came with his draught horse to pull it out before they could change the wheel and get going again, and all the time the farmer making remarks about newfangled machines and horses being so much better.

Everyone came back to the house for soup and a sandwich – Dymphna and Mary O'Hare had got the house ready – but it was a quiet affair because there were no good stories to tell about the deceased, the way people usually do.

Father Iggy stayed all day and told a very funny story, which lifted the

71

mood and everyone enjoyed. Irish wakes are happy occasions usually. We don't see death as the end, and the sadness is for those left, not the person gone. So it's common to hear laughing or even singing at a good wake. My parents' wake was the best party for miles, I remember. Even though I was heartbroken, it was good to have so many people tell such nice stories about them. I'll tell you Father Iggy's story if you like. It might make you laugh and be a brief respite from the misery of this letter.

Two brothers were at the wake of an old lady, and they had a bit too much of the free whiskey and ended up dancing around and breaking the glasses and being nuisances. So late in the night, they were thrown out of the house by her son. Well, they were very indignant at this insult, so they decided to get revenge on the family of the deceased.

Now the son had a big orchard and it was late autumn, so the two drunk brothers decided to go in and steal all the apples from the orchard to sell at the fair, so they got two big bags and started filling them into the bags. As they left the orchard, one brother saw that the other had a bigger bag full and began complaining loudly at this injustice, and it was the early hours of the morning by now.

So to keep the peace, the brother with the bigger haul suggested they go into the graveyard, where there was a big tomb, and they could put all the apples out on the flat surface and divide them evenly.

Unsteady on their feet and full of whiskey, they managed to drag themselves and the two big bags of fruit up onto the graveyard wall, the gate being locked at night, but as they did, two apples rolled out of the bag and landed below on the ground.

The two brothers considered going back for the two stray apples but decided that it would be too hard to get back up again, so they'd count what they had and collect the two that had fallen on the way out.

They emptied the bags onto a big tomb and started dividing. 'One for you, and one for me,' one of the brothers intoned loudly. 'One for you and one for me.' Over and over he did this.

Well, a local man, walking home from the wake, got the fright of his life, hearing this deep voice coming from the cemetery, 'One for you and one for me,' over and over. He was sure it was God and the devil sharing out the souls of the dead. Panicked, he ran for the priest and woke him up. Of course the priest wasn't too happy about this given the hour, but he agreed to go down to the graveyard because the man was so convinced God and the devil were below.

The priest and the local man crouched behind the graveyard wall, and sure enough they heard it. 'One for you and one for me, one for you and one for me...'

The priest was nervous but willing to face the devil himself to save the souls of the people of his parish, but then the counting stopped and all they could hear was another deep voice saying, 'We have them all from here, and that's fair, but what about the two out by the wall?'

The priest and the man ran screaming up the lane, never to be seen again.

Maybe it seems strange that there would be fun and laughing at a wake, but it's how we do it. The canon is so dour and miserable, but Father Iggy is mischievous and kind, nothing like his superior. I'm sure the canon would not approve of Father Iggy telling a story like that, but everyone loved it.

The Warringtons could only stay for an hour, as they had to be back at the hospital in the morning, and when they left, they made a big point of saying they were leaving me in peace to rest because my leg must be sore, which worked a treat – the house emptied of neighbours. Dymphna washed up the last of the cups before she went, and Tilly took her mother home in the horse and cart.

Then Declan, who had been helping, came to tell me he and his father were going as well, and did I want him to run me my bath before I went, because Dr Warrington had said my leg was paining me...

Richard felt a pang of something. This Declan guy seemed to always be there, on hand, helping Grace. He wished it could be him and not McKenna.

...but I asked him to bring his father into the kitchen, because I had something to say to them, meaning about Agnes's confession.

So we had another pot of tea, and I got out the sweets Bríd had left for me. For ages I couldn't think where to start, so we just chatted about the funeral and how it had gone well, and they seemed happy enough to be there in the warmth as it was freezing outside, but they must have been wondering why I'd asked them to stay.

Then finally I got up my courage and I said the reason was that I had something very serious to tell them. And I blurted out all about Agnes's deathbed confession.

Richard, I can't believe I poured the whole thing out like that, with no warning given. I suppose it had been on my conscience, that it was my own sister who had done this to them, but that's no excuse for springing something like that on those poor men out of the blue.

Declan stood and paced the floor, while Charlie sunk his head in his hands. He looked so old and weary, though he is only fifty. He said this was very hard to know, that years had gone by, and even if this Father Noel Dempsey was still alive and in New York, how could we find him in a city that big? And that if we did find him, why would he tell us the truth?

Then Declan said darkly that he knew how to get at the truth, that he was going to find the canon in Tipperary and would drag it out of him, whatever it took.

Charlie got upset and begged him not to go threatening the canon. The Church is so powerful, the state would lock him up and throw away the key. Declan said he was going to do it anyway, and I felt so awful for causing all this hurt. The only way I could think to stop Declan getting in terrible trouble was by begging him to wait until I'd written to you first, to see if you could help.

He wasn't happy about it at all, but eventually we got him to agree.

Richard, I know I must seem so gauche and naive, and I am, I suppose, but do you know anyone in New York who could help us?

If this is a daft question, I'm sorry, and if you are rolling your eyes now, I wouldn't blame you. It's probably like asking me if I know someone who could find someone in Dublin.

And yes, I know New York is a lot bigger than Dublin, and looking for one person in it would be like looking for a needle in a haystack, only worse because there's a good chance the needle isn't in the haystack at all, but dead or moved on...

A few smudged words followed, as if more tears had fallen.

Richard, I'm a fool. I've just realised New York isn't just a city, it's a state. So please just ignore me. Obviously it's an impossible task. It's only I was so worried for Declan, but by the time you've read this, I'm sure Charlie will have talked sense into him, so don't mind me.

I'm sorry this letter has been such a litany of woes. If it's any consolation, I'm feeling a lot better right now. Just writing to you helps to get it all off my chest.

Richard, if you've read this far, thank you for putting up with me.

Grace

PS If you want to picture the scene, and I know you like hearing about my day-to-day life in Knocknashee, I'm finishing this letter sitting at the kitchen table and it's half past ten in the morning. Outside the rain is relentless – February can be like that, so wet you'd think it could never again be sunny – and the robins in the cherry tree are drenched.

I'm still in my dressing gown, which makes me feel guilty, but everyone has been so kind to me, leaving baskets of stuff on my doorstep early this morning without even knocking. There were eggs and a loaf of home-made bread from the O'Hares, and tea and sugar, and a jar of marmalade from Biddy at the grocer's, and a pat of the home-made salty butter wrapped in a cloth, which I think was from Mikey O'Shea's parents. So I've just made a slice of toast on the ring of the range, and I've smothered it in the butter, which has melted into the holes, and I've piled marmalade on top.

I know it's selfish of me trying to cheer myself up after the business with the McKennas yesterday, but I slept so late and I'm starving and I'm feeling so down about everything.

I'd never have dared lie in so late when poor Agnes was alive. Saturday was always her day to get the 'house in order', which meant both of us up at seven to start polishing and mopping, and I kept it up after she had her stroke to keep her happy.

If the poor woman knew I wasn't even dressed yet, she'd be spinning in her grave at the sin of sloth, which to her was the deadliest of the seven sins.

I do miss her, you know. Life without her is hard to get used to; the house seems very big and quiet. And it does make me think about my future. Is this it for me now? Running the school, until I retire or die? Living here in this house, the last of my family? Because I don't think Maurice is ever coming home. He is all I have in the world, but he's gone on the missions and has not been seen since. He didn't even come back when Mammy and Daddy died – more Masses and prayers arrived in the post instead. So while I know I'm not entirely alone, as Tilly says, my brother is as much use to me as a chocolate teapot.

And here I am, pitying myself again!

Just ignore me.

Your self-pitying Irish pen friend,

Grace

Richard folded the letter and propped it in its envelope back against the ketchup and sat thinking for a while.

Poor Grace. But also, what a coincidence.

Only this evening, after a couple of beers, Jacob and he had discussed – a bit tipsily – going all the way to New York, over eight hundred miles, to talk to the foreign editor of the *Capital* in person and try to convince him to send them to Europe, instead of just communicating by letter and constantly getting ignored.

So maybe he could look for this Father Noel Dempsey himself, and at least alleviate one of her worries?

Next week wasn't possible. Gideon Clarendon, editor of the *Savannah Morning News*, had commissioned him to write a review of *Strange Cargo*, Clark Gable's new film after *Gone with the Wind*. He'd found the movie boring and didn't like Joan Crawford much, so it was a struggle. He was planning to see it again during the week and hopefully come up with something 'punchy and precise, entertaining and astute', because no editor would pay for fluff. Every word had to pull its weight, as Gideon Clarendon was fond of pointing out.

He'd also gotten to write a feature for the *Savannah Evening Press* on a meeting of the South Georgia Farmer's Association on the subject of onions. Apparently the twenty-four million crops planted in the state would come to harvest before the huge Texas onion crop, and so there would be enough for one onion for every third American. Mainly yellow Bermudas, though some white Bermudas were also being planted. He could see why onions made people cry. But apparently this mattered to people. He was a newspaperman and didn't get to pick what he covered.

He'd be free, though, from the following Monday. He and Jacob could set off on Sunday evening and travel through the night. They'd get to New York on Tuesday to meet the editor on Wednesday – they'd send a telegram to let him know they were coming. He knew Jacob had a movie festival to cover back in Savannah over the weekend and would have to head back straight away, but he could stay on by himself for a few days and make an effort to find this priest.

He'd never been to New York, and the prospect of going to explore that city and do Grace Fitzgerald a favour at the same time was appealing.

Of course the favour involved keeping the ever-helpful Declan out of trouble... But that was a good thing, Richard told himself sternly. The guy was a friend of Grace, and any friend of hers should be a friend of his.

Meanwhile, he'd write a short note back to her commiserating about her sister, along with the article he hoped to send to the *Capital* to see if she liked it.

It was the one she'd given him permission to write ages ago, about the letter to St Jude she'd thrown into the ocean in an empty bottle, which had ended up on the beach near the house in St Simons. Maybe it would help to cheer her up. It would be his equivalent of Tilly sending a dozen eggs, or Biddy leaving a pot of marmalade, or the pat of salty home-made butter from the O'Sheas.

As he daydreamed briefly about being in Knocknashee, there was a clatter and sound of hasty feet on the back step. The kitchen door flew open with such a bang that even old Doodle came blearily awake and looked up from his comfy bed, which despite what Sarah had said wasn't flea-ridden at all. Esme aired it on a regular basis, much to the old dog's annoyance; he preferred it smelly.

Sarah stormed in through the door first, and Jacob followed, looking annoyed. Clearly they'd had some sort of a row.

Richard decided it was best not to ask, and anyway, his mind was still full of New York. 'Jacob, I've been thinking – let's just head up to the Big Apple on Wednesday. I'll pay for both of us if your cow dollars have run out. I've got a couple of things I want to do up there myself, so after we've seen this guy Falkirk –'

'Don't encourage him, Richard,' snarled Sarah, pulling off her coat.

'Great idea, Richard. Let's do it. Goodnight.'

And to Richard's surprise, Jacob slammed out of the kitchen and up the stairs; on the landing above, Richard could hear him head into Nathan's room, and that door closed as well, more quietly, though, out of respect for Esme, who had already gone to bed. Meanwhile Sarah beat a path to the fridge and grabbed her own beer, joining Richard at the table, slumping down crossly in a chair, her arm thrown over the back of it, her dark eyes moody and dark-brown curls in disarray.

'So what was that all about, dare I ask?' he asked.

'Jacob sleeping in Nathan's room? I assume he "wants to be alone",' said Sarah, doing a passable imitation of Greta Garbo, then she slugged back her beer.

Richard got up and fetched himself another bottle from the fridge, flipped the cap, then sat back down, waiting. He found, if he left his sister space, she would tell him what was troubling her in the end.

Eventually she said, 'I don't want you two going to New York together.'

He stared at her, surprised. 'Why not? Sarah, it's just for work. We're seeing Jacob's editor about being sent to Europe, and Jacob will have to come home straight away afterward – he has a festival to cover.'

'But that's just the point,' she burst out. 'I don't want him to go over there!'

He was still confused. 'To Europe? But...why not? It's all he's been talking about for months.'

'But I never thought it would happen!'

'Sarah, relax. It's a good career move –'

'Oh, for God's sake,' his sister snapped contemptuously. 'A pair of dumb kids playing at going off to war, not giving a damn about who you're leaving behind, and that's all it is to you? A good career move?'

He tried to reassure her. 'We're not going to war. Nothing's happening. We're just going to talk to a few people about their experiences, if this guy will send us, which he probably won't. Jacob won't be in any danger.'

'Because of course he's going to stay away from where Jews are being persecuted?' She raised a cynical eyebrow. 'Is that not exactly what he wants to go over there to document, to show everyone what's happening?'

'Well, yes, but... I mean...being press and Americans and everything will protect us.'

'Will it? If America goes into the war like Roosevelt wants?'

'Yes, it will,' he said, with more conviction than he felt. 'And look, Jacob will be OK. He's smart. He'll make sure not to do or say anything to get the wrong kind of attention.'

'Until he meets up with other Jews, which is absolutely his intention, then he'll get so riled up...' She let out a long, shuddering sigh. 'Look, I get it, I do. And I agree with a lot of what he says, but being a Jew here is one thing. Sure, there's prejudice. Sure, our parents wouldn't have him to dinner or in their clubs. But over there, if what you wrote in that article about Mr Schlisser and his family is only half true...'

'We're not going to Germany, Sarah, we're hoping to go to France. And it's not likely to happen, so this fight is probably for nothing anyway.'

'And that's another thing. How the hell do either of you expect to find your way around or talk to people when you can't even speak the language?'

'I'm sure the newspaper will put us in touch with someone to help us...or...' He softened his voice and said coaxingly, 'Maybe you could give us some lessons before we go?' Sarah had been to finishing school in Switzerland and was nearly fluent in French and passable in German; she had a knack for languages like she had for numbers. Richard had been taught French in school, but he hadn't learnt any; there'd been too many other interesting things going on – parties, and girls, and cars.

He knew how much it annoyed Sarah, the clever one, that all she was expected to do was marry someone like Algernon Smythe, while Nathan got to be a doctor and Richard was offered a career in their father's bank.

Now she looked at him for a long moment, her eyes narrowing, like something was going on in that brilliant head, but instead of answering him, she shrugged and picked up the letter leaning against the ketchup bottle. 'Your Irish girlfriend?'

'Not my girlfriend, Sarah.' He knew she wasn't being serious, but somehow her comment annoyed him; he wasn't sure why.

'Everything OK with her?'

'Not really. Her sister died.'

'Oh. Sad.'

'Yes, it is.'

She turned the envelope around in her hands without trying to look in it, like she was still thinking about something else. Then she said, 'You know, I think this Grace girl was part of the reason Miranda dumped you.'

'What?' He was so taken aback, he laughed. 'Why on earth…?'

'I think she felt a bit jealous or something.'

He scoffed. 'That's total nonsense, Sarah. And if she ever said that to you, it was just an excuse to make her look less calculating. The fact is she wanted me to go into the bank and I wouldn't, that's all there is to it. No point picking over the past anyway. She's happy with Algy now. He's much more her sort.'

'You mean, her family's sort,' she said, still turning the envelope.

'Well, Miranda was always one to do what her family wanted.'

'Mm…' She propped the letter back against the ketchup. 'But I don't blame her for that, and nor should you. It's a hard decision for us girls to make, who we hitch ourselves to for life. We're not allowed to make our own way in the world. We have to chain ourselves to some man and hope he's got what it takes to make us happy. Do we want a wild adventurer, or somebody safe and secure?'

He looked at her in surprise. The Sarah he'd known all his life was a mischievous albeit hugely privileged girl, always with a rebellious glint in her dark-brown eyes. But now she seemed subdued and self-doubting.

'What's up, Sar? You don't wish you'd married Algy yourself, do you?'

She shuddered. 'God no. I don't want children who look like fish.'

'For sure. And you know, he might have thrown you a few yacht parties for a while,' he said soothingly, 'but after he inherited the business and had to knuckle down, he'd want you to do nothing, just sit there at home being bored all day, like a good little wife.'

'Says the man who's about to run off to Europe with my boyfriend, leaving me to sit at home bored all day...'

'Ah now, Sarah, that's different.'

'Is it? All men are the same underneath. Whether they're off to make money or off to change the world, all they want is to have a little woman who waits for them until they graciously choose to reappear, and then they'll let her fuss over him and make him a cocktail and warm his slippers or whatever it is she's supposed to do to keep him happy, never mind if she's happy or not.'

He looked at her, shaking his head, amused. 'I don't think you'll ever be that woman, Sarah.'

Her eyes flashed. 'Then what sort of woman will I be? You know, I'm beginning to wonder if that friend of Grace Fitzgerald's has it right – just doing her own thing, not bothering about getting a man. I'd live like that if I could.'

'Be a farmer?' He tried to suppress a grin at the idea of Sarah tilling her own little stony fields, and butchering her own lambs, and getting honey out of hives while surrounded by angry bees.

'Yeah, of course, a farmer, that's exactly what I mean. I wonder if she ever read that book I sent her?'

He pulled an apologetic face. 'She did, actually...'

'Oh! Why didn't you tell me? Did she say what she thought of it?'

'Mm...' He didn't want to disappoint her. After all the effort she'd gone through to buy the thing – apparently it was very hard to find and normal bookshops didn't stock it – it seemed a bit mean to tell her Tilly hadn't liked it much.

'Was she offended by it?' She looked suddenly concerned.

'No, nothing like that.' He wondered why she would think Tilly might be offended by a piece of fiction. 'But I'm afraid she only said it was OK.'

To his surprise Sarah cheered right up. 'She said it was OK, did she? Interesting.'

'Interesting? Why interesting?'

She winked at him, draining her bottle of beer. 'Never you mind, little brother. You just stick to your own charming *Gone with the Wind* romance with your Irish girlfriend.'

He sighed. 'She is *not* my girlfriend.' Really, his sister was incorrigible.

CHAPTER 7

*G*race pulled on the new red coat she'd treated herself to from Peggy Donnelly's, and it was as warm as toast.

She and Peggy had had a hard time finding one to fit her. She was only four foot eleven, and everything made her look like a child playing dress up.

'God, Grace, there's not a pick on you, girleen. Ye're such a dainty little thing.' Peggy had sighed as she waddled up and down the rails, hunting through her new stock. 'And I like a ball of butter then. 'Twould be easier to climb over me than walk around me these days.'

It was true Peggy was getting larger with every passing year. As a childless widow, she was lonely and had resorted to eating her troubles away. She didn't seem to care about her weight, though. In fact she'd confided to Grace that it was a good thing when you were selling clothes, as people felt less self-conscious buying from a fatter woman.

But as for Grace being dainty...well, it was nice of Peggy to say it, but she hardly felt that way with the clumsy calliper and ugly black built-up shoe. In the end they'd settled on a child's duffel coat with a hood, a padded lining and large bone buttons.

After doing up her coat, Grace wrapped the matching scarf – that

Peggy had thrown into the bag 'for luck' – around her neck and pulled on a multicoloured hat she had knitted herself from the usual odds and ends of wool. She suspected she looked like one of the small lumpy snowmen the children built in the schoolyard in January, but she didn't care. She would be protected from the freezing February blast coming in off the ocean, flattening the pale early daffodils.

She let herself out the front gate and limped in the early morning light down the main street, the shops all still closed, the street deserted. It was a good hour and a half before she needed to be in school. At least it wasn't raining today, though the clouds over the ocean were dark and threatening. It might blow over, though, one never could tell; the weather on the coast was nothing if not unpredictable.

The gulls were cawing, wheeling in the air above, waiting for the fishermen; the rooks were competing from the yew trees around the church. Shrill sparrows and warbling robins filled in the top notes, and the layers of birdsong lifted her troubled spirits; it felt as if they were encouraging her to make this visit.

Grace's parents, and now Agnes, were buried in the graveyard on the side of the hill that gave Knocknashee its name – 'the hill of the fairies' – overlooking the town and the ocean. It was as beautiful a spot as you'd find anywhere in the world, Grace was sure of it. Not that she'd been anywhere beyond Cork, but the rugged majesty of the Dingle Peninsula was surely singular. Winter or summer, it was wild, beautiful and dramatic.

The hill used to be such a hard slog for her, but she felt it easier these days, since she'd been doing the hot water treatment. Either side of the path, the yellow furze that in summer would give off a sweet coconut scent was stark and spiky. Intertwined around it was traveller's joy, a kind of climbing clematis with a puffy grey flower that bloomed in winter.

The surrounding mountains were rusty with dry heather, dotted only with a few mountain sheep that had thick wool coats that could withstand the cold, but in the summer those same mountains would be ablaze with purple rhododendron and yellow gorse, and the small fields, separated by unmortared stone walls, would bloom with pale-yellow buttercups, bright-yellow iris and blood-red fuchsia. Lambs would gambol and cattle would graze.

A blackbird came to rest on the branch of a bare hawthorn tree, singing its song. She opened the rusty gate to the graveyard, hanging on by one hinge – the salt in the air here rusted everything – pulling her coat over her hand before touching the freezing metal. Picking her way across the uneven ground, she was careful; a fall would be a disaster up here, as nobody might come for ages.

The cemetery had been in continuous use for centuries. There was a standing stone from the days when the pagans walked these mountains, twice the height of a man, pale green and yellow-white with different lichens. She, like everyone here, grew up with such reminders of Ireland's ancient past all around them. Stories of the Fir Bolg, the Tuatha Dé Danann, the Fomorians, the ancient magical people of this island. Celtic ring forts with their underground souterrains were their playgrounds; dolmens, marking places on the landscape for four or five thousand years, their significance often lost in the mists of time, were just part of their everyday lives. The monks of the seventh century built their beehive huts out here, the perfect location for their desire to be close to God, unencumbered by the trappings of man. This was an ancient place, and every stone, every blade of grass, every mountain and waterfall and cliff had a story to tell.

The small, stunted limestone headstones from Christian medieval times were packed so tight, it was impossible not to step on them as she passed. She apologised as she always did and offered a prayer for the unknown incumbents, their inscriptions long worn away by the salt winds. Newer graves were squeezed in between the ancient ones; there was no pattern to it. The Fitzgerald grave backed onto the family plot of the Duggan family, last opened in 1847 for a man and his wife and two children, all dead in the same year, the worst year of famine. And squeezed between the bare strip of earth beneath which Agnes lay and the wall of the cemetery was the grave of a baby boy who died in 1540, a lonely little stone, only a few inches high, with just the name 'Fergus' and the dates carved crudely on it.

Yet despite the haphazard nature of the place, Grace found it gave her a sense of order, the continuity of time and people of this place, of her place.

One day she would be lowered into this earth at her father's right hand, the way Agnes lay next to their mother, and then Maurice would go down next to Grace, if he decided to be buried here, and there would be an end to the Fitzgeralds, because Agnes had died childless, and Maurice was a celibate priest, and no one was going to marry a woman crippled by polio.

Last autumn some American visitors had come to Knocknashee to find the Duggan grave. They had called to the school wondering if there were any records of their family. A handsome brother and sister with American accents, tall and well fed, with the look of the Irish in their tanned faces, black hair and dark-brown eyes. Their ancestors were the surviving children of the last to be buried here; they had made the trip to America in 1847 – uneducated, without English – showing such temerity and strength, and now their well-heeled descendants had come back to see where it all started. Grace hoped all the Duggans buried in this grave were looking down and smiling. It had moved her at the time, thinking about it.

When Grace took them to see the headstone, which she knew well, the man had looked sheepish. 'I guess you guys laugh at us Americans coming over here looking for our roots, huh?'

'Why would we?' she'd asked, puzzled.

'Just that you all know your ancestors, and it must seem kinda lame, us coming back saying he was a Duggan from Kerry or whatever?'

She'd smiled then. 'But they were our ancestors too. For every brave boy or girl that got on the emigrant boat, there was a mother, a father, a brother or sister left behind, like your relatives buried here. We would never laugh at you for wanting to know where you come from. Sure we all have the same blood in our veins.'

Now, once she reached her family plot, Grace perched on the flat rock at her father's right side, as she always did. This stone was not a grave; it was just an outcrop of the limestone beneath the soil that surged to the surface everywhere in this rocky land, like white teeth growing up through the grass and heather.

Her parents' stone stood out from the rest; it was black marble and very large. Agnes had chosen it so the wind and rain wouldn't weather it, but Grace felt it always looked out of place and kind of showy, as if the Fitzgeralds were worthy of a better stone than anyone else, when her parents weren't a bit like that.

In memory of
Edward John Fitzgerald 1880–1932
And his wife, Kathleen Mary Fitzgerald (née Moriarty) 1883–1932

Grace found it cold and impersonal, and when the earth had settled on her sister's side of the grave and Agnes's name was added to the headstone, she was going to ask the stone mason for a little prayer or a quotation as well to soften the look of it. *Ceol na n-aingeal go gcloise siad*, something simple like that, that they might hear the angels' music.

Gathering her red coat over her knees, massaging her bad leg with her hand, she greeted her parents as she always did. 'Hello, Mammy and Daddy. 'Tis early in the day for a visit, I know, but I couldn't sleep for thinking and *chíonn beirt rud nach bhfeiceann duine amháin*,' she began with a smile. That was another of Mammy's sayings – two heads will see things that one won't.

She stopped then, feeling awkward. It wasn't just her parents in the grave now; her sister was buried there as well. And if her parents could hear her, so could Agnes.

Thinking about what to say, she turned her face to the weak, pale morning sun, which was doing its best to break through the blanket of heavy grey clouds and failing. There was a smell of rain in the air; if she sat here much longer, she was going to get soaked. She took a deep breath.

'Mammy, Daddy…and Agnes…' It felt very strange to be asking advice from Agnes after all that had gone between them. But then again, why not? This situation had everything to do with her dead sister. 'The thing is, I'm not sure what to do, if anything at all…'

And she poured it all out, the situation with Charlie and Declan, and how she didn't know if she'd done the right thing by telling them.

'I wish I could be sure, Agnes, that Father Dempsey was in New York. He might have moved, he might never have been there at all, and maybe you meant the state, not the city – they're two different things. And on top of that, we don't even know if he is still alive. I wrote to Richard asking him for advice on how to find a missing priest. He must think I'm mad or a fool. I'm sorry, I've no idea what I'm asking you… Oh!'

A large drop of rain had just fallen on her head, and then another and another. The heavens were ready to open; time to be getting back. She said goodbye to her parents, placing a kiss on the black marble as she always did, and then another goodbye and a kiss for Agnes. It felt so strange, as she'd never kissed her sister in real life; Agnes wouldn't allow it, said it was silly sentimentality. Then she made her way back carefully across the graves, the raindrops coming faster now, tucking up her long auburn curls into her woollen hat.

As she set off down the hill, she met Charlie cycling up the stony lane towards her on his early postal round, his sack of letters over his shoulder, his collar turned up against the shower. Rain, hail, snow, gales – it didn't matter; Charlie McKenna delivered the post. There were several cottages beyond the graveyard, and the O'Hare farm as well. He cycled miles every day, so the hill was no bother to him.

'Morning, Gracie!' he called as he neared her.

'Hello, Charlie. 'Tis early you're out and about.'

To her surprise he got off his bike, leaning it on the ditch, and started rummaging in his bag.

'Ah, Charlie, don't worry. If I have post, give it to me later. Get on to the O'Hares', and they'll take you in for a heat up and a cuppa before you get soaked.'

'No tea for me. I've the whole round to do yet, and another as well. 'Tis more soaked I'll be getting. Now here you are.' He pulled out a letter covered in American stamps. 'Put it in your pocket, Gracie, before it gets wet, but don't be expecting an answer to your question about that priest. There's wicked disruption to the post from abroad since the Emergency started – it would be a miracle if your last letter got there before your friend wrote back, not unless you have someone looking after you from above.'

Grace sighed and felt bad about the whole thing again. 'I suppose you're right.'

The postman nodded and pulled his cap down over his eyes as the raindrops fell faster. 'And there's going to be more delays to the post by the looks of things if that madman Hitler keeps this up. If I see Tilly, will I send her down with the horse and cart to take you home out of the rain?'

'Do not, Charlie, she has enough to be doing. My leg is fine. I'll be home in no time.'

'Right so. God bless.' And he was gone up the hill on his bike.

Grace kept the letter in her inside pocket as she limped home through the blustering rain. It wasn't unusual of Richard to send a second letter before he'd heard back from her; it was common for both of them to drop each other another line after the first had gone – some funny story about Knocknashee she'd forgotten to tell him, or in Richard's case, a newspaper clipping of an article he'd got published that he wanted her opinion on.

Judging by the thickness of the letter – she felt it again – that was the case in this instance, because it was very thin.

CHAPTER 8

$\mathcal{B}$ack in the welcome heat of the kitchen, Grace pegged up her coat, hat and scarf to dry on the washing line slung across the corner of the room to dry, made herself a cup of tea and a bowl of porridge sprinkled with Biddy's sugar and slit open the envelope with a butter knife. Instead of the newspaper clipping she'd expected, there was a closely typed sheet of flimsy paper, along with a short letter.

She read the letter first.

Dear Grace,

What a terrible shock. I'm deeply sorry for your loss. Agnes was your sister, and she was a huge part of your life, and the story she told you on her deathbed explains so much about the way she was. It's hard to believe anyone could be as evil as Canon Rafferty. He seems to have blighted so many lives in Knocknashee—your good friends Charlie and Declan McKenna, as well as your sister's. And I know he treated your friend Tilly very badly as well. Sarah sends her regards, by the way.

I'm glad the funeral went well, and I'm not at all surprised the whole of Knocknashee showed up for you. You have such good friends and neighbors, and you're a good friend and neighbor to them.

Grace, I don't know how long this note will take to reach you, or how it will travel to you. The shipping routes are so disrupted. In fact I'm amazed your letter found me this quickly, but it's just as well it did, because...

Well, I'm going to New York ten days from now!

I haven't been to the Big Apple before – I wonder why it's called that; I must find out – but I'm traveling with Jacob to try and persuade the foreign editor face to face to send us to Europe, a crazy idea of Jacob's that won't work, I'm sure of it, but we're doing it anyway. And I now intend to stay on for a few extra days to search for your priest myself. So my next letter will be a lot longer than this one, and will tell you whether I have succeeded or failed.

In the meantime I'm enclosing that article about the bottle we discussed before. I'm intending to send it to the features editor of the Capital, *with some pictures taken at the scene by Jacob and that photo you sent me of yourself, but I don't want to do it without your permission.*

Please let me know what you think as soon as you can, and as soon as the battle in the North Atlantic allows.

I know it's taken me forever to write this piece, but after things changed with your sister's stroke, it took me a long time to feel my way back into it from a different angle. I think I have it straight now, and it feels like the right time for it as well. No doubt I'm flattering myself, but I think it could be important with everything heating up over there in Europe and the big discussion about whether America should enter the war.

See if you think the same. And if you don't care for the piece, please say so – you don't have to explain yourself, and we'll never talk about it again.

Grace, I hope this isn't an imposition, and please accept all my sympathy for your sad loss.

Richard

Grace sat smiling in amazement and thinking about poor Charlie on his rounds as the rain bucketed down outside, rattling off the slates of the little bath house and running down the window in opaque sheets, obscuring her view of the back yard.

So Richard was going to New York to see an editor, and he was going to stay on to search for Father Noel Dempsey? How generous of him. She longed to rush over to Charlie's cottage, a thatched two-up, two-down to the right of the post office, and tell Declan the news at once. But as quick as the urge came, she suppressed it. She'd caused the McKennas enough heartbreak and uncertainty already; she would wait until Richard's next letter to see whether he'd found the mysterious priest or not.

And that was fine, because even though Charlie McKenna knew she'd got a letter from America, he didn't expect it to contain any advice from Richard about Father Dempsey, because he didn't think there'd been enough time for Grace's letter to reach America before this one was sent. 'Not unless you have someone looking after you from above,' he'd said.

She still had another hour and a half before she needed to be in school, so she poured herself a second cup of tea and settled down to read the article Richard Lewis had sent her, which was closely typewritten on thin paper. It was the first time he'd asked her opinion on an article before it was published, and it felt like a huge responsibility.

The opening paragraph made her eyes widen in astonishment.

She is nineteen years old and very beautiful; she lives between the purple mountains and the vast ocean in the wild, remote west of Ireland; she speaks Irish—don't call it Gaelic—as well as English; she plays the piano and the tin whishtle; she reads every book she can lay her hands on, especially the old Irish legends of gods and heroes; and the tales she tells me of her everyday life make me laugh out loud.

How did I meet her? I have never met her in person. But by chance—or was it fate?—we were thrown together and have found a common purpose: to believe in each other and support each other's dreams.

Two years ago, when she was seventeen, this young girl poured all the frustrations of being young and longing to escape from what she called the smallness of her world into a letter written to St. Jude, the patron saint of hope and champion of lost causes. Then she pushed that letter into an empty bottle and flung it into the Atlantic Ocean, never expecting to hear of it again.

Months later, I found it. Or rather my dog found it, digging it out of a pile of seaweed, washed up on the beach at St. Simons Island.

I am a young man from a wealthy banking family. I was raised in Savannah, the jewel in Georgia's crown. It's genteel, not rugged, a well-

planned city of elegant mansions, with smooth roads and wide sidewalks, not a haphazard collection of thatched stone cottages spilling onto a single muddy cobbled street. When it's dark outside, I switch on the electric light—a utility unheard of in rural Ireland. When I buy my food, I have no idea where it came from. When she buys food, she knows exactly which neighbor's hens laid those eggs, or bees made that honey, or cow gave that milk. When I want to go somewhere for entertainment, I drive my Buick to the movies. She saddles up an old pony named Ned and takes him to the beach, and she watches the cormorants dive for fish and seals pop up their heads from the waves and crabs scuttle sideways across the sand.

Yet when I read her letter, every word rang inside me as if it were a bell.

Why did I feel such a connection to an unknown Irish girl, far across the ocean, in a place I couldn't then find on a map?

I felt it because we were both young, both had hopes and dreams. Both of us longed to live our lives as we wished to live them, not follow the path others had chosen for us.

In other words, I felt it because we were both human.

And like humans everywhere, we desired to be free, and we desired to be happy.

So I replied to her, told her about my own dreams, and since then many letters have crossed that ocean, the vast Atlantic.

Is it possible to care deeply about a person you have never met, who lives far away on the other side of the ocean, who maybe speaks a different language, or who was raised in a different religion, who plays different sports? I used to think it wasn't possible, but now I know I was wrong.

Because, like the Atlantic Ocean, our common humanity unites us more than it divides us.

Europe at the moment is fighting for its freedom, it is fighting for hope, fighting to live life as it wishes, fighting not to be crushed beneath the heel of Hitler's boot.

It is easy to think of that continent as a place far away, divided from us by the vast Atlantic. But the ocean unites us as much as it divides us; a message cast into the water on the western shores of Europe will one day wash up on the eastern shores of our own continent.

So in a way, this is a love story.

Not the one everyone has been talking about for the last year, Scarlett O'Hara sweeping down cantilevered stairs in a flowing crimson gown, Rhett Butler smouldering at her, beautiful women, handsome men, longing and lust pulsating beneath the surface and a full orchestra playing in the background.

No, this story is not like that.

It is the love story of two different worlds, and the principal players are America and Europe. And Europe is the one sending the message across the ocean, addressed to the patron saint of hope and champion of lost causes. Impossible ideals, like democracy and freedom.

We are different people, from different worlds, but the ocean unites us.

History separates us, yet we are united in mind; culture separates us, yet we are united in heart; distance separates us, yet we are united in spirit.

And we belong together. We have to belong together. We have to love and support and help each other.

Otherwise, for the world, there will be no happy ending.

Grace's hands trembled as she laid the typed sheet down on the table on top of the handwritten note. She tried to steady her breath as she read that first sentence again...

She is nineteen years old and very beautiful.

Her cheeks burnt; her mouth was dry; her heart pounded in her chest.

Stop it, Grace, she told herself sternly. *You're being silly. Stop trying to read between the lines.*

Richard Lewis had made it perfectly clear this 'love story' was about Europe and America, and how what happened on one continent could wash up on the shores of another. He'd spelled out that he wasn't talking about a classical romance, nothing like *Gone with the Wind*, with its 'longing and lust pulsating beneath the surface'.

He'd simply made the story of Grace writing to St Jude into a way of getting people's attention, making the impersonal seem personal. That's what all good writers did when they wanted to get a message across.

But still, she read the first sentence again... *She is nineteen years old and very beautiful.*

Did he mean it? He couldn't mean it.

Even if he did, then if he ever met her in real life, he'd be quick enough to change his mind.

She'd only ever sent him one picture, one she and Tilly had had taken by a seaside photographer the day after they went to see Cullen's Celtic Cabaret in Dingle, but that was only of her head and shoulders, so she supposed she looked normal enough. What it didn't show was the twisted leg, the limping walk, the built-up shoe. She'd told Richard about her polio, she hadn't lied, but maybe he didn't understand how bad it was. If he saw her in real life, he wouldn't think her beautiful.

And anyway, he didn't mean it. He couldn't. He was only telling a story to get the reader's interest so they would keep reading.

Agnes had lied about a lot of things, but she was right about Grace being destined to grow old alone. Since the polio, the possibility of her ever finding someone to love, or for someone to love her, seemed as unlikely as a white blackbird. People like her didn't attract men. Men wanted wives with working legs, who didn't limp everywhere, who didn't get tired after a short walk. Men wanted a real woman, not one so small that she took a children's size in coats.

And on top of that, Richard Lewis wasn't even an ordinary man. He wasn't a farmer or fisherman's son from Knocknashee. With his trust fund, and his own house by the sea and his motor car, which he'd even mentioned in the article to show how different he was from her, and his friends with yachts and his father who owned a bank, there was no way on God's green earth he'd be interested romantically in someone like her.

She reread the short handwritten note again to steady herself. It was kind but matter-of-fact. Suitably sympathetic about Agnes and very generous about looking for Father Dempsey, all the sorts of things she'd come to expect of him, but not a hint of romance.

Grace's cheeks grew hot again at the thought of that photo being published. But then she pulled herself together. Of course the article needed pictures to illustrate it. It helped the readers to imagine the scene. And what did it matter what a load of strangers she would never meet thought about what she looked like? Anyway, it was a very small photograph, only two inches square, so they'd hardly notice.

Please let me know what you think as soon as you can, he'd written, and then he'd mentioned the difficulty of getting a letter across the North Atlantic these days. He'd be amazed to learn how fast his letter had got here. Just as fast as hers had got to him…though there was no guarantee that would ever happen again, as Charlie was saying it got less likely every day.

We support each other's dreams, he'd written. Well, she was proud to support him.

Her red coat was still wet on the outside, but it was good-quality wool and lined, so it was dry inside. She found a different hat on the hall stand – a dark-green oilskin one that Tilly had left behind the other day – and a different, pale-blue scarf that had belonged to Agnes. In her mind she asked her sister's permission and thanked her for the loan of it as she let herself out into the street.

The rain was still relentless, bouncing up off the cobbles as she crossed the road. She did have an umbrella back at the house. Lizzie had insisted on giving her one that someone left in the hospital – it was pouring one of the days she was in Cork last year, and it had been great for keeping her dry. But here in Knocknashee, exposed to the ocean, the umbrella would be blown inside out and destroyed by the time she got to the post office, so she kept it for her visits to the Warringtons and the rest of the time left it in the hall stand.

As she pushed open the door, the little bell jangled and Nancy O'Flaherty looked up.

'Grace, in the name of God, what has you out on a morning like this? You wouldn't put a milk churn out in it,' she fussed as she came around the public side of the counter; sure enough there was nobody else there.

'Hello, Mrs O'Flaherty.' Grace smiled as she removed her oilskin hat, shaking off the drops. 'I know, I'm daft as the crows, but I have to send an urgent telegram to America.'

'Well, let you sit down over there and write it out, and I'll send it right away,' Nancy said, and Grace knew the postmistress would be as good as her word. Nancy O'Flaherty was a very chatty person and happy to talk about all the goings-on in the town, but she never commented on people's postal business. If you got a cheque or a summons to appear in court in the post, or you needed to send a telegram of a private nature, the people of Knocknashee were confident it stayed with Mrs O'Flaherty and wasn't the subject of discussion with everyone who came in to buy a stamp. 'Just remember now, the shorter you can make it, the better.'

But Grace had already decided what to write, and it was very short indeed. She intended to send the exact same telegram that she had sent to Richard from this very post office what seemed like a lifetime ago.

Back then he'd had quite a different idea of how to write about finding the empty naggin of Paddy's whiskey washed up on St Simons beach, with Grace's letter to St Jude rolled up in it. Then it was going to be a human-interest story with a polio angle, nothing about Europe or the war. He might even have written a follow-up piece when she got there – she'd been going to go to the hot springs the president of America went to.

That particular dream came crashing down when Agnes had her stroke, and Grace had to return the first-class ticket to America that Richard had sent her. They were fated never to meet, it seemed.

After writing a simple YES on the form, she handed the postmistress the slip and the address. Nancy took it without remarking on it, accepted the fee of one penny and sat down to send it.

Once the telegram was gone, they had a brief chat, mainly about the weather and how the cattle would need to be kept in for another few weeks at this rate, which would be hard on the farming families because if they were inside, they needed feeding and that was expensive. Then Grace put her hat back on and stood to go.

Just as she reached the door, Mrs O'Flaherty called her back again. 'I'm not being nosy now, Grace, but I was wondering, would Dymphna be free to take a new job if it came available?'

Grace looked at the postmistress in surprise. It seemed unlikely Nancy was planning to offer Dymphna a job as a postwoman, bicycling up and down hills in the early morning with a big sack on her back. That was surely not a job for the stick-thin, careworn widow. The postal round in Knocknashee was getting bigger. People were sending more letters now that their children were going to school and could write them for their parents, and she knew Nancy had been short-handed after Declan left his job as junior postman to be a teacher. But she had replaced Declan in October with Paddy and Eileen O'Flynn's second-oldest son, Fiachra who was literate and numerate, knew the whole area like the back of his hand from all his childhood jaunts and these days had a good, sensible head on his shoulders.

'I don't know, Nancy. You'd have to ask her?'

'But what I mean is, is she indispensable to you, Grace?'

'Oh, I see...' Grace hesitated, not sure how to answer.

She would never say this to anyone, but now that Agnes was gone, she was only employing Dymphna because the poor widow needed the money to feed her children. And it was getting awkward with how little there was for Dymphna to do. So far she'd made new curtains for the entire house, mended every rip or tear in every sheet and pillow slip, cleared out the pantry that had gone neglected and done everything she could think of to be of use. She also helped clear up after the art classes on Friday, but once Janie became a monitor, that job would be gone too.

'Honestly, Mrs O'Flaherty, it's up to Dymphna. I love having her around, but I wouldn't want to stand in the way of her getting something better,' she said diplomatically.

'Well, I thought so. I had an idea,' said Nancy.

'Go on.' Grace sat back down next to the table on which she'd filled out the telegram form.

'Well, Kit Gallagher,' began Nancy, with a conspiratorial glance towards the door, not that it was likely anyone else would turn up in this weather. 'You know she was really for the canon, and between you, me and the wall, she's starving poor Father Iggy and that new curate, Father Lehane, half to death. She refuses to bake, and for dinner they're getting one chicken leg or maybe a chop, or half a mackerel each in season, and only two potatoes with it, not big ones, and a few leaves of cabbage, and no butter or gravy at all.'

'I know, and Father Iggy really should say something to the bishop.' Grace sighed. 'I do have him over for tea as often as he's free, and I feed him a good few of Dymphna's buns – he loves them. I suppose I should start doing the same for Father Lehane, only he's so shy, and I suppose I didn't notice him losing weight because he's rake-thin already.'

'Yes, Father Iggy told me about the buns. Which brings me to my next point,' said Nancy, leaning with one elbow on the counter. She was wearing the same brown skirt and cream blouse she wore every day, brightened by a pale-pink cardigan from Peggy Donnelly's, the same colour as her cheeks and nose. 'Have you ever met Kit's sister, Margaret?'

'No. I know she moved to Waterford when she married, that's all.'

'She did, she married some kind of a solicitor or something, but you wouldn't remember that. Sure you were only a baby if you were even born at all. But I remember her well growing up – we're the same age. And if you think Kit is a long string of misery, you should meet Margaret. God forgive me, but even as a girl she always had a puss on her that would turn milk sour. Anyway, her husband recently died, there's no children, and now she's alone in the world.'

Grace wondered anxiously where this was going. Surely Nancy wasn't going to suggest Dymphna O'Connell move all the way to Waterford, which was over one hundred miles away, maybe even two, to keep house for a woman even more bad-tempered than Kit Gallagher? 'I don't think Dymphna would want to uproot the children, Mrs O'Flaherty. They're very settled at school.'

Nancy's broad, kind face broke out into a wide grin, and she held up her hands. 'Ara, don't be thinking I'd wish such a fate on poor Dymphna, though God knows she'd probably start feeling as sorry for that Margaret as she did for your Agnes...God rest her soul,' the postmistress added hastily, suddenly remembering who she was talking to, and also that Grace's sister was recently dead so shouldn't be spoken ill of. 'No, no, Margaret already has a housekeeper and a cook and all the rest. It's Kit she's after inviting to go and live there with her.'

'She asked Kit?' Grace was astonished.

Nancy pulled a face, her squinty eye turning even more inwards. 'Sure I know it seems strange. Kit Gallagher never left Knocknashee in her whole life except for one time years ago when she went to care for a sick aunt in England. But Margaret has a big old house in Waterford town and is rattling around in it on her own, so she wants the bit of company, I suppose. And maybe she hasn't much in the way of friends and neighbours, though I have an acquaintance of my own in the post office there, and she tells me there's over twenty thousand people in the town – imagine.'

Neither of them said the obvious, that if Kit Gallagher was the best option you could come up with for company in a place of that size, people mustn't think very well of you.

'But will Kit go, do you think?' Grace asked doubtfully. 'She's never said anything kind about Margaret?' She was putting it politely; in fact Kit Gallagher could often be heard denouncing her older sister for all sorts of sins, pride being the foremost of them, having married a wealthy man.

'She's in two minds about it, she says.' Nancy sighed. 'She says there's all sorts of wickedness and men in a city. She says she'd be *sceoined* going around. But it's a fine house, bigger even than the parochial house. And she's a bit younger than Margaret, and she and the husband had no family, so the lure of being the sole beneficiary when the time comes would be a powerful one.'

'So she could be persuaded?' Grace wondered. 'Maybe if we told Father Iggy to put his foot down over the food...'

'Ah, Grace, Father Iggy couldn't put his foot down on an ant. Every time Kit mentions leaving, he feels he has to let on that he'd be devastated to lose her and all the rest, so I was thinking' – Nancy dropped her voice further, with another glance towards the door – 'that if we could help out and give your woman a bit of a nudge, then Dymphna could go as housekeeper to the two priests.'

'But what can we do to help?' The idea of Kit Gallagher leaving

Knocknashee and Dymphna taking over minding the priests would be marvellous, if it could be managed. Apart from the starving of the two priests, Kit was notorious for withdrawing access to the clergy from the people. If you called to the parochial house wanting to see any one of them, you'd have to state the exact reason to Kit, even though it was not her business, and the chances were she'd deny you.

'Well, I've made a start already,' confessed the postmistress, looking both a bit guilty and pleased with herself. 'When the bishop told Father Iggy the parochial house should have a fresh lick of paint now that the canon is gone, and Father Iggy got young Pa Creedon from the pub to do it, I told Pa to paint both the housekeeper's sitting room and the kitchen pale green. Kit hates that colour apparently – she says it's the colour of envy, sure she should know.'

'But I suppose she could paint it again herself, with a less sinful colour?' Grace pointed out.

'Ah, she won't. She's too mean to spend her own money. Anyway, I've done more than that. I've joined the altar committee myself, which she doesn't like one bit. She was always in charge of the altar, as you know, and saying how much work it is, so I suggested to Father Iggy he ask for volunteers to take some of the burden off, and when he did, I jumped in. Kit won't like sharing the limelight, and I'll make sure there are plenty of wild daffodils, which she doesn't like either, and I've a few people planted to admire the new flower arrangements, so that might nudge her a bit too.'

Grace laughed out loud. 'And to the untrained eye, this place looks like a perfectly normal village. Little would anyone guess the skulduggery that goes on behind the scenes.'

'Ah, Father Iggy needs feeding up. He doesn't throw a shadow if he stands sideways these days, the poor *crathur*.'

'Well, if there's anything I can do to help...' Still laughing, Grace started to get up from her stool.

'Well, there is,' said Nancy, with a big wink of her squinty eye. 'And that's the other reason I wanted to speak to you, apart from making sure 'twouldn't put you out to lose Dymphna. Kit Gallagher told me the other day it would be better if you kept the windows closed when the children were learning the tin whishtle, because the noise – she called it noise – was very grating and she could hear it all the way up in the parochial house.'

'Did she now? Well then, we'll need a daily tin-whishtle practice for the Easter concert, I think,' Grace said, with a mischievous grin. How dare Kit insult the children? They were wonderful little musicians, and it would be a delight to anyone to hear them play. She stood, pulling her hat down over her bouncy curls. 'Between us, we'll have her on the train to Waterford by the end of the month. Oh, and Nancy, I was forgetting – a stamp for America, please.'

* * *

DEAR RICHARD, wrote Grace as soon as she got back to the house. *Your article is so well written and so lovely, I applaud you, and I'm glad our friendship was able to give you a jumping-off point, as it were, for an important piece of writing about the relationship between America and Europe. I'm lighting a candle for you that the features editor will put it in straight away, and I'm sure he will.*

She decided not to thank him or say anything about him calling her beautiful. The more she thought about it, the more she knew it was just a way of drawing the reader into his story.

I have to admit I'm a bit daunted about the idea that my picture might be published, but I'm comforting myself that it's only very small, and as Pádraig O Sé, who is surely the rudest man alive, says to anyone who worries about whether their old shoes are still in fashion, 'Sure who'd be looking at you?'

I hope you're successful in persuading the Capital to send you to Europe if that's what you want, and if you do get to go, I'll say a prayer for you both every day that you'll be safe. I know Jacob Nunez is a Jewish man and might not need Catholic prayers, but some god will need to look out for him over there.

It's so generous of you to offer to stay on and look for Father Dempsey yourself. It seems like an impossible task, but it's so kind of you to try.

In other news, we – me and Mrs O'Flaherty in the post office – are hatching a plan to save poor Father Iggy and his curate from starvation. We are trying to subtly get Kit Gallagher, the priests' housekeeper, to go to her sister, Margaret, in Waterford and put Dymphna in the job instead. The sister has a big house that Kit would inherit if Margaret goes first, which is likely as she's a lot older, but then there might be years of them having to live together first, so she's very on the fence about it.

So we're trying to develop what Charlie calls push factors here, which will hopefully make her feel she'd rather face living with her sister than stay in Knocknashee. It involves painting her sitting room in the parochial house pale green, which she hates, and covering the altar in wild daffodils and having the children play their tin whishtles very loudly.

Oh dear, my news of this place must seem so silly and provincial to you after all the big issues you write about.

Richard, I think you're marvellous, and you write so well – I'm sure you are on the cusp of something really big.

I don't think I have any other news right now, except it's freezing cold and it feels like it will never stop raining. Some people are saying that fuel could be rationed if the Emergency goes on much longer, but it's hard to see how it could affect us here in the west of Ireland. We mostly burn turf anyway – coal is expensive.

Another thing people are worried about is sailing across the Atlantic because of U-boats, but of course any Irish ship is painted with EIRE on both sides and flies the tricolour fore and aft. You can see it's a ship from a neutral country, and the shipping companies seem to think the Germans will respect that. They'd hardly risk a big expensive ship if they thought it was going to be blown to kingdom come.

I suppose that's the same for America as you're not in the war either?

I look forward to your next letter and hearing all about how you got on in New York, and please don't worry if Father Noel Dempsey is nowhere to be found. If it's meant to be, it's meant to be. It would need someone looking down on you for sure.

Thank you for all you do to help me.

Grace

She glanced up at the clock, it was time she was at school, so she sealed the envelope and went to begin her day,

CHAPTER 9

*I*t was ten in the morning in New York, and Richard and Jacob were sitting in the sumptuous office of Guy Falkirk, foreign editor of the *Capital*. The newspaper's headquarters were on Fifth Avenue in Manhattan, and traffic noise and bustle rose from the street below.

'So you're the guy who wrote the piece about the bottle washing up on St Simons Island and somehow turned it into a plea for America to go to war?' Falkirk placed the copy of yesterday's paper on the desk in front of him, open to the double-page spread across which the features editor had run Richard's words and Nunez's photographs.

As soon as Grace's telegram arrived, with its one word – YES – Richard had rushed to post his article and Jacob's pictures, plus the very small one of Grace, off to Ed Irwin, the features editor of the *Capital*.

He'd assumed it would be at least a week before it was printed, if it was used at all, but when he bought the paper yesterday from a news-stand at Washington Union Station while changing trains on the way to New York, there it was, run across two pages under a massive headline.

AMERICA AND EUROPE, A LOVE STORY

He and Jacob pored gleefully over it, sitting side by side in the second-class carriage.

Every word he had written was there, instead of half the story getting slashed as usually happened. And Jacob's pictures had been used.

The one of Doodle with the original bottle had come out well. Jacob had smeared the bottle with a ton of bacon grease from that morning's breakfast to get the ever greedy Labrador to dig it up enthusiastically out of the seaweed, tongue lolling and ears flapping. They'd used the portrait of Esme uncorking the bottle and given a good amount of space to the one of Richard reading the letter in his bedroom, stretched out elegantly on his bed, leaning back with one knee cocked, wearing his white linen trousers, the letter flattened by one hand against his thigh, his other hand behind his head, ruffling his slightly too-long blond hair.

The best photo by far, though, in Richard's opinion, was the one Grace had sent of herself, sitting on a bench by the water, her face in profile, her hair adrift in the wind, and it seemed the features editor had agreed with him, because he had blown it up way bigger than the others. In fact, to Jacob's mild annoyance, it took up almost half of one of the two pages.

'Some two-bit seaside photographer, stealing my thunder,' he'd grumbled, not too seriously, though. 'Your girlfriend's gonna be impressed anyway. Imagine, her face all over the *Capital*. Hollywood will be after her next.'

'She is *not* my girlfriend,' Richard had said, rolling his eyes good-humouredly. No amount of teasing could upset him today. He'd only started out as a newspaper writer last year, and already he had a double-page spread in the features section of the *Capital*.

'Anyway, hopefully it will impress Guy Falkirk into sending us to Paris.' Jacob yawned as he leant back in his seat and closed his eyes. It was midnight, and there were still seven hours to go until they arrived in New York.

Richard had wanted to purchase bunks in the first-class sleeping carriage, but Jacob had pooh-poohed the idea. 'You want to rough it around Paris speaking to real people? Better toughen up and stop acting like the spoiled rich kid who can't live without getting a hot shave at the barber shop every other day.'

His Jewish friend was the sort of fellow who cut his own hair rather than give a barber twenty-five cents to look presentable. 'You got spare cash in grandma's trust fund? Save it for Europe. You never know, we might need it for something that's actually important.'

So now Richard was sitting in this plush carpeted office of the man he hoped would give him the opportunity of a lifetime, and instead of being alert and ready for any question that might be thrown at him, he was thoroughly exhausted, his hair and clothes dishevelled.

'You wanna go with this guy to Europe, huh?' asked Guy Falkirk, narrowing his blue eyes that sagged and had big puffy bags beneath them at Richard while jerking his thumb at Jacob, who looked annoyingly bright-eyed and breezy, though with a slight shadow on his chin. 'And you wanna go on my dime?'

The foreign editor had a jowly face and broken veins in his purple cheeks, and he was overweight, with heavy rounded shoulders and a completely bald head, but he had the intimidating presence of a man who had seen and done a lot and took no prisoners.

'I do, sir, very much, sir.' Richard straightened his shoulders and tried to look confident.

'Call me Kirky, everyone does.' The man glanced down at the open newspaper on the desk in front of him and slapped it with the palm of his hand. 'So what are ya?'

Richard glanced in panic at Jacob. What was he? What did that mean? 'Um...'

'Features, news, what are ya? Why should I send you to Europe? Any experience with reporting on foreign affairs?'

'I...am... Well...I mean...er... I've covered a lot of local politics down in Georgia...'

'Like?' barked the editor.

'Um…there's a really important debate going on about onions and fertiliser…'

'Load of crap,' snapped Falkirk, not realising that he'd just hit the nail on the head. Richard was so nervous, he didn't feel the urge to smile, but Jacob spluttered slightly, earning him a ferocious glare.

'Come on, kid,' snapped the editor, turning his attention back to Richard. 'Give me something to work with. Any experience with reporting on politics or local government, something like that?'

'I wrote a piece about a Jewish family who escaped from Germany,' said Richard desperately.

'Published in…?'

'The *American Jewish World*.'

The editor waved this information away with his large, pudgy hand. 'Parochial stuff, only of interest to the Jews. What experience have you got that would be relevant to a national newspaper like the *Capital*?'

'Well…' Richard made a desperate gesture towards the pages lying open on Falkirk's huge mahogany desk. 'I mean, that piece I've had published in yesterday's *Capital*, I mean it's all about Europe…'

Falkirk snorted loudly, scrunched up the newspaper and flung it into the huge wastepaper basket beside his desk. 'Yesterday's paper, today's garbage. And that sentimental claptrap you wrote doesn't qualify as news. Ed Irwin only ran with it because it gave him a chance to feature a picture of a pretty girl – readers love that.' He steepled his fingers in front of his thick purple face and studied Richard with his small blue eyes. 'You Jewish too?'

'No, sir, I'm –'

'Enough with the sir business, kid, you ain't in the South now. It's Kirky. I don't expect to have to tell you things twice.'

'No, um, Kirky, I'm Episcopalian…'

The man snorted. A laugh? Maybe. Richard had no idea how this meeting was going.

'OK…' The big man drummed his chubby fingers on the desk.

'OK...' He looked from one to the other of them. 'Well, seeing as you took the trouble to come over eight hundred miles to see me in person, you're hungry for this, so OK, I'm gonna take a chance on you both, but you need to listen carefully. You can go. We'll pay you and take care of everything. But Nunez, you're to keep away from the communists and especially the communist Jews. I don't want that. You hear me? You're a great photographer, but you're a wild card, and I won't have you leading Lewis here astray. In particular I do not want to pay for a bunch of garbage about how great Russia is, or the down-trodden proletariat. People here don't want to read that. They want to know how this war will affect them and what likely impact it's going to have on us here in the States, on business, on transportation, on the postal system. I want straight reporting, not a bunch of ideological sentimental claptrap, and I'm relying on you both to make sure that's what I get. And stick to France, maybe Belgium and Holland in a pinch – don't go wandering off anywhere dangerous. And if things get hairy, you're to get yourselves back here on the next boat. We clear?'

Richard's heart hammered with nerves and excitement. This was it; they were going to Europe. 'Yes, um...Kirky,' he said. He tried to sound nonchalant, but he wanted to get up and punch the air.

'Nunez? We clear?'

'Oh yes, absolutely clear,' said Jacob, with a bright smile.

Falkirk scowled at him. 'Do I detect a note of insincerity, Nunez?'

'Not at all, Kirky.'

'Good.' Another glare. "Cos I can't sell a bunch of commie claptrap to the board – they won't print it. And if that's all I get, I'll have wasted a lot of dough and time on you two, and it'll be the last time you get any work off me, you hear me?'

'I hear you, Kirky.'

Falkirk gave another suspicious glare, and for a terrified moment, Richard thought Jacob had ruined it for both of them and the foreign editor was going to change his mind. But then the big man relaxed and the slightest hint of a smirk played around his full lips.

'Good. Go downstairs to Lucille. She'll take care of all the paper-work you need, press passes, tickets, accommodation, expenses and all the rest, and send them out to you when they're ready, whenever that is – don't ask.' He shooed them with a wave of his hand, while with his other hand he picked up the receiver of the enormous phone on his desk and started barking orders at some poor unfortunate called Jones.

* * *

EVEN THOUGH JACOB NUNEZ had a rich uncle in Manhattan, the one with the jewellery business, he'd insisted they book into a boarding house in Harlem.

'I'm just not ready to face my uncle yet. He always puts me under such pressure to leave photography and join him and get rich, and I will, I will, but...' He stopped and shrugged.

'But not yet, I know,' Richard finished for him, with an inward sigh for Sarah.

Harlem was like no other neighbourhood he had ever seen. People of every skin tone and nationality milled around, and it was a shock to him how confidently the coloured people went about their business. In the South, coloured people kept their heads down and didn't make eye contact with white folks unless absolutely necessary. Walking past groups of men who looked him and Jacob up and down as if they were the ones who didn't belong was unnerving.

'The Jews and the Italians used to own this part of the city,' explained Jacob, keeping up a running commentary as they made their way through the crowded streets in search of their hotel. 'The Blacks came up from the South in the last forty years, escaping Jim Crow laws. Up here they got a chance, better education, better jobs, no chance of being lynched. During the last war, there was so much work since all the white boys were drafted. It's around seventy percent Black here now, mixed in with some Puerto Ricans.'

The change in ethnic composition clearly fascinated his photographer's eye. It was in this place that he'd found his calling, spending three summers as a kid working in his uncle's friend's photo studio on the Lower East Side of Manhattan. The photographer, a Mr Goldstein, had, to Jacob's uncle's horror, encouraged the boy's natural talent, and when he died of TB, he left his youthful protégée all his expensive equipment.

The boarding house turned out to be as seedy as it was cheap. Richard had never set foot anywhere as grim, not even Jacob's apartment in Savannah. He didn't say it out loud, as he didn't want to give his frugal friend further proof that he was too soft for this job. But he left his clean clothes in his leather suitcase rather than hanging them up in the filthy closet with half an inch of dust and cobwebs inside, and he kept well away from the pile of heavily stained towels bundled up in a corner of the bathroom. He was one hundred percent sure the bed had bedbugs, but that was something he'd have to navigate later.

As soon as they'd dumped their bags, they went out to celebrate their success with hamburgers and a few beers in a jazz bar off 155th Street, where whites were definitely in the minority. They found a small table in the corner and listened to a Black woman singing about love and hardship in a deep, emotional, gravelly voice.

'You ever heard of the Harlem Renaissance?' Jacob took a long draught of his beer.

'No?' Richard took a gulp of his own, then coughed; the beer was strong.

'It's an exciting Negro movement, poets, playwrights, artists, so many from the South – Georgia, Alabama, Florida, Tennessee. In the South, trying to make a living as an artist is hard enough, even if you have white skin. I mean, you know that – you've met the guys who hang out in my apartment. But they're the privileged ones. If you don't have white skin, you can forget it.'

'This area doesn't look very prosperous, though.' Richard risked another mouthful of his beer.

'That's what makes it cheap for artists to live here. The Depression hit it hard. It hit everywhere hard, but the marginalised, they're always the first to suffer. Domestic work, manual labour – rich folks can't afford to pay their staff, and there's always a group less well-off who will work for cheaper. It's a race to the bottom, the poor getting poorer and undercutting each other, fighting for the scraps from the master's table. We need to stop competing with each other, the Jews, the Blacks, the Chinese, the Italians, the Irish, the Russians, and we need to pull together and turn on the rich who profit from our labour and see us all the same. Imagine what a world we could make.'

Richard didn't reply – he suspected this was exactly the kind of thing Kirky didn't want – but Jacob didn't notice; he was quite happy to do all the talking when it came to politics. He signalled for a second round of beers and started talking about the armistice between the Soviet Union and Finland, and his worries that Finland would team up with Nazi Germany.

Later, drunk, they managed to find the boarding house again and both fell into their beds at midnight, bedbugs and all; Jacob was used to them, and Richard was too drunk to care.

When he woke in the morning, Jacob was gone. His train for Savannah had left at seven in the morning, and the energetic photographer, who seemed to be able to drink anything and sleep anywhere, had no doubt leapt out of bed as fresh as a daisy. It was now eight thirty, and Richard's head pounded, his mouth was as dry as the bottom of a bird cage, and there was an ominous itching all over his legs.

After splashing his face with cold rust-brown water in the filthy sink and dabbing with a wet linen handkerchief at his insect bites, he dressed in the clean white shirt and grey suit he'd left folded in his suitcase and went downstairs to pay the bill. The lobby, which seemed to double as a dining room, was empty, and he rang the little bell on the counter. Five minutes later a young girl emerged from the kitchen carrying a plate with a congealed fried egg and two dubious-looking strips of bacon, and she seemed very insulted when he declined. It turned out there was no need to pay the bill because Jacob had covered it.

On the street outside, he hailed a cab and went straight to the St Regis hotel on Fifth Avenue. With Jacob out of the way, he was going to take a long, luxurious bath and have something to eat that wasn't going to give him dysentery.

His parents always stayed in the St Regis if they came to the city.

His father knew Jack Astor, who built it; they had studied together at Harvard, one of the few times in Arthur Lewis's life he'd willingly gone north of the Mason-Dixon line. Sadly Astor was lost on the *Titanic*; his son Vincent now owned the hotel, a sumptuous place where rumour had it the maids carried their keys on strings of real pearls and one needed to spend three figures just to dine there.

The hotel's ethos was to keep all but the wealthiest people out, and he worried slightly that his shirt and grey linen suit might get him shown the door – not because they were of poor quality, they weren't, but because they hadn't been pressed. He needn't have worried. The manager who came out of his office to check him in registered the name and the accent.

'Are you anything to Mr Arthur Lewis of Savannah, Georgia, sir?' he asked, his pen poised over the form, his elegant eyebrows raised.

'I am,' Richard confirmed. 'He's my father.'

'Then let me upgrade you to one of our better suites. Mr Lewis was a great friend of the owner's father, and Mr Astor would insist on it.'

'Thank you. That's very kind of you,' said Richard as the manager handed over a large silver key. No actual figures were discussed, but even with the free upgrade, his stay here was bound to be eye-wateringly expensive.

He could afford it, of course; his trust fund was invested in the stock exchange and had grown exponentially as America climbed out of the Great Depression. That was another thing Jacob liked to grumble about – the way people with inherited wealth could get even richer without having to lift a finger.

He made his way through the expanse of marble and huge greenery to the ornate elevator, operated by an expressionless boy in a neat blue uniform with gilded buttons, and rose to the top floor.

The room he'd been allocated was beautiful, huge windows overlooking the city, original oil paintings on the walls, a bed so soft he could sink into it. First he phoned room service for two aspirin to cure his hangover, some soothing cream for his bedbug bites and for a maid to iron his clothes. Then he took a long bath scented with lavender and softened with bath salts, thoroughly washed his thick blond hair in case of fleas and got dressed again in his freshly pressed shirt and suit.

After that he ate a hearty late breakfast of a perfectly cooked omelette with triangles of warm buttered toast and strong coffee in the Viennese roof garden while rereading his own article in the day-before-yesterday's paper – he was going to have to clip it out and send it to Grace – and wondered how to set about finding Father Noel Dempsey.

* * *

HE FINISHED breakfast and had the idea to ask the helpful manager, the one with the elegant eyebrows, who was at the reception desk sorting his way through a pile of mail.

'Excuse me, do you know how I would go about finding a Catholic priest in New York?'

'Any priest or a specific one, sir?' asked the man smoothly.

'Specific.' He felt a bit foolish.

The manager took a sheet of hotel notepaper and wrote down a name and address. 'Go and see Canon Devine in St Patrick's Cathedral off Fifth Avenue. He's a very busy man, but you can say Mr Astor of the St Regis would appreciate it if he would take a moment out of his day to speak with you.' He went back to sorting letters as Richard stepped out into the bright sunshine and instantly started shivering.

He wished he'd thought to bring his overcoat from home. He hadn't realised New York could be this cold, colder even than yesterday or the day before. There were men on the street walking by in light jackets like his, but to him, raised in the warm, scented South, it was freezing. In his head Jacob's voice berated him for being too soft, and he grimaced. He supposed it was true. He would need to toughen himself up a bit if he wanted to be a gritty foreign correspondent.

That said, there was no point in suffering, so he ducked into Saks and bought a navy wool overcoat, lined with scarlet paisley silk. While he was there, he also bought a beautiful navy fedora and a pale-blue scarf. As he paid for the purchases, he told the gentleman waiting on him that he'd wear them, so no need to wrap them up. He would no doubt be quizzed by Jacob about the cost of the new items, which he would have to halve, or even quarter, and even then Jacob would roll his eyes at the decadence.

CHAPTER 10

St Patrick's Cathedral was impressively huge. Richard walked through the elaborately carved bronze doors to find a vast gilded interior containing intricately carved columns and blazing windows of stained glass.

The Episcopalian church he attended in Savannah, Christ Church on Bull Street, looked nothing like this. It did have one simple piece of coloured glass behind the altar, but the rest was plainly built and painted white, nothing like the ornate artwork and design of this House of God. He'd always imagined Catholic churches to be poorer than Protestant ones for some reason, but the place oozed money, even more so than the St Regis.

There were several solitary people kneeling in prayer, and the only person he felt he could approach was a dark-haired Spanish-looking lady in a scarf, polishing the tiled aisle of the church. She was deep in concentration on her task, and Richard had to clear his throat several times before she turned on her knees and raised an eyebrow.

'I'm sorry to disturb you, ma'am, but I'm looking for Canon Devine.'

He wondered at first if she'd understood him, but then she said in heavily accented English, 'Go around to the cathedral parish house. Somebody there will help you.'

'Thank you, ma'am. And that would be where?'

'At the side.' She returned to her polishing.

As he walked back up the aisle, another man at the point of leaving went down on one knee facing the altar and crossed himself; out of politeness Richard did the same before he left.

Outside he followed the wall of the cathedral around to the right and found a two-storey house with Romanesque windows and gothic peaks; like the church, to which it was physically attached, it too looked very ornate. He knocked on the door, and moments later a short, stout lady in her sixties opened it with a welcoming smile.

'Can I help you, dear?' she asked, in what he thought might be an Irish accent, he'd only ever heard one other Irish person, a guy who tended bar in a place in Savannah, though it was very soft and melodic.

He smiled. 'I was looking for Canon Devine, and I was told to say Mr Astor of the St Regis would appreciate it if he would give me a few moments of his time.'

She opened the door further to admit him, and he found himself in a hallway, which was thankfully warm.

'The canon is in the sacristy – let me take you to him. I think he's got a few minutes before Mass.' She looked at her watch. 'We'll have to hurry, though. Follow me. We'll go through the deacon's sacristy and into the main sacristy this way.'

He followed her through several passageways, then two rooms, both with glass cabinets full of liturgical vestments. The air smelled sweet, of something burning, like dead flowers.

They reached a closed door and she turned to him, her knuckles poised to knock. 'What was your name, dear?'

'Richard Lewis, ma'am.'

'Richard Lewis…' she repeated to herself as she rapped and then entered, leaving him to wait outside. Through the half-open door, he could hear the low hum of conversation but not what was being said.

Then she was back. 'Go right in, but as I said, he only has a few minutes.'

In the sacristy, a tall, thin, greying priest was in the process of dressing for Mass, pulling a long purple and gold vestment over a white robe.

'How can I help you, Mr Lewis?' he asked briskly as he straightened his dog collar. 'I'm Canon Devine. I know, ridiculous name for a priest, but my dad is one of a long line of Devines who came over from the old country, so there was nothing I could do.' His eyes twinkled, and his accent was very like Guy Falkirk's – pure New York.

'Hello...um...' *What do you call a canon in the Catholic Church?* 'Um...Father...' *Isn't that how Grace refers to Canon Rafferty?*

'Presbyterian?' asked the priest, noticing the uncertainty.

'Episcopalian, and thank you for seeing me, Father.'

'No problem. Shoot.' The canon was clearly a nicer man than Canon Rafferty, but he wasn't going to waste time. Richard was beginning to see why his own father hated going north. He could hear Arthur Lewis complain. 'Everyone is in too much of a hurry up there. We're all dying at the same rate. What's the rush?'

'Well, the thing is, Father, I have a friend in Ireland, and she's trying to find a priest, but she just has a name, no address. His name is Father Noel Dempsey, and we think he might have been in New York fifteen years ago.'

'What parish?'

'I'm sorry, I don't –'

'City or state?'

'I, er, don't –'

'You don't know much, do ya?' The priest glanced at his watch, once more reminding Richard very much of Guy Falkirk.

He reddened. 'I'm afraid not, Father.'

'OK, here's what you're gonna do. Go back to Mrs McHale, ask her to show you the parishes directory. Hope that helps. Now, duty calls. And you do not want to tick off my boss.' He briskly patted Richard's shoulder as he passed.

Mrs McHale had disappeared. He retraced his steps through the heavily scented rooms and passageways until he found her busily sweeping invisible dirt off the carpet on the stairs.

When she saw him, the stout little woman straightened up stiffly with her dustpan and brush in her hands. 'How did you get on with the canon, Mr Lewis?'

'He told me to ask you to show me the parishes directory, that I could search for a priest I'm trying to track down there?'

The Irishwoman looked extremely doubtful. 'That will take hours and hours, two whole days at least. You'll have to trawl through it, and who knows what good it might do you. If he's a serving parish priest in the archdiocese, he'll be listed, but if he's a curate, or in any other role, he won't be.'

Richard winced. 'Still, I don't have any other ideas, ma'am, and I told my friend I'd try. She's not here in America to do it herself, so however long it takes...'

'And where is your friend from if not America?' At least this softly spoken Irishwoman was prepared to speak at much greater length and give him more time than Canon Devine. She must not have been in New York for too long.

'Ireland, ma'am.'

'And whereabouts in Ireland?'

'I doubt you'd know it, ma'am. A very little place called Knock-nashee. It's in –'

'County Kerry! I know it well!' cried Mrs McHale, waving around the brush and pan. 'My grandfather came from Dingle, that's near there, and we used to visit the homeplace when I was a child. Beautiful, just beautiful...like nowhere you've ever seen, and that God's own truth. Well, now, that's surely a sign I'm supposed to help you. Come into the sitting room and I'll make us a nice pot of tea, or maybe you'd prefer coffee? I can't stomach the stuff myself. I'll get the directory, and we'll go through together. You can take the one page, I'll take the other, that way we might have it done by tonight – sure it's not lunchtime yet. The canon is going out visiting all day after the morning Mass, he has three stations to do, and Father Connor is taking over, so there's nothing I have to do aside from clean, and sure the place is already spotless. I was going to go buying myself a new pair of sheepskin slippers – my feet do be sore with the arthritis, and the softness and the lanolin does them good – but sure the slippers can wait, because today I met a friend of a woman from Knocknashee...'

So completely unexpectedly, the rest of Richard Lewis's day was spent sitting on the parochial house sofa next to a woman whose heart still seemed to belong in the west of Ireland and whose eyes occasionally misted up as she told him about the mountains, the bogs, the stone-walled fields.

Occasionally she bobbed up and down to make more tea for herself and a coffee for Richard, or a mighty ham sandwich, or a slice of cake, but most of the time the two of them spent running their fingers slowly down the pages of the register, Richard taking the left-hand page and Mrs McHale the right, as outside the parishioners streamed home from morning Mass, then afternoon Mass, then evening, then as dusk gathered and the cathedral windows threw long vibrant shadows across the lawns, and then as the sky became the rich starless orange of a city night.

By the time they got to the last page, it was ten thirty in the evening, and between them they had located six Father Noel Dempseys.

One had passed away in 1937. One was alive and serving in St Peter and St Denis Parish in Yonkers, and the other three had retired to smaller churches in remote little clapboard towns in far-flung corners of the state. The last had been a parish priest in Brooklyn but was now in a retirement home.

Six. Well, five living. It could have been worse, but it was still daunting.

Mrs McHale sighed as she inhaled what must have been her hundredth cup of tea. It amazed Richard how much tea the Irish-woman could drink; he'd refused the last twenty coffees she'd offered him. 'So five. Well, at least he's not called Patrick Murphy or we'd have hundreds to deal with, but 'tis a shame you haven't more to go on. About how old might he be?'

'I'm afraid I don't know that, ma'am.'

'Do we think he's from Ireland? First or second generation? Third maybe?'

'I don't know, ma'am. I suppose by the name, he's of Irish descent, but if he's actually ever set foot in Ireland, I don't know.'

'So your friend never met him?'

'No, ma'am. It was my friend's sister who met him, years ago, on this side of the Atlantic.'

'And can your friend not ask her sister a bit more about him, like where was his church or what did it look like even?'

'I'm afraid the sister is dead.'

'Is that so.' She looked at him thoughtfully. She clearly guessed there was a lot more to this story than what he was telling, but in the end all she said was, 'Well now, God rest her soul. Is there no other clue?'

Richard thought back to Grace's letter and that confession on Agnes's deathbed. But he knew from Grace how the Church protected its own, so he wasn't going to say that this priest might have been involved in buying and selling an Irish child – he didn't want Mrs McHale to show him the door. 'Nothing, really. I'm so sorry, ma'am.'

Her mouth twitched. 'Don't be. I love a good mystery.'

'So it looks like I'll just have to go and see all of them?'

Mrs McHale tutted and shook her head. 'Sure that will take a week at least, presuming your Father Dempsey isn't the one buried already, God rest him. Have you a week to spare?'

He wanted to say 'I've as long as it takes,' but that wasn't true – the *Capital* might want him to sail to Europe in a month or two, but it could be just a few days. Lucille had said it all depended on the paper-work, and with Europe in the state it was these days, how long it would take to arrange was uncertain. If the call came sooner rather than later, he couldn't let Jacob down, not over a wild goose chase, not even to help Grace. 'I have a couple of days anyway, maybe a bit more.'

'And you can't tell me anything of what this meeting between this priest and your friend's sister was about? Sure when you meet the man himself, Mr Lewis, what will you ask of him to know whether he is the one you're looking for?'

It was a very good question, one he hadn't considered. 'I suppose I might ask, did he ever meet a woman from Knocknashee... No, wait, I wouldn't start like that...' He knew from Grace how Canon Rafferty had refused to reveal the truth for all these years. There was no reason to think this priest would be any better; after all he might be just as guilty as Rafferty in this whole thing. Richard had no idea. If the priest knew Richard's visit was to do with Knocknashee, then maybe he would close up and pretend to know nothing.

'If you can't ask him that, then what will you ask him?' The chubby little housekeeper looked at him, fascinated.

'I think I could just ask if he ever met my friend's sister, her name was Agnes. I think it was in 1925 she came over here, in around May?' He blushed then because what he was about to say was a lie. 'I think my friend misses her sister and would like to connect with people who knew her, and her sister had a friendship with this Father Dempsey, she thinks.'

Mrs McHale dropped her eyes and tapped her lips with her fingers, thinking, and with a sinking feeling, Richard just knew she was going to tell him to leave and would never open the door of this house to him again.

'Look, I shouldn't really call her so late, 'tis nearly eleven,' said the Irishwoman, with a little shake of her shoulders, 'but I know she's a terrible night owl, so hold on one minute...' She went to the telephone and dialled, and after a few seconds gave Richard a thumbs up as she spoke into the receiver.

'Maura, I didn't wake you, did I? No, I thought not... Anyway, 'tis Patricia. Yes, I knew you knew it was me. Come here to me, your Father Noel Dempsey – don't bother the poor man, but do you know if he ever had communications with a woman in Ireland at all? A woman called Agnes Fitzgerald?'

She glanced at Richard as she said this, her cheeks going a little pink. 'Yes, I'm asking for a new member of our congregation. He's trying to make the connection. The woman has passed on, but her sister back in Ireland wants to be put in touch with Father Dempsey, but she lost the address, so she asked a friend to try, and he's here with me now. I'm so sorry to bother you with this, Maura...'

She paused, then relaxed and chuckled. 'Ah, I know it, 'tis child's play for the likes of us. The poor men don't know if they're coming or going, everything has to be written down for them. Sure I sent Canon Devine out today with a list of all his visits and stations, and I still have my heart in my mouth wondering if he'll make it home again by midnight. Yes, I'll wait on the line...'

She put her hand over the receiver and whispered to Richard, 'She's just going to check his address book and the parochial house diary. She's been with him since he was in New York, but he was retired out to a little place in the middle of nowhere three years ago, and she's bored stiff, sits up reading all night. Pass me my tea, Mr Lewis, if you'd be so good.'

As she sipped at what seemed like her hundredth-and-something cup, resting on the chair by the phone, Richard sat in drowsy silence on the sofa, thinking half about Father Dempsey and half about his comfortable bed in the hotel suite. Ten minutes later the dumpy little housekeeper shot bolt upright in her chair and gave him another cheerful thumbs up; this time he noticed her thumb was a little crooked with arthritis.

'Right... Oh yes, of course... Right... You're certain of that? No better woman. Thanks, Maura, God bless.' And she hung up. 'Well, that's one down. No Agnes Fitzgerald in his address book, no note in the diary from 1925 of meeting with any Irish girl. Now,' she went on, as Richard started to thank her, 'that's just the beginning. I won't be phoning any of the other housekeepers at this hour, but I'll get straight onto it in the morning, and if you come in to me around eleven in the morning, hopefully we'll have your list whittled down some more.'

CHAPTER 11

The housekeeper was as good as her word, though she looked worried for him. 'The one in Yonkers is a definite no. He was in Africa all his life, only came back three years ago. And the other two out of town, well, there's nothing about an Agnes Fitzgerald in their address books either, or their diaries, which leaves only two Noel Dempseys, and I'm afraid both their housekeepers have passed away, God rest them. One of those priests is in the Calvary Cemetery in Queens, and the other is in the retirement home in Jamaica, also in Queens, so at least he's alive, but who knows what he'll be able to remember or tell you?'

Not very much, suspected Richard, thinking about the disappointing letter he would have to write to Grace later that day. 'Well, who knows, there might be something. Thank you so much, ma'am. I'm so grateful.'

'You're welcome. Even if this turns out to be a dead end, I hope your friend manages to find out what she needs to know one day.'

'I'm sure she will. And thank you again. I really do appreciate it.'

'And don't forget to tell her a woman who spent all her summers in Dingle is thinking of her.' Mrs McHale's voice was wistful.

'I sure will, ma'am.' He handed her the Macy's shopping bag he was carrying. He'd breakfasted at nine, smoked salmon and scrambled eggs, with a glass of freshly squeezed orange juice – nothing as good as you'd get in Savannah – to give himself time to pop over to the iconic New York store and buy the best pair of sheepskin slippers they had in stock. 'And you have a nice day now. I'm much obliged.'

Leaving her almost crying with happiness over the soft, pliable slippers, which by a happy coincidence had been made in Ireland, Richard stepped back out into the freezing New York sunshine.

The address he was looking for, which Mrs McHale had handed to him on a neat sheet of lined notepaper, was St Xavier's Retirement Home, 1165 95th Ave, Jamaica, Queens, New York. Deciding not to attempt the subway, he hailed a cab and tried to relax and enjoy the view of the city as they crossed the East River and drove through the leafy streets of Elmhurst and Woodside to Jamaica.

The home for retired priests was a beautiful place, set in its own manicured grounds. He paid the cab driver and tipped him a dollar for luck, then walked up between smooth green lawns to the main entrance, sporting a pair of fine oak doors not unlike the doors of a church, and rang the bell.

No answer. He tested the doors; they were locked. But then the handle moved a little, and the right-hand door creaked open. The wrinkled face of a very old man, presumably a priest, appeared in the gap.

'Hello. I'm looking for Father Noel Dempsey?' Richard said quietly, but the man looked puzzled, putting his hand to his ear.

He tried again, a bit louder. 'Father Noel Dempsey?'

The man still looked puzzled, but he shuffled aside to let Richard into the reception area, which smelled pleasantly of beeswax and polished floors. There was no one around; the space behind the desk was empty. Small statues in alcoves lined the walls; one figure had blood pouring from his hand, and another was of a man stuck full of spears. They seemed to him kind of grotesque, not the sort of thing with which to surround the elderly and dying.

The old man leant heavily on his cane, glaring furiously at him.

'What are you doing here?' he asked, in a loud, booming voice. 'Who is it you want?'

'I'm looking for Father Noel Dempsey,' Richard said, equally loudly, and the man winced and recoiled indignantly.

'There's no need to shout, young man. I'm not deaf. That way.'

Richard thanked him at normal volume, eliciting another puzzled frown, and went in the direction he'd been pointed, down a long corridor leading to the right off the hallway.

Several doors lined it, but they were all closed except the one at the very end, which led into a large sitting room overlooking the grounds. Two men sat in the room; one was even more ancient than the priest who had let him in, sleeping peacefully in a wheelchair. The other, sitting in an ordinary armchair at a small square table, sat gazing intently at the chessboard in front of him.

Richard approached the man with the chessboard. 'Excuse me, sir...' he began, but the man, who clearly had no problem hearing him, held his hand up to silence him.

'Queen's pawn to D3,' he muttered to himself. He made the move and seemed pleased, then turned his head to look at Richard. 'Yes?' he asked, in a bored, vaguely irritated voice.

He looked no more than seventy years old; his thick grey hair and bushy beard still held traces of red from younger years. His skin was translucent and pale, and his eyelashes and eyebrows had faded to be almost invisible. But his arms, their elbows resting on the table, shirt sleeves rolled up, were lean and muscular; he was once a man of strong physique and was still far from frail.

'My name is Richard Lewis, sir, and I'm looking for a Father Noel Dempsey?' Richard wondered how many times today he'd have to repeat that sentence.

'Are you now,' the man answered calmly, his eyes returning to the board. 'Well, you've found him. So what do you want with him?' His accent was that of this city, not of Ireland.

After Richard had recovered from his surprise, he thought long and hard about what to say next. If the man he wanted wasn't lying under the ground in Calvary Cemetery, there was a good chance this was the one he was looking for. He'd thought he would mention the canon and see how the man reacted. He hoped that even if the priest denied knowing him, he'd give something away and Richard would be able to spot it. It was a long shot but all he had.

'I was hoping to find a distant relative of my mother's. He's a priest in Ireland, and she's lost touch with him – they moved house and lost the address. But she thought he was related to a priest in New York called Father Noel Dempsey, so I looked you up.'

'And who is this priest in Ireland your mother is related to?' Richard couldn't see the man's expression; his red-grey head was lowered over the chessboard.

'A Canon Rafferty. Michael Rafferty.'

'Is your mother related on the Rafferty side or the O'Connor side?'

'I honestly have no idea, sir…I mean, Father. He's just a distant cousin of her father's. My grandfather's name was Fitzgerald…' Grace's surname was the only Irish one that came to mind. 'But that's all I know.'

'Michael Rafferty is at the parochial house in Ballypatrick, County Tipperary,' said Father Dempsey quietly, resting a finger on a black rook but not moving it.

'Thank you, sir, I really appreciate that.' He hesitated, not sure where to take this next. 'Well, my mother will be really pleased to be able to get back in touch…'

'You sure about that?'

Richard blinked. Had he misheard the priest's muttered question? 'I'm sorry, what did you say, sir?'

The priest looked up from his game once more, his pale-blue eyes raking Richard's face. 'I said, is your mother sure she'd want anything to do with Michael Rafferty?'

'Er…Canon Rafferty?' This was unexpected.

'Yes, Canon Rafferty! Were you raised a Catholic, Richard Lewis?'

'Er, no, sir… I mean, Father…'

'I thought not. Sit down. And take off that damn hat.'

His head spinning, Richard did as he was bid, removing not just the fedora but his coat and scarf as well, then brought over a small blue padded stool and placed it on the other side of the table from the priest. Between them on the board, only a handful of white pieces were left standing; black was winning.

'Do you play chess, Mr Lewis?'

'A little, sir.' Sarah had taught him the game when he was a child, and he enjoyed it and considered himself rather good at it.

'Take over as black.' The priest twisted the board around, presenting Richard with the superior side.

'Er...um...' This seemed unfair to the priest.

'Just move, Mr Lewis.'

He did, taking a hapless pawn with his knight.

'Good. Now, back to Canon Rafferty, who I suspect is no relation of your mother's, seeing as she made no effort to raise you in the Church. I wonder, did you know he was moved to the back of beyond by the bishop for thieving from the Church funds and the school funds as well?'

'I did, er, hear something,' Richard admitted cautiously, watching the other man move his queen sideways for no obvious reason.

'Then I suppose you know he was in the business of selling babies?'

'*Babies?*' He jerked up his head and stared in shock at the priest's pale face. All he knew about was Siobhán McKenna. 'You mean... more than one baby?'

'Yes. Babies. Plural. More than one. Don't they teach grammar in school any more?'

'I...er...well, of course...'

'And why stop at one, when it was such a lucrative trade?'

'I...um...'

'And did you know that he blamed me?'

Richard felt a light sweat breaking out across his forehead. 'I did not know that, sir, no.'

'Really? Doesn't it strike you as strange that I'm in a retirement home at my age when there's many a priest far older and frailer than I who are still in their jobs, serving God, while I am here playing chess against myself because the rest of the deaf, senile old men in this gilded prison haven't one functioning brain between them? Your turn.'

'Oh…right…' He scanned the board blindly.

'It all began with a child who was truly an orphan,' said the man across the table. 'A mite of a thing Rafferty wrote to me about. We knew each other from the seminary in Maynooth before I was moved to New York. Rafferty was sent to Galway, until he disgraced himself there, something I knew nothing about, and was shipped down to Knocknashee, where it was thought he'd do less damage.'

'I don't think he did less damage, sir,' said Richard, a bit sharply, thinking of Agnes and Grace, and the McKennas, and all the inhabitants of Knocknashee whose lives had taken a serious turn for the worse as a result of the Church sending Canon Rafferty to a place where 'he'd do less damage'.

'You're right, Mr Lewis. Knocknashee was where he branched out into the baby business, starting with the orphaned child of a local farm labourer and his wife. He wrote to me asking me did I know of any good Catholic family who were childless and would like to adopt a baby girl, and give her a better life, and I did – a couple in their thirties, Joey Maheady, a good, devout Irishman, and his wife, Sylvia, of Italian extraction. They were unable to have children of their own, and I knew they would love to offer a home to this poor little girl who had no family. It's still your turn, young man.'

His mind reeling, Richard took a second pawn, with his bishop this time. 'What happened then, sir?'

'Rafferty wrote back saying that there would be expenses to pay and that he would be sending over a very reliable and respectable young woman – her parents were the local schoolteachers in Knocknashee. I was happy to help. The Maheadys were hard-working people – he was a fireman, she was a nurse – and they were saving to buy their own house in Brooklyn. They weren't worried when I warned them about expenses. Sylvia was so excited. She began to tell people she was expecting and wore something under her clothes to suggest she was.'

The priest stared at the board, tapping with his fingers on the edge of the table, then moved his knight. 'A few weeks later, I collected this woman and a baby from the boat – Miss Fitzgerald was her name, I never forgot her, drove her to the Maheady house and left them all together until it was time to drive Miss Fitzgerald back to the dock to board the ship back to Ireland. I admit I sinned, Mr Lewis, by churching Sylvia Maheady one week later as if she was a woman who had just given birth, but in my defence, I thought I was doing the right thing. Such a pretty little baby she was. I think the Fitzgerald woman was fond of her too – she seemed very low on the way back to the boat. Your turn.'

Richard focussed on the names as he kept his eyes on the board. *Joey and Sylvia Maheady*, he kept repeating in his head. *Joey and Sylvia Maheady, Brooklyn.*

'Though they didn't buy in Brooklyn after all,' said the priest. 'They moved out to a smaller area by the ocean called Rockaway Beach.'

Rockaway Beach, Richard corrected. *Joey and Sylvia Maheady, Rockaway Beach.*

'When I asked why they were moving, they said they could no longer afford a house in the middle of the city. After that I didn't hear much from them again. A card at Christmas every year, signed by themselves, then by themselves and the little girl, Lily...'

Joey and Sylvia Maheady, Rockaway Beach, with their daughter Lily. He moved a pawn, carelessly placing it in the sights of Dempsey's queen. If Dempsey took the bait, Richard had his bishop lurking in the background, ready to swoop.

'And then I heard, as can happen, a few years later, they had a natural-born child, Ivy.'

Joey and Sylvia Maheady, Rockaway Beach, with daughters Lily and Ivy...

'At least it didn't cost them the price of a house that time. Can you imagine, Mr Lewis, three thousand dollars for a child? In 1925? Lily Maheady was the first, but a woman called Kit Gallagher brought over three more at least. Always the same story, orphans, nobody to care for them, but I wasn't involved.

'I thought it was a one-off, until years later when I was called in for questioning by the bishop. Someone had complained to the diocese about the price. Neither the bishop in Ireland nor here knew of these transactions. Canon Rafferty named me as the go-between and said it must have been me who took the money. That wasn't true, Mr Lewis.'

'I believe you, sir.' There seemed no reason for this man to tell a lie. The Church had punished him already by hiding him out of sight.

'I only ever acted on behalf of the Maheadys. They never said anything to me about being charged any money, only said they were grateful, but if the racket started with them, it would explain why they couldn't buy their house in Brooklyn. The bishop said it was a murky business and I shouldn't have been involved. Gave me a choice of being defrocked or retiring here. Your turn.'

Richard looked down at the board. Father Noel Dempsey had fallen into his trap, taking Richard's pawn with his queen, and Richard felt bad taking his queen with the bishop. But then the priest took Richard's queen in return and declared with a slight grin, 'Checkmate.'

* * *

HE DECIDED he would send a telegram.

Leaving the grounds of the residential home, he strode briskly down the cold, sunny street, his hands in the pockets of his coat, scarf wrapped around his neck and tucked down inside the coat over his chest, the felt fedora crammed down over his ears.

Later, in the comfort of his hotel, he would write Grace a long letter telling her all about the extraordinary Father Dempsey. And about the *Capital* sending him and Jacob to Europe. And enclosing the cutting of his article about the bottle.

But surely she would want to know as soon as possible about Siobhán McKenna? Or that's what he told himself, though to be honest, the truth was he was so proud of himself, he couldn't wait to tell her.

Passing a large central post office, he hurried in and asked for a telegram form.

Have found Siobhán, he wrote. *Adoptive parents Joey and Sylvia*

Maheady, Address Rockaway Beach, New York. Daughters Lily Maheady (née Siobhán McKenna) and Ivy. Letter to follow.

But after filling it out, he had a sinking thought. Supposing there were millions of Maheadys in Rockaway Beach...

Only one way to find out. He asked the woman behind the counter for the telephone directory for that area and scanned it hurriedly. There were a lot of Irish names in Rockaway Beach – there must be a big Irish community there, he thought – but thank God, there was only one Maheady family.

Joseph and Sylvia Maheady, 12 Sea View Terrace, Rockaway Beach, New York.

Charlie's baby – now a fifteen-year-old girl – was living on the coast of New York state, with nothing between her and the land of her birth but the wild Atlantic.

His hand shook as he made out the telegram form again.

Have found Siobhán. Adoptive parents Joseph and Sylvia Maheady, Address 12 Sea View Terrace, Rockaway Beach, New York. Daughters Lily Maheady (née Siobhán McKenna) and Ivy. Letter to follow.

* * *

BACK AT THE St Regis in time for a late lunch, he ordered himself a crab salad and a glass of Sancerre – Jacob would be horrified, but he deserved it – and asked for a pen and a pad of St Regis notepaper, with its gorgeous golden masthead. Now he'd write the letter that was to follow.

Dear Grace...

He stopped, tapping his pen on the paper. Where to start?

Begin at the beginning, he decided. Tell her about the excitement of finding his article in the paper, and what Jacob said about her picture, how Hollywood would come calling for her next.

Then the meeting with Guy Falkirk, where the editor said the only reason Ed Irwin had used the bottle feature was because he thought Grace was 'a pretty girl, and the readers love that'.

Then the coincidence of Mrs McHale knowing Knocknashee and

how helpful she'd been as a result, and the even more astonishing revelation from Father Dempsey.

In the end, instead of going out sightseeing as he'd promised himself, he found himself so wrapped up in the story, he ended up sitting there until the staff had cleared everything away and were getting the dining room ready for the evening meal.

Later he went up to his room and leant on the balcony for a while, until the cold drove him in, and then he warmed up with another hot bath and threw himself on the bed, restless, his mind going round and round. He should go out to a show…

His mind wandered back to Grace.

He'd finished the letter for now, but probably he should wait to send it until he was certain of the dates.

He'd asked Lucille about the route, and she'd said it was unlikely they'd have a stop in Ireland. He and Jacob would probably sail to England and from there cross to France.

But no matter how it happened, he was going to find a way to see Grace, a girl so beautiful that the features editor of the *Capital* had blown her picture up and placed it right in the middle of the paper. He was going to be on her side of the Atlantic, for eight weeks at least.

Surely in that time he could find a way to see her?

He closed his eyes.

CHAPTER 12

KNOCKNASHEE, CO KERRY

*N*ancy O'Flaherty had dropped the telegram to the house while Grace was at school, and Dymphna brought it over when she came to help clear up after Friday's art class.

She was still working for Grace because Kit Gallagher was still on the fence over going to her sister's in Waterford, even though she was very unhappy about the pale-green paint and the wild daffodils on the altar, as well as the grating noise of the children on their tin whishtles as they prepared every morning for the Easter concert. This year they'd practised so often, there wouldn't be a note out of place.

Grace read the telegram three times, standing in the middle of the classroom, surrounded by paintings of pink blossoming trees. They had been reading *The Selfish Giant* by Oscar Wilde, and she had ended up telling the children all about Savannah, Georgia, where the countryside was covered in peach trees, just like in the giant's garden.

Have found Siobhán. Adoptive parents Joseph and Sylvia Maheady, Address 12 Sea View Terrace, Rockaway Beach, New York. Tel: EH 129. Daughters Lily Maheady (née Siobhán McKenna) and Ivy. Letter to follow.

Every night since writing to Richard about the priest, Grace had tossed and turned into the small hours, reliving the scene in the kitchen after the funeral, worrying that she'd made a terrible mistake by telling the McKennas about Agnes's confession when clearly it would lead nowhere, only down a dead-end street.

And now, out of the blue, he had found Siobhán.

It was incredible. Unbelievable.

'Will you finish off here, Dymphna? I've a message to run.'

'Of course I will, Grace, and Paudie and Kate will help, won't ye, lads?'

'Yes, Mammy, yes, Miss Fitz,' chorused the O'Connells, busy rolling up all the newspaper that Grace had put out to cover the tables.

After pulling on her red coat and scarf and multicoloured woollen hat, Grace limped over to the postman's cottage, where yellow daffodils were flourishing in the little front garden, waving in the sea breeze. She knocked and went straight in, the way people did in Knocknashee. Both Charlie and Declan were at the kitchen table, listening to the news on the radio and eating bowls of Charlie's famous mushroom soup; he was up so early as a postman, he was always finding clumps of wild mushrooms in the fields and woodlands, with the dawn dew still on them.

Charlie switched off the radio – it was an item about a British civilian getting killed in a German air raid, the first time that had happened and hopefully the last – and pulled out a chair for Grace. 'Sit yourself down there, Gracie.' After moving the chair, he put his hand to his ribs, wincing.

'Have you hurt yourself, Charlie?'

'Pulled a muscle cycling up past the cemetery to the O'Hare place, I think – I must be getting old.' He grimaced. 'But will you have a bowl of soup and a hunk of Mary's home-made soda bread that Tilly gave to me in sympathy for me hurting myself?'

'Not yet, Charlie. I've something to tell you.'

She sat down with him and Declan at the table and explained about the telegram as gently as she could, then showed it to them.

Charlie went white as a sheet, and once more Grace wondered if maybe she shouldn't have said anything at all. But it wasn't her decision to make, she knew that. This was a miracle, for better or worse, and she hadn't the right to keep it from them.

'So what do we do now?' Declan asked, agitated. Just like last time, he jumped up and paced the room, running his fingers through his floppy dark hair.

'That depends on what we want, I suppose,' Charlie said softly, almost to himself, as he rubbed his sore ribs.

'We want her back, obviously. I want my baby sister and you want your daughter back here in Knocknashee where she belongs.' He looked at his father as if debating the issue was ludicrous.

'But she's not a baby any more, Declan.' Charlie's voice was low and trembling.

'I know, because this has gone on far too long already. We need to go and get her as soon as we can. And don't worry about the money – Peggy Clifford heard about the hot water thing I made for Grace, and she asked me to install four of them in the hotel. I have three done already and she's going to pay me well, so we can use that. There'll be plenty enough for the two of us to travel in steerage, and buy a single ticket for Siobhán coming back with us.'

Charlie sighed long and deep. 'What I was trying to say, son, is that the baby you remember is now a fifteen-year-old American girl, and that life is all she's known. She won't remember anything of Ireland. She probably doesn't even know she's adopted. As far as she knows, Joey and Sylvia Maheady are her real parents. She has a sister called Ivy. We don't even speak the same language as she does. I can manage in English of course, but it's not my native tongue. I might be her father, but in every way that would make any sense to the poor girl, I'm a stranger.'

Declan looked at his father in astonishment, like he didn't know him. 'But you must love her! You can't want to abandon her all over again?'

'A mhic, I never abandoned her! She was taken from me, and I think of her every minute of every day. I would give anything to have

her back, to have my two precious children under my roof again...'
Charlie's voice cracked with the emotion of it. 'But Declan, I won't
disrupt her life for my own benefit.'

'So you still want to do nothing, is it? Like always, you just accept
it, take it lying down like you've done all these years. Are you so
blinded by the priests that you can't even see what they've done to
you? What they did to your children?' Declan's jaw was clenched and
his fists balled by his sides; Grace had never seen him like this.

She was amazed. It was so unlike the young man she knew. He was
patience and kindness personified in school, especially with the children that struggled a bit, he was gentle and full of praise for even the
tiniest accomplishment, and he loved his father.

'I didn't take anything lying down, Declan,' Charlie said, his kindly
face careworn and sad. 'I really tried.'

'Oh yeah, I forgot, you did try, you *tried* to drink yourself to death.
Well, that did a lot of good, didn't it? That really helped me and
Siobhán when we were abandoned by everyone...'

It was time for Grace to intervene. She could not stand by and let
Declan pour all of his pain, however understandable, on his father.
'Charlie did everything he could,' she said, standing up and placing her
hand on his arm. 'He didn't just abandon you to your fate, and every
day you were gone was a torture for him. It's not fair or right to blame
him. He was up against the Church. They are powerful and they get
their way, you know that.'

Something about her tone at least stopped the tirade. But then
Declan roughly shrugged her hand away and stormed out of the back
door into the yard.

'Don't walk out on Grace. She's only ever tried to help you,' his
father called after him, and went to follow his son, but Grace stopped
him.

'Let me.' She left Charlie standing in front of the range, holding his
ribs and breathing hard.

Outside, Declan was leaning against the wall of the house,
smoking.

She leant beside him. 'Your father loves you, you know,' she said quietly.

He didn't reply.

'I know it must feel like everyone forgot about you, but that's just not true,' she added, her eyes on the damp ground where little green shoots of bluebells were pushing up everywhere. 'Your father humbled himself before the only one who could help. He went cap in hand to Canon Rafferty, only to be cruelly dismissed. Not once or twice, but over and over. He didn't give you up easily, he was forced to.'

A long silence passed and then she heard him, speaking so quietly she had to strain to hear. A lonely tear ran down his face as he spoke.

'They beat me for wetting the bed at the start. I was so lonely and confused. My mammy was dead, and my daddy and sister were gone, and I was all alone in this cold, hard place, and I didn't know what I'd done wrong. They used to make me stand all day with no food and the wet sheets over my head, and everyone would laugh at me. By the time I left, I'd had so many hidings. I didn't know what it was for most of the time. I didn't care. It didn't matter. They were cruel, Grace, more than cruel. It was like they enjoyed it. They got their pleasure from us. And nobody could stop them. It's no place for any child.'

Grace swallowed. She had never heard Declan speak this way before, and she put her arms around him, his wracking sobs the only sound in the cold spring air.

'Supposing Siobhán isn't happy,' he gasped. 'Supposing that rich couple died, like your parents died, and she's in an orphanage. I can't bear to think she might be over there alone and abandoned.'

Grace's heart went out to him. The poor young man was in such a dark place, perhaps the same sort of place in which Dymphna's husband, Tommy, had found himself on the night he walked into the sea to end his pain. She shivered at the thought and said a prayer for the poor man, traumatised by his time in the orphanage. Poor Tommy lay in the *cillín* now, with the unbaptised and the lost.

'I've an idea, Declan. Why don't you write to the Maheadys and say you think you might be a distant cousin of the father or something. Americans are always coming to find their ancestors here, like that American brother and sister who came to look at the Duggan grave. The Maheadys will think it's really normal. Then you and Charlie can at least get to visit and see her, and you can make yourself sure whether she's happy or not?'

She didn't know if Charlie would approve of the plan, but it was the best she could come up with.

Declan stood, wiping his tears. 'Writing back and forwards, though... I know from seeing you and Richard write to each other, it all just takes so long, and they're not going to tell a blank stranger the truth. And every day she's away...'

Grace knew he meant how every day for him was horrific and if he could have been rescued even one day earlier, it would have been better. The scars of his childhood ran deep.

'Sure it doesn't always take forever, sometimes it's quite quick. We'll write today. Come back inside, Declan, see what your father says to the idea.'

Charlie listened, and his face softened as Grace explained the plan, and finally he nodded. 'OK. We'll write to them, and if they agree to see us, we'll go and visit them. But son, if she's happy and loved and cared for, promise me that we'll let her be. Just knowing that, well, that will have to be enough to do us.'

'And if she's not?' Declan said, agitated again. 'If she's unhappy, will we take her then?'

Charlie plunged his fists into his pockets, threw his shoulders back and spoke with such conviction you could never doubt him. 'If Siobhán McKenna is anything less than totally content, then I'll tell you this, and I give you my solemn word. Wild horses won't stop me getting my little girl home.'

The clock on the dresser ticked in the silence as Declan absorbed his father's answer. 'If you'd have found me...' he said at last. 'And I know you tried, and I'm sorry for saying you didn't. I know you did. But if you'd have found me and asked me was I all right, I would have lied and said I was.'

'Why would you have done that?' Charlie asked in amazement.

'Because I was so scared of them and what they'd do to me if I ever said a bad word against them.' He shrugged. 'There used to be a welfare man, I don't know who he was, but he would come once a year and we'd have to have the place shining. We'd all get new shirts and trousers. I got a pair of shoes one time, the first pair that had ever fit me properly, but they were taken away the next day.'

The way he said it, so matter-of-fact, touched Grace. Declan was a peculiar mixture of strength and vulnerability. Though he was only a year older, in some ways he seemed younger than her – and in other ways so much older.

'Was he there to check you were all right?' Charlie asked, and she could hear the dread in his voice at the answer.

'I suppose he was, but we were all well schooled. Nobody got a beating the week before, so there were no fresh bruises. I had a yellowing one on my back, but I was told to say I got it playing football.' He laughed then, a hard, cold sound. 'As if we were ever allowed to play football.'

Declan had barely said a word about his experience in Letterfrack, a snippet here and there was all they had heard, but a picture was forming and it was a grim one.

'So we told him the food was fine. It wasn't and there was never enough. That we went to school. We didn't really. We worked most of the time. They hired us out to farmers, big estates. We never saw any wages of course. We were told to say that we had clothes and boots and winter coats, and that we were well treated.'

Charlie's face was a mask of anger as he took his beloved son in his arms, though Grace noticed him wince with pain as Declan hugged him. 'What happened to you won't happen to Siobhán, I promise you, son. We'll make sure she's safe and really loved, not scared or being hurt, and if she's not happy, then we'll find a way to get her back. I promise you that, Declan. I swear on your mother's grave.'

* * *

GRACE AND DECLAN composed the letter to the Maheadys together, and Declan wrote it out, using the new neat handwriting that Grace had managed to teach him. He'd had a terrible time in the sporadic classes at Letterfrack. He was left-handed but they beat it out of him, and he was too traumatised to hold a pen with it ever again. He still found writing with his right hand slow work, but he was getting better and better with practice.

In the letter he introduced himself and his father as distant cousins several times removed from the Maheady family and asked if it would suit to visit in April, just to say hello.

* * *

THREE DAYS and a visit to Dr Ryan later, and Charlie's painful ribs turned out to be shingles, which could last for two months. Another delay. Grace wasn't sure Declan could stand it but didn't know what to suggest.

He came into her room after she'd been cleaning the chalkboard at the end of the day and stood there with an envelope in his hand.

'What have you there?' Grace asked, drying her hands on the towel she kept hanging on a nail beside the basin.

'See for yourself.' He passed the envelope to her.

She opened it and inside were two tickets, from Cobh to New York, leaving on the fifth of April and returning on the twenty-fifth. A few days each side of the Easter holidays.

'But America will never let Charlie in with the shingles, we know that? Even if he was fit?' Grace said, gazing at the tickets in confusion.

'That's true,' Declan said.

'So why did you buy him a ticket? Will you get your money back? They must have cost every penny you had.'

'I didn't get a ticket for him. I got one for you.' He looked at the floor then, clearly shy.

Grace could hardly believe it. This was the second time in her life someone had bought her a surprise ticket for America. 'For me? But why, Declan?'

'Please come with me, Grace. My father will worry less what I'd get up to if you're there, and I'm...well, I'd feel better if you were with me too. I'm less likely to get myself in trouble.' He smiled to show he was joking.

'But the school... Bad enough you'd be gone...'

'Most of the trip is in the Easter holidays. I'm sure Father Iggy and Janie and Dymphna will help with the few extra days if you ask them. But please, I have to go, Grace, I can't wait. And Dr Ryan says Da could be out of action for even longer – with shingles it's hard to predict, and he has a bad dose of it. I just have to go, and you're the only one I can ask to come with me.'

'I'll be in your way, Declan, I walk so slowly. Maybe you'd be better taking Tilly?'

'She has the farm – it's spring and the sheep are lambing. And you wouldn't slow me down. You're so much better these days, and we can stop whenever you want. We can get buses or trains or whatever they have – we won't need to walk everywhere. And you're so much better at talking to people than I am...'

Grace looked at the man who had become such a dear friend, and once again he seemed younger than his years. He so desperately wanted to do this. She could go and help, she supposed. Or at least try to.

He looked agonised as she hesitated. 'I couldn't afford first class. I know that's what you should have had last time, but the man in the travel agent's said the *Lady Anne* was a nice ship and the cabins are well kitted out, and if you say yes, I'll change one ticket to a second-class cabin for you, so you'll be comfortable.'

'Ah, Declan, there's no need for that...'

'There is and I will, I promise.'

She thought of another problem. 'But you haven't heard back from the Maheadys yet. What if they're away in April and you've wasted your money on me?'

'Well, if they're not there, I'll save up again and go back,' said Declan firmly. 'I won't ever stop looking till I've found her.'

She sighed, torn about what to do. 'Well, if I come with you, what I

141

need you to promise is this – if your sister is fine and happy, will you promise to stick to your father's wishes and not disrupt her life?'

He squared his narrow shoulders and looked her straight in the eye. 'All I need is to see for myself, Grace. I told the inspector at Letterfrack I was fine and happy, and I was far from it, but if I can find my sister, and see with my own two eyes that she's got a good life and they're good people who are rearing her, then I'll leave her be. I promise you that, Grace, and I promised Da the same thing. But I have to see for myself.'

Grace believed him. Despite the scars he carried from being reared in the orphanage, Declan was as honest as the day was long.

'So will you come?' he asked.

The question hung between them.

The McKennas had been so good to her. And Charlie had been her father's dear friend. Eddie Fitzgerald had tried all he could to help at the time when Declan and Siobhán were taken from Charlie; he would want Grace to do this.

'I will,' she said.

And suddenly she was enveloped in a hug. Declan wasn't normally demonstrative, he was reserved and quiet, so she was taken aback.

'Thanks, Grace, you...you've no idea what this means to me, and to my da. I promise nothing bad will happen. I'll be very calm and reasonable.'

After he'd gone Grace sat down behind her desk and rested her elbows on the wood, thinking. How amazing to think that she would be in New York so soon. All this time Richard had been talking about maybe the foreign editor of the *Capital* sending him and Jacob Nunez to Europe, but it had never happened, and from what he'd said in his last letter, it wasn't likely to happen. But now she was going to New York!

Perhaps Richard could come up and visit? She wouldn't suggest he do it specially, that would be too much to ask, but she would write tonight and tell him the dates she would be there, and he could make up his own mind.

Maybe he'd meet her and Declan off the boat... At the thought of it, her heart fizzed with excitement, and she couldn't wait to sit down at her kitchen table with her fountain pen and bottle of lilac ink.

She hadn't heard from him since his telegram. He'd said he'd write soon, and she was waiting on his letter, but everything was so delayed. And nothing had come from the Maheadys yet. She hoped they would hear from them before it was time for her and Declan to leave.

And hopefully her letter back to Richard would also reach him in time.

CHAPTER 13

8th of March 1940, Knocknashee
   Dear Richard,

   I don't know, did you even get my last letter yet? Nothing is certain these days about the post. But I hope you get this one in time, which is why I'm writing it in a hurry.

   I can hardly believe I'm writing these words, but I am going to New York!

   As soon as your telegram arrived, Declan McKenna wrote to Siobhán's family, introducing himself and Charlie as distant Irish relatives, cousins several times removed, the usual thing, and asking to visit with them in Rockaway Beach. I know it seems duplicitous, but I really do think it's for the best. That way Declan and Charlie could make sure that Siobhán/Lily is happy and well looked-after, without upsetting her by saying who they really are, so then, assuming she's fine, they could go back home to Knocknashee and live out the rest of their lives in peace.

   Well, Richard, that all fell through when Charlie got shingles. America would never let him in, so Declan asked me to go instead. Poor Charlie. He's in a bad way, it's a horrible thing. But I can't help being a bit excited on my own behalf. I never thought I would get this opportunity a second time, after your wonderful offer before Agnes's stroke.

   We, Declan and I, we'll be sailing from Cobh in Cork on the fifth of April and we'll be in New York from the twelfth to the nineteenth, and if you happen to be in 'the Big Apple' around then – and I know that's so unlikely, but still if by a miracle you were there when I was there, it would be silly to pass each other 'like ships in the night' as they say, without realising it – I would be so delighted to finally meet you.

Your globetrotting friend,

Grace

PS I have an update on that daft story I was telling you about Kit Gallagher, the housekeeper at the parochial house, that might make you laugh.

I was leaving the sweetshop yesterday – I had a grá for a bit of toffee – when I heard my name being called, and there was Nancy O'Flaherty beckoning me over. When I got to her, she ushered me in and shut the post office door, sliding the latch and turning the sign to closed.

'Is everything all right, Mrs O'Flaherty?' I asked.

She beamed at me. 'Well, it's wonderful, Grace! We did it! Guess who is on the train to Waterford next Saturday?'

Well, I couldn't believe it at first.

'And are you sure of this?' I asked. 'Because I was talking to Father Iggy only yesterday, and he didn't think Kit was going to go at all. He was very glum about it, though he was trying to hide it.'

'Oh, 'twas touch and go, but it's true,' she assured me. 'It was Pádraig O Sé who got it over the line for us. He was overheard by the lady in question. She was outside the door on her way in to collect Father Lehane's shoes that were being resoled. She heard him talking about her, saying no wonder the poor priests were starving to death, that she had no idea how to feed a man, that there was more meat on a spider's elbow than on her, that she was so skinny that one eye would do her – you know the way he goes on. Nobody is the right weight for that man – everyone is either too fat or too thin. But anyway, she took great umbrage and rounded on him.'

Nancy rubbed her hands in undisguised glee. 'Well, she let rip, told him that she's seen a better head on a brush, he was so ugly, and how people would rather have holes in their boots than go into him and face his nasty remarks.

'Well, before Pádraig could reply, she turned and saw loads of the kids

outside enjoying the drama and they all laughing, so out she goes in high dudgeon, roaring like a bull that this is a desperate place altogether, with children only half reared and only big, thick, ignorant cábogs to be dealing with and that she was getting out of it for once and for all.'

I was all agog. 'Do you think she intended to say it?'

'I don't, but Pádraig has a way of needling people, you know he has, and he really annoyed her. And she has it said now, so she can't lose face. She was in here this morning telling everyone her ticket was got, and what a big house her sister Margaret has, and how the people of Waterford are a better class of people altogether.'

So, Richard, it seems that our straight-talking and extraordinarily rude cobbler was the straw that broke the camel's back. Between that and the green paint and the flowers on the altar and the sound of the tin whishtle, we got her to go. A community effort, I suppose you could call it. It will be great for Dymphna to have a secure position at the parochial house for life, and the priests will be delighted – she's a wonderful cook – and Kit Gallagher will inherit a house, so everyone wins.

And that's all from me, Mr Lewis!

Your parochial friend,

Grace

CHAPTER 14

SAVANNAH, GEORGIA

March 5, 1940, The Beach House, St. Simons Island
  Dear Grace,
You're not going to believe this! I'm going to Europe! I'm not sure when. I wanted to wait to mail this till I was sure of the dates, but that's taking a while, so I'm sending this now and will give you the dates later. It might not be till May at this rate.

Anyway, it seems like Jacob's mad scheme of travelling over eight hundred miles to see Guy Falkirk actually did the trick. He seemed impressed with us because of it.

Jacob thinks getting the article in the paper also helped. I didn't even know the features editor had used it until we stopped at Washington Union Station on our way to the Capital office.

I've enclosed the article. It's a double-page spread, so everyone will read it.

Kirky (as Falkirk insists we call him) said Ed Irwin (he's the features editor) only put it in because you were so pretty, and he sure must think so because he used your picture but blew it up so everyone can see you. Jacob had a bit of a grumble about being outdone by a seaside photographer, but he was good-humored about it and said Hollywood would be knocking on your door next. I have to agree!

Anyway, it looks like we will be in Europe for eight or nine weeks depending. We will go to England first and from there to France.

Our accommodations in London will be all arranged and paid for, the woman who arranges this stuff at the Capital told us. Her name is Lucille. She's terrifying. We will have a budget for accommodations in France, but since there is no way of knowing what it is like there, or how we can get around, we will have access to cash, though Lucille said Kirky always wants receipts for "every single dime" and it was to pay for "legitimate work expenses, which do not include alcohol, women, clothes for women, alcohol for women, or anything not directly and strictly necessary for the story."

Goodness knows what this newspaper's reporters and photographers usually get up to abroad, but I don't think Jacob has eyes for anyone but Sarah, who is still crazy about him, though she still says she won't marry him until he's safely in the jewelry business.

As for me... Well, I very much doubt anyone there will catch my eye.

I don't know what the situation is regarding travel from England to Ireland or vice versa, but perhaps I could get to somewhere in Ireland even for a day?

I looked on a map and saw that Knocknashee, or at least Dingle—Knocknashee wasn't marked—is somewhere near the ports of Dublin, Cork, or Wexford. Whichever way we do it, I can't fathom the idea that I would be there and you were so close and for us not to meet.

Anyway, we'll discuss all this further when we know the actual dates. For now I'm sure you're more interested in how I found Siobhán McKenna, or Lily Maheady as she is called by her adoptive parents.

You were right when you said finding Father Dempsey in New York City might be like looking for a needle in a haystack, but the hotel receptionist sent me to a Canon Devine in St. Patrick's Cathedral, and I struck gold when I met a lady who works there, Mrs. McHale.

She was an Irishwoman who spent all her childhood summers in Dingle at her grandfather's home, and as soon as I told her I had a friend in Knocknashee, she dropped everything to help me, and by the next morning, I was playing chess with Father Noel Dempsey in his retirement home in Queens.

The guy was around seventy years old but with a mind like a steel trap, and once he found out I wasn't a Catholic, he told me he was only in the retirement home because otherwise he'd be defrocked (Is that the word? I heard that someplace but I'm not too sure. You know what I mean anyway, right?) because—you'll never believe this—Siobhán McKenna wasn't the only baby sold by Canon Rafferty.

There were other babies brought over after, by a woman named Kit Gallagher, who I suppose is the awful housekeeper you wrote to me about.

The way Father Dempsey got the blame was because someone had complained to the bishop about the three thousand dollars being charged, and Canon Rafferty named Father Dempsey as the go-between and said it must have been him who took the money, which Father Dempsey is adamant is not true, and personally I believe him. He was involved in Siobhán McKenna's adoption only, not any of the others—he only heard about them when the bishop started to investigate.

The Maheadys were in his congregation, a childless Irish-Italian couple who sound nice. He's a firefighter and she's a nurse. And Father Dempsey genuinely thought Siobhán was an orphan and had absolutely no idea your sister was going to ask them for three thousand dollars. The Maheadys only had it because that was the price of the house in Brooklyn they were saving up for, which is why they moved outside New York City to Rockaway Beach instead, a small place on the coast.

I got the impression from Father Dempsey that she had a nice life and they were good people. I hope that's the case.

I'm going to visit my parents later this week to tell them I'm going to Europe. They haven't cared about my writing career up to now. I don't know how they reacted to the piece I wrote about us, and drawing an analogy for Europe and the States. They were very much against America getting involved last time we spoke, so I'm sure that didn't go down well. All they want is for me to give up and come back to the bank, but I suppose I should at least let them know what I'm up to. I am their son, even if they have stopped my allowance and keep threatening to cut me off altogether. They don't know much about love or loyalty or trying to make a real difference; with them everything boils down to money.

Sarah is sulking about Jacob going and keeps telling me to make sure he stays out of trouble. I've no idea how she expects me to manage this. Keeping him out of trouble is like keeping a moth away from a flame—you can flap your hands all you like, but they'll still find a way.

I sent a card to Nathan to say goodbye for now. I don't know what he'll think about me being a war reporter. He's also very against the idea of America getting involved in this war. As he always says, "Old men quarrel and young men die, and doctors like me are left to pick up the pieces, literally."

Not that I'm off to fight a war, but he might think I should just ignore the whole thing.

OK, I'm gonna sign off now. See you somewhere in Europe very, very soon.

Richard

CHAPTER 15

*S*ix days later, at half past noon on a Saturday, Richard parked his Buick outside his parents' house on Jones Street and climbed out. Unlike in freezing New York, the early spring weather was warm and fragrant. Already the wraparound porch was covered in trailing bougainvillea and begonias, and lilies bloomed in pots. The peacock-blue double swing with its immaculate snow-white cushions creaked in the gentle breeze.

He'd not seen his parents since Miranda and Algernon's wedding, when Nathan and Sarah were there to take some of the heat off him. He'd hoped Sarah would be here this time – she still spent a lot of time at the Jones Street house – but she was off goofing around on St Simons Island on a yacht with some friends of hers, including Miranda, with whom she was still very friendly. Nathan rarely came south these days, to either St Simons Island or Savannah; it was so far from Detroit, and he was very busy. He'd just earned a very prestigious promotion to hospital consultant, and he and Rebecca had bought a nice house in a fancy suburb with a huge yard for the children.

In response to Richard's card, he'd written a very nice note, complimenting him on his article in the *Capital* and saying how pretty

Grace was, and asking if she'd ever seen Sister Kenny. And he said the Europe thing had changed his mind a little bit, that maybe there was such a thing as a 'just war'. 'But whether you're right or not,' he wrote, 'I'm proud of you, so take care of yourself and don't do anything stupid. And by the way, I love you.' It was a very touching thing to say, especially as they'd been raised to not show affection.

It felt strange to knock on the front door of his home, but it felt stranger to just walk in. So he knocked. As he waited he fought the urge to just walk away.

The door opened and Delores, their maid, stood there. She was a tiny, wizened Black woman who could have been any age between fifty and eighty. Unlike Esme, who had practically raised him before she went to live permanently at the beach house to mind the decrepit Doodle, he and Delores had never been close. He was always polite – it was very crass and screamed new money to be rude to the help was one of his mother's mantras – but Delores neither invited nor shared confidences.

'Good afternoon, Mr Richard,' she said, politely holding the door open.

'Good afternoon, Delores. Are my parents in?'

'Yes, sir, they are about to dine.' Her slow, drawling Southern vowels were long and melodic.

'I'll just go in then, thank you,' he said, walking past her into the entrance hallway. It wouldn't be fair to make her decide whether to announce him; once his parents sat down to eat, visitors were supposed to be shown into the living room to wait. But he'd timed his visit deliberately for this hour, because that was the only time they were likely to be found together.

Nothing had changed in the house. It still was clean and tidy, a huge bowl of fresh lilies on the entrance table, the wicker fan rotating overhead. He went through the large double-width stained-glass doorway into the large living room, where the cream damask sofas still sat facing each other, a low glass and mahogany coffee table, with a large Waterford Crystal bowl filled with lemons, between them.

His father's voice, deep and sonorous, wafted through the double doors that led from the living room to the dining room.

'Sumner Welles doesn't think much of von Ribbentrop by all accounts, and he met Hitler too, who seems to be under the impression that Britain wants to destroy Germany...'

Arthur Lewis didn't have conversations, he gave sermons. The gospel according to himself.

Richard's mother murmured something noncommittal. It had been this way all of Richard's life, his father making pronouncements about the world at the dinner table and nobody ever contradicting him.

'Maybe he's right, who knows?' It was not a question in search of an answer. 'Welles was right on the subject of the Jews. The British wanted to give their quota of immigrants allowed into the US to the German Jews, and Welles said it was a mistake...' Father droned on.

Richard was glad Jacob wasn't here. To hear anyone describe Adolf Hitler as anything but the devil incarnate would send him into a spin, and on the subject of the sluggish international response to Jewish refugees, he was incandescent with fury.

Taking a deep breath, he walked in, trying not to show how unsettled he was.

Both his parents looked up, his father midlecture, his mother midserve of a bowl of collard greens.

'Richard, this is a surprise. What are you doing here?' His father's tone was neutral, though his eyes betrayed a glint of curiosity.

His mother merely raised her eyebrows. It was no effort to her to keep her emotions in check – she'd had years of practice, since she was a little girl. Sometimes Richard wondered if there were any emotions left in there at all or if they'd atrophied due to lack of use.

'Hello, Father, Mother. I won't keep you long, and I don't want to disturb your dinner, but I thought you might like to know I am sailing for Europe on the second of April. I got the dates this morning. I'm going as a war correspondent for the *Capital*.'

Caroline Lewis served her greens and replaced the serving spoon in the dish, while his father sat impassively, folding and unfolding a corner of his napkin.

Long seconds passed, and Richard began to wonder if he should just turn and leave. But then Arthur Lewis broke his silence. 'I saw you stayed at the St Regis while you were in New York?'

'Well, yes...' How had his father known about the hotel? He'd paid his own bill, not charged it to the Lewis account, even though he'd been offered that as an option.

It was as if his father could read his mind. 'The manager called me, checking everything was to your satisfaction, but really to tell me he had upgraded you because you were my son. You know Yankees – no good deed goes unheralded.' He smirked under his magnificent moustache at his own wit.

'What do they charge per night there now, Richard?' his mother asked coolly.

'I don't recall exactly, Mother...' He was confused at the turn the conversation had taken. It was very unlike his mother to inquire about the price of things; it was another mantra of hers, that if you had to ask how much, you couldn't afford it.

'How fortunate for you to be in a position not to know.' The barb was there. *Subtext: Your rebellion is not a real rebellion since you are still doing it on the family's money.* Even though they'd cut off his allowance, his grandmother's trust fund still gave him a financial cushion – well, more a featherbed than cushion, if he was honest.

'It was just for two nights. I needed to see the foreign editor in New York,' he said through gritted teeth. His mother could raise his hackles like nobody else.

'And the *Capital* wouldn't pay for you? I thought you were their war correspondent.' The slight note of mockery in her voice grated on him.

'I am now, but I was there for an interview.'

'And are you going alone?' It was his father's turn to put him on the spot, but there was something different in the way he asked his question. Not so much contempt. Even a little...concern?

'No. I'm going with the newspaper's photographer. He's pretty experienced.'

'The same one who took the pictures for your piece in the *Capital*?'

'Oh, did you read that?' He couldn't help feeling a burst of satisfaction. It was the first time either of his parents had even acknowledged his career.

'I did. Earl Tomkinson – he's an absolute king in the insurance world, his son married one of the Stanway girls – he pointed it out to me at the golf club, said he agreed with the sentiment even though it was in a damn Yankee paper.' Was that a hint of pride in his father's voice? He was certainly stroking his moustache, something he only did when pleased...

'I take it you know that Jacob Nunez is Jewish and known to mix with...well...not our sort of people? I'm very surprised at you, Richard, that you allowed him to stay at the house on St Simons, particularly with Sarah staying there.' His mother's voice was sharp and accusing, and Richard's stomach turned over. Oh God, if they found out Sarah was dating Jacob, they'd never forgive her, her life would be ruined...

'I...er...is he?' he parried feebly. 'I mean, Nunez, that's a Portuguese name?'

'I have it from Miranda's mother – there's no doubt about it. He goes to the synagogue. I hope he was in your dear grandmother's house no longer than it took him to take those photos.'

Richard felt his shoulders relax. Of course, that's how she knew Jacob had been in the house. Two of the pictures were taken inside, in the kitchen and Richard's own bedroom, and the one with Doodle on the beach nearby.

'No, of course not, Mother. We have a working relationship, that's all. We're colleagues, not friends. We don't socialise.'

He felt bad for disowning a man who had become a good friend, but it was as much in Jacob's interests as his that his parents didn't know the extent of Sarah's relationship.

'I'm glad to hear it. I believe your "colleague" mixes with *artists and anarchists*,' his mother stated, in a tone that she might have used had she said 'murdering rapists'.

'I wouldn't know about that. As I said –'

'Well, maybe you should make it your business to know. And maybe you should be more careful who you mix with in the future, and that includes peasant girls in Ireland who throw messages into the sea, if – God forbid – that bit of the story is really true, which I sincerely hope not. I asked Sarah as soon as I saw her – I hardly see her from one day to the next these days, even when she's here at home and not at the summer house with you – and she assured me it was only "poetic licence", whatever that is, and the picture is posed by a model, which is obvious when you look at it. No peasant girl would look like a Hollywood actress. So that's what I told Nancy Tomkinson when we met to play bridge. She was very concerned about you –'

Richard attempted to interrupt – it was one thing to disown Jacob Nunez but another to disown Grace – but Caroline Lewis held up her hand, her rings, diamond and sapphire caught the light.

'No, Richard. If this Irish girl does exist, I don't want you to tell me. I would rather exist in a state of blissful ignorance. It is hard enough not knowing where your sister is half the time. A mother's lot truly is a heavy one.'

Making it clear that was her last word on the subject, Caroline Lewis helped her husband and then herself to a slice of rare beef from a platter on the table. Both began eating. Neither of them offered for him to stay and join them.

Still, he hesitated. 'Well, um…Mother…Father… Well…I just wanted to let you know I was going…' He found it hard to just walk away. A big part of him wanted his parents to tell him to take care of himself, to be safe, not to do anything to get himself in trouble. He wanted them to care.

He had to face the fact that they didn't.

It was so difficult to understand. He knew his mother was angry about the wedding, and his failure to marry the eligible Miranda. His father didn't care so much about that, but he was furious at Richard's refusal to follow him into the bank. But surely now that he'd told them he was going to Europe, after everything that was in the news, didn't they care if he put himself in danger? Didn't they even care if he died?

'Can't you see your father and I are dining, Richard? Don't just keep standing there gawking. It's rude and unnecessary.' His mother sighed, as if Richard were being a particularly tiresome six-year-old who had tested her patience too far this time.

It took him right back to his childhood, to when he was that six-year-old boy, trying to get her attention. His mother was never the warmest. She wasn't a cuddly mother, and they were not a hugging family; they never said the actual words 'I love you'. And yet...as a child, he'd assumed she loved him anyway. All mothers loved their children, didn't they? That's what he'd thought. Maybe he'd been wrong. Maybe she hadn't loved him even then. She certainly didn't now.

'Well, I'll go then.' He turned to the door.

His mother said not another word, but Arthur Lewis called after him, 'Yes, thank you for coming by.'

Delores stood in the entrance hall, the front door already open for him.

'Goodbye, Delores,' he said, swallowing the lump in his throat.

'Goodbye, Mr Richard. You take care now.' Even Delores had a kinder word to say to him than his parents. What kind of a cold couple had raised him?

'You too, Delores.' And for the first time ever, he dropped a peck on the old woman's cheek, which clearly surprised and even pleased her a little, because she smiled a tiny, wrinkled smile.

As he strode down the steps of the house, his emotions in a whirlpool of grief, sadness, fury and hurt, he heard her close the door behind him. But then it opened again, and he heard someone descending. Arthur Lewis said in a lower voice than usual, 'Richard, wait one moment.'

Half of him wanted to walk on without looking back, to hell with his parents, but the lost, ever-hopeful little boy in him stopped and turned.

'Well, Richard,' said his father, gazing seriously at him. 'I can't help being anxious at the thought of you going to Germany with a Jewish companion. They're not a very popular people, and I'm not sure you should associate yourself –'

'Not Germany. France, Father. There's no war in France. The French have a line of fortifications along the French-German border called the Maginot Line, and that will keep the country perfectly safe.' He'd been desperate for his father to care about him, but he didn't want to worry him unnecessarily.

'Oh, very well. You know best, I'm sure.' His father, not used to being contradicted, seemed lost for what to say. But then he managed, 'Well, anyway, good luck,' and proffered his hand.

Richard shook it. 'Goodbye, Father,' he said again.

'Good, yes…good…' Arthur Lewis hesitated again, stroking his moustache, then abruptly turned on his heel and remounted the steps to where Delores was waiting with her hand on the door. He went into the house without a backwards glance, and Delores closed it again behind him – though not without another tiny smile in Richard's direction.

Richard climbed into his Buick and drove through the handsome city and out into the flat countryside, where peach orchards stretched as far as the eye could see, already coming into blossom; soon the vast landscape would turn a vibrant almost purple-pink.

He felt comforted somehow by that handshake – though it still hurt like hell that his mother had dismissed him from her presence without a word of love. He stuck out his chin as he was driving and told himself he didn't care any more than his mother did.

A short while later, after crossing the causeway to the island, he let himself into the house. There was nobody home. He figured Sarah must still be out sailing with her friends, including Miranda, and Esme had perhaps gone shopping, maybe with Jimmy the gardener in his truck. Only Doodle waddled to greet him, then crashed in a soft, panting heap at his feet.

On the table in the hall was a letter from Grace – no, two letters! The war in the Atlantic was playing havoc with the post from Europe;

everything went by boat now and took ages. She couldn't have had time to receive his last letter yet, so this must be a response to the telegram.

Not wanting to be disturbed if Sarah returned with her yachting crowd for cocktails, he ran upstairs to his room, kicked off his shoes and flopped back on his bed, unconsciously adopting the very same posture Jacob had captured him in for the *Capital*, his right knee bent, his other hand behind his head, ruffling his slightly too long blond hair.

He opened the first letter of the two and flattened it on his thigh.

2nd March 1940, Knocknashee.

Dear Richard,

Your article is so well written and so lovely, I applaud you, and I'm glad our friendship was able to give you a jumping-off point, as it were, for an important piece of writing about the relationship between America and Europe...

They came from different worlds, but she'd understood exactly what he was trying to say. Though he hoped she knew he meant it when he said she was beautiful, that it wasn't just for the sake of the story. Maybe he should tell her straight out – well, he had, sort of, in his last letter to her, saying how Kirky had called her a 'pretty girl' and Jacob talked about Hollywood calling.

I have to admit I'm a bit daunted about the idea my picture might be published, but I'm comforting myself that it's only very small...

She did doubt her looks then. Well, wait until she saw what Ed Irwin had done with that two-inch-square seaside photo. Surely she would see for herself then how beautiful she was, without anyone having to tell her.

It's so generous of you to offer to stay on and look for Father Dempsey yourself. It seems like an impossible task, but it's so kind of you to try.

She would have his telegram by now; this letter was posted before he sent it. But he wanted to spin out the pleasure by reading it all the way through first.

In other news, we – me and Mrs O'Flaherty in the post office – are hatching a plan to save poor Father Iggy and his curate from starvation. We are trying to subtly get Kit Gallagher, the priests' housekeeper, to go to her sister, Margaret, in Waterford and put Dymphna in the job instead...

If it was the same Kit Gallagher who brought over the babies for the canon after Agnes sold Siobhán so successfully, then maybe that was a problem solved. Surely the evil woman needed only to be threatened with exposure to run away from Knocknashee as fast as possible.

I don't think I have any other news right now, except it's freezing cold and it feels like it will never stop raining. Some people are saying that fuel could be rationed if the Emergency goes on much longer, but it's hard to see how it could affect us here in the west of Ireland. We mostly burn turf anyway – coal is expensive.

Another thing people are worried about is sailing across the Atlantic because of U-boats, but of course any Irish ship is painted with EIRE on both sides and flies the tricolour fore and aft. You can see it's a ship from a neutral country...

I suppose that's the same for America as you're not in the war either?

This was something he hadn't thought about, the chance of getting blown up in the middle of the Atlantic. A very, very childish part of him pictured his parents getting the news and being devastated... Or, more realistically, not.

He read to the end of the letter and immediately reached for the second, eager for her response to his telegram.

8th of March 1940, Knocknashee

Dear Richard...

I can hardly believe I'm writing these words, but I am going to New York!

He read on in amazement.

WELL, Richard, that all fell through when Charlie got shingles...so Declan asked me to go instead... I never thought I would get this opportunity a second time, after your wonderful offer before Agnes's stroke.

We, Declan and I...

Declan and I. Declan and I. Why did that bug him so much?

...we'll be sailing from Cobh in Cork on the fifth of April and we'll be in New York from the twelfth to the nineteenth...

If by a miracle you were there when I was there, it would be silly to pass each other 'like ships in the night' as they say...

Then there was a PS about Kit Gallagher, which would normally entertain him hugely, but he didn't care enough right now to even read it.

He let his hand with the letter fall limply to his side, lowered his knee and just lay flat, staring at the ceiling. Grace was arriving in New York on the twelfth of April. But by the second of April, he would be gone. He'd be in Europe, leaving Grace sightseeing in New York hand in hand with Declan McKenna, who would probably be delighted Richard Lewis wouldn't be there to greet them when they got off the boat.

Of all the hurts he'd endured today, this one was most like a punch to the gut.

Grace Fitzgerald. Declan McKenna. It had been only a matter of time; even from this distance, he'd known it. Why else would Declan ask her to go to New York with him, when he could have waited just a few weeks for his father to recover from the shingles, as she wrote on to explain? What was five or six weeks when Siobhán had been gone fifteen years already? Tickets were easily exchanged.

No, the reason was clear. Declan McKenna was in love with Grace Fitzgerald. And she was probably in love with him – even if she didn't know it yet or was too modest to think it before the man proposed or something.

'Oh, for God's sake, pull yourself together,' he snarled to himself as he sat up and swung his long legs off the bed.

As he'd said time and time again, both to Sarah and Jacob, this Irish girl was *not his girlfriend*. She was his pen pal and confidante, supporter of his career, teller of funny stories, a breath of fresh air. And she deserved to be happy and flourish, get married to someone who understood her and where she was from.

And *as her friend*, he should be happy for her. She and Declan had so much in common. They were both teachers, he lived across the street, he was the son of her father's friend. Of course he was her ideal husband...

Downstairs the front door opened and there was a clamour of girlish voices as the young women poured into the house, giggling and demanding cocktails. The next moment Sarah was calling up the stairs, 'Richard? Richard? Are you in?' and then a moment later saying to someone, 'He must have gone for a walk. He likes the beach at this time, I'm sure he won't be long...' The voices ebbed into the lounge where the cocktail bar was, and someone put a record on, the Glenn Miller Orchestra's 'Moonlight Serenade'.

In the privacy of his bedroom, Richard dashed the hot salt tears of disappointment from his eyes, then walked over to his writing desk, pulling a chair across the wooden floor. He sat down and scribbled a hasty note, something to restore his pride after his last letter, where he had gushed like a fool over seeing her in England or Ireland.

Dear Grace,

How unfortunate. It would have been great fun to meet you and Declan McKenna in New York, but I'm afraid duty calls.

As you know already from my last letter, Jacob Nunez and I are off to Europe for a couple of months. I have the dates now. We sail from New York very early on the second of April and arrive in Southampton on the night of the eighth, and I can hardly think of anything else but getting ready and packing.

Of course, it would have been nice to catch up with you in Ireland, but it was clearly not meant to be.

Do try and do a little sightseeing in New York while you're there.

I stayed on myself for a couple of days after completing my mission, and I recommend the Statue of Liberty, the Coney Island Cyclone, and the boating lake in Central Park, which is a great spot for courting couples. And be sure to have a hot dog!

Yours,

Richard

He read over what he'd written and thought about scratching out the words 'courting couples', but then told himself it was only the truth. The lake was a common rendezvous for lovers; when he was there, he saw a young man and his girl in every other boat.

And if he was right, and Declan was going to propose, it would be the perfect place...

To his annoyance, he found there was a lump in his throat. If only he'd told her how he felt sooner, but then it was only the mention of Declan that made him so jealous that he realised just how much this Irish girl had come to mean to him. He was that dumb. And now it was too late.

Someone knocked on the door. 'Richard, I heard you moving around, so I know you're in there. Stop hiding.' It was Sarah. 'Come on down. The girls are all dying to see you. Especially you-know-who.'

He stayed silent.

'Richard, open this door or I'm coming in!'

Hastily folding his note to Grace and stuffing it in an envelope for mailing, he glanced in the mirror, smoothed his hair and opened the door.

Resisting Sarah was futile, so he followed her downstairs. Five or six girls Sarah's age – he recognised most of them, Southern belles in the making – were enjoying their last days of freedom before their mamas found them a suitable spouse.

They chatted and flirted and teased him about never going to anything as Sarah put an old-fashioned into his hand.

Miranda sat on the swing on the porch, watching him. She was as pretty as ever, not a hair astray, her cream linen dress looking like it had been pressed five minutes ago. Pearls at her ears and throat, she looked like a carbon copy of her mother, only younger. Elegant, pretty, smiling and perfectly groomed.

He extricated himself from the main body of girls who wanted him to dance and joined Miranda on the porch. He could feel all their eyes bore into his back. Sarah, to her credit, turned up the music and started a conversation about the Easter Ball at the yacht club so he and Miranda could talk without eavesdroppers.

'Well, if it's not our intrepid reporter, coming to mingle with the rich and empty.' She grinned and sat back, appraising him.

'Well, I do live here, Miranda.' He sat down opposite her.

'I heard. And Sarah says you're off to Europe?'

He nodded, taking a sip of his cocktail. It was too strong; Sarah always made them that way.

'Be careful, won't you? She says you're going with the Jewish photographer.'

'I feel fairly sure she didn't describe him like that.' Richard gave a small admonishing smile.

'No, she was all starry eyes and broken-hearted actually, but you know Sarah.'

'I do. Not practical and sensible like you, who would never let the heart rule the head.' He smiled fully then to take the sting from his words.

She didn't tease him back about being a penniless bohemian; instead she sighed deeply. He felt bad.

'Maybe I should have.' She took a sip of her vodka and tonic with a lime wedge. 'Too late now but…maybe I should have.'

He didn't know what to say, if he should ask about her new marriage or not. He threw propriety to the wind. They were old friends if nothing else. 'How are things with Algernon?'

She made a face, a forced smile, and she raised her perfectly arched eyebrows. 'On the wrong tack, Richard, I'm afraid.' She laughed at her nautical humour, knowing he'd get the joke. God knew they'd teased Algernon enough about his sailing obsession over the years.

'I'm genuinely sorry to hear that. I did hope it would work out for you,' Richard said, and meant it.

'I know you did, and I'm grateful for it, but it was a mistake. You know how it is. I think our parents had fewer expectations of marriage. Your mother listens to your father pontificate over dinner and in return gets to get her hair done four times a week. Mine accepts that the only sight of my father she's ever likely to see is the top of his bald head behind a newspaper. Algy's father is an even bigger bore on the subject of the damned boats than his son is, but his mother only cares about her flower garden, so he rambles on about jibs and hulls and what have you while she chatters about hydrangeas and begonias and wisteria. There's no connection, no friendship even, but they didn't expect it and so aren't disappointed.' She shrugged. 'It's all very transactional and it works, for them anyway, but I think I need more.'

'In what way?' Richard asked, half knowing the answer.

'I've taken a lover. Algy suspects but he doesn't care, I don't think. I'm very discreet. My husband is going off around the Caribbean next month, and then he's got a trip to Panama after that, and the idea of me tagging along…well, neither of us wants that.'

Richard tried to hide his shock. He knew it was ridiculous, but men having affairs was one thing – but women…it was unheard of.

'And this, er…lover…he's all right with the arrangement?' He tried to sound nonchalant.

'He is,' she answered blithely. 'He's Costa Rican, very handsome, and entertaining me is infinitely more pleasurable than picking peaches, so it suits us both.'

Richard felt a profound sadness for her. This was not what she wanted, not really, he knew that, but she was doing what she always did, making the best of a situation.

'Just be careful. If the Smythes get to hear about it, or your parents…'

'To hell with them.' He was surprised at the coldness in her tone. 'I was used, like a bargaining chip. You heard my father at the wedding – two dynasties, the Logans and the Smythes. They never gave a damn about me or what I wanted, so I won't care about them now.'

'But I thought… Well, I know your family would prefer Algy to me, given my choices, but I thought you were of the same mind? You couldn't live without all the…' He waved his hand; she knew what he meant.

'I didn't think I could either, but love isn't something to be squandered I now realise.' Her gaze fixed on his. 'I was in love and I gave it away, and now…' Her shoulders rounded in defeat as she took another sip of her drink.

'And with the…Costa Rican guy…is that love?' Richard asked.

Miranda's familiar chuckle, and he felt a wave of affection for her. 'No, Richard, nothing like love. But he's nice, he's funny and kind and heart-stoppingly handsome, and most importantly he doesn't know the hull from the stern of a boat.'

She clinked her glass off his and they smiled.

'I'll tell you what, though.' She leant in, and he could tell she was a little drunk. 'I wish I'd been a little less prim when we were together.'

He smiled, thinking of those nights in his car when she allowed kissing and over-clothes touching but nothing more.

'I'm not sure I'd have known what to do if you'd not stopped it.' He laughed ruefully.

'Oh, I think we both know that's not true, Mr Lewis.'

Richard felt that lurch of raw attraction in the pit of his stomach. A thought occurred to him that if he asked Miranda to go upstairs with him now, she probably would, willingly, and there would be no rules. Tempting as it was – and it really was; she was so beautiful – he dismissed it from his mind. That wouldn't solve anything and would complicate everything.

'You could leave Algy if you are really miserable.'

She patted his hand, as if he was so naive, it was adorable. 'I won't do that, we both know it, but I'll find a way to live.'

'Sounds like you already have,' Richard said quietly.

'In the absence of a much better option, I guess I have.'

CHAPTER 16

'More rhubarb crumble! Oh, Tilly, your mam really shouldn't...'

'I'm afraid you'll have to get used to it, Grace. It's growing everywhere now that the weather has warmed up, huge green stalks all around the cottage like a forest – you can hardly get in and out – and Mam is trying to use it all up.' Tilly had just come in the back door as usual and was emptying a sailor's duffel bag of goodies onto the table, including the big pan of crumble.

'I'm not complaining – it's delicious. I'd have it for every meal forever if I could. It's just she should be selling it at the market, not wasting it all on me.'

'Oh, Mam's doing that as well, along with her soda bread and apple tarts. Don't worry about it. But the rhubarb is too much – it's a jungle out there. Oh, and here's a few scones she sent down for you for our tea...and I've brought these as well. These are for the Warringtons when you and Declan stay over there on your way to America.' Digging down to the bottom of the duffel bag, Grace's best friend produced six pots of honey, the waxy pieces of the honeycomb still in the jar, and a Jacob's biscuit tin stuffed with soft hay in which two dozen fresh eggs were carefully stored.

'That's perfect, Tilly. Thank you so much.' The Warringtons would never take payment from Grace for putting her up in their downstairs front room, and now she'd asked for Declan to have the spare room upstairs for a night as well, so this was a good way of paying them back. 'What do I owe you?'

'G'way out of that, Grace. The hens are laying non-stop with the fine weather and we're falling down with honey, so don't you dare offer me money.'

'Well, I'll get you back somehow...' Sometimes it was hard when no one would take payment for anything.

'I'll tell you what you might do. When you write to your man Richard next, ask him if his sister knows is there any other book by that woman Radclyffe Hall, something like the first one she sent me, and if so, where could I get it.'

'Radclyffe Hall is a woman?' asked Grace in surprise. Last year Richard's sister, Sarah, had posted over a novel called *The Well of Loneliness*, which for some reason she said Tilly might like because of the way Grace had described her in one of her letters. Grace had assumed the book was by a man and about farming and horses or something, and Tilly had been quite reticent about it, only saying it was all right. She must have enjoyed it, though, to ask for another by the same writer.

'Course she's a woman, why not?' asked Tilly, slightly belligerently.

'Well, I don't know why not... I suppose Americans do have funny names,' said Grace mildly as she took the kettle off the range and brought it quickly to the boil on the gas. 'But yes, I will ask him. So you enjoyed the trip to Dublin?'

Tilly had finally got to see her older sister, Marion, at the weekend, after having to postpone her journey for weeks because of Agnes dying and then the funeral. She'd wanted to get it in quick before the spring lambs started coming.

'I did. The baby is sitting up already. Only that eejit sister of mine is after getting herself pregnant again, like she hasn't enough to do with seven already.' Tilly lit a cigarette, her favourite bad habit.

Grace smiled. 'Ah sure, she's happy as Larry, though, isn't she?'

'She is, the poor blind fool.' Tilly snorted. 'And him even more so, with six children of his own from that poor mad wife of his, God rest her soul, and no one left to mind them. I'd say he was very glad to meet and fall in love with our Marion. Anyway, Mam's delighted she has another grandchild on the way, though she's mad about Colm's kids, to be fair, and Marion is doing a great job on them all. They're nice and chatty but not spoiled.'

'I don't know, I think maybe who loves and rears the child has as much or more to do with it as who its natural parents are,' said Grace as she got down the brown earthenware teapot to make the tea. She'd been thinking a lot about Siobhán McKenna and hoping if Declan saw his little sister was loved and looked after, then he'd be happy for her.

'Well, Mam's happy anyway. Sure she'd given up on me or that *óinseach* brother of mine ever giving her a grandchild, so Marion was her only hope.'

'You're still set against ever marrying?' She and Tilly were the spinsters of the parish, her friend joked, and while it was obvious why that was the case for her, she didn't know why Tilly didn't take up any of the many offers she got.

'That's completely correct. Not a chance of a snowflake in hell I'd lumber myself with some gom of a man and a screaming baby to ruin my life, and Alfie always said the same – he's too busy saving the world. But looks like Marion won't be happy till she has a football team, so that will have to do for Mam.'

'Have you heard from Alfie?' Grace asked, pouring out two cups of tea and slathering a couple of the scones with home-made butter from the O'Shea farm and a dollop of blackberry jam from Biddy's.

'A letter two days ago. We weren't expecting any post at all, it was so late in the day when young Fiachra O'Flynn came cycling up the hill. The poor *garsún* is doing the whole round now that Charlie is laid up with the shingles, and it's a lot.'

'I know, he's a martyr. And is Alfie still in France?' The last she'd heard, Tilly's hot-headed brother was in Paris.

'He is, and God alone knows what sort of people he's after getting himself tied up with now. Half the letter was about the fact that Stalin was making a deal with that Hitler yoke, which he says was a terrible sell-out for the French communists, who thought Russia was great up to then. And the other half was about this French girl he's met, and that he is mad about her...'

Grace laughed. 'So maybe there will be a few French grandchildren one day after all.'

'Not a bit of it. She'll go the way the rest of them go. That boy, I don't know, *a míshocracht a chuir fonn taistil air.*'

Grace suspected Tilly was right, there was a restlessness in Alfie O'Hare since he was a *garsún*; he could never settle. While Tilly, unusual as she was with her men's clothes and insisting on never marrying, had her feet firmly planted on the land and no intention of going anywhere.

'But he's been in Paris for a while now?' she asked.

'Long enough to give us his address and all, so at least that,' said Tilly, her mouth full of scone.

There was a rattle on the front door, and Grace went to open it. It was Fiachra O'Flynn, skinny and freckled, his carroty hair stuck to his forehead with sweat. 'Three letters for you, Miss Fitz,' he gasped. 'Sorry I'm late, it's just...'

'An awful big round to do all by yourself, I know, Fiachra. Will you come in for a cup of tea or something?'

'I've no time for the tea, but if you could let me have some water please, Miss Fitz.'

Grace went to fetch him a glass, and he gulped it down gratefully before he handed her back the glass and cycled off again, the big postman's sack slung over his thin shoulder, nearly bigger than himself.

Grace looked through the letters as she went back to the kitchen. One was her cheque from the Department of Education, a lot more substantial now that she was a headmistress and not just a lowly assistant teacher. The second made her heart glow – it was from America. And the third...oh, it was from America as well!

'What are you blushing for, Grace Fitzgerald?' teased Tilly, finishing her scone.

'Ah, nothing...'

'Do I spy American stamps?'

'I suppose they're just from Richard. The Emergency is making a right *hames* of the post these days. Charlie says stuff from America can get here in any order.' She checked the dates on the postmarks to make sure she opened the first letter first. Biddy O'Donoghue had got a Christmas card from her cousin in Boston last week, posted last November.

'Oh, "just Richard". That's the Richard who's the millionaire with the film-star looks?' Tilly was a terrible one for teasing.

Grace willed herself to stop blushing. 'I don't think he's a millionaire, but anyway, yes, him…'

'Well, open it then.' And when Grace hesitated, she added, 'Oh, come on, you can read me aloud the bits that aren't' – she made a silly face – '*private.*'

'There's nothing private in our letters,' protested Grace, blushing even worse.

'Then you can read all of it out to me so.'

Her face burning hot now, Grace tutted and tore open the first envelope. There was a folded newspaper clipping inside, which she put aside on the table for later, and she scanned the first paragraph of the letter.

Her heart leapt with pleasure for him. 'Oh, the *Capital* is sending him to France!' She felt so proud of him. She would always support him, no matter the teasing from Tilly.

Tilly looked delighted as well. 'Well, that's great. Give him Alfie's address in Paris, would you, Grace, and ask him to check on him. Sure my brother will probably know all sorts of people he and his photographer friend might like to speak to. And tell him to get Mr Nunez to get a snap of Alfie so I can see what he looks like now – oh, and one of this girl of his as well, always supposing they're still together.'

'I will ask him, yes,' Grace agreed happily as she read on. 'This is such wonderful news. He says the editor liked that they came all the way to New York to see him, and Jacob Nunez thinks some article they'd had published helped as well…'

'This one?' asked Tilly, unfolding the cutting.

'Maybe.' Grace looked up, smiling. And then her mouth fell open.

Tilly was holding up not one but two pages of newspaper, printed side by side, and running across the top was a headline saying AMERICA AND EUROPE, A LOVE STORY. Underneath was the picture taken of Grace in Dingle by the seaside photographer, and paid for by Tilly, that time they went to watch Cullen's Celtic Cabaret.

But the photo of Grace was no longer a modest two-inch square. Somehow it had become huge and took up nearly half of one of the pages, bigger even than the one on the other page of Richard Lewis reclining on a bed, looking impossibly handsome and seeming to read a letter.

'Look at this – it's you, in a newspaper!' Tilly's own eyes were round with amazement.

'Oh my goodness, I don't believe it...' Grace felt breathless with shock.

'Grace, you look amazing, really and truly. That photo!' Tilly gazed at it, and Grace blushed.

'Well, that bit's not too bad, but they don't see my twisted leg.'

'Yerra, would you whisht. You look gorgeous and you better bloody well know it or I'll have to beat it into you. No wonder he's writing day and night.'

'He's not, we're just friends and –'

'Grace Fitzgerald, look at him. Seriously, take a good look.' Tilly shoved the photo of Richard nearer her face. 'Tell me any fella around here is as good-looking as him.'

'He's handsome, I know he is, but it doesn't matter. That's not what...' Grace tried to protest, but Tilly was right; there was something about Richard Lewis that made women look.

'You'll have to get Declan to make a frame for it and hang it on your wall!' said Tilly.

'Well, I don't know...'

'Actually, better not drive him out of his head entirely. God, Grace, you'll have to get a ticket system going, the admirers you're gathering.' Tilly laughed and took a big bite of scone. 'Declan mad about you here, Richard mad about you over there, and Pádraig O Sé told me three days ago that you were in front of him at Mass on Sunday and your lovely hair was the only thing stopping him nodding off at Father Lehane's sermon about St Paul's letter to the Thessalonians. You're spoiled for choice.'

'Well, at least I'd have a good heel on my ugly black built-up shoe if I married Pádraig.' Grace giggled, the notion so preposterous. She was used to Tilly telling her both Declan and Richard were mad for her, which was not true, but she didn't bother to object.

'So when is lover boy coming to this side of the ocean?' asked Tilly.

Still shaken by seeing her picture in the paper, Grace went back to the letter, reading on further. 'He doesn't say, he doesn't know yet. All he says is maybe in May. They're travelling first to England, then to France…' She gasped. 'Oh, Tilly, he wants to meet me in Ireland! He has absolutely no idea – he imagines he can get to Knocknashee easily from Dublin or Wexford…'

'That man is so rich, he can probably buy a car or a horse or some-thing,' said Tilly, cheerfully brushing aside any obstacles. 'I bet you can't wait to meet him. Open the second letter. Go on – it might have more about when he's coming.'

The second envelope felt thin. Just a short note, probably about the dates… He would surely have got her own letter by now, about going to New York. Maybe he would come and see her there instead. She'd been hoping for that anyway, though she hadn't wanted to pressure him. It was clear he really wanted to see her, and Savannah to New York was surely easier than London to Knocknashee.

It was far too much to expect both.

Smiling, she scanned the few paragraphs rapidly…

Her world crashed down, and she sank onto a kitchen chair.

'What? What is it?' asked Tilly anxiously, standing. 'You've gone white – what's the matter?'

Grace pushed the short letter across the table towards her. There was nothing private in this one. It was curt, cold and short, like she was more of an acquaintance than a friend.

Tilly picked it up and read it, her face getting longer and longer, and then she came over and gave Grace a big, strong hug, the letter still in her hand. 'Oh, what? He's going to be here when you're over there? Ah no...that's not fair...that's terrible...'

Grace swallowed hard, determined not to burst into tears. 'Yes, it is. Well, for me anyway. He doesn't seem to mind.'

Tilly scanned the short, curt note again, a small frown between her eyebrows. 'I'm sure he does mind, Grace, but...'

'Oh, look, you don't have to say that to make me feel better. He's got this big job now, an international journalist travelling the world. I'm sure he's not being deliberately cold, he's just very busy. And it was nice of him to take a moment to give me some sightseeing tips.'

'Will I tell you what I think?'

Grace nodded.

'I think he heard you were going over with Declan and he thinks you two are together. Why else would he tell you about that lake or boat or whatever it is?'

'But we're not, and anyway, why –'

'He's sweet on you. The dogs on the street can see it, but you can't. And he's a bit jealous because you're going over there with Declan and not waiting here to see him.'

'But I didn't even know –'

'You said yourself the letters are all messed up. He thinks he's missed his chance and you're with Declan now.'

It was such an absurd idea, Grace laughed despite her disappointment. 'Don't talk nonsense, Tilly. Richard could have any woman he wanted. He's not going to fall for a cripple no bigger than a child.'

'Will you stop putting yourself down, Grace? Look at you. Just... *look* at you!' Tilly dropped the note on the table and picked up and brandished the newspaper article. 'You're like a film star! Of course he's jealous that you're going to be sightseeing in New York with a different man.'

'Firstly he's not jealous, and secondly he has nothing to be jealous about.'

'Oh, will you stop, Grace? Declan's mad about you,' scoffed Tilly.

'He is not,' Grace said, startled. Tilly teased her all the time, but she sounded serious now.

'He is, Grace.'

'He really is not.'

'And if you ask me, you should give him a chance. He's gorgeous, he's kind, you work so well together...'

'Tilly. Please. Stop. This isn't making me feel better. I'll be pure awkward with him on the boat if you put this into my head.'

'All I'm saying is' – Tilly had started to read Richard's first letter now – 'you don't have to go around thinking you'll be an old maid, like that sister of yours kept telling you. Oh, look at this – that Falkirk man thinks the features editor only used the article because your picture is so pretty, and his friend Mr Nunez thinks Hollywood is going to come knocking on your door! Looks like Richard isn't the only one who could have anyone they wanted.'

* * *

LATER, Grace wrote back, a polite, friendly note, thanking Richard for his sightseeing tips and wishing him luck on his own journey.

This is where Alfie O'Hare lives in Paris, she added, after writing down Tilly's brother's address, which Tilly had given her earlier.

Tilly says her brother is in touch with lots of interesting people he can introduce you to. He was in Spain before moving to Paris. His mother thinks he's daft as the crows, running towards war when if he had a hair of sense, he'd be running away from it, but he's always been restless.

I hope you don't mind, but Tilly wants me to ask you for a photo of Alfie, if your friend Mr Nunez wouldn't mind taking one, and if you have a chance, a picture of the girl he's friendly with, if he's still seeing her. She also wants to know, did Radclyffe Hall write any other book, and if so, where could she get it? Maybe you wouldn't mind mentioning it to your sister if you get this before you leave America.

Yours,

Grace

PS That is so awful about Kit Gallagher and the other babies. I'm so glad she's gone from Knocknashee. I'd never be able to look her in the eye again.

PPS I have absolutely no idea what a hot dog is. I'm a bit afraid of dogs to be honest, being unsteady on my feet. Nonetheless, I am willing to try one if there's no fear it could jump up and knock me over.

She was pleased with her letter when she'd finished it. She felt it made her sound cheerful and normal, and not like some lovesick girl with a crush on her fairy prince. Which of course she wasn't.

CHAPTER 17

*T*he ship, the *Lady Anne*, wasn't a luxury liner, but it was simple and clean. As Declan had promised, he'd paid for her to have a second-class cabin, while he stayed in third.

The lady in the next cabin, a single woman in her fifties, knocked on Grace's door as Grace was unpacking her bag and putting her clothes in the drawers provided, in between looking out of the port-hole at the Irish coast that was gradually receding into the distance and in general taking in her strange new surroundings.

'Good morning, my dear. My name is Abagail McKinnon. I'm from Pittsburgh, Pennsylvania.' The woman extended a hand. She had iron-grey hair cut in a severe style and was dressed in a navy skirt and pullover.

'Grace Fitzgerald, from Knocknashee, County Kerry.' Grace took the hand to shake; the woman had a firm, cool grip.

'Nice to meet you, Miss Fitzgerald. I had a very nice time in your country. My mother came from Belmullet, County Mayo, and I was over there visiting distant cousins of hers, the Sweeney family of a little place called Blacksod. My mother is too old to travel now, but she wanted me to go over there to help sort out a misunderstanding about an inheritance. The family in Ireland were the beneficiaries of a small bequest from the estate of my uncle in Philadelphia, but a distant relative Stateside felt it should not go back to Ireland, though it was my uncle's expressed wish. My mother was most adamant that it should, so I delivered it. It was not a huge sum, but it is the principle that is important.'

Grace was a little taken aback. That was a lot of private information to give away to a total stranger. Maybe Americans were like this, forthright, open. If so, it would be an interesting experience going there.

'Anyway, I just dropped by to say I won't lock the bathroom door from my side apart from when I'm using it, and if you'll agree to the same, we should both enjoy a pleasant voyage?'

Grace had no idea what Abagail McKinnon was talking about, and her face must have reflected that, because the woman smiled and added, 'Your first time, eh?'

'Er...yes...'

'Well, you see, your cabin and mine share a bathroom. It can be accessed from either side, and some people lock the door from their side for the duration. It's mean and not really neighbourly, but that's some folks for you.' She shrugged.

'Oh, I won't do that...I...'

'Yes, I can see you're not that kind of person at all,' Abagail said warmly, her eyes crinkling in a smile. 'Are you travelling alone too?'

'Not exactly. I have a friend who is travelling with me, but he's in third class.'

'Very chivalrous to allow his sweetheart the comfort of a private cabin. I approve already of your young man, Miss Fitzgerald.'

'Oh, he's not my young man. We're family friends. It's just that he felt I needed the privacy, well, because...' She indicted her disfigured leg, with the calliper and black boot, and waited for the woman to flinch. She was used to people staring, nervous that she might be infectious all these years later.

The woman just nodded. 'Oh, I see. So you'll want your hot bath every day – I hear that's very good. Our president enjoys Warm Springs.' Her nonchalance about the disease was refreshing. 'Is that where you're off to, Georgia?'

Grace felt a slight pang. One day last year, that was exactly where she'd been going. 'No…'

'So on vacation then?'

'No…not really. There's someone we need to meet…' She didn't want to blurt out the whole tale to this stranger, but after Abagail McKinnon had been so open with her, it felt churlish to be curt.

'And where are you headed?' the woman asked, leaning on the doorframe, clearly in no rush to go anywhere.

'Well, Rockaway Beach, but we'll be staying in New York…' The Maheadys had written back saying they'd be delighted to meet Declan and Charlie in April, which was still the plan at the time, but that they were away with their girls in Maine for the first week of Easter. This left only a couple of days when they were back and Declan and Grace would still be in America. It was enough, if all went well, Grace hoped, but it left a few days to fill.

'The Big Apple, eh? I lived there for a few years.'

'Do the people who live there call it that?' Richard had used the term a couple of times, but he was from Savannah where they didn't seem to like Yankees. It was to do with the American Civil War, but she hadn't been sure of the details of it.

'They do, and would you believe, it was a friend of mine who started it. He has the same name as you – John J. Fitz Gerald. He's a sportswriter for the New York *Morning Telegraph*. He heard two stable hands at the New Orleans Fair Grounds calling it that because of the large prizes available at horse races in New York, and he began using it in his column and it caught on.'

'Oh, that's so interesting!' She made a mental note to tell Richard and then remembered with a sinking heart that she had no address for him; he was just somewhere in Paris now… Unless she wrote via Alfie? But Richard hadn't answered her last letter yet, if he even intended to, and she didn't want it to seem like she was chasing him.

She'd never stopped herself before from writing a second letter almost straight away after the first. But things felt different now.

'Anyway, I hate the place now, too many people, too much noise, but most people love it. I'm sure you will too.' Abagail patted the doorframe and left.

Grace went back to staring out of the porthole in between folding away all those lovely light summer dresses that Lizzie had insisted she buy before her trip to see Richard in America, the trip that Agnes's stroke had put an end to.

She wondered if he was sailing this way right now, on this same ocean, or if he was in Southampton already. So odd to think their ships might pass each other. It seemed unlikely they'd ever get another chance to meet. The war was heating up, not tailing off, according to Lizzie Warrington, so who knew what the future held for anybody these days.

Over dinner in Cork last night, the doctor's wife had said she was worried about the German U-boats prowling the North Atlantic, even after Grace pointed out that the papers had said nothing about any attacks on neutral shipping, or any shipping really.

'But we're told nothing, Grace,' Lizzie Warrington said, her round, pleasant face creased with anxiety. The Warringtons were putting her and Declan up for the night; they sailed the next day, on the morning tide. 'Mr de Valera has censored the news completely. It's only from reading the foreign papers in the ladies' reading room that I know anything about the war. He's going to keep us in the dark for the duration, that seems to be his tactic.'

Declan looked up from his lamb chop and roast potatoes. 'So do you think there is a real definite risk and we've not been told? Maybe Grace should stay here?'

'I'm just so worried it may not be safe...'

'We'll be fine, Lizzie, and Declan, don't you dare talk about me staying behind,' said Grace. She had no intention of missing out on America a second time. 'The *Lady Anne* has been going backwards and forwards with no trouble at all since everything started.'

Hugh Warrington, who was less worried about things than his

wife, possibly because he had no access to the ladies' reading room, strongly agreed that there was nothing to worry about, and as it happened, he and Grace were right, and the voyage passed uneventfully; there was no talk or sight of any Germans.

There weren't even any storms; the days were mainly warm and sunny. And after she got used to the constant motion, Grace found being gently rocked to sleep every night in her bunk very soothing. She took a bath twice a day, having checked with Abagail – they were now on first-name terms – that she didn't mind, which she didn't. She did her exercises religiously; she needed to be as fit and as flexible as she could be when they got to New York.

She and Declan walked around on the deck, and when her leg got tired, they played chess. Declan, who had a brilliant, analytical mind, won every time, until he insisted on teaching her how to play it properly, and after that she improved enough to win maybe one game out of ten.

They also played cards, mainly Spades, until a young American man called Henry Carter taught them poker, which Grace was better at than chess because she could smile happily even if she had a terrible hand; maybe it was all the years of having to put a brave face on things.

After winning her fifth game in a row – they were playing for matchsticks – Henry insisted on buying them a beer in the second-class lounge bar. Grace had never tasted it before and didn't like it much, but Declan said he enjoyed his, and the American drank several. He was on his way home from a minor diplomatic posting in Marseille, where he said the food was good and the wine even better, and that he was sorry to be leaving but his parents were worried about him being there when the Germans invaded, not that that was going to happen because of the Maginot Line.

The days and nights passed in an easy blur of conversation, reading, eating and drinking, though alcohol was not an attraction for her or Declan, unlike many of their fellow passengers.

She would sometimes wake from the hum of the engines or the

sound of chains or something being pulled, and she would lie there, thinking her thoughts.

Declan and she were becoming closer, and she wondered about what Tilly had said, that he was sweet on her. She'd thought at the time that Tilly was mad – why on earth would he be – but she was beginning to wonder if her friend was right. God knew she'd never even held hands with a boy, so how would she know the signs, and for the most part, Declan just seemed nice and friendly. But sometimes the way he looked at her…

If he did like her that way, should she consider him? He was very good-looking. It wasn't just her thinking it; she saw how the local girls were, not just Sally and Maura, when he walked up the aisle at Mass each Sunday. His silky dark hair, his long curling dark lashes, his blue eyes that sort of mesmerised, the way his clothes hung from his slight but muscular frame, the smattering of freckles on the pale skin of his face. He reminded her of Buster Keaton, the actor; she'd seen his picture in a magazine once.

And he was so kind to her always, and they enjoyed each other's company – was that what love was?

He didn't make her heart flutter with excitement, but maybe that was girlish nonsense.

The last morning of the voyage, she stood with him on the deck, leaning on the railings. Water in every direction, no seabirds yet, and the sea was calm. She'd left her cardigan in the cabin and wore just an emerald-green short-sleeved dress with a cinched-in waist. All the fashion now was shorter and tighter due to the lack of fabric. She'd put a green ribbon around her hair because the salted sea air was playing havoc with her already unruly mop of corkscrew curls.

'Can you believe we're really going to be there soon, Grace, you and me in America?' Declan said.

She squinted into the misty lilac distance, hoping to catch a first sight of land. The ship had made surprisingly good time; they were half a day ahead of schedule, the cabin crew had informed them.

'I know, it's exciting. But I keep thinking of poor Charlie. I hate he's missing out, but I'm glad to be getting the chance. Imagine, twice in my life I had a chance to go to America, and I thought Cork was the furthest I'd ever go in my life.'

Declan was serious now. 'You can do anything you want to, Grace, you know that.'

'Oh yes, Antarctic explorer, circumnavigate the globe, invent a cure for cancer...' She laughed. 'The sky's the limit for me and my bandy leg.'

'You joke, but I think you could. You set your mind to it, and nothing could stop you.'

'You overestimate me, Declan.' She nudged him playfully.

'I don't actually.'

'Well, who knows, maybe we will both do amazing things. There's time yet.'

He gazed off into the distance, in the same direction as her. 'I suppose it will be sad for you to be in America and not get to see your friend Richard?'

She shrugged. 'It would have been nice, but I don't know if we're that friendly any more.'

'Really?' He glanced at her. 'I thought you wrote regularly?'

'We did, but he's got more important things on his mind now than writing to me...'

'But what's more important than you?'

She laughed. 'Oh yes – I'm fierce important.'

'Oh, you're definitely important enough, so it's his loss...' He turned and looked at her then, and she realised his eyes were the exact azure of the Atlantic Ocean stretching behind him. 'He's a fool to let you go.'

'Well, I'm not being let go of, considering we are just pen friends, but thanks.'

She thought he was looking at her in that way again but dismissed it. But then she remembered all the pretty girls setting their cap at him and mentally rolled her eyes. 'How much longer are you going to make Sally O'Sullivan wait for you before you ask her out?' she asked teasingly.

'Sally?' He looked surprised. 'She's not for me, I don't think.'

'She would be if you'd have her.'

'Oh, I'm the catch of the parish right enough.' He chuckled self-deprecatingly.

'Well, you make a fine flutter of the girls every Sunday. They all admire you, and Maura Keohane is mad for you altogether.'

'Maura is a nice girl, but she's got a fine few acres coming to her and she an only child. So I think Donal Keohane might have bigger plans for his daughter than an assistant teacher.' He winked at her.

'Oh, about that, I meant to say, I've written to the Department about your wages, and Father Iggy has as well as chair of the school board. We've both told them you should be paid properly. You're not entitled to the qualified rate, but there's an allowance if you're acting as a fully qualified teacher and there's nobody else available. Father Iggy looked into it for you. It should be enough to support a wife and family, if that's what's stopping you.'

He laughed then, a deep throaty sound. 'Are you trying to marry me off, the pair of you? Good luck with that.'

'Do you like Maura, though?' Grace asked.

'I like her well enough – she's a grand girl – but not like that.'

'I don't know, Declan McKenna. Are you a lost cause like myself?' She sighed. 'The spinsters and bachelors of Knocknashee, you, me and Tilly.'

'Well, Tilly wouldn't take a present of a man, that's for sure.'

'True enough. She could have anyone, but they all get the harsh negation, as my father used to say. Maybe you should ask her yourself. She likes you a lot, I know she does.' She didn't tell him Tilly had said that when Tilly was trying to persuade Grace to give Declan a chance.

He pulled an amused face. 'Yerra, I'd say Tilly has her own plans, and they don't involve us lads at all.'

'I know, and she's made a great job of the farm and the markets and everything. She's a great businesswoman. It's a pity she doesn't marry really. If she got the right man, they could really build that farm up into something.'

Declan looked at her then, and she could see he was weighing something up, whether to tell her something or not. He wasn't as good as her at keeping a poker face; his pile of matchsticks always ended up on her side of the table.

'What?' She cocked her head to one side and gazed at him.

He hesitated a moment more, then said, 'Nothing. And what about you? Did you never have a thought about getting married yourself?'

'Not a bit of it. The school's enough family for me. Now will we get an ice cream even though we're only just after having our breakfast?' she suggested, seeing the man come on deck with the ice cream truck; she loved their creamy treats, always strawberry for her, chocolate for him.

He shrugged and smiled again. 'We will, Miss Fitz, and nobody can stop us, because we have money in our pockets and nobody to give out to us.' He offered her his arm theatrically, and she took it. Declan always did that, and it helped with her leg to have him to lean on.

SAILING into the harbour of New York that afternoon, Declan beside her at the railings of the ship, was far more emotional than Grace had imagined it would be. She had never seen so much activity, and the height of the buildings astounded her. She tried to commit it all to memory to tell the children when she got home.

Seeing the mighty Statue of Liberty, her lit lamp aloft, gave her a lump in her throat. She had memorised the poem, 'The New Colossus', engraved on its plinth.

Not like the brazen giant of Greek fame,
With conquering limbs astride from land to land;
Here at our sea-washed, sunset gates shall stand
A mighty woman with a torch, whose flame
Is the imprisoned lightning, and her name
Mother of Exiles. From her beacon-hand
Glows world-wide welcome; her mild eyes command
The air-bridged harbor that twin cities frame.
'Keep, ancient lands, your storied pomp!' cries she
With silent lips. 'Give me your tired, your poor,

Your huddled masses yearning to breathe free,
The wretched refuse of your teeming shore.
Send these, the homeless, tempest-tost to me,
I lift my lamp beside the golden door!'

How many souls had passed by this monument of welcome, from every corner of the globe, praying, dreaming, terrified, excited? And here she was, Grace Fitzgerald, orphan, polio survivor, standing where they stood. Life was strange.

The harbour was a hive of activity – steam ships, tugs, passenger ferries, other ocean liners, all going to and fro, horns honking endlessly. The buildings were the tallest she'd ever seen, one after the other, piled up like children's towers of bricks. There were cars everywhere, a large number of them yellow, and she was shocked at how close to the city they were. Large lit-up signs were on the sides of the huge buildings advertising things Grace had never heard of.

Charlie had once told her that her father, Eddie, had always wanted to go to America. He never got the chance. 'I'm here for you, Daddy,' she whispered into the light evening spring breeze.

There was a smell of damp in the air, and she wondered if it was as wet on this side of the Atlantic as it was on her side. Sure enough, a few minutes later the rain came down, and she retreated below deck to get her umbrella, hoping it would be more use to her here than in Knocknashee, where it just blew inside out.

The huge immigration centre on Ellis Island was the noisiest, busiest place Grace had ever been. The entire interior was made of white tiles, and the cacophony bounced off the hard surface and reverberated all around. In every part of the cavernous structure, people were waiting or being processed. The teeming crowds, speaking every language imaginable, skin all different colours – from black to white and all the shades in between, many dressed in clothing she'd never seen before – were lined up in queues between metal bars. She had never seen a person who wasn't fair-skinned before, and she had to force herself not to stare.

Declan was off out of sight in the third-class queue, which was long and slow; she was being processed in a line with other second-class passengers. She hoped she would have a slightly less hectic passage through, and Declan had told her to wait outside for him before they took the boat to the main quay.

Moving slowly up the snaking line to a pair of officers, she limped heavily with the weight of her bag, then started to panic that they wouldn't let her through, not when they saw she was crippled by polio; people were so afraid of the disease. She wore a long skirt to cover the steel calliper and she was using the umbrella as a stick – they were under shelter now, so she didn't need it for the rain – but the limp was unavoidable.

Dr Warrington had given her a letter on hospital letterhead to say she was in perfect health and that she was not infectious, and second-class passengers were subjected to less medical scrutiny than those in steerage, but she still couldn't help being worried. What if Declan found himself alone in America, and her on the ship home? It didn't bear thinking about.

A moment later Abagail took her arm and her bag, and that helped her walk straighter and easier, more like a normal person, though she still leant on the umbrella. Reaching the male officer, she handed over her brand-new passport with the harp of Ireland on the front, and he glanced at it while the female officer checked Abagail's.

'And what's the purpose of your visit to the United States, Miss Fitzgerald?' the man asked briskly.

'I'm visiting a friend, and I have a return ticket for six days' time.' She handed over her ticket, hoping the fact she was leaving the country again so soon would work in her favour. She couldn't be much of a risk surely.

He looked puzzled and unconvinced. 'This is a long way to come for such a short vacation?'

'Well, you see' – she pulled out a letter from Father Iggy, saying she was on leave as headmistress of Knocknashee National School and expected back in the classroom on the 26th of April – 'I need to get back to work.'

'And your infirmity?' He nodded at her leg; he'd clearly noticed her limp.

'I had polio as a child, but I'm no longer infectious. I have a letter from my doctor here.' She handed over the letter from Dr Warrington.

He scanned it and returned it to her. 'Enjoy your stay, Miss Fitzgerald.' And he waved her on.

Abagail had passed through with no questions, and together they walked out onto American soil.

CHAPTER 18

*R*ichard and Jacob's sailing had been delayed by nearly two weeks. The hull of the ship they were due to travel on had been accidentally damaged by a U-boat and came back into port for repairs before setting sail again nine days later.

But now they were going at last. As they walked up the quayside at the New York Passenger Ship Terminal – they had been directed to Pier 88 on the Hudson River between West 44th and West 54th Streets – with their duffel bags over their shoulders, it started to rain even more heavily, and Richard pulled his fedora down over his eyes. Arriving passengers being taken from Ellis Island passed them coming the other way; they were being dropped off at Pier 86 about three hundred yards below them. They disembarked, wet and cold and tired, dragging luggage, their own hats pulled down, hoods up, umbrellas over their heads as they passed the line of passengers leaving.

It was difficult. The flood of people fresh off the boat pressed along the quay, splashing in sudden puddles, and he and Jacob moved aside and stood between two bollards. A man in his twenties hurried past, then a Jewish family, the father in a long black coat with a tall hat and ringlets growing from his temples, all around him a collection of people speaking Yiddish, Richard thought, elderly people, children, his wife. He watched the teeming masses, as the poem said, and hoped America was kind to them. Then an older woman with short grey hair, and then a couple, a red-headed girl leaning on the arm of a very handsome young man who was holding up an umbrella to shelter her from the downpour.

As they passed, the girl glanced at Richard from under the umbrella, then looked away, then glanced at him a second time over her shoulder. Although he could barely see her face between the umbrella and the rain, for a strange moment, Grace came into his mind. That was ridiculous, of course, even if such a mad coincidence was possible among all these people; her ship wasn't even due until tomorrow morning.

'Richard, come on, let's go!' Jacob tapped his arm.

'Coming…' he said, still looking back. The girl was disappearing into the jostling crowd.

'*Richard!*'

'I said I'm coming.' But then he realised it wasn't Jacob who had spoken the second time, it was a girl's voice. He turned to find his sister grinning at him, and Jacob stood staring at this apparition in utter bewilderment, running his hands through his dark hair.

'Sarah, what are you doing here?' Jacob choked out.

'Waiting for you two.'

Richard was equally astonished. 'You came all the way to New York to see us off?'

The three of them had said goodbye in Savannah, and Sarah had been quite snarky, muttering about boys having all the fun, but now she seemed sunny and happy despite the teeming rain, which she was keeping at bay with a huge blue umbrella.

'I'm not seeing you off, I'm coming with you,' she said brightly.

'*What?* No… You can't!'

'I can. You need a translator in France. In fact I don't know how you thought you could manage without me.'

'But the newspaper has only paid for the two of us…' Jacob was clearly reeling.

'Which is why I bought my own ticket. You're always telling me to put my trust fund to good use. Jacob, please close your mouth when you're staring at me.'

'I... But... How did you...' Jacob struggled to get the words out.

'It was in the paper that your ship was delayed because of the U-boat, and I realised it was a sign from the stars or something, a sign for me to stop complaining and take charge of my own life.'

'No, Sarah, you can't.' Richard tried to inject steel into his voice. 'We're going to France, maybe Belgium and Holland too. What if the Germans invade?'

'Then I suppose the German I learnt in my Swiss finishing school will come in handy as well.' She winked at him as she brandished the huge blue umbrella aloft. 'Now, come on, get under this, it's big enough. See? I'm being useful to you already.'

CHAPTER 19

NEW YORK CITY

*A*pril 1940

The Westchester Inn was modest but clean and centrally located opposite Madison Square Garden on 8th Avenue between 49th and 50th Streets. She and Declan had two rooms adjoining each other, each with a single bed, a washstand, a small chest of drawers and a wardrobe. There was a bathroom at the end of the hall.

Neither of them had ever stayed in a hotel before, so they were unsure what the etiquette was, but they soon realised the young man who helped them with their bags wanted some money for it. They had no idea how much they should give, so Grace asked him.

He looked surprised to be asked. 'A nickel?' he suggested. 'Five cents,' he added helpfully.

She had no idea what a cent was but pulled out an Irish penny. 'Is this enough?'

'I wouldn't know, miss. I've never seen a coin like that before.' He looked unimpressed.

'Oh, of course, sorry...' On the ship one could use either currency,

American or Irish. She put her penny back in her purse. 'I don't have any American coins yet – I just arrived. But how about I give it to you when I get some? Would that be all right?'

He didn't look like it was anything close to all right, but he had no choice, so he turned on his heel and left.

'That went well,' Declan said with a grin.

Grace laughed. 'We're the real country mice here, aren't we?'

'Well, so far my travels in life have taken me from Knocknashee to Letterfrack, from Letterfrack back to Knocknashee, so this is a bit of a leap all right.'

'Well, I went from Knocknashee to Cork, then back to Knock-nashee. So you've been further than me!'

For some reason, nerves, exhaustion or something else, they both found this hilarious, and they laughed until they were breathless.

'Now,' said Grace, still chuckling and wiping her eyes, 'I'm going to get washed and dressed, and I'll meet you downstairs. We'll ask how to change some money, and where to post a letter to the Maheadys saying when exactly we're coming, and how to get something to eat, because I'm starving.' It was three in the afternoon, and they had not eaten since breakfast on the ship at seven that morning.

She unpacked and hung up her clothes, then freshened up at the sink; she'd have a hot bath down the corridor later. The lady at the desk downstairs had said it was unusually warm for the time of year so she put on one of the light summer dresses Lizzie had bought for her in Cork. Despite the earlier shower, it was very warm in the city, and she was very glad she'd brought them, although originally they were intended for Georgia, where the polio treatment centre was. And Richard's house on St Simons Island...

She thought back to the tall man in the fedora, the one she'd seen standing on the quay beside his shorter, darker companion with thick wavy hair.

It couldn't have been...

Obviously not, as his ship sailed nine days ago. She needed to stop thinking about Richard so much; she was starting to see him everywhere.

The lady on the reception desk had said to come to her if they had any questions. Declan was downstairs waiting for her in the hallway, and together they approached her.

The woman looked up. 'Good afternoon, can I help?'

'We were wondering where we could change some money and post a letter to Rockaway Beach, and also if we could have something to eat?' Grace asked awkwardly. She didn't know how that worked in a hotel. Did they have food available all the time or was it just during mealtimes, and if so when were those?

'Well, the post office will help you with the first two, and for the last, our kitchen is closed now, but this is New York City, Miss Fitzgerald – you can eat whatever you want whenever you want,' said the woman with a smile. 'What sort of food would you like?'

Grace was nonplussed. What did she mean, what type of food? The type you ate? She had no idea how to answer that question, and it must have shown on her face, because the woman laughed.

'OK, if you go out and make a left, you pass a post office, and then there's Nedick's restaurant. They've got hamburgers, doughnuts, coffee, their famous orange drink…whatever you want.'

'That sounds wonderful, thank you,' Grace said gratefully. She liked that both the places they needed were close by and right next to each other. It wasn't much different from Knocknashee after all.

Though there were a lot more people.

Outside, the sun was shining and the footpath was thronged. Once again Grace had to force herself not to stare. A very tall man with very curly hair and skin blacker than anyone she'd seen in the queue at Ellis Island was washing the windows of the hotel while whishtling. A group of girls wearing coloured dresses to their ankles and who had their heads covered in scarves all wound the same way talked animatedly in some foreign language. Two swarthy brown-skinned men with dark-brown eyes were having a heated argument about something that involved a lot of hand gestures. How could a place be so huge, so busy, so full of different people?

'She definitely said turn left?' Declan too was gazing around, taking it all in as they walked. 'I can't see a post office.'

'Well, maybe it's further than we thought.' As they walked along the street, the buildings were taller than any they'd ever seen, with shops and businesses on the ground floor of each one. Some of the names over the windows were ones she recognised – McManus, Spillane's – but many others were strange to her – Silvio's, Garcia's. Many of the shops had shades that overhung the street to protect the goods on sale from the sun, and in lots of cases, there were steps outside that she assumed led to living quarters upstairs.

They passed a huge building called Madison Square Garden, which was advertising a big boxing match. Next was a place with 'Liggett's Drug Store' painted on the window. 'What do you think that place sells, Declan?'

'Medicine, maybe?' He pulled a doubtful face.

'I suppose so.' But when she glanced in, there were people sitting on high stools, eating ice cream and drinking funny-looking drinks.

A woman who looked a bit odd wandered past, her hair matted. She wore bottles around her neck and seemed to have lots of layers of clothes on despite the warm weather. Grace could smell her body odour as she passed them. She was talking, but not to Grace, just to herself. 'Welcome to Hell's Kitchen… You don't wanna be here… It's hell, all right…'

Grace was beginning to worry that the post office was too far and wondered if they were going the right way at all; with her leg, anything over half a mile away was a long way off.

Just then the post office came into view, and she was able to limp the last few yards, leaning gratefully on Declan's arm. It was huge and there were several counters, all manned by different people. It was hard to know which queue to join, but Declan made her sit down while he joined one. He got to the top of it eventually and came back without the letter and with an envelope of dollars that he'd exchanged for some of their pounds.

'She said she'd put it straight into the post bag and it would definitely get there tomorrow,' he said, looking both pleased with himself and nervous. 'It will be there waiting for them when they get back.'

Nedick's was only a few shop fronts beyond the post office. It wasn't like any place Grace had ever seen, not the fish-and-chip shop in Dingle or even the restaurants in Cork. Everything was bright and with hard surfaces, and everything was either orange or white. The menu was written up behind the counter on a huge chalkboard, with a logo of a cartoon man with a bald head saying 'Good food isn't expensive at Nedick's.' And another huge sign in the same colours saying 'Always a pleasure.'

'What should we order?' Declan asked as they took a seat in a booth.

'I really don't know?' She scanned the menu of unfamiliar foods. Thankfully the prices were listed beside each item, so she knew they could afford it. Declan had the money from Mrs Clifford, she had some savings of her own, Charlie had given them five pounds, and the Warringtons had insisted on giving Grace ten pounds as she left, however much she tried not to take it. Each pound was worth about four dollars, so they had enough, but they would have to be careful at the same time.

Near the bottom of the list was written 'hot dogs with everything', priced at ten cents. So a hot dog was something you could eat. Well, every day was a schoolday. Richard had said she should try one.

A waitress arrived to their table, dressed in an orange and white uniform with a frilly apron over it. The dress was short, shorter than any Grace had ever seen, and she was in her forties at least. Agnes would have had a canary.

'What can I getcha?' The waitress was brusque and businesslike. The place was busy, so she clearly had no time for dithering.

'Hot dogs,' Grace said decisively, eliciting a startled glance from Declan.

'Two dogs...' The waitress wrote it down. 'Pickles? Relish? Mustard? Onions?'

Bewildered, Grace answered yes to everything.

'And to drink?' She looked at Declan this time.

'Er, milk please,' he said, frozen to the spot.

'Sure, and for you?' She turned to Grace.

'Tea please?' she said.

'Iced tea.' The woman started to walk away.

'Er, no...no...' Grace called after her, alarmed.

'You don't want iced tea?' The waitress snapped around, impatient to get to her next customer.

'I don't know what that is,' Grace said honestly. 'But I'd like a cup of tea, hot.'

'Hot tea?' The woman's brow furrowed, and she called back to the kitchen behind. 'Hey, Marv, we got hot tea?'

A huge man in an apron and a white chef's hat shook his head.

'Coffee?' asked the waitress.

'I'll try the iced tea,' Grace said, embarrassed now, as everyone in the restaurant seemed to be watching, including a group of policemen who were in the restaurant having coffee and doughnuts and who kept bursting into raucous laughter – she hoped not at the sight of herself and Declan being clearly lost and confused.

The woman shrugged and moved on.

'What is a hot dog? Is it made of dog meat?' whispered Declan, looking horrified.

'I don't think so... Surely not?' She hadn't thought of that and felt a bit ill at the idea. Alfie had written to Tilly and his mother about the French eating horses and donkeys, but she hoped nowhere in the world ate dog, and surely Richard wouldn't anyway – he wrote very fondly about his old Labrador, Doodle. Doodle's picture had been in the paper too, licking the actual bottle, an empty naggin of Paddy whiskey she'd found in a cave at Trá na n-Aingeal. It was amazing it had survived in one piece all that way.

The waitress appeared again with a tray and two enormous bread rolls that had sausages poking out either end. Fried onions and the selection of sauces Grace had ordered were squeezed inside the roll with the sausage.

She set the plates down in front of Declan and Grace, along with two huge glasses, one of milk, the other containing a golden-brown liquid with big cubes of ice and slices of lemon floating on top.

'Is that tea, cold, with lumps of ice in it?' Declan peered at her drink.

'I think so,' she said, then put the straw in her mouth and sucked. To her surprise it was delicious, like tea but cold and sweet and with a hint of lemon too.

'It's actually really nice, try it.' She passed him the glass and he took a sip.

He winced but took a second sip. 'It's strange but not bad.'

She took up the hot dog and took a bite, not really knowing what to expect and sincerely hoping it was just pork or beef or something...

It was like nothing she'd ever tasted before. The meat was smoked, and the skin, which showed signs of being chargrilled, seemed to almost crack when she bit into it. The combination of the smoky sausage with sweet onions, crisp pickles, creamy hot mustard and a tomato-based relish was like an explosion of flavour in her mouth. The bread was soft and white, nothing like the brown soda bread they ate at home, and the entire combination was magical.

'Oh my goodness...' she managed after her first bite. 'Declan, these are delicious. Have some, you'll see.'

Cautiously he took a bite of his and was soon clearly enjoying it too. 'Mm,' he kept saying, his mouth full.

'Excuse me for disturbing you, but I couldn't help overhearing you talking – you two from the old country, eh?' asked a man with a strong American accent.

One of the police officers from the raucous table stood over them; he was big and beefy but had a warm smile. His colleagues were at the counter, paying their bills – he must have paid his already – and they were all of the same build, tall and brawny.

'We're here from Ireland.' Grace smiled, hoping that was what he meant. 'We just arrived today, our first time here.'

'Yeah, I thought so. You sound new.' He stuck his hand out and shook Declan's. 'Brendan McGinty, nice to meet you.'

'Declan McKenna,' Declan said softly, unable to hide his shyness.

'Grace Fitzgerald.' A moment later her small hand was enveloped in his large one.

'Hey, Grace Fitzgerald. Like Grace O'Malley, right? The pirate queen?' He kept hold of her hand. 'You got that great red hair like she had – I read it in a book. I read a lot about the old country. I'm Irish too. You got a beautiful smile, but I guess all the Irish guys tell you that, huh?'

He was openly flirting with her, which made her feel like laughing. He was funny if a bit mad.

'Where in Ireland were you born?' she asked, gently retrieving her hand. She thought he must have come over a long time ago considering he had no trace of an Irish accent, only a very strong American one, but he did have the red hair, shorn almost to his scalp, and the pale, freckled complexion of a typical Irishman.

'Nah, I was born here, 11th Avenue. My old man and all of my uncles were longshoremen.'

'Oh, I see,' she said, having never heard of a longshoreman. 'So it was your father was born in Ireland then?'

He laughed. 'He ain't never been over the Hudson, never mind the ocean. Nah...I think my great-great-great grandfather? Somethin' like that. He came from Dublin, two steps ahead of the law the old story goes. He sure would be rollin' in his grave if he knew I was a cop now.' He chuckled again.

Grace thought it strange to identify as Irish when the link was five generations old, but she made sure not to show it in her face, using her poker expression. 'That's interesting.'

'You know any McGintys back there, eh?' he asked.

'I'm afraid I don't, but that sounds like a name from a different part of the country.' She didn't like to disappoint him.

'Don't matter. Now do you and your boyfriend need any help getting around the place?' He towered over them, smiling at both of them but mainly at Grace. His arms were the size of legs of lamb. He didn't look like a man you would try to get the better of physically, but he was not at all threatening.

'Oh...er...Declan and me, we're just friends,' she said, with a quick smile at Declan.

'Is that so?' The policeman winked over at his colleagues, who had finished paying now and were smirking and nudging as they watched.

'Then you wanna catch a movie later? Or go boating? Or we could go to Coney Island if you want, ride the Cyclone?'

Richard had mentioned the Cyclone on Coney Island. And the boating lake. She blushed as well as laughed. 'I… Thank you…but no thanks.'

'C'mon, I don't bite. I'm a nice Catholic boy. You sure you won't come on a date with me tonight? Where you stayin'? I'll come pick you up? I swear I'm a good guy. I won't say or do nothin' the Reverend Mother wouldn't approve of…' He winked again and his blue eyes twinkled.

'I'm sorry, Brendan. We're only here for a week, and we have lots of important things to do.'

He looked astounded and suddenly serious. 'Only here for a week? How will you find your way around? Well, that's no good… You won't have time to see a thing without me to help you. I know, what about I bring the two of you out to see the town, hey, Declan? Show you around together? I have a car, so I can take you on drives around the city, showing you the sights. I'm off tomorrow, so I'll come and get you about ten? Where are you staying?'

'I…er…'

Again she glanced at Declan, who to her surprise answered, 'The Westchester Inn.'

'OK…I know where that is…great. I'll see you there.'

* * *

AFTER THEY'D PAID the bill and were walking back to the hotel, she asked him why he'd given Brendan McGinty the address of the hotel. 'I'm not worried, I don't think there's any malice or bad intentions in him, but I wasn't sure you liked him?'

He cast her a look with his azure eyes. 'I don't think I have to like him. It's you he's interested in, Grace, and I wouldn't want to stand in your way.'

'Stand in my way of what?' She was puzzled.

'Of him asking you out. Even though it was a bit ridiculous…'

'Of course it was ridiculous. He was just doing it for a joke. He clearly had a bet with those other people he was with.'

Declan looked vexed for a moment. 'I didn't mean it was ridiculous that he'd want to ask you out, but just that it was so quick. Sure is there anyone in Knocknashee who would ask a girl out they didn't know for years?'

'Well, even if that's not what you meant, it still is ridiculous,' she repeated, amused.

'No, it isn't.' He became very solemn, gazing down at the pavement beneath his feet as he walked. 'You've no idea the way other people see you, Grace. You just see the polio and the calliper and all of that, but nobody else does. People like Brendan look at you and they see a beautiful woman…'

'Now it's you who is being ridiculous.' She grinned at him as they reached the Westchester Inn. 'And I'm off for a nice hot bath for my gammy leg.'

CHAPTER 20

*B*rendan McGinty was as good as his word, and it was lovely to have someone show them around for the few days while they waited for the Maheadys to return from Maine.

The young policeman continued to be a terrible flirt, and every time he got Grace alone, he would announce that he was madly in love with her and that he was going to show her such a good time in New York that she wouldn't want to leave. In response she would just laugh at him, which didn't seem to bother him in the slightest. He was charming to Declan as well, so much so that the shy schoolteacher relaxed and started to enjoy his silliness.

Brendan McGinty was so huge, Grace felt even tinier than normal beside him. He was six feet four and weighed, he said with pride, two hundred and thirty pounds. The muscles on his arms were broader than her legs, and his chest was like a wall. He lifted weights and worked out in a gym, where he also boxed. He explained that being a cop, you needed to be able to take care of yourself, and he could take on anyone and come out not too bad.

'I think I might not have ticked the brain box in the training, but I sure ticked the brawn one,' he joked, but Grace contradicted him.

Brendan was far from stupid; he was in fact very sensitive and funny, and she liked him a lot.

Declan still suspected Brendan had a real crush on Grace, but Grace laughed that off and said she was sure it was just that the fifth-generation New Yorker was so enamoured with the whole idea of them being Irish that showing around two people who were actually reared in Ireland was a big thing for him.

He certainly loved his Irish heritage and made a much bigger thing of it than anyone who was from Ireland did. He had some funny ideas of what it meant to be Irish, like the foods he assumed they ate, something called corned beef and cabbage cooked together, which Grace had never heard of, or the songs they sang, like 'Too-Ra-Loo-Ra-Loo-Ral', which were totally new to her and Declan.

On the first and second day, he took them up to the top of the newly built Rockefeller Center, on a boat out to see the Statue of Liberty and even to see a show on Broadway – his mother's friend worked front of house and got them in for free. Driving them in his car over the Brooklyn Bridge, he taught them the chorus of 'Who Threw the Overalls in Mrs Murphy's Chowder?' And by the time they were on the right side of the river again, all three of them were singing at the tops of their voices.

Declan and Grace conversed in English around Brendan – it would be rude not to – but alone they spoke in their own language, and when Brendan overheard them, he got them to teach him a few Irish phrases.

Given the young policeman's propensity to go rushing in where angels feared to tread, Declan suggested, 'Is minic an béal a bhriseann an srón' – often the nose is broken by the mouth. When he explained the meaning, Brendan found it uproarious and insisted on learning how to say it. After that, every day he learnt a new phrase.

They'd laughed when a waitress in a coffee shop – everybody in New York, it seemed to Grace, knew Brendan McGinty – commented how he was quieter than usual. 'An rud is annamh is iontach' he replied. And she was perplexed.

'I'm speaking the Irish of my people, Charisse,' he said proudly. 'It means that what is rare is wonderous.'

'You're a lot of things, McGinty, but wonderous sure ain't one of 'em,' she'd called with a chuckle as they left with their iced teas.

The fourth day, just as they were beginning to worry the Maheadys might have been delayed in Maine or changed their mind about meeting them or something, the woman at reception handed Declan a letter with a Rockaway Beach postmark.

Grace and Declan read it over the hotel breakfast of orange juice and coffee and very creamy scrambled eggs with soft white bread, all of which they were getting used to.

12 Sea View Terrace, Rockaway Beach, New York.

Dear Mr. McKenna,

My husband and I are very excited to be meeting you tomorrow, and we hope you will eat with us and stay for your last two nights to save traveling. We're sorry your father was too ill to come, but we are looking forward to meeting your colleague from the school, Mistress Fitzgerald.

If you are happy to stay, Joey can come to the hotel in our car tomorrow afternoon, Wednesday, and collect you and your bags, and then take you to the ship on Friday morning to save you the expense of two more nights in the hotel.

Our house isn't big, but our daughters can bunk in together, so Mistress Fitzgerald can have Lily's room, which Lily promises to make neat and clean.

If you don't mind, Mr. McKenna, we will put you up on the couch in the living room. It's a large couch, and we often use it for visitors. We won't have to disturb you, as the kitchen will do for us to sit in; it's where we usually sit anyway.

We are so looking forward to hearing all about Ireland. I will make corned beef and cabbage, which Joey says he knows you would like to eat, and after dinner maybe you can teach our daughters some Irish songs, as they're very interested in their heritage, just like their father.

Joey is sitting here, and he wants me to tell you how excited he is to meet you, and I do understand why. The Italians also love family, and I have so many cousins I've never met. One day I would love to take the girls to

Naples, where my great-grandmother was from. And maybe one day we could take the girls to Knocknashee so they can visit their Irish roots.

Yours, Sylvia Maheady

Passing the letter back across the table to Declan, Grace looked at him with her head to one side. 'Are you feeling all right about meeting Siobhán... I mean, Lily?' She knew she mustn't slip up and call the girl by the wrong name. This child had always been Siobhán in her mind, but then in her mind Siobhán was a little baby, so maybe it wouldn't be that hard to see the fifteen-year-old girl as a totally different being.

Declan shrugged. He was paler than usual but not overly agitated. 'If you're asking whether I'm going to tell them I'm a lot closer relative than a distant cousin, no, I'm not. They seem nice, and they don't need a bomb going off in the middle of their lives. I really do just want to make sure she's happy and well cared for and...' He shrugged again. 'Well, Sylvia seems nice.'

It was the calmest she'd seen him about it, and she wondered if Brendan taking them around the past few days had been a help. Declan had been able to see how wealthy Americans were, how confident and full of opportunity, which must have made him feel better about his sister's future.

When Brendan arrived midmorning, he was crestfallen to hear this was their last full day and became unusually quiet, then said he needed to run home for half an hour but would be back. When he returned, he took them to a diner for chicken and waffles, a peculiar mixture of food to Grace and Declan's taste, but it was surprisingly delicious. He insisted on paying for them, and afterwards he took them to Central Park, where they ended up at the boating lake.

Here he asked Grace if she'd like him to row her across the lake. There was only room for two in the little rowboats, and Declan said he didn't mind sitting this one out and settled himself with a copy of the *Capital* under a tree to read about the war in the North Atlantic, which unlike the Irish newspapers, the American press took seriously.

Brendan rowed out to the middle of the lake in record time; it was almost comical the speed of it. He was so strong, they left a wake behind them as they passed other boats just bobbing along, couples chatting together. Once they were in the middle of the lake, though, he balanced the oars on the sides of the boat and they bobbed around gently on the water, like everyone else. His huge bulk took up the entire seat opposite her, his legs like tree trunks, and Grace found herself wondering what it would be like to live life in a strong, powerful body like his.

After a quiet minute or so, while she enjoyed the sunshine, he reached out his hand to her. Smiling, she took it, assuming this was some kind of formal goodbye. He kept hold of it, though, which made her blush but was also nice. This man knew about her bad leg, saw how it was and still wanted to hold her hand.

'I guess there's no point in, er...' – he was not his usual brash, confident self – 'askin' you to stay?'

'How do you mean?'

'Here, in New York... Like, ah...you gotta go back? To Ireland?' He looked suddenly bashful.

'I do have to,' she explained. 'I'm the headmistress of a school. They're expecting me back...it's my job.'

'We got schools here, y'know?' He put his head to one side, squinting against the strong, bright sun. 'You could move here, and we'd see each other every day?'

She chuckled. 'If I said I would, I think you'd have a heart attack, Mr McGinty.' She was used to his flowery ways now.

But to her surprise, he didn't quip back with some witty rejoinder like he usually did. 'No, I would not. I know you came over on some kinda mission, and I know once that's done, you're gonna take off back to Ireland, but I... Look, I know I come over all wisecrackin', but I ain't never met nobody like you, Grace, and I really like you...and I...' It was his turn to blush; his ears went pink, which clashed with his hair, and Grace felt a wave of affection for him.

'Brendan, you're very nice to say those things, but I know I'm not the kind of girl men go for. But thank you.'

'Are you nuts? You're a knockout, and I don't care about the polio. My aunt has it too, it's no big deal...'

She smiled and didn't answer.

He backtracked, clearly thinking he'd offended her. 'I don't mean it ain't serious or nothin' to have it, and I know you said you had to be a long time in the hospital. I just mean if you were my girl, I'd feel like the luckiest guy in New York, in America – hell, in the whole world. And I was trying to get up the guts to tell you, and I asked my old man this morning, and he said just say it. Just tell her straight and she'll either go for it or she won't. So here it is. I'm just startin' out, still live with my parents, and I don't make big money or nothin', but I got plans for promotion. I got my own car, and I'm gonna buy a place of my own, not fancy and not in Manhattan, but in the city, Queens maybe or Long Island, and I'd be good to you, Grace, if you'll have me.'

Grace sat stunned. The water lapped against the little wooden boat as Brendan McGinty offered her a life with him, here in this amazing city. He clearly wasn't joking; she'd never seen him so serious in the five days since she'd known him.

'My old man is a good guy, y'know, treats my mom right. He don't stay out at the bar, or go with women or nothin' like that, and I'd be the same. I'd be a good husband, if that was something you could consider.'

'Brendan, we've only just met…'

'I know, and I know it's too quick. Normally I'd take a bit longer, let you get to know me properly, not just the goofin' around stuff. But you're gonna up and leave any day now, and I'm scared I'll be losing the best girl I ever met, so I gotta take the opportunity of a lifetime in the lifetime of the opportunity, y'know?' He smiled, and she could hardly believe what was happening.

Before she had time to speak, he produced a small box and opened it. Settled on a velvet cushion was a single solitaire diamond. 'This is Grandma McGinty's ring. Before she died she said I was to give it to the girl I fell in love with for life. That's what I went home for this morning. And it's probably not the style you like, but we can get it remade however you want…'

Grace felt lightheaded. Was this a marriage proposal? It really was.

A man, a kind, nice man was asking her to marry him. After Agnes telling her for years that obviously nobody would ever want her, it was a total shock.

Brendan gave her a hopeful, wobbly smile. 'So what about it? You think you could be married to a big New York cop with a smart mouth but a soft heart?'

Grace tried to recover from the shock and gather her thoughts. 'Brendan, I never thought in a million years that anyone would ever want to marry me, let alone someone as wonderful as you...' She paused, trying to formulate the words.

'I'm waitin' for a but...' he said sadly.

She nodded. 'But I can't. I have to go home.'

'You're breaking my heart here, Grace...'

'I'm sorry, and I might be making the biggest mistake of my life – you seem lovely – but it has to be a no. I'm sorry.' He looked so woebegone, she leant forwards in her seat and hugged him.

And then, in the middle of the lake, with people rowing by, he leant forwards himself, tilted her face up by placing a finger under her chin and kissed her softly on the lips.

Grace had never imagined being kissed ever, but to have been kissed, by an American, on a lake in New York City, well, life was very strange.

He sighed and put the ring back in his pocket, then rowed them back across the lake. Later, when he dropped her and Declan back to the hotel, he got out of the car and came around to help her out, not that he really needed to. American cars were so much bigger than any she'd seen in Ireland, and it meant getting in and out was less cumbersome with her leg.

After the three of them had shaken hands, she stood smiling at him for a moment. 'I have loved meeting you, Brendan McGinty. Thank you for showing me your wonderful city. I will never, ever forget it, or you.'

'So long, Grace Fitzgerald. I'll never forget you either.' His voice cracked with emotion, and within seconds he was back in his car and driving away. She stood outside the hotel, waving until his car went around the corner.

Declan waited for her as she limped up the steps of the hotel. 'Was Brendan all right? He looked very unhappy to be leaving you.'

'Of course he's all right,' she said firmly.

CHAPTER 21

The following morning, they waited with their bags for Joey Maheady on the sidewalk outside the hotel, the warm sun on their faces, the sounds and aromas of the city relentless and insistent.

Grace kept stealing glances at Declan, worried in case he was tense or upset, and he noticed and smiled back at her reassuringly. 'I'm grand, Gracie, don't be worrying about me. I just need to meet my sister and ensure that she's happy, that's all. If I can be assured of that, see her with my own eyes, talk to her, then you have my word I'll leave her in peace.'

Before she had a chance to reply, they heard a honk, and a large American car, a Chevrolet Master, drew up at the kerb beside them. A tall and thin man in his fifties, with thinning brown hair and pale-blue eyes, climbed out of the car and went straight to Declan.

'Hello, I'm Joey Maheady, and I'm guessing you're Declan, from the old country?' He had a wide, open smile.

'I am indeed, and this is my friend, Grace Fitzgerald.'

Turning to Grace, the tall man first looked startled, then laughed. 'You are Mistress Fitzgerald? Goodness me, you're nothing like any schoolteacher I remember.'

They'd worried whether Joey Maheady or his wife would remember meeting Agnes all those years ago and make the connection with the surname, but since Grace looked nothing like Agnes and it was years ago, and since Fitzgerald was a very common Irish name, they hoped he wouldn't make the link.

He shook their hands gently, not pumping them like Brendan would have done, then looked closely at Declan. 'Cousins, hey? You sure do remind me of someone, just can't think who right this moment. Sylvia might remember. I didn't bring her and the girls with me – there wouldn't be enough room in the car for all of us.' He threw open the boot. 'Let's get your bags in the trunk.' She smiled as she added that to her long list of words that were different over here. Faucets and trunks, sidewalks and sweaters, cookies and soda, the list was growing by the day.

The journey to Rockaway Beach took almost an hour, and thanks to Brendan, Grace was familiar with some of the landmarks as they drove down the banks of the Hudson. Crossing the bridge and seeing the skyline of the city made her sad. This was the last time she would ever see this sight, and somewhere in that city, doing his job, was a big, brawny New York policeman called Brendan McGinty who, if he was to be believed, was nursing a broken heart.

Once they were over the Brooklyn Bridge, the traffic moved a bit more freely, and the roads took them through a warren of smaller streets, businesses on the ground floors of the walk-ups – as she had learnt houses over shops, with stairs on the outside, were called.

Joey Maheady, who kept up a stream of conversation, explained this was a solid working-class area, where everyone helped each other out. Grace peered out of the window at the little children playing on the streets with bicycles and dolls and prams, or playing what Brendan said was called baseball, and it did seem cosier and more neighbourly than the area around the Westchester Inn, but certainly the people here enjoyed a standard of life that would have been considered luxury in Knocknashee. Not posh or anything, nothing like Richard Lewis's lifestyle, but with indoor plumbing, electricity and public transport; people took things like that for granted here.

They passed the Brooklyn Botanic Garden and a large building with Greek columns, which Joey Maheady said was a museum. She stored this information away for when she was teaching the children about Greek architecture and how it had influenced so many public buildings all around the world. They loved learning about the Greeks and the Romans and the Celts.

They drove all the way down the other side of the river to Coney Island, where she, Brendan and Declan had had such a wonderful time, and Joey Maheady explained how Rockaway Beach, where they were headed, had a big Irish community that made him feel at home.

Grace knew by now that a big Irish community meant people like Brendan. They were of Irish extraction, not people actually from Ireland, and she wasn't surprised to find Mr Maheady's Irish roots had left Ireland almost a hundred years earlier, not long after the famine.

The area was nice, though, on the shore, and in clusters all around the streets were more bunches of children playing. Eventually they pulled up at a single-storey house on its own plot, with a small, neat front garden. 'Here we are. Sylvia's waiting for you. She's Italian and she makes great coffee, but if you prefer, as you're Irish, she can make you tea...'

Grace perked up. It had been a while now since she'd had a proper cup of tea. Joey and Declan got the bags out of the boot. She could see Declan was on edge, and she gave him an encouraging smile. He smiled back weakly as they followed Joey Maheady up the path and stood behind him as he inserted his key in the front door, the top half of which was opaque glass.

'Please, come in.' He stood back and allowed them to enter his home.

It was bright and beautifully decorated. In various frames were pressed flowers, and the house smelled of baking and – yes – coffee.

A woman appeared then. She was very tall, almost as tall as her husband, with black hair set in waves and an open, pleasant face. She had an apron over her clothes that she was rapidly untying.

'Hello, Mr McKenna, and...er...'

'Grace Fitzgerald, but call me Grace,' she said, accepting the woman's handshake. 'Thank you for having us.'

'Oh...you're welcome...' Sylvia Maheady's eyes widened slightly as she took in Grace's small stature and young face. Like her husband, she must have been expecting a headmistress who looked more...well, more like Agnes. 'Do come on through to the kitchen. Lily and Ivy are at my sister's – she just lives up the block – but they'll be here in just a couple of minutes. They're excited to meet you too – we love family. Can I get you a drink? Coffee? Tea?'

'Tea would be lovely, thank you.'

'Gee, it's hot today.' She led them into a sunny kitchen and dining room that overlooked a little back garden where a swing made from a tyre hung from the bough of a tree, and in another corner was what looked like a rabbit hutch.

'So, tea... I can tell you're from Ireland. The Irish love their tea, don't they?' Sylvia was busy taking down a set of matching tumblers, each with yellow lemons on them, and placing them in the centre of the table, and Grace and Declan exchanged an amused grimace. It looked like it was going to be iced tea again, sweet and lemony.

Brendan, despite his 'Irishness', had also been surprised when Grace asked where she could get a cup of hot tea; apparently in America hot tea was for the elderly or infirm.

When Sylvia opened the refrigerator, as the Americans called it, Grace noticed there were several rather good drawings stuck to its door, one of a rabbit with every bit of fur delineated. When Sylvia saw Grace admiring them, she said, 'Both the girls love their art. Now where... Oh, here they are!'

And moments later two girls burst in through the kitchen door.

CHAPTER 22

*T*he girls immediately launched into a story about how Aunt
Gaby's cat was going to have kittens any day now and how
Aunt Gaby said they could have one each. 'But Momma and Daddy
have to agree and can they just say yes now pleeeease?'

Sylvia tried to calm them down, but the kittens were too exciting
and it was difficult to break through the chatter with stories of
cousins visiting from abroad.

'We'll talk about it later, girls, I promise, but now I want you to
meet a distant relative of your father's. Remember I told you they
were coming?'

She pointed the two girls towards Declan, and they both
approached him without a hint of shyness.

Grace knew exactly why Joey Maheady thought he'd seen Declan
before. The taller girl, Lily, was the absolute image of him. Same sleek
very dark-brown hair, in her case escaping from a bun, tendrils falling
around her heart-shaped face, those same piercing indigo eyes – it
was from their beautiful mother they had got them. She was lithe and
slim, with straight white teeth, and the only difference was her skin
was more tanned from living all of her life in the heat of New York
summers.

Her ten-year-old sister had dark hair too, but wavy, and brown eyes, showing her Italian heritage, as well as a wide white grin.

'Lily, Ivy, this is Mr McKenna and he's from Ireland,' Sylvia announced.

'Hello, Mr McKenna,' Lily said brightly, and Ivy echoed it. Grace got the impression that Ivy adored her big sister and followed her in everything.

'Declan, please,' he said, shaking their hands.

'And this is his friend Miss Fitzgerald, who will be staying in your room, Lily. She's a headmistress, so I hope you have it tidy.'

'I do, Mom.' Lily smiled, and Ivy echoed, 'She does, Mom...and I helped.'

'And you've been in Maine all week at a swimming gala?' asked Grace, keeping the conversation going as Declan stood tongue-tied from looking at his own image in the mirror of a fifteen-year-old girl.

Lily nodded, went to a set of shelves hanging on the wall and returned with a medal and a big grin.

'First place in the two-hundred-metre freestyle. I didn't think I'd make it – there's a kid from Queens, she's like a dolphin – but I just squeaked past her, three tenths of a second,' she said proudly.

Ivy piped up, not to be beaten. 'And I got picked for the softball team in school.'

'You didn't?' Grace pretended to look aghast. 'Well, look out world is all I can say, the Maheady sisters are coming for you.'

They giggled at that, delighted.

'That looks like an amazing swing you have out there,' Grace said to the younger child as Lily went to put her precious trophy away on the shelves, which she now saw were covered with other trophies.

'Daddy made it for us. You wanna go on it?' Ivy asked.

'I'd love to try,' Grace said, 'but I have a wonky leg, so I don't know if I can.'

'Sure you can.' Lily smiled, holding out her hand. 'We'll help you. C'mon. Declan, will you come too?'

'Let's all go. I'll bring the iced tea out into the garden,' said Sylvia. 'Joey, grab that tray there and get some bowls of ice cream.'

Joey looked slightly startled and gave himself a shake; he'd been staring at his daughter talking to Declan and seemed a bit faraway, but now he came back and picked up the tray of glasses.

Outside in the sun, Lily helped Grace into the tyre swing. Ivy pushed her gently while the older girl went to the rabbit hutch and extracted a huge floppy-eared rabbit, the one in the picture stuck to the fridge, and showed him to Declan.

'This is Chomper. He's old now. I got him for my birthday when I was twelve.' She sounded so New York, it made Grace smile.

'He used to have a wife, Cinnebun,' Ivy called over, 'but she died. We buried her over there, under the vegetable patch. Me and my dad grow carrots and squash and strawberries and all sorts of stuff there.'

'That's great. Everyone where I come from grows their own vegetables too,' said Declan, smiling at the younger girl; his nervousness seemed to be fading. He turned back to her older sister, who was putting the rabbit back in his hutch. 'So you're a fast swimmer, are you?'

'I am. I love swimming. I could swim before I could walk, Mom says. Do you live near the beach?'

'I do. I live right beside a long white beach, in the most beautiful place in the world.'

'That's what Dad says about Ireland, my grandma and grandpa too, though they ain't never been there, but maybe I'll get to go sometime. And do you like to swim?' she asked.

'I do. When I was a small boy, my daddy taught me to swim, so like you I can't ever remember not being able to.'

'My dad taught me too.' She grinned, glad of the connection. 'And how to dive. We got some diving rocks out toward Rockaway, and we go there sometimes. Mom hates it, she thinks they're too high, but it's fine. Me and Ivy both dive off them.'

His face had shadowed slightly when she said 'my dad', but then he smiled again. 'And do you like school?'

She shrugged. 'It's OK. My teacher this year is nice, Mrs Siloh, she's left-handed too, so she makes sure I'm sitting on the left side 'cos

I write better with that hand, every other year they tried to make me write with my right.'

Sylvia was pouring out the iced tea, and Joey appeared with bowls of ice cream; it was getting warm.

'Dad, can we take Declan to the beach?' Lily asked, in between scoops of ice cream and sips of iced tea. 'Declan says he loves to swim. He lives near the beach too in Ireland.'

'Well, honey, I don't know. Maybe he's not as keen as you are. It's still a bit chilly this time of year,' Joey replied hesitatingly.

'Compared to Ireland, this is the tropics,' Declan replied with a laugh. He seemed genuinely relaxed and enjoying himself now. 'Only thing is, I didn't think to bring a swimsuit.'

'I can give you a swimsuit, I've a few pairs. Should be OK – we're both skinny.'

'If it's all right by Grace...' Declan glanced at Grace. He knew she swam as well at the height of summer, but he also knew she did it in private, with only Tilly to watch. She wouldn't want to be having to fuss with the calliper in public.

'Grace can sit on the sand with me,' said Sylvia comfortably. 'She can tell me all about Ireland, and I'll tell her all about Italy.'

Joey clapped his thin hands. 'OK, it looks like we're all going to the beach.'

Everyone fussed around, getting picnic rugs and towels, and within ten minutes, they were all piled into Joey's Chevrolet Master. The car was overcrowded, but as Joey said, it was only a short trip this time. Ivy sat in front between her parents and Lily behind between Grace and Declan.

The beach wasn't thronged but it was busy enough. The hot dog stands and ice cream sellers were doing a brisk trade, and though some people were wearing jumpers and coats, the weather was warm by Irish standards, where you'd never go willingly into the Atlantic in April. Maybe if it hadn't been for all the people around, Grace would have been tempted; she did love the sensation of being weightless and not dragged down by her steel, the same way she enjoyed riding on the old pony, Ned.

As soon as they hit the sand, Ivy and Lily stripped down to their swimsuits and bolted for the water. Declan and Joey changed under the long wooden platform they called a boardwalk, and Sylvia fetched two deckchairs so she and Grace could sit on the beach and watch.

Joey entered the water in a mad rush, then frolicked and dived, while Declan played easily with Ivy, who seemed to be stuck to him, the two of them throwing a beach ball back and forth. The other two joined in, Joey making mad splashes when throwing himself around after the ball and Lily leaping high in the air.

It was a lovely family scene, and it struck Grace that Joey was a great father, always urging his daughters on, full of fun. The woman sitting beside her, Sylvia, was kind and nurturing. A perfect combination. She hoped Declan could see this and emotionally let go of the baby sister who had haunted his thoughts all these years; she hoped he could see that the newborn child who had once been Siobhán McKenna had grown up into a very happy and lucky girl with two loving parents and an adoring younger sister, and that back in Ireland he would reassure his father of all this so Charlie could sleep at night knowing his beloved child was safe and secure.

'It's funny, isn't it,' said Sylvia suddenly, 'that your friend is such a distant cousin he doesn't even know how many times he's removed, and yet he fits right into the family.'

'He really does, it's lovely to see.' Grace, who had been thinking the same thing, turned to smile at her. But Sylvia wasn't smiling; her eyes raked Grace's face.

'I mean he looks so like Lily, doesn't he?'

A slight chill ran down Grace's spine, but she kept the poker face she was so good at, smiling gently. 'I noticed that a bit,' she said. 'It's definitely the Irish in them. It's a type in the west, black hair, bright-blue eyes, pale skin. They get called the Black Irish. People say they're descended from Spanish sailors shipwrecked off the west coast of Ireland during the Spanish Armada of 1588.'

'Mm...' Lily's mother – because that's who she was – kept looking at her closely, but Grace kept smiling blandly. And then she said, looking away at the ocean, 'Well, I suppose you've noticed we're not young parents.'

Grace hadn't really. Life in rural Ireland could be very tough; a woman like Dymphna O'Connell, who was only thirty-seven, could look old. Grace had been surprised to find out the woman behind reception at the hotel was in her fifties and looking forward to retirement; she didn't look any older than Dymphna to be honest. To her eyes, Joey and Sylvia looked fresh and healthy.

'I was forty-two when I had Ivy,' continued Sylvia, still without looking at her. 'We couldn't have kids of our own, or we thought we couldn't, and Lily was like a little miracle. We couldn't believe that God would bless us with such a sweet child. We love both our girls, Miss Fitzgerald. We love them both exactly the same. They are our children, and to lose one of them now...well, it would be more than a mother could bear.'

'But you won't lose either of your girls,' said Grace quietly.

Sylvia's gaze came back to her, resting on her face...not exactly with suspicion, more as if she were trying to see into Grace's soul. 'Do you promise me that, Miss Fitzgerald? I met another woman called Miss Fitzgerald once. She didn't look like you, but she said she came from the west of Ireland, the same as you. And she promised... Grace, she promised... I don't know how to explain, but she assured me everything was in order.'

'I suppose she did,' said Grace, her face giving nothing away.

'I don't know if you ever knew this woman, Miss Fitzgerald? She was a teacher too, I think.' Her dark-brown Italian eyes brimmed with pain and fear.

'Please call me Grace.'

'Did you know this woman, Grace?'

Grace thought of all the things she could say to this loving mother. That yes, she knew Agnes Fitzgerald, that the woman was her sister, and that she was dead now but before she died, she had confessed her guilt and finally told the truth.

And that's why she and Declan McKenna were there.

But instead, her face expressionless, she said, 'No, Sylvia, I didn't.'

CHAPTER 23

PARIS, FRANCE

*M*ay 1940

The trip so far had been arduous and fascinating in equal measure. After a number of delays, and getting fired on by a U-boat but thankfully not damaged this time, they landed in Southampton. It was difficult to get a sailing to France, so rather than wait, they headed to Holland, their press passes allowing Jacob and Richard to travel freely, with Sarah posing as their official interpreter.

In Holland everyone they met was carrying on as normal, confident the Germans weren't going to invade because they were a neutral country. It was even rumoured that Bernhard von Lippe-Biesterfeld, who had married Dutch Princess Juliana three years ago, was a member of the Nazi party.

It was the same in Belgium, which they passed through on their way to France; their King Leopold was not unfriendly to the Germans, and most people didn't really believe anything bad was going to happen.

In Paris Richard decided to do a piece on the abdicated and

disgraced king of England and his American divorcee wife, Wallis Simpson – they were living in Paris and also known to be friendly with the Nazis – but as a lowly American reporter, it was hard to find an entry to that kind of society. His father had known Mrs Simpson's first husband, a US Navy officer, in some capacity, but he thought that might not be the best way to introduce himself.

In the meantime they found a surprising number of Americans still enjoying life in the French capital.

It seemed that thousands of their fellow countrymen had ignored the ambassador's advice to go home, and he and Jacob made a point of seeking them out and began to build up quite a portfolio, asking them about their motivations for staying and what they thought might happen next. Kirky would be pleased, they hoped. It was a good angle; Americans would be interested to read about their fellow countrymen and women and would be fascinated about why they weren't afraid of what looked, from the other side of the Atlantic, like a precarious future. The reasons were many and varied – love, business, politics, ideology, disillusionment with life Stateside, the list went on – but each story was compelling in its own way.

They sent the copy and photos to Kirky, and to Richard's relief and astonishment, Kirky thought it was great and wanted them to stay on. The stories of regular people, not politicians, were being gobbled up by the public.

Along with Kirky's reply came another letter – this one from Grace. It had been sent to St Simons Island, and then – thanks to Esme – to the *Capital* offices in New York, from where Lucille had forwarded it to their PO box in Paris.

It was bright, friendly and breezy and showed no concern about the fact that Richard was in Europe while Grace was in New York. She seemed to have only written to him because Tilly wanted to know if Radclyffe Hall had written any more books, and she also gave him an address for Tilly's brother, Alfie, in Paris.

Jacob was delighted. He'd been complaining that they should meet someone with deeper political connections than the Americans they'd been hanging around with, so he was keen to meet Alfie and his friends. They were probably just the sort of people whose opinions would annoy Kirky, Richard pointed out, but Jacob laughed and Sarah told him not to be such a goody two-shoes – did he want to be like Hemingway or not, she'd asked.

The address Tilly had given Grace turned out to be a fourth-floor attic not far from Canal Saint-Martin, and Alfie was at home, along with a girl called Constance, who sat looking very serious on the edge of their unmade bed; she had mousey-brown hair cut roughly to her jaw, a wide face, dark eyes and a small, pert mouth.

Alfie was initially very suspicious, but as soon as they mentioned Tilly O'Hare from Knocknashee and explained about the letters, he relaxed.

Alfie had all the look of a man who'd left the Spanish Civil War to come to Paris. He was of average height and athletic build, with a week of stubble and deep-set dark-grey eyes. His hair was badly in need of a barber, standing up in all directions. He wore moleskin trousers held up by a length of leather and a shirt with no collar. His boots had once been military issue.

Jacob took a picture of Constance and Alfie, as Tilly had requested, and then Constance went off to help her sister Bernadette, who'd just had a new baby that was keeping her awake all night.

Alfie brought them to a traditional Parisian café on the Place du Combat, where he allowed them to buy him cheese and bread. He bolted it down, clearly starving, and drank most of a carafe of white wine.

'So you're the famous Richard Lewis, the fancy American!' His beautiful grey eyes lit up. Despite his scruffiness, he was a good-looking lad, with high cheekbones. And when he smiled, he had a crooked tooth, which added to his charm. 'Tilly says you published an article about Grace, which was really about America needing to join the war? You should come and talk to some people I know.'

He explained that while the official line in the newspapers was that the French army could stand against Nazi aggression, the reality was that they would look away so long as he kept going east. In the

brasseries of the City of Light, however, there was a different understanding, should he turn west.

'I'll bring you to meet some people there. So you're Sarah...' He
turned his beautiful grey eyes on Richard's sister. 'Are you the Sarah
who sent Tilly the book?'

'I am, and I hear your sister is looking for another one by the same
author, so if you're writing back, tell her I'll find her one as soon as
I'm back in the States.'

'No need to wait,' said Alfie, throwing back the last of his wine.
'There's an American woman I know who owns this English-language
bookshop, Shakespeare and Company.'

'Hemingway's friend Sylvia Beach?' asked Jacob excitedly. 'You
know her?'

'I know everyone interesting in Paris.' He winked as he stood, and
he threw a few centimes on the table as a tip. '*Merci*, Armand, *au
revoir.*'

'*A bientôt*, Alfie,' the young barman replied.

Alfie O'Hare patted Richard on the back and ushered him out of
the brasserie. 'Let's go.'

They crossed the city, Richard wishing Alfie would allow them
time to take it all in. He'd never been anywhere as beautiful in his life.
Gold statues, civic buildings that looked like something from a fairy
tale, four-storey buildings with tiny wrought-iron balconies, where
people lived in this magical city.

On every corner people sat outside cafés, smoking and drinking
coffee or glasses of a liquid that seemed to go cloudy when water was
added. He wondered what it was, but Alfie was in such deep conversation with Jacob about the communists and the Jews and the fascists
that he didn't dare interrupt.

The language was beautiful and baffling. And cross as he might
have been initially at her muscling in, hearing Sarah navigate in fluent
French, asking for directions and actually understanding what people
said to her, he realised that without her they would have been in dire
straits, as Algernon might say.

They traversed Rue de Rivoli and crossed over the Seine via the

Pont d'Arcole, the beautiful Notre-Dame church on their right. The bookshop was on Rue de l'Odéon, several blocks away from the left bank of the Seine. Tiny gardens on street corners, closed with ornate gates, tiny little stores selling all manner of curiosities – Richard vowed to walk back when he had some time just to wander.

Sylvia Beach was charming and gracious to them; she had no idea who Richard and Sarah's family were and didn't seem perturbed by the fact Jacob was a Jew – she judged them on their own merits. She found Sarah a copy of *The Unlit Lamp* to send to Tilly and let Richard interview her about publishing James Joyce's *Ulysses* and her friendship with Ernest Hemingway.

Afterwards Alfie took them on the metro across the city to a seedy place in Pigalle in the red-light area of the city where artists and dropouts could be found and introduced them to another interesting person. In this case, Gigi, a lady of the night.

Gigi was determined to go to Chicago – it had to be the Windy City for some reason – so she was willing to spill the beans on a clandestine communist meeting that night for American dollars and a chance to practise her English, which was nonexistent, so it was as well they had Sarah there to translate for them.

Alfie declined to go. He and Constance had left the Communist Party after the Stalin-Hitler pact last August and he didn't want to end up having an argument with his old comrades, but he said he'd meet them afterwards in the Papillon Rouge. And if they wanted to bring anyone from the meeting along with them, that was fine by him. Not all French communists agreed with the Comintern line, which was against fighting Hitler.

The meeting turned out to be in the back of the café where they'd taken Alfie for lunch, in the Place du Combat.

A man stood and spoke with such passion, Richard wished he'd paid more attention to Monsieur Laval, the French master at school. But at the time, France might as well have been the moon for all the use Richard saw in learning that language.

'What's he saying?' he asked Sarah quietly.

'He's talking about the role for women in the party, how equality cannot just be along political or economic lines but along lines of gender too.' She nodded, looking very pleased with what she was hearing.

There were several women in the room, all dressed in working clothes, their heads covered by scarves, the complete opposite of Gigi in Pigalle. The prostitute had terrified him, frankly, with her red lips and lacquered hair.

The meeting broke up shortly afterwards, and when he looked around for Jacob, he found him talking with one of the working women. She was in her mid-twenties and plain-looking and reminded Richard of the young men and women who hung out in Jacob's flat in Savannah.

'Can we take you for a drink or something to eat, Amelie?' Jacob asked her, and he gave Richard that look, the one that said 'I've caught something here, let's reel it in.'

'No. Thank you, but no. I must return. To my house.' Her English was halting but good.

'Are you from Paris?' Richard asked, joining the conversation.

She looked directly at him, her cool green eyes unreadable. 'Yes, but I was down in the south. Now I came back.' One of her shoes had a hole at the toe, and her dress was patched several times.

'We're going for a beer now, to the Papillon Rouge, if you're sure you won't join us? We just would like to talk about the current situation, we don't want anything else. We can buy you a meal and a drink if you like?'

'Why?' she asked plainly, her face full of suspicion.

Sarah came to the rescue in effortless French, as she had repeatedly in the past few days. He caught 'journalists', 'American', 'important', 'Paris'.

'Why?' the woman asked Richard again, but her face changed, a tiny melting.

Richard answered in English. 'Well, because Americans are debating what we should do in this war, if anything, so we want to get a sense of what it's like so we can write about it and maybe help people to decide.'

'And you want I tell you my story now? So Americans will decide to come in the war?'

'Well, they can make their own minds up about it, but we'll just show them the facts.'

'I don't have money,' she said bluntly. 'It is why I say no.'

'Well, that's all right because we do,' said Sarah, 'and we agree with equality and sharing and everything like that, so don't say no again.'

* * *

THE LOW LIGHTING of the Papillon Rouge, a bar and café on a side street beside a church, was ideal for talking clandestine politics over cigarettes and beer and onion soup. Alfie stood and waved when he saw them, and they made their way over through the spindly chairs and tables, and the five of them sat down together.

Amelie Boucher told them she was the daughter of a trade unionist and – like Alfie and Constance – used to be a confirmed communist, until Stalin signed his pact with Hitler. She had grown up listening to the inequalities of life from her parents and their admiration of Lenin and Karl Marx, and the Molotov-Ribbentrop Pact had shocked her.

Her mother didn't seem to know what to do with herself after the pact was signed; she'd gone back to Strasbourg and wasn't in touch.

'And your father?' Richard asked.

'In prison.'

'Prison?' Richard was surprised at the matter-of-fact way she said it.

She shrugged. 'The authorities worry the communist trade unionist leaders will sabotage war production.'

Richard waited for further explanation, but none was forthcoming. 'What do you think will happen next?' he asked, after a few seconds.

She shrugged again, that very Gallic gesture Richard had come to expect from the French. 'Hitler, he is worry. The British and the French army was making pushes to the Western borders, before Poland fell, but only with heavy artillery cover, horses, men marching

– it is too slow. Once Poland is captured, they send so many back to Western borders again. He has the agreement with Stalin, so there is no threat from the east, so he can now look to us. We are easy target.'

She took a sip of her beer; she'd polished off the onion soup and bread Sarah had bought her in record time. 'He will be afraid – we fought such a hard fight last time. But he will do it, I think...but different.'

'In what way?' Richard was hanging on her every word now. In the time they'd been talking, he'd come to realise Amelie was more knowledgeable about the war than anyone he had met so far in Paris.

'He will not want the same as before, in the Great War, trenches, long time, many deaths. He will want fast, complete...over quickly with France conquered.'

'But how? We know he has fewer resources than the Western Allies. He'd need tanks, men, weapons,' Jacob said, repeating what he'd been reading in the press. 'And you have the Maginot Line...'

'I know, the Maginot is...they say is...*impénétrable*.' Her brow furrowed as she searched for the right word.

Sarah intervened. 'It's the same word, impenetrable, can't get through it.'

Amelie smiled. 'Ah, yes. So this they think, but I don't know.'

'What do you think?' Richard found this young Frenchwoman fascinating.

'Only old men guard this line, and it is from a different war, different technology. The French government don't want to hear it, but some people think we are in very grave peril.'

'But the Ardennes as well, in both Belgium and France, dense forest, fast-flowing rivers, deep ravines... They won't be able to do there what they did in Poland surely?' asked Jacob.

Again the shrug. 'Maybe, maybe not. But they are gathering at the borders of the low countries, and along our border, and that is not for nothing. And they have now this panzers, much better than old tanks, so...we will have to fight back with the same. In France we believe in liberty, equality, fraternity. *La solidarité féminine*, sisterhood as well – you heard at the meeting tonight. We believe in equality of every person. Gender, religion, nationality – this means nothing. Every person is equal. Hitler does not think like this...always he lies.' She was getting angry now, even thinking of the Nazi regime, and she reverted to her native language. '*Crois-moi, tout ce qu'il t'a dit c'est des conneries.*'

'Everything he says is bullshit,' Sarah translated helpfully.

Amelie stood then and pulled on her threadbare jacket. 'Thank you for the food and the beer.'

'And thank you for your time,' said Richard. 'Politicians talk on and on, but I think your voice speaks better to the ordinary people of our country and helps them understand what's truly happening here.'

'Then will America join the war?' The question was blunt and honest, and Richard glanced at his sister and his friend. They had been asked this question often since arriving.

'I think it's looking a bit more likely than it was,' Richard said slowly, 'but the isolationists hold a lot of power, and they believe America should stay out of foreign conflicts. The attitude is that we have enough problems at home to deal with. Woodrow Wilson promised an end to wars if we did our bit the last time, and that promise feels empty now. People are disillusioned at how little the sacrifice meant, so getting the American public behind another big European war is a tough sell honestly.'

'But your article will help them to understand why they must?'

The easy thing here would be to say yes. That was what she wanted to hear. But he had to be honest. 'Our articles will try to explain how things really are, then people will make up their own minds. Our president believes that if Hitler isn't stopped somehow, then that threatens American interests, to have a powerful dictator controlling Europe, if that eventuality comes to pass. We all hope it won't of course...'

'But you will try to make the American people understand like your president understands?' Suddenly she looked much younger than he had initially judged her to be. A desperation lurked behind her eyes.

'I will try, we both will,' Richard promised.

CHAPTER 24

PARIS, FRANCE

*T*he area around the Gare du Nord in Paris was nothing like the wide open and breathtakingly beautiful boulevards of the city, nor was it quirky and arty like Montmartre, or even seedy but exciting like Pigalle. Here was where the working people of this beautiful city lived.

Constance had brought Richard and Jacob to meet her sister, Bernadette, and Bernadette's Jewish husband, Paul.

They arrived at a four-storey building in a street of identical buildings that had been subdivided into apartments. Constance brought them to the third floor and knocked on a door already slightly ajar.

'*Entrée!*' a high female voice called from inside, and they pushed open the door.

'Ah, *bonjour*, Constance – where's Alfie?' She was a pretty blond woman of ample proportions, barely five feet tall and curvy.

'Still sleeping off last night's wine,' said Constance in French.

'Ah...' She turned to Richard and Jacob. '*Je m'appelle Bernadette. S'il vous plaît, entrez, asseyez-vous.*'

'*Merci, je m'appelle Richard*,' he answered in halting French with a Savannah drawl. He'd tried to order coffee and a croissant this morning, and the woman in the café actually winced at his efforts.

And Jacob added, '*Merci de votre hospitalité*.' A bit better but not much.

However horrific it sounded to the natives, they were trying their best; Sarah had been encouraging them both to make the effort.

'You're welcome here, gentlemen. Constance has told us what you are doing, and we would like to help if we can.' It turned out that her English, though accented, was fluent, which was just as well, as Sarah had declined to come because the Dreyfuses had a newborn baby, Odile.

Sarah couldn't stand babies. As a young woman, people were always foisting their babies onto her, expecting her to know which way up to hold them and to coo at them and even change their revolting diapers. But she wasn't that sort of woman, so as she told Jacob, if he was looking to marry brood mare, he could look elsewhere.

The room was a large one and served as a kitchen, dining room and living area. It had tall, wide windows looking onto the street. The furniture was mismatched and tatty, but there was a lovely, relaxed feel to the place. Rag rugs covered the floor, and the fireplace had a huge mantle on which were several photographs, knick-knacks, books and cigarettes. There was clutter everywhere, shoes under the table that was piled with newspapers and a string hanging across the top of the room on which clothing dried. The room was scented by something that smelt sweetly delicious, and Bernadette went back to taking a tray out of the oven.

Moments later a short, balding man appeared from the corridor to the right, cradling a baby in his arms. Before they could say anything, he whispered, 'Shh...' and smiled. Bernadette crossed to him, moved the white blanket and kissed the baby's head.

'This is Odile, our daughter,' she whispered proudly. 'And last night she did not sleep for more than twenty minutes at one time, so we are both exhausted. Lucky for her we love her, otherwise she would have been thrown out of the window last night.' She laughed and ran her finger down her baby's perfect cheek. 'We take in turns to walk with her. Our neighbours' – she pointed upstairs – 'do not like babies and will complain to the owner if we are loud. Odile knows this – she is clever, our child – and she likes for us to walk with her, so she squawks and we walk.'

'And I walk her as well,' said Constance in French. 'I love her.' Unlike Sarah, she clearly didn't have a problem looking after other people's babies.

The man laid the baby in a crib by the fireplace and then extended his hand to shake theirs. 'Paul Dreyfus, nice to meet you.' He smiled, and his warm, intelligent eyes lit up. 'Now, it is eleven, so we will have coffee. Bernadette has made her special *chouqettes* and her famous *tarte aux amandes*.'

Constance made the coffee and served it in tiny cups, and Bernadette served up a cake that Richard had never tasted anything like. The buttery, almond-flavoured confection melted in the mouth. As well as the cake there were tiny little pastries with a light but creamy custard filling and pearlised sugar crunching on top.

'My wife is a *chef pâtissiere*, the best for five hundred kilometres. It is the main reason I love her,' Paul joked.

Bernadette swiped him with her tea towel.

He laughed. 'Only a little joke, *ma cherie*. I would love you if you could not fry an egg.'

'If I could not cook, we would starve, so be glad we do not have to rely on your terrible efforts at food.'

'Totally correct.' He grinned and crammed another *chouquette* in his mouth.

The baby stirred, and Bernadette rushed over to soothe her back to sleep.

'So you are writing a piece for American papers about why they should enter the war, yes?' Paul began in a whisper. His English also seemed excellent.

'We think if we just write as we see and hear it, then people at home will naturally come to realise that they have to get involved,'

Jacob explained quietly, while Richard finished his exquisite mouthful. 'Nazism is a horrible and disgusting ideology. We just have to explain it to them.'

'I think you're right…'

When Paul spoke passionately about the need to defeat Fascism, he was articulate. He punctuated his rhetoric with examples he'd seen in Germany, about what daily life was like for not just Jews but trade unionists, communists, Jehovah's Witnesses. And then he spoke of the physically and mentally disabled, how Hitler's ideas of the Aryan race did not include defects, and how people deemed flawed were of no use to the new Reich.

Richard sat listening to the two Jewish men talk and hoped what he wrote for the *Capital* would really have an effect. To them it was obvious why the world had to intervene; no expense should be spared to stop Hitler.

But neither of these men had sat at the dinner tables of the wealthy and powerful as Richard had and listened to the 'America first' rhetoric that was so popular. How often he'd heard the argument. If America was invaded by, say, Mexico, would Britain be in a rush to send men and ships and everything? And actual American boys dying in Europe was not something the mothers and fathers of the United States would agree to lightly. Roosevelt was going to have to use every power of persuasion he possessed to get America into this war in a meaningful military way, even if Hitler turned west.

'Do you think there is any chance that Hitler will be content with the expansion he has achieved so far?' he asked, picking up his pen.

Bernadette snorted. 'Satisfied? Never will he be satisfied. You can see it in his eyes.'

She had picked Odile up, who was awake now and very vocal, and was preparing to nurse her.

'Well,' Paul went on, 'she is right. Hitler has always been audacious. He annexed Austria and removed the chancellor, who was insisting on putting the Anschluss to the people. Unsurprisingly, once the Nazis controlled everything, the plebiscite showed overwhelming support for the annexation. That would most certainly not have been the outcome before. Mussolini was frightened of him, so he signed a non-aggression pact. Stalin is not scared of him, but neither one trusts the other, so a non-aggression pact there is the best option for both too. The British and the French did nothing when he marched into Austria. He fooled Daladier and Chamberlain at Munich into believing they had achieved peace by letting him take the Sudetenland, this far and no further. But what did he do then? Took the rest of Czechoslovakia, and still they did nothing. So you see, his audacity has paid off each time. He will lie into their faces, and they are stupid enough or selfish enough or scared enough to believe him.' He shrugged. 'Even when he went into Poland, claiming it was about Danzig, it was never that. He knew his opponents were weak. Britain was under-resourced and had no stomach for another war, and France was still thinking they could appease him. They foolishly don't think he will turn his panzers on us. Declaring war on him was not as devastating for Herr Hitler as the world might have thought – he cares nothing for what people outside of his precious Reich think of him.'

Richard admired the clear-eyed view Paul had of such a murky situation and took rapid notes. He'd been teaching himself Pitman shorthand, and it was proving invaluable.

'So this is perfect for him,' Paul went on. 'No threat from the east, the Siegfried Line to the west and Britain and France too nervous to do what is needed. This is why America is vital. If he is not stopped decisively and soon, the future looks very bleak indeed.'

'And what do you think of the League of Nations?' Richard asked, and Dreyfus laughed grimly.

'Does the League of Nations have an army? No. Then it is just pretty words, meaningless. The only possible thing they could do, and they won't do this, is block oil. An army can't function without oil. But they will never do that.'

'Will he invade France, do you think?'

He shrugged. 'Probably. Why would he not?'

'The Maginot Line?'

Paul Dreyfus laughed again, even more derisively. 'A defence for a different war, different technology,' he said, as Amelie had said.

'And what will you do if he does invade?' Jacob asked then.

Paul glanced at Bernadette, who was gazing lovingly at her daughter who was feeding from her breast.

'I don't know.' He sighed. 'I am outspoken, so are Bernadette and Constance. We have campaigned, spoken at rallies. We have tried to tell the people what Hitler is like, what his real ambitions are, so' – that Gallic shrug again – 'if they come, it will be for us they look first.'

CHAPTER 25

PARIS, FRANCE

*M*ay 29, 1940
In May, Belgium and Holland surrendered to a German invasion and the French army collapsed, and on the 26th of May, the British Army began to evacuate from Dunkirk.

An urgent telegram came from Kirky, ordering Richard and Jacob out of France, followed by orders from the American embassy, which threatened not to renew their papers if they stayed. They had to go.

* * *

THE GARE DU NORD was a sea of people desperate to get away from the city. The fear of bombing, the risk to Jews and anyone Hitler deemed beneath him – everyone wanted to get away. All around, people were embracing, children crying, soldiers leaving for the front, wives and girlfriends clinging to them. The cacophony was immense – the fumes from the engines, the whishtles blowing on other platforms. Faith that the French government would help or defend the people was negligible; nobody believed a word Prime Minister Paul Reynaud said any more.

The day before they left, they'd bumped into Amelie; she had heard from her mother in Strasbourg that when war was declared, in two days the French moved all of the Jews to the southwest of France and the university to Clermont-Ferrand in the Massif Central. The city was now a ghost town, with only soldiers garrisoned there inhabiting the place. The French government said they didn't fear an invasion, but why move everyone from the border if they really believed that?

Richard and Jacob had been sent tickets by Lucille, first class; Sarah bought her own, also first class, and boarded with them. Even in the first-class carriage, it was a crush as people made their way onto the train, some carrying all they owned it looked like.

They found their compartment, which had seating for four, two facing two, and stowed their bags on the rack overhead, leaving a space for another case; no doubt someone else would join them soon.

'Richard! Richard!'

Was that his name being called, in the French way, 'Reesharde'?

He peered out of the narrow window, back down the crowded platform, to see Alfie's girlfriend, Constance, pushing through the crowds all weighed down with bags and cases. The next moment she climbed on board the train, into the first-class carriage, and then appeared at the door of the compartment.

She smiled. 'I had to come to say goodbye.' She was carrying a soft brown leather bag with two worn handles, and she put it down as they all stood to hug her. Nobody was checking tickets yet, and the aisles were packed with people. 'Alfie, Paul and Bernadette all send their love.'

'Have you made up your minds yet?' He'd seen them all only two nights ago, over red wine and Bernadette's cassoulet of duck, sausage and white beans in a rich sauce, with green beans and fresh bread; Richard thought he would never again taste anything as delicious. 'What are you going to do? Are you going to leave?'

She shook her head, a determined jut to her jaw. 'No, we've

decided. We are Parisians, this is our city. We will stay and fight if we have to.'

'But Constance...' Sarah was as anxious as he was. 'It's going to be dangerous.'

'I know, but as I say, this is our city. We know it in a way that no *boche* ever will. If we do not wish to be found, so we will not be. We will leave the apartment, and...' She shrugged.

But before they had time to say anything further, ticket inspectors appeared, making their way along the aisle, checking tickets and ushering everyone without one off the train. An elegant woman with a bird in a cage squeezed into their compartment, past Constance; she placed the bird up on the rack with a cloth covering the cage and settled herself next to the window.

'I must go.' Constance reached up and kissed Richard's cheeks, one each side, and did the same for Jacob and then Sarah. '*Bon chance mes amis*, and thank you.'

'Wait.' Richard dug in his wallet and extracted a wad of US dollars. It would require some creative accounting on their part to explain, but he didn't care. The dire warnings that the expenses were not to be spent on alcohol, or women, or alcohol for women rang in his ears. He'd figure something out, even if he had to supplement it himself. 'Take this.'

Constance didn't hesitate. '*Merci*,' she said, nodding and placing the money in an inside pocket of her coat.

He longed to do something else that would protect this brave girl, but there was nothing. He was insulated, being an American, but Constance and Alfie, like all the other Parisians, would have to stay and face what was coming...or try to flee, but where was there to go?

She hugged them one last time and was gone.

The crowds on the platform were a mixture of people waving, some wiping tears, others in stoic dry-eyed silence, watching as the train pulled out to the Gare de Nord in Paris, the passengers leaving the City of Light, having no idea what kind of city they would return to, if they ever would.

Jacob took pictures as he always did, out of the window, catching the myriad of human emotion as the train gathered speed. Richard took out his notebook, capturing smells, sounds, images that he would use later to paint a vivid picture of this scene. He was where history was being made, here in Paris, France, just before Hitler's jackbooted soldiers marched on the city. This was something he would remember all his life, he knew it.

As he searched his vocabulary for a word, something that would sum up a combination of grief, fear of the unknown and despair, he lowered his head into his hands. And then he saw it, the brown leather bag with two worn handles, poking out from under his seat.

'Wait, no… Constance left her bag. Damn!'

'Too late,' said Sarah, looking up from the book she'd begun to read, the one she'd bought for Tilly, *The Unlit Lamp*, as Jacob continued to take pictures, this time of rolling green countryside and red-roofed farms. 'Maybe we can mail it to her. Is it heavy?'

'Quite heavy.' He drew it out from under the seat.

'What's in it?'

'Books? I don't know.' He started to undo the buckles, and a lusty squawking filled the air.

CHAPTER 26

*T*here were three envelopes pinned to Odile's soft white knitted blanket. One was from Bernadette and Paul, promising to come and get the baby from them as soon as France had beaten back the Germans. The second was from Alfie asking them to deliver the baby to his sister in Ireland, with hand-drawn maps and advice about transport.

Best thing to do, he wrote, *is give her to Mam and Tilly. Tell them the truth, but tell everyone else she's my daughter. That will make her an Irish citizen just in case there's any problem with that. I know you are probably a bit shocked, but we have to go to ground, and she's a noisy little thing, as you know, so we have to send her away. Bernadette and Paul are heartbroken, but I've assured them she'll be fine. I mean, me and Constance, we're practically married, so she'll be with family, much safer. Richard, you and Sarah both have the surname Lewis, so write in 'Baby Odile Lewis' on your own passport, Richard, and travel as a married couple. I've enclosed another letter to Mam and Tilly, to explain things to them.*

The third letter was addressed to 'Mrs and Tilly O'Hare, Knocknashee', and Richard left it unopened, his mind in a whirl. Seriously? Alfie expected him to deliver this baby to Knocknashee?

Sarah was panicking. 'This can't be happening,' she kept moaning.

'We're on one of the last trains out of the city for Calais, with someone else's baby? What the hell are we going to do with her? Richard, do something, stop her crying...'

Odile wasn't just squawking now; she was howling lustily. Richard tried to pass her to his sister, who recoiled, and then to Jacob, who also flinched away, and then tried rocking her on his chest. Thankfully she stopped crying, her fat little cheek pressed against his coat as she chewed her tiny fists.

He peered over her downy head into the bag; there were three bottles of milk, a big tin of powdered milk, some folded towelling squares and several changes of clothes.

'I think she's hungry. Pass me a bottle, Sarah.'

Sarah passed him one of the bottles from the bag, and he uncapped it and stuck the nipple in the baby's mouth.

To his relief she sucked it furiously until it was all gone, and when it was finished, she relaxed in his arms and settled again. He looked up with a proud smile to find the woman with the birdcage staring at him from her seat by the window.

'*Ta fille?*' she asked doubtfully. She had very short hair, almost cropped to her scalp, and wore a black turtleneck sweater and huge pearl earrings; her bony hands were adorned with rings. She turned to Sarah, who was huddled defensively in the opposite corner by the door, looking anything but maternal. '*Es-tu la mère?*'

'Sarah, whatever she's asking you, explain it somehow,' begged Richard.

'Oh God... OK...' She sat up and smiled at the elegant Parisian. '*Oui, je suis la mère du bébé.*'

'*Et tu la portes toujours avec toi dans un sac?*'

'*Oui, c'est normal de porter des bébés dans un sac aux Etats Unis.*'

'What are you saying to her?' asked Jacob.

'That I'm her mother and it's normal to carry babies in a bag in America.'

Odile was wriggling and mewing. She wasn't yelling her head off like before, but she wasn't happy either and there were certain signs... 'Sarah, you have to help me. I think she needs her diaper changed.'

His sister looked horrified. 'Well, I'm not going to do it! Jacob?'

'I don't know how!' protested the photographer.

'And neither do I! Just because I'm a woman doesn't mean I was born with a diaper-changing gene. Richard, you try it.'

He frowned into the contents of the leather bag, trying to imagine what to do with those towelling squares. The bird woman glared at him again, and then at Sarah. '*Es-tu certaine que c'est son bébé?*'

Sarah smiled even more brightly. '*Cette femme était notre nounou, elle s'est toujours occupée du bébé elle-même mais maintenant elle refuse de quitter Paris avec nous et je n'ai aucune idée de ce que je fais et mon mari non plus…um…et cet autre homme n'est que le chauffeur.*'

As Richard and Jacob stared at her, she translated for their sake. 'I'm telling her that woman was our nanny, that she always took care of the baby herself but now she's refusing to leave Paris with us and I have no idea what I'm doing and neither does my husband, and that other man is just the chauffeur.'

The woman arched an eyebrow at all of them and muttered something to herself in rapid French; the only word Richard thought he recognised was *Amérique*. Then she reached for Odile and snatched her away.

For a scary moment, Richard thought the woman was going to go running off down the carriage with the baby, calling the guards for help, and Jacob must have thought the same thing because he stood up sharply, and even Sarah seemed alarmed. But instead, the woman lay Odile across her lap, using a square of muslin from the bag as a changing mat, and rummaged for a fresh napkin, a long pin, some cotton wool and a little bottle of oil.

Holding the baby with one hand on her tummy, she expertly whipped off the soiled diaper, wiped her bottom with the cotton wool and oil and deftly folded the clean square of cloth, and within seconds she had pinned it together to form a diaper.

The train journey, normally about two and a half hours, took eight, as the train kept having to stop for ages at a time. Nobody knew why, but maybe it was for the best, because at least by the time they got there, the French woman had taught Richard how to change nappies, and wind a baby when feeding her, and to make up a new bottle with boiling water, which Jacob went to beg from the station café.

Sarah was absolutely no help; she refused to have anything to do with it. And Jacob was almost as bad. He didn't mind holding Odile when she was asleep or running the odd errand, but when asked to change a diaper, he would say, 'Well, she's not *my* daughter, Mr Lewis. I'm just your chauffeur,' and laugh his head off.

CHAPTER 27

KNOCKNASHEE, CO KERRY

*J*une 1940
Grace dropped into Charlie's cottage on her way to the bus; Declan had stuck his head in earlier just as she was sitting down to lunch of home-made soup – bones from the butcher, carrots and parsnips from the school garden.

'Dad's got something to show you, Grace – come round when you're free?' He seemed happier, more light-hearted than he'd been in a while.

'I will, give me twenty minutes.'

After finishing her lunch and eating a slice of fresh soda bread slathered in home-made butter, she washed the dishes, picked up her overnight bag from where it was waiting in the hall and headed across the road, pausing only to take a deep breath of the fragrant sweet peas clustered over the gate and fence at the front of her house.

It was hard to believe that nearly six months had passed since she'd been scattering snowdrops from this garden on her sister's grave.

The McKennas were in their kitchen listening to the radio as

British Foreign Secretary Anthony Eden described the evacuation of Dunkirk. According to him four-fifths of the troops had been saved, but despite his valiant tone, this could not be seen as anything but the disaster it was.

'The British Expeditionary Force still exists, not as a handful of fugitives but as a body of seasoned veterans,' Eden intoned. 'We have had great losses in equipment. But our men have gained immeasurably in experience of warfare and in self-confidence. The vital weapon of any army is its spirit. Ours has been tried and tempered in the furnace. It has not been found wanting. It is this refusal to accept defeat that is the guarantee of final victory.'

'That's one way of looking at it, I suppose,' Charlie said, switching off the radio as the bulletin ended. 'Will you have a cuppa, Gracie?'

She sank onto a stool, still shaken. 'So Hitler is well on the way to controlling most of Europe. We never thought it would come to this.' She was struggling to absorb what she'd just heard. She prayed Richard was in America, safely away from France. How long had he said he was going for? Eight weeks? Nine at the most? He'd sailed on the second of April...so he'd be home by now.

'We'll have to watch out too that Hitler doesn't come for us next.' Declan was filing the rough edges off a cut length of copper pipe; the word had got out about his water heating machine, and now he was doing a nice sideline business, supplying them to guest houses in Dingle.

'But we're neutral. Why would he come for us?' Grace asked, still trying to absorb the latest awful news.

'So were Holland and Belgium and Luxembourg neutral. Besides, it would be just the thing for Herr Hitler to occupy land to the west of Britain as well as to the east, make them face a two-front war, like they did to the kaiser the last time.' Declan lifted the pipe and blew through it.

'Ara, that won't happen...' Charlie shook his head.

'I don't know about never.' Declan didn't share his father's confidence. 'Your man Hitler doesn't give a damn about neutrality or borders or who owns what. If he wants something, he just takes it, he's proven that.'

'Well, we'll just have to pray he doesn't come knocking for us, because we've no way of stopping him if he does. Anyway, Gracie...' After moving the kettle to the hottest plate on the range, Charlie took a letter off the shelf. 'This is what I wanted to show you. It came this morning.'

The envelope was covered with American stamps, and Grace's heart missed a beat, though she did her best to look calm and relaxed. Richard hadn't written to her since that last cold note in March. He'd sent no reply to her letter giving Alfie's address, and she'd begun to despair of ever hearing from him again.

She took the envelope and glanced at the postmark; it had taken six weeks to get to Knocknashee. Inside was a single folded sheet that enclosed two photographs.

At the top of the sheet, in very neat cursive script, was written *12 Sea View Terrace, Rockaway Beach, New York.*

Torn between disappointment at it not being from Richard and happiness for Charlie that the Maheadys had written to him, Grace read on.

Dear Mr. McKenna,

We were delighted to meet your son, Declan, this April. Lily and Ivy very much enjoyed spending time with their cousin and have talked about nothing else since. Lily especially says she would love to come to Ireland one day. Of course this seems very unlikely with the war, and who knows what the shape of the world will be after it ends, whenever that might be.

We're so sad for you, Mr. McKenna, that you were too ill to come to America with Declan, although we were pleased to meet Miss Fitzgerald. I enclose two photographs that I thought you might like to see.

Joey, Lily and Ivy send their best wishes for your speedy recovery, and Joey wants me to tell you that you have a fine son. But I'm sure you know that already. You must be as proud of him as we are of both our daughters.

Hopefully one day we will all meet together.

Yours,

Sylvia Maheady

Grace looked at the enclosed photos and smiled. One was of both the girls, Lily pushing Ivy on the garden swing, and the second was of Lily by herself, with a medal around her neck, beaming into the camera.

'She's the head cut off my Maggie,' Charlie said, his voice husky with emotion, as he set a mug of tea in front of Grace, then stayed behind her to stare over her shoulder, his hand resting on her back. 'The same hair, same eyes, same everything. Sure Maggie was only a bit older than Lily is now when I met her first.'

'She's such a lovely girl, Dad, so full of life and fun,' said Declan, looking up from his polishing with a smile.

His father nodded and swallowed. 'Letting her there is the best thing, I know 'tis, but it's hard that I never got to lay my own eyes on her.'

'Of course it is. She's your child, Charlie. Yours and poor Maggie's, God rest her,' said Grace, placing her hand on his. 'And you never know, maybe someday she will sit here at this table, like Sylvia says.'

'Maybe, but either way, I won't hate anyone.'

Grace could only nod and hand him back his letter. Tears brimmed in his eyes, and her heart broke for him, but she was also glad Sylvia Maheady had sent the photos. After their talk on the beach, she had a feeling the Italian woman guessed that the McKennas were related by blood in some way to her adopted daughter, so it was brave of her to write.

She slowly sipped her tea and admired Declan's metalwork, and then realised it was time to go. It was a quarter to two, and it would take her a good seven minutes to walk to the bus stop, especially as she had an overnight bag with her.

She and Tilly were going to Dingle for the day, catching the two o'clock bus, and they would eat fish and chips and visit the shops and maybe even scandalise the locals by having a beer in a pub. Grace didn't like beer – she'd discovered that on the journey to America – so she always had a lemonade, but Tilly liked to make waves, so she had taken to ordering a pint of Guinness for herself. Not even a half, which while still outrageous was more fitting for a woman.

They planned to stay over in the boarding house with the friendly landlady who was always delighted to give them a room in exchange for two jars of Tilly's honey and three loaves of Mrs O'Hare's soda bread, and they would come back on the bus the next day.

Declan walked her to the door, and as she was going, said, 'Is the dress new?'

'It is,' she said, and he smiled shyly and said nothing more.

The little village square, with the huge tree the children loved to climb, was full of her pupils. They all waved and shouted hello as she walked past, shouting, 'You look lovely, Miss Fitz!'

She laughed as she waved back to them. 'Thank you!'

They were used to seeing her in her headmistress clothes, a long dark skirt and buttoned-up blouse, but today she was wearing the dress that Dymphna had made her for her birthday, which was beautiful, far too nice to wear to school.

She'd been worried at first when the priest's new housekeeper showed her the lovely fabric she planned to use – a deep red with tiny white flowers – because Agnes had always said red was too flashy a colour for a lady and that besides, Grace could never wear red with her red hair. But Dymphna said that was rubbish and that anyway Grace's hair wasn't red, it was a beautiful rich copper, and that Grace would see how well red suited her when she had the dress on. Dymphna's confidence had greatly increased since she'd started minding the two priests instead of minding Agnes – they were always saying how much they loved her cooking, Father Iggy was getting as round as ever, and even the rake-thin Father Lehane had colour in his face these days.

And the finished dress was, Grace had to admit, lovely on her. It had a white collar and was fitted around her waist, and Dymphna had made the flared skirt long enough to hide the calliper. There wasn't anything to be done about her built-up black shoe, but at least from the feet up she looked passable.

Or maybe more than passable? Maybe, actually, quite nice?

After getting dressed that morning, she'd allowed herself a moment to admire her reflection in the mirror – something else poor

Agnes would have been horrified by – then brushed her hair and tied it back in a low bun, though some copper corkscrew curls escaped around her neck. Then she'd taken a little box out of the drawer by her bed.

Tilly had made her buy a lipstick the last time they were in Dingle. A lady in one of the shops was giving samples and insisted Grace try one, and Tilly decided she should buy it. It was a lovely coral colour. She'd never worn lipstick in her life apart from that one day, but she thought she might, just for today. She had it in her bag.

Tilly wasn't at the bus stop yet, and the walk had been quicker than she thought it would be. Her leg was so much better these days, nowhere near as sore as it had been; the bathing and exercises were really paying off.

Seán O'Connor was standing in the door of his pub, looking up and down the street. 'How's our big adventurer?' he asked as Grace set down her bag at the bus stop.

'Great altogether, Mr O'Connor,' Grace replied. Her travels in America were still the subject of much talk in Knocknashee, and there was no point in disavowing her neighbours of her worldliness; she and Declan had been so much further than anyone in the place.

There were another few minutes until the bus would arrive, if by some miracle it was on time, which almost never happened. Bobby Spillane, the driver, was a hard man to get out of bed, and even if he did get up, he was known to pop into the odd funeral house midroute to pay his respects – or in other words, to finagle a glass of whiskey.

The tantalising aroma of fresh toffee wafted out of Bríd Butler's sweetshop next door, so she decided to use the time to buy some for the journey.

'Well, you look lovely in that dress, Miss Fitz. Would that be American fashion then?' Bríd asked as she bagged up four ounces of the still-warm toffee.

'It is, Mrs Butler. I brought Dymphna back a magazine, and she made this for my birthday.'

'Oh, I'd say America is only smashing, with all the style and the cars and the Hollywood stars and all. And would the buildings in New York be twice as high as ours, Miss Fitz?'

'At least twice, Mrs Butler.' She didn't bother telling her that Hollywood was on the other side of the country, so it wasn't commonplace to see Clark Gable or Bette Davis roaming about on Fifth Avenue. The memory of the city always brought Brendan McGinty to mind, and she smiled at the thought of her time with him.

The sweetshop owner shook her head at the idea. 'I wonder how they stay up at all.'

Back out on the cobbled street, the bus stop was still empty except for her bag sitting there. A little further down the road, Peggy Donnelly was out hanging up some of her pastel cardigans from the awning of her shop; they were going like hotcakes now that the weather was nicer. 'You look beautiful, Miss Fitz,' she called out. 'That colour is perfect on you.'

'Thank you, Mrs Donnelly.' Grace coloured but was pleased. Peggy Donnelly had good taste – Grace had one of her silky-soft white cardigans in her overnight bag – so maybe Bríd Butler hadn't just been being polite. It was an unusual sensation to be admired.

Pádraig O Sé appeared in the doorway of his cobbler's shop, his wild hair looking more stuck on than ever. 'Who's looking beautiful?' he sneered, and Grace braced herself for him to pass one of his horribly rude remarks, probably about how a redhead like her should never wear red, that would bring her back down to earth. But instead he looked her up and down and merely grunted before going back inside.

Peggy Donnelly met Grace's eyes and grinned in amusement at the idea that Pádraig O Sé for once in his life had found nothing negative to say.

A loud whishtle pierced the sunny air. 'Since when did Rita Hayworth move to Knocknashee?' called Tilly in her strong, confident voice as she strode up the cobbled street. She nudged Grace teasingly as they walked back to the bus stop together. 'You're a knockout. Brendan McGinty was right.'

Grace had confided in her friend about her admirer in New York, and Tilly had been very kind. 'Isn't that what I've been telling you for years, Grace? You are lovely. Everyone but you sees it. I'm glad you didn't stay there, but if not Brendan McGinty, then someone else will catch your eye, Miss Fitz, you mark my words.'

A small crowd had gathered at the bus stop by the time they reached it. Buses were so important now that petrol rationing was strictly enforced. Clergymen, doctors, vets and commercial travellers all had special petrol allowances, but there was no point in most people even thinking of going anywhere by car. The teacher's union had begged for teachers to be included in the special arrangement, but even they were denied. The master out at Ballyferriter had to cycle fifteen miles every morning to school, rain, hail or snow.

Biddy O'Donoghue of the grocer's was in the queue, with a small suitcase beside her. She was off to visit her sister in Dingle, and for once she'd managed to get her husband, Tom, to stay home to mind the shop instead of him finding an excuse to sneak off to Cork, where rumour had it he got up to all sorts with the ladies.

'We got a letter from the Department this morning to prepare for rationing of foodstuffs,' she complained to Grace and Tilly as they waited with her. 'From Seán Lemass himself, if you don't mind. That auld misery Churchill tried to bully Dev, tried to get him onto their side, and when we refused, he decided to make us pay.'

Biddy O'Donoghue had a deep dislike of Winston Churchill. She, like many others, never forgave him for sending the dreaded Black and Tans to Ireland during the War of Independence. And for pressuring Michael Collins to sign the Anglo-Irish Treaty of 1921, effectively dividing the country.

'If the cat had kittens, Biddy O'Donoghue would blame Churchill,' Charlie was often heard to quip.

So much of the Irish agriculture industry relied on British imports of feed and fertiliser, so they did hold a lot of the cards, and it was true that Churchill was furious over Ireland's neutral status. He seemed to have no understanding whatsoever that Ireland couldn't ally itself to a nation that had subjugated and tortured the people for eight centuries. It was a typical British response, that Ireland should just forget the past and step up to 'do the right thing', as they saw it.

'At least Dev got the treaty ports back. Imagine if the British Navy were using Irish ports?' John O'Shea, a local farmer who was also waiting for the bus, interjected. 'Hitler would blow us all to smithereens.'

Grace had taught the children, John's son Mikey included, how the ports of Cobh, Lough Swilly and Berehaven had been retained by Britain under the Anglo-Irish Treaty but that Mr de Valera had negotiated their return with Neville Chamberlain and that this was very good for Ireland because it meant the country could be truly neutral.

'Ah, Chamberlain is not the worst. A bit of a gom, believing that little maggot Hitler over in Munich when he said that he was going to behave himself, not like that other *looder...*' Biddy grumbled. Nobody was in any doubt who she meant.

'So what's going to be rationed, Mrs O'Donoghue?' Grace asked.

'Everything, I'd say. Meat, tea, butter, sugar, everything. Tough times are coming for us all, but we'll survive, like we always do...'

The crowd waiting for the bus muttered and looked none too pleased at this new development, but nobody was surprised. So much of the produce came from England, and so if Churchill wanted to punish Ireland, he was going the right way about it.

'Sure you were lucky to get to go when you did, Miss Fitz. It looks like we're all going to be affected much more than we thought by the Emergency,' said Nóirín Dunne who was carrying a small toddler. She still looked thin, but she'd recovered from her time in hospital in Tralee; it hadn't been the consumption after all, just a bad infection after childbirth.

'I think we are,' Grace agreed. Thinking of what Declan had said earlier, though, about Hitler maybe invading, she thought things wouldn't be too bad if the whole thing would just stop at rationing.

The bus finally came around the corner at the end of the street by the parochial house and stopped outside O'Connor's pub and undertakers. Everyone gathered their belongings and stood back as the passengers alighted, most of them familiar faces from neighbouring villages like Dún Chaoin.

There were only two strangers, the last to get off, making their way awkwardly from the back of the bus. One was a tall, blond man carrying a small white bundle, and the other was a slight, dark fellow in horn-rimmed glasses who was grappling with all the rest of their luggage.

The one carrying the bundle got off first, holding it very carefully, as if it was fragile. Bobby Spillane helped down the other fellow, who was struggling with two duffel bags, a huge camera case and a brown leather holdall, all of which were very scuffed and had clearly seen a lot of travelling.

As the blond man scanned the crowd, smiling slightly, the locals stared back at him with unashamed curiosity, forgetting their hurry to be on the bus.

And Grace grabbed Tilly's arm, unable to speak.

A moment later the young man's eyes met hers and widened. He took a step towards her, moving the bundle from being cradled in the crook of his arm to resting against his shoulder. He towered over her – he must be about six foot tall, it seemed – and with the high afternoon sun behind him, shining in his thick blond hair, she thought he looked like an angel.

'Hello, Grace,' he said, in a soft American drawl. 'I'm Richard Lewis, and I know we've not been introduced, but I'm sure I've seen your photograph…'

Grace gazed up at him and opened her mouth to speak, but no sound came out.

A moment later Tilly stuck out her hand and said loudly, 'Mr Lewis, you're welcome to Knocknashee. Excuse my friend here – I think she's a bit surprised to see you. I'm Tilly O'Hare.'

'Well, this is ideal at least. You must be Alfie's sister.' The smaller man with the horn-rimmed glasses dropped his bags and shook Tilly's hand vigorously, ignoring Grace. 'Richard, this is great. Let's get out of here. We can take this bus on to Dingle instead of waiting for the next, and we'll be much more sure of getting the last train to Cork for the boat.'

'Jacob, quit being ugly,' said Richard Lewis, laughing, his gaze still resting on Grace's face. 'We'll be fine waiting for the next bus. Grace – it is Grace, isn't it? – this is my friend Jacob Nunez. He's having himself a hissy fit about how long it took us to get here.'

'Oh, just give her the baby.' The dark-haired man took the bundle from Richard's arms and handed it straight to Tilly, leading her away from the fascinated crowd. Grace and Richard followed, and Bobby started encouraging his passengers onto the bus.

'What on earth?' Tilly looked down at the sleeping child.

'It's a girl, eight weeks, name's Odile Dreyfus, also known as Odile Lewis, your brother's niece…'

'My brother's…*what*?' Tilly looked down, utterly bewildered, at the little white bundle in her arms, which was beginning to wriggle and squawk. 'Oh my God, Grace, look, it's a baby…'

'Of course it's a baby. I told you, she's Alfie's niece. Well, she will be once he marries her aunt. That's why he's sent her to you. You should take this as well,' said the man, handing Tilly the leather holdall. 'It's got all the baby stuff and a letter from your brother explaining every-thing… Well, I assume it does. I haven't read it. Oh, and there's this…' He opened one of the duffel bags, pulled out a book called *The Unlit Lamp* and stuffed it into a corner of the holdall. 'Can you manage all that? Perfect. Richard, please stop staring at that woman. Let's get this bus while it's still here. Remember how many buses we've had to wait hours for just to get here and some of them never turning up at all?' He added with an eye roll to Tilly, 'We were planning to get here four days ago, but it's been hell. Easier in France with the Germans coming. Of course they're there now. *Richard!*'

'Jacob,' said Richard firmly, still looking at Grace. 'We're not just going to rush off again, so forget it.'

'But it's the last boat! If we miss the train, we'll miss the boat and we'll never get back to America!'

'Don't worry about that, gentlemen,' said Bobby Spillane, who like everyone else had been watching the free show in fascination. 'Everyone here will tell you that I'm never late.'

'You were late today!' snapped Jacob.

'That is a *very* rare occurrence. It was to do with a car coming the other way on the road,' said the bus driver, bristling.

The baby was beginning to whimper now, and Richard broke eye contact with Grace for the first time since he'd set eyes on her, turning to speak to the baby in Tilly's arms. 'Shush, shush, shush, little girl...' he murmured soothingly, running his finger down her soft cheek. 'Could we go somewhere, Grace? I think Odile needs feeding.'

'Oh... Yes... Of course, yes, of course. Come over to my house. You must be famished. I have soup and bread.' Grace had finally found her voice. 'It's just up the street.'

'Of course it is. I feel like I know the place like the back of my hand already. Come on, Jacob, grab all our stuff. Mr Spillane, we'll see you at six on the dot.'

And under the astonished gaze of the inhabitants of Knocknashee, Richard Lewis and Grace Fitzgerald walked side by side up the road to the house next to the school, trailed by Jacob Nunez carrying two duffel bags and his camera case, and Tilly O'Hare with Odile in her arms.

CHAPTER 28

'"*D*ear Mam and Tilly",' read Tilly to the assembled company in Grace's sitting room. Mrs O'Hare was there as well now; Declan had gone for her on his bike and brought her back in the horse and cart.

'"Odile is the daughter of Bernadette, my fiancé Constance's sister, and her husband, Paul Dreyfus. He's Jewish, so there isn't any chance of him getting papers to get out of France, and Bernadette wouldn't leave without him, and Constance wouldn't leave without Bernadette, and so we're all staying in France to fight.'"

'Oh, St Anthony in heaven, that young fella will be the death of me, I swear he will,' groaned Mrs O'Hare, shaking her head. 'Why does he want to be fighting with your man Hitler? That man is…well, he's a… he's a right nasty yoke.' It was the worst insult she could come up with for the German dictator.

'He is, Mam, a right nasty yoke,' agreed Tilly. 'And we'll just have to hope Alfie survives him like he survives everything else.' She went back to reading the letter aloud. '"So if you wouldn't mind looking after Odile while I'm busy at that, I'll see you after the war. If it's easier to say she's my daughter, do that, in case there's any problems with paperwork or citizenship or anything. I'll leave it up to you. So thanks, both of you, and Mam, I know you'll do a great job. You did a great job with me, didn't you? Ha, ha. Well, Constance thinks so anyway. Don't be worrying, Mam, I'm like a cat I've so many lives. There's no fear of me. Love, Alfie.'"

The baby was sleeping quietly in Mary O'Hare's arms, in the armchair by the fire; the old woman seemed to be the only person apart from Richard who could settle the fractious little girl.

'She really has taken a shine to you, Mam,' Tilly said as she put Alfie's letter aside and went to bend over the baby. 'So you see, blood isn't always thicker than water when it comes to children, no more than it is with Marion's six stepchildren, who she loves as much as her own.'

'I suppose you're right.' Mary nodded as she gently rocked the sleeping baby. 'And I can see it's meant to be, God wills it, you and Grace being the first people these two men set eyes on in Knocknashee after bringing the poor *leanbh* all the way to us from France, without a woman to help them.'

'Well, we did have my sister with us as far as England,' said Richard honestly.

'Not that she was any help,' corrected Jacob.

'And there was a lady on the train as far as Calais who showed me how to change a diaper and make a bottle. Just as well – what I know about babies could fit on the back of a stamp,' Richard added, with another of his enchanting smiles at Grace.

She smiled back at him while trying not to stare like a lunatic. He had a beautiful mouth, even white teeth, tanned skin, blond hair – he was ten times as gorgeous in real life as he was in his photos. His accent was like honey, slow and drawling and deep. She could listen to him all day.

'But we were completely on our own from Dover, Mrs O'Hare,' said Jacob, who was clearly still traumatised by the whole thing. 'Sarah had to get her own boat back to the States. It's hard to get out of Europe these days, so our newspaper got us tickets. Sarah had to take whatever one she could. We had to get a train to London and then to Wales and the boat over to Dublin, and then we got a variety of vehicles to get here. It took days and days.'

'You didn't do too bad, to be fair to ye, for a pair of *garsúns* who never held a baby.' The old woman chuckled. 'She's still alive anyway.'

As if on cue, Odile let out her high-pitched screech, and Mary laughed as she cradled her in her arms.

'*Céad míle fáilte go* Knocknashee, Odile. You are very welcome here, and we'll get along fine the two of us.' She took a silver coin from the deep pocket of her skirt and placed it gently in the baby's fist, closing her tiny fingers around it.

'Oh, she doesn't need... I can send you money for her upkeep, of course, and I'll leave you some now as well,' Richard said quickly.

He was sitting on the sofa beside Grace, and she put her hand on his arm; it felt like a natural gesture. 'She's hanselling the baby, don't stop her,' she said quietly.

'She's what?' asked Jacob, staring over from where he was sitting on a low stool, eating yet another slice of bread piled high with butter. The two Americans had been famished – they'd been living on very scant rations – so Grace had served up the rest of her soup along with soda bread and home-made butter, and both of them had declared that they had never, ever tasted butter that good.

'It's an old tradition,' Grace explained to Jacob, 'to give a baby a silver coin when you first meet them. It brings them good fortune.'

'Well, she's sure gonna need that, because she's gotten off to a real rocky start.'

'And don't worry about sending money, Richard,' said Tilly proudly. 'We can manage. We live simply here, but people are kind. Nobody is on their own in Knocknashee, and this child is our family, so everyone will mind her.'

'I can see that,' said Richard, smiling as he looked around the room. A scramble around the village meant that within two hours, Odile had a new crib, plenty of napkins and clothes, spare bottles, a highchair, rattles and soft toys. Dymphna had found an old pushchair in their shed that Tommy had made when their children were babies. It was a bit rusty and worse for wear, but Declan had said he'd clean it up and have it ready by the morning.

Declan had made himself very useful collecting everything – including Mrs O'Hare – but he'd gone now, saying there were too many in the room and the child would get unsettled. Grace thought it was more that the presence of Richard had made him very awkward, the way he could be around strange people. There was such a contrast between the shy, dark Irishman with the azure eyes and pale skin and the big, golden American with the warm, confident smile.

'So is it true what your friend is saying, Mr Lewis, that you really have to go on the six o'clock bus?' Mrs O'Hare asked him, settling the baby again. 'And you only just got here?'

Richard nodded, with a lingering, regretful glance at Grace. 'We do. We have passage booked on a ship out of Cork tomorrow morning, but our office in New York had to pull all kinds of strings. Civilian travel is more or less stopped now for all but complete emergencies. If we miss it... Well, we can't miss it.'

Grace gazed back at him, keeping her face calm and smiling. Her poker face. Inside, she had a tight feeling in her chest, a churning in her stomach. Sensations she had never experienced before were flooding her body. Something hard to define but so powerful, and a knowledge that she never wanted to let this man go.

'Of course you can't miss it.' She smiled.

'But is that Bobby Spillane as reliable as he says he is?' asked Jacob, his mouth full of bread and butter again. 'He smelled of whiskey to me.'

'Ah, ye'll make it. Someone's looking after ye from above to get ye this far.' Mary winked.

'I'll tell you what, Grace,' said Tilly suddenly. She was standing with her back to the empty fireplace, and she'd been very quiet this past while, looking at Grace and Richard sitting beside each other on the sofa, a little distance between them. 'Why don't you take Richard down the strand and show him where you threw the bottle in all that time ago.'

'But he's only an hour, Tilly, and I walk so slow...'

'Sure the bus goes by there. Bobby can pick him up on his way to Dingle.'

'I would love that, if it's all right with you, Grace?' said Richard hesitantly, getting to his feet and offering Grace his hand to stand.

'Great idea, I'll take some photos.' Jacob was also on his feet, reaching for his camera.

'No, sorry, you can't go as well,' said Tilly sharply, in her most commanding voice.

The photographer looked at her, startled. 'Why – what?'

'You need to bring the luggage on the bus.'

'I could carry it to the beach...'

'But Mr Nunez, you'll miss out on a plate of my rhubarb crumble with fresh cream straight out of the cow.' Mary O'Hare smiled brightly at him.

'Let you sit there, Jacob, and I'll bring it right out to you,' added Tilly, with a wink.

The photographer hesitated, then sighed and sat down again. 'Mrs O'Hare, you and your daughter are both hard women to argue with. I can see Odile is going to be brought up just fine.'

* * *

As they walked through the town, she pointed out to him every landmark that he already knew from her letters and brought him up to date on every story. The shops were closing up now, but every shopkeeper was out sweeping his or her step like it couldn't be clean enough, and fascinated children peered down from tree in the town square.

'This will give the town something to gossip about for a month,' she murmured, with a sideways smile. 'You have to be the most exciting thing to have ever happened here.'

He laughed. 'It's exciting for me too. I can't believe I'm here, actually here in Knocknashee.'

'I can't believe you're really here either. I just can't take it in.' She felt so mesmerised by him. It made her feel stupid, like he could have

259

been reading the shipping forecast and she would be hanging on his every word.

'And you, your house, Knocknashee – it's all even better than I imagined.'

She winced apologetically. 'I was so afraid you'd think us...well, a bit backwards, not modern like America is. We don't even have electricity.'

He smiled his beautiful smile down at her, linking her arm with his, helping her walk steadily. 'I find it delightful, and I find you delightful.'

She willed herself to look calmly amused, to treat it as the light-hearted, throwaway remark it so obviously was. 'I think you're fairly delightful too.'

'Yeah, it honestly feels like I've gotten to that place over the rainbow or something, that rainbow Judy Garland sings about...'

'That's what I've always thought about where *you* live!' she exclaimed. But then she cringed; she was behaving like an imbecile. She thought she really must stop agreeing with everything this man said.

'By the way, that photograph didn't do you justice,' he added in a lower voice, looking intently down into her face. 'You have the greenest eyes, with flecks of gold, and I love your hair, it's like copper, and your skin...'

'You look better in real life too...' As soon as she heard the words come out of her mouth, she was ready to die of embarrassment. At this rate he would think her mind was as twisted as her leg. And she was horribly, acutely aware of how twisted that was as she limped along beside him.

He laughed, a lovely rumbling sound, clearly assuming she'd said it as a joke.

Oh God, that laugh...so deep. He was so...well, male. She had other men friends, of course, Charlie and Declan and Father Iggy, but none of them seemed as manly as Richard.

She pulled her eyes away from him. 'Oh look, there's Father Iggy!'

She waved, and so did Richard, and the little priest waved back at them from the door of the church, the sun glinting off his huge round glasses.

'I see he's put on weight again,' said Richard approvingly.

'He has. And there's the hill – up there is the graveyard where Agnes is buried with our parents, and beyond is Tilly's farm...'

All the rest of the way, she prattled on, desperate not to give her emotions away.

* * *

At Trá na n-Aingeal – the beach of the angels, as she explained to him – she led him to the big flat rock where she normally had her picnics with Tilly. The gulls cawed overhead, and puffy white clouds scudded across the Kerry sky as the warm summer sun glistened on the azure sea.

He sat beside her on the grey slab, a foot apart. 'So is this the exact spot you threw the bottle in?'

'I think it was more over there.' She pointed out the rocks where as usual the seals lay sunning themselves. 'And I came down every day for weeks for fear it would be washed up and Agnes would find out about it. Now look what I have...' She pulled the bag of toffee out of her pocket. 'They're a bit squashed and not warm any more, but they're another thing from your dream, Bríd Butler's toffee.'

He smiled as he reached into the paper bag, taking a toffee. 'Mm... Talking about dreams... Do you know, I thought I saw you in New York? In the rain, on the quay, while I was walking to my ship.'

She blinked at him, finding it hard to believe her ears. 'No... But... Seriously? That's so strange. That happened to me, I thought the same... On the quay, in the rain... But it wasn't possible, you'd sailed on the second.'

He looked equally bewildered. 'No, our ship was delayed by nine days. But yours wasn't due until the twelfth?'

She stared at him. 'We made good time. We were one day early.'

'My God.' Sitting up, he ran his hands fiercely through his thick blond hair. 'Do you think...' And then he looked away to the ocean and laughed, almost bitterly. 'Isn't that great? A few seconds on that side of the Atlantic…a few hours on this… Would you think that means we're fated to meet or to keep missing each other?'

'To meet, I hope?' Her voice came out all foolish and weak. Ugh, she was doing it again, mindlessly repeating his words. She gave herself a shake. He was from a different world.

He grinned ruefully. 'I guess so. I hope, by the way, that you had a wonderful time in New York with Declan, and he seems like a nice guy.'

'We did. It was amazing. And thank you for all the detective work you did.'

He looked at her, a slight sadness in his face. 'Sure, it was my pleasure.'

She closed her eyes and squeezed her hands, getting herself calm again. *Smile, Grace, smile.* She opened her eyes, smiling.

He was looking back at her, also smiling, yet somehow frowning slightly at the same time, as if she were the most puzzling thing to him in the world.

'Richard! Richard!'

An American voice, calling across the strand. 'Richard! Hurry up! The bus is here!'

'The one time he's early, huh?' said Richard Lewis softly, looking at his expensive wristwatch.

'Just our luck.' Grace sighed, longing to throw her arms around him and not let him get on the bus.

'We're going to miss the train!'

Grace glanced towards the entrance to the strand. The bus was parked there, where Tilly usually tied up the horses, and a figure was jumping up and down, wildly waving his hands. 'Richard, you have to go.'

'In a minute. Just a minute. Look at me, Grace.'

She did, and all those unknown sensations she'd felt before, both tightness and looseness, washed through her body again. 'Richard,' she said weakly, 'you've got to go.'

'Wait.' Slowly, delicately, he reached out his hand towards her face, touched her nose, then with his fingertip traced the curve of her mouth. 'Let me just remember you, here, in this moment.'

'Richard!' screamed the voice in the background.

'All right, all right, I'm coming...' With a sigh and a careless shrug, Richard stood up off the stone and held out his hand to help Grace to her feet.

'No. I'll slow you down. You better run,' Grace said.

'You'll write, I hope?' He looked like he didn't want to go either.

'I will, of course,' she assured him.

'And next time we meet, maybe it can be for a whole day?'

She laughed. He was being light-hearted again. 'Definitely. It seems to get longer every time. Maybe by the time we're old, we'll have worked it up to a week.'

He hesitated, torn. He stood on one foot, then the other, then glanced at Jacob. Then briefly – it was infinitesimally brief – he dropped the lightest kiss on her mouth...and ran.

As he got nearer to the bus, the engine roared into life and Jacob Nunez started jumping up and down again, even more frantically. 'Come on, come on, we're going to miss the train! Run! Run!'

Grace watched from the beach as Richard sprinted to the bus and was pulled inside it, leaving her and Knocknashee behind.

EPILOGUE

DOURDAN FOREST, FRANCE

JULY 1940

The woman placed her hand ever so slowly across her mouth, terrified the slightest movement would alert them overhead, but also worried the sound of her breath would be enough to give them pause.

The crawlspace beneath the floorboards would not have accommodated her before, but mercifully she was just thin enough to squeeze in. She'd lost a lot of weight in recent weeks. Her breasts ached as she pressed herself flat to the earthen floor, the milk filling them painfully, each wave of pain a reminder of what she no longer had. She cast the image from her mind. She needed to stay alert to stay alive. There was no time for sentimental reminiscing or tears.

A boot rested inches from her face. She could see the highly polished leather through a missing knot in the wood. She could hear them, not just the words they spoke but every breath, every creak, every footstep. There were three of them, one senior and two junior, judging by the tone of voice. She didn't understand a word. Were they looking for someone or something, or had they just stumbled in here for shelter from the downpour?

The earthy smell of the forest filled the air, mixed with the dank odour of wet earth, rodent droppings and wood. There was nothing in the little cabin to suggest anyone lived here now. Whoever had once stayed in this home was long gone, their few possessions probably loaded onto a cart as Parisians departed the city ahead of the German invasion.

She'd slept on the one remaining damp mattress last night.

Their voices were low and genial, no barked orders. They dragged the two kitchen chairs that were in the cabin across the floor, and she heard them creak as they bore weight. One of them lit a cigarette; she could smell the tobacco. She was sure they could hear her heart thumping in her chest. Sweat cooled between her shoulder blades as she lay face down. How long would they stay? How long could she lie here like this?

A tickle in her throat. Panic. *Do not cough.* She didn't even dare swallow. She forced the cough to abate by sheer willpower. She would not get caught. Not today. She would survive. She had to. She was needed. Her child needed her. She ignored the pain in her shoulder, stiff from being held in one position for so long.

The rain drummed relentlessly for what felt like an eternity as they chatted, their conversation occasionally punctuated by a laugh. She was sure they could hear her stomach growling – hunger threatened to give her away – but they seemed relaxed and comfortable, not on the lookout. Eventually the men rose. The chairs scraped on the floorboards again, a fine dust falling between the cracks right in front of her face, the floorboard itself dipping under the weight of a man, pressing on her right buttock. She held her breath.

Maybe the shower had eased off. A boot crushed the butt of the cigarette as they made for the door. It creaked on its hinges, the wood stiff and swollen from the wet weather. She moved her stiff arm down slightly, her shoulder rubbing the underside of the floorboard.

All movement stopped.

She heard one of them ask, *'Was war das? Hast du etwas gehört?'*

<u>*The End*</u>

IF YOU ENJOYED THIS BOOK, and I sincerely hope you did, you will be happy to hear the next book in this series, History's Pages, is available - here.

If you would like to join my readers club, to get a free novel to download, access to my weekly letters, sneak previews of books in the works and the occasional special offer, then pop over to www.jean grainger.com and sign up. It's 100% free and always will be and you can unsubscribe any time.

To get a sneak preview of the next book, read on!

History's Pages

The Knocknashee Story - Book 3

Chapter 1

KNOCKNASHEE, CO KERRY, IRELAND

AUGUST 1940

'Now then, *a stórín,*' Grace Fitzgerald cooed softly as she laid Odile into her pram, a sturdy contraption of wood and leather that Dymphna's late husband, Tommy, had made for their two small children out of an old drawer and bicycle wheels.

Paudie and Kate O'Connell were eight and six now, and the pram had been in their turf shed for the last few years, but Declan McKenna, her fellow teacher, had cleaned off the rust, and Pádraig O

Sé, the cobbler, had donated a fresh piece of leather for the rain cover where the old one got cracked with the bad frost last winter, and Dymphna had made new cushions.

'We're going for a nice sunny walk to meet your Aintín Tilly off the bus,' Grace continued as she tucked the bag of bottles and napkins and clean folded baby clothes into the foot of the pram. 'And she'll take you back to the farm, where your Mamó Mary will be delighted to have you home again.'

Grace's best friend, Tilly, had gone to see her sister, Marion, in Dublin, and Mary O'Hare's rheumatism was very bad at the moment, so Grace had been minding the baby for a few nights. Having the company of another human being in the house, even one as small as Odile, had been lovely. Since Dymphna O'Connell left to be house-keeper to the priests, the place could seem very empty during the day. And even Agnes, bitter as she had been, was another person in the house at night, but now there was nobody. She wasn't nervous – Charlie and Declan McKenna were just across the road, and her neighbours all were close by – but it did feel lonely at times.

She sighed. 'I'm going to be lost without you, Odile.'

Odile gurgled, smiled gummily up at her and waved her tiny fists. Her blue eyes had turned to brown, and her fair hair was darkening too. At four months old, the sturdy Parisian baby was thriving in Knocknashee and showed no signs that being dragged halfway across Europe in a leather bag and landed in the southwest of Ireland had taken the slightest toll on her.

Grace laughed. 'I know, a stór, life is good and I shouldn't complain.'

Straightening up from fixing the baby's blankets, she caught her own reflection in the hallstand mirror. The summer sun had lightly tanned her skin and added threads of gold to her flame-red curls, which tumbled below her shoulders now that Agnes wasn't here to say she was 'making a show of herself' by letting it hang loose. And her new dress of emerald-green cotton was the exact colour of her eyes.

She'd made it herself. Peggy Donnelly at the draper's had slipped her six yards of the material with a wink and a nod, well outside the rationing restrictions, so she'd been able to cut the skirt long enough to hide her right leg, which was shrunken by polio. Everyone said the dress looked very smart on her.

She'd first worn it when she turned twenty in June, at a little party for her birthday that her friends gave her. Dymphna O'Connell had brought a lemon cake, which she'd saved up her sugar ration to ice, and Tilly arrived with a whole honeycomb in a wooden box and a cream lamb's wool cardigan knitted by her mother. Father Iggy presented her with a pretty silver cross on a delicate chain, Charlie McKenna brought her a rose bush for her front garden, and Declan gave her a book about the Aztecs and told her she looked lovely in green.

After that she'd only worn the dress for Sunday Mass, taking it off the moment she was home. But lately she'd had a thought. She wasn't likely to be going anywhere fancy, well, ever, so she might as well wear it on other days also and get the good of it.

She had new shoes as well. Dr Hugh Warrington, her polio consultant in Cork, had sent her a calliper he'd ordered from England, and it was lighter and less cumbersome than the last one he'd found her, so she'd asked Pádraig O Sé to make her a different pair of shoes to go with it, of soft blue leather instead of stiff ugly black. The right shoe still had to be built up and had holes in the heel into which to slot the steel, but they were comfortable and looked quite nice.

She left the house, pushing the pram down the stone path. The light sea breeze off the ocean was lovely and warm, and fragrant with the scent of the sweet peas clustered over the fence and the rose bush Charlie had planted in the corner. The bush covered the patch where Agnes had burnt their parents' things, leaving a scorch mark on the wall.

Through the gate from her garden into the schoolyard, she could see Patrick O'Flynn, a lanky, freckled twelve-year-old with ears that stuck out like a toby jug, sitting on the steps of the schoolhouse; he was earning a few pennies by watching his father's six skinny mountain sheep as they ate down the grass and weeds, getting the place ready for when school started again. Ned the pony kept the grass short in the field behind, but the playground was better cropped right down. Mountain sheep were the best for that, though they needed watching like hawks; they were right divils for leaping walls.

Eileen, Patrick's mother, had stopped Grace after devotions last Sunday night to thank her for giving him the job and letting the sheep have the grass in the yard. With eleven children and only three small rocky fields, everything was scarce in the O'Flynn house. The two oldest girls had gone into service as soon as they turned fifteen, one with Dr Ryan and another with an old lady in Dingle; their oldest boy was apprenticed to a fisherman and often came home with a few mackerel or a salmon; and their second son, Fiachra, was the junior postman. But that still left six young ones under ten, and Patrick who was twelve.

As Grace walked slowly down the cobbled street, Charlie McKenna came out of the thatched post office, ready for his second postal round of the day after sorting out the letters with Nancy O'Flaherty, the postmistress.

'Nothing for the O'Hares, Charlie?' she asked. 'Save you the spin out – I'm meeting Tilly off the bus?'

'No, Gracie, still nothing.' Charlie looked sympathetic; he knew that Tilly and Mary O'Hare were anxiously waiting to hear word of their brother and son, Alfie, who was in Paris, fighting the German powers of occupation of that city. Or at least they hoped he was, and not already captured by the Germans or something awful like that. Charlie added comfortingly, 'There's no postal service to speak of out of the occupied places these days, so he probably can't get word out.'

'I'm sure you're right, Charlie,' she agreed, praying that was true.

'I'd say the letters from America are disrupted as well,' he added, now leaning over the pram and delighting Odile by shaking the little wicker rattle Declan had made, with the dried berries inside. 'Though Peggy Donnelly heard from her brother in Boston today, so it's hard to tell which ones will make it across or not.'

The postman said this last part very kindly, but Grace felt a stab of sadness. She had been hoping the reason she'd not got a letter from

Richard Lewis, only a telegram to say he'd got home safely, was because of the battle in the North Atlantic, so it was hard to hear there were others getting through. She understood why Charlie had let her know; it was better to be prepared if Peggy mentioned it. But it still hurt.

She'd almost collapsed with shock when Richard arrived out of the blue in Knocknashee a few weeks ago with his friend Jacob Nunez, handed Odile to her and Tilly, then left again three hours later to get his ship back to the United States. His telegram had arrived a week afterwards, saying he would write soon, so she'd waited and waited, but nothing ever came.

She'd repeatedly gone over those few hours in her head, when he'd sat in her house and then walked with her to the beach to see the spot where she'd thrown the bottle containing her first letter into the sea. It had been like a dream, it was all so strange, and sometimes she was sure she'd imagined the whole thing. He was even better looking in real life than in his photos, and he'd said the same to her – that she was more beautiful than her photo. But everything had been so fast, so rushed, it was impossible to know if he seriously liked the look of her or was just being nice.

Probably just being nice, given her bandy leg and the way she wasn't quite five feet tall while he was a six-foot athletic young man. She could picture him now, running long-legged across the beach towards the bus, where Jacob Nunez waited impatiently for him to board the bus.

Her last sight of him, the sun in his blond hair.

And now he was back in America and might as well be the man on the moon in terms of how far he was from her. Not just geographically but in every way. He was like a bright star that shone, and she'd got to sit in his glow for a while, but then he was gone.

'So I'll see you later, Grace,' said Charlie, taking his bike from where it leant against the post office wall and slinging his leg over the crossbar. He was thoroughly recovered from the shingles now. 'Will you come over for a bite with myself and Declan later, before the two of ye look over the new books that arrived for the teaching course? I have a couple of rabbits I snared earlier and carrots and potatoes from the garden.'

'I will, Charlie, sounds lovely.' She smiled. 'And I'll bring over one of the Madeira cakes Dymphna brought up to me earlier.'

She and Charlie's son, Declan, who was a year older than Grace and taught the senior children in the two-room school where Grace was headmistress, were starting a correspondence course in September, with a tutor called Miss Harris who was based in the Drumcondra Teacher Training College in Dublin. It wasn't unusual in rural schools for teachers not to be officially certified, but Grace felt it was important to read up on the theory as well as learn from experience, and it would mean Declan could earn a better wage as a qualified teacher. At the moment he was being paid as an assistant teacher and would never be able to afford a wife and family – though he always claimed not to be interested in any of the girls who chased after him, swooning over his brooding dark looks.

As the postman cycled away, Grace limped on through the village square, leaning on the handle of the pram. A few of her pupils were using sticks to knock conkers, as they were called, out of the big horse chestnut tree, then stripping off their prickly green coats and making holes in the burnished nuts with a nail and a hammer to thread them with string. They would then do battle with the conkers, whacking them off each other while trying to crack the opponent's. Knuckles got a right walloping in that game, and she'd been scared to play it as a child, but Tilly had had a twelvie, which meant a conker that had smashed twelve of her opponents' offerings. Nothing scared Tilly.

As soon as the Angelus bell rang out from the church, they would be called home for their tea, but until then the children were making sure to enjoy the last week of the summer holidays.

Two little girls from the infant class, May O'Shaughnessy and Dearbhile Deasy, were sitting at the side of the road plaiting daisy chains to wear as necklaces. Another group had made squares on the ground with twigs and were playing hopscotch, while a swarm of boys raced up and down the cobbles after Patrick O'Flynn's football. Patrick had got that ball for his tenth birthday and had passed it down to his younger brothers. It was a treasure for the whole village, where a real leather ball was a rare sight.

'Hello, Miss Fitz! Hello, Odile!' chorused several of the boys and girls when they spotted her coming with the pram, rushing across to coo over the baby. Mikey O'Shea, eight years old himself now, leant over the pram, swinging his conker on a string, grinning as Odile tried to grab at it.

'Is that a tooth coming through?' Áine Walsh gasped, pointing at the bud beginning to poke through Odile's lower gum.

'It is, Áine, and isn't she being good about it?' said Grace. 'She's not complained once.' And it was true. Odile was such a funny, sunny little thing most of the time, though she had a fiery temper too. When she was hungry and didn't get her bottle soon enough, she could be heard two parishes away.

Patrick's younger sister, Máire, stroked the baby's round cheek with her finger. '*Is leanbh álainn thú*, Odile,' she said. Odile gurgled in agreement, and all the children laughed.

'Sure, listen to her,' said Mikey. 'She'll be talking in no time.'

'She will,' agreed Grace.

Though she wished there was someone in the village who could speak French as well as Irish to Odile. The O'Hares had let everyone believe Odile was Alfie's daughter. Nobody questioned it, because Alfie was so unpredictable and wild – nothing about him could shock anyone, not even him marrying a Frenchwoman called Constance and sending their newborn baby home to be minded while they stayed in Paris to fight the Germans. Sergeant Keane, a decent man, had called up to the farm and said technically the baby should have some paperwork or something. But he said he understood about the Emergency, and that if Mary O'Hare, who knew all about herbs and had cured his wife of a terrible cough, said her son was the baby's father, then that was good enough for him.

But Odile's real father was a Parisian Jew called Paul Dreyfus, who was married to Constance's sister, Bernadette. And when the French couple came to find their baby after the war, which would take some explaining in itself, it would be hard on them if their child spoke only

Irish, and maybe a bit of English if she'd got as far as going to school...
though surely the war wouldn't go on for another five years?

She walked on, but when she got to the bus stop outside the
undertaker's, it was deserted. She had arrived with time to spare, and
Bobby the Bus was usually at least half an hour late anyway, so she
pushed the pram on down the street past the shops so Odile wouldn't
get bored. The baby didn't like to be still.

Bríd Butler came to the door of her sweetshop as Grace passed.
She also exclaimed over the new tooth and insisted on giving Odile a
tiny spoonful of strawberry ice cream, making the infant coo with
delight.

'Mrs Butler, you'll spoil her. She's too young for sugar,' protested
Grace mildly.

'Ara, Miss Fitz, a little bit of ice cream is good for the teething. And
sure isn't it full of real strawberries and cream? As healthy a treat as
you can get. And thank God we have local milk and fruit here – it
means I can get past the rationing for lots of the ingredients.'

All the businesses and shops were suffering with the shortages,
though at least in the rural areas, there were fresh vegetables, meat,
fish and milk to be had.

'Will Mr de Valera keep us out of the war, do you think?' Grace
asked. Looking at Odile and thinking about the baby's parents in
France, sometimes she had doubts that staying neutral was the thing
to do.

Biddy O'Donoghue joined in the conversation from the door of
her grocer's shop. 'Well, with petrol and everything else rationed and
tax gone to seven shillings in the pound, we're in it after a fashion
anyway. But the English are scared stiff the Germans will do a deal
with the republicans and we'll have Germans here and England will
be facing them on two sides.'

'It's awful, isn't it?' asked Grace. 'I keep thinking about those girls
in Campile in Wexford last Monday.'

"'Twouldn't do you good, so it wouldn't.' Biddy· shook her head.
'They thought first that 'twas because the creamery there was
supplying butter to British soldiers, but now they're saying it was just

that the Germans were running out of fuel and needed to drop the bombs to get home, without a thought who might be under them, even though we're a neutral nation, much to the vexation of that other *óinseach…*'

Grace didn't need clarification that the 'other *óinseach*' was Winston Churchill. In Biddy's book, there wasn't a hell hot enough for the British prime minister.

Bríd had glanced up anxiously at the clear blue sky as Biddy spoke, and Grace looked up too. Could a German bomber fly over them and drop a bomb, either on purpose or by accident? It had happened in Wexford, so maybe.

'More lies from London. The Germans wouldn't do that. It's so close to Wales there, the pilot might have thought he was over Pembroke,' said Pádraig O Sé, joining in the conversation as he made his way to his cobbler's shop. He was one of those who considered England's enemies to be his friends and didn't like to think the Germans would deliberately drop a bomb on Ireland.

He'd been especially outraged when the *Irish Times* tried to tell men how to join the British Army in a way that sought to outfox the government censor. An anonymous contributor wrote that he'd been told there was a nudist colony in Belfast, at 72 Clifton Street, and men were queuing up to become members. Upon arriving there, he described stripping down completely, and 'then we, nudists, filed out and along the coconut matting to the stairs. At the top, five doctors set to work to test our fitness for His Majesty's forces!' Of course 72 Clifton Street was a British Army recruitment office, and the newspaper was rapped sharply on the knuckles for publishing the address under the pretence of telling a funny story.

All of the Irish newspapers were subject to the government's say-so on what could be printed these days. The country was divided between those who were on the British side and those like Pádraig who saw 'England's difficulty as Ireland's opportunity', so T.J. Coyne, the Controller of Censorship, insisted that all coverage stay clear of the controversy, which meant the press had become very sparse on detail and circumspect on opinion about what was happening.

Grace had learnt a lot more about the progress of the war from Richard's previous letters and the clippings he sent her when he was reporting for the *Capital* from Paris, before the Germans invaded. It was another reason she wished he would write; he had a real knack for telling the story of the conflict through the eyes of those actually living it, making you feel like you were there.

'Hello, Grace!'

It was Declan, his voice snapping her out of her reverie as she walked on. He was coming uphill towards her from the direction of the strand, and he had a pretty girl on his arm – Bridie Keohane, Nancy O'Flaherty's niece, who was usually so light on her feet she could dance like a butterfly but at the moment was limping badly and leaning on Declan.

'Hello, Declan, hello, Bridie. Goodness, what's happened to you? Did you hurt your foot?'

'I did, and it's fierce sore, Grace,' said the girl in her sugary voice.

'I was down for a swim,' said Declan, 'and Bridie appeared on the strand just as I was getting out of the water. Then she slipped and twisted her ankle on the rocks, so I'm helping her home.' His indigo-blue eyes creased in a warm smile as he stopped in front of Grace, his damp dark hair curling slightly over his pale, lightly freckled forehead.

'I don't know what I'd have done if you weren't there,' simpered Bridie, gazing up adoringly at him. Bridie had set her cap at Declan and made no bones about it, finding all kinds of reasons to hang around him, flirting outrageously; it didn't at all surprise Grace that Bridie had managed to find herself on the beach just as he was coming out of the water.

Not that Bridie was the only one. All the local girls had their eye on Declan. He was a fine catch, especially now that his pale face had lost the brooding darkness that had hung over him when he first came home from the reform school in Letterfrack. These days he was relaxed, serene and calm, with a sardonic and quirky sense of humour.

'Where are you off to with the little boss?' He tickled the baby and made her giggle, while Bridie pouted and fidgeted and seemed to forget which ankle was sore.

'Just as far as the church. We'll light a candle and then back up the hill to meet Tilly off the bus. Odile will only get restless if I don't keep moving.'

She walked on with a wave and a smile, leaving him to the mercies of the lovelorn Bridie, who clearly planned to have him bring her all the way to her father's farm on the far side of the village. John Keohane had a fine few acres that would all be coming to Bridie as the only child, and maybe she was hoping the sight of so much land would melt Declan McKenna's heart towards her and encourage him to propose.

And why wouldn't he marry her? Grace asked herself as she walked on past the parochial house. Bridie was very pretty, and she would have money, even if Tilly did say the girl was 'too sweet to be wholesome'. But Tilly was an unusual person and believed in straight talking; she was not the sort of girl to flutter her eyelashes at anyone.

Outside the church Father Iggy was standing in the sunshine with his hands behind his back, the afternoon light twinkling off his bottle-top spectacles. When he saw Grace, he came over.

'Hello, Father Iggy,' she said, happy to see him.

'Well, 'tis yourself, Grace, and young Miss Odile. She's growing every time I see her, God bless her.'

'Indeed she is. She's a sweet little thing, though, so long as she gets her own way.'

'Ah sure, that's women for you.' The priest winked to show he was joking as he dangled his rosary beads in front of Odile.

'Oh, we won't listen to that talk, will we, Odile? And women running every house in the parish?' She smiled at the priest as she shielded her eyes from the bright sunlight. 'We were going to light a candle. We're waiting for Tilly off the bus.'

'Righto, in with ye so, and say a prayer for me while you're there. God knows I need it.' He put his rosary beads back in the pocket of his soutane. Grace knew he kept a few toffees in there too and wondered if Odile would still be here when she was old enough to get one. The

276

children would crowd around him as he walked down the street in hopes of a treat.

She and the baby went inside, and Grace lit the candle, whispering prayers for her parents, for her sister Agnes and then she said a special prayer for Odile's parents, Paul and Bernadette.

When they emerged into the sunshine once more, Father Iggy was still outside. 'I'll join you in the walk if you ladies don't mind?'

'We'd enjoy it, but if it's a message you need doing, I'm happy to save you the trip?'

'I need the exercise, Grace,' said the chubby little priest, patting his waistline. 'I'm a bit too round again now that Dymphna is our house-keeper. She keeps on baking these wonderful cakes, God bless her. Sure only last week Pádraig O Sé said to me, '"Twould be quicker to climb over you than walk around you these days, Father." I can't understand how Father Donnchadh manages to stay so thin.'

Father Donnchadh Lehane was the new curate. He was nice and tried to help out where he could, but he lived on his nerves and was very timid. Father Iggy had confided in Grace that the curate was an only child who was much cosseted by his mother, and he'd got a terrible shock when she died and his very religious father sent him off to the seminary at ten years old.

'But I think Father Lehane has a bit more colour in his face these days, Father Iggy?'

'Ah, he does. Dymphna has been wonderful for him in other ways than food. She understands grief and talks to him a lot about his mother, and she tells him how sad her children were when her Tommy died. Talking of which, I'm thinking of having a little cere-mony and wondered what you might think about it?'

Grace smiled. 'I'm no expert on religious matters, Father.'

'But you have a warm heart and a good head on your shoulders, which I sometimes think is every bit as good,' Father Iggy reassured her. They were true friends, Grace and the priest, and it was a big part of the reason the town went along so harmoniously now.

When Canon Rafferty was the parish priest and Agnes Fitzgerald ran the school, Knocknashee had lived in terror, with the children being beaten daily and terrorised parishioners being denounced in the canon's snaky, whispery voice from the pulpit every Sunday. Now that Agnes was dead and the bishop had moved the canon to a parish in Tipperary, and Father Iggy was in charge of the school board and Grace was headmistress, it was as if the pall of fear had been lifted off the village. Even the bad-tempered Pádraig O Sé was in a better mood these days.

'So what were you thinking, Father?'

'Well, I've a notion to bless the *cillín* and say a requiem Mass for the repose of all the souls buried there. I know a lot of them are not known to the people of the parish, but some are, and in particular I was thinking of Dymphna and her children. I know God has taken Tommy to himself. Our Lord understands the terrible pain he was in when he died, but I think it would help Dymphna a bit if I blessed his grave here on this earth.'

Grace felt a huge rush of affection for the brave little priest. He was so different from the apologetic curate he'd been when he arrived, bullied and put down by Canon Rafferty; he was a more confident man now in lots of ways. But he'd never become arrogant, never lost that personal, caring touch he'd always had, and it showed in how he wanted to help Dymphna heal her broken heart.

When Tommy O'Connell walked into the sea, leaving a note saying how sorry he was, the canon had refused Dymphna's husband a funeral, saying those who took their own lives died in a state of mortal sin and therefore could not be laid to rest in consecrated ground. So Tommy was buried by his neighbours in the *cillín*, the unofficial graveyard that had served for centuries as the final resting place for unbaptised infants, new mothers who died before being churched, beggars, strangers and anyone the Church deemed unworthy of a Catholic burial.

'I think that's a wonderful idea, Father,' she said, feeling tears prick her eyes. Dymphna was slowly recovering now from her awful loss, but for a long time she had looked so careworn and tired; grief, financial worries, the shame that some people – including her own mother in Dingle – had made her feel about the way Tommy died had all taken their toll.

Father Iggy nodded, satisfied. 'Sure I don't know if it's strictly Church protocol, but I can't imagine the bishop would mind, as long as we don't make a big thing of it.' He chuckled. 'And sometimes 'tis easier to ask for forgiveness than permission if you know what I mean.'

'I know exactly, and it's a good, kind thing for you to do, Father. Like you said, I'm sure God has Tommy at his right hand already, but it will be a great comfort for Dymphna.'

As they strolled past the draper's shop, Grace noticed Peggy leaning on her counter, absorbed in reading a letter. She looked up with a smile. 'Hello, Miss Fitz! Hello, Father! Isn't it a lovely day? My brother in Boston has written to me. He went down to Florida for his holidays. Do you know there are alligators in America? Grace, that dress is lovely on you!'

'All thanks to you finding me the material, Peggy.' Grace smiled, feeling another pang about Richard's lack of correspondence but able to hide it, thanks to Charlie forewarning her.

'Sure it was in the back room for years. It was either you or the moths,' lied Peggy, with an airy wave.

'It's getting away!'

The swarm of small boys who had been playing around the square earlier was rushing towards them; someone had kicked the football too hard, and it was bouncing down the cobbled street towards Grace and the priest. Quick as a flash, Father Iggy trapped the ball with his right foot and, with a cry of triumph, took off. His soutane was blowing in the wind as he raced towards the square, dribbling the ball in front of him, holding up his black robes, pursued by whooping children, their young clear laughter ringing out around the village.

It was so good that Father Iggy was the head of the school board now instead of Canon Rafferty. When the canon used to come to check her pupils' catechism, they would sit in terrified silence, afraid to move a muscle in case they got beaten. But when Father Iggy came in, which he did almost every day to do lessons with anyone who needed extra help, all the children clamoured to tell him what they'd been learning. He even taught a bit when he had time, his personal passion being history.

He'd had the older ones enthralled last term when he told them that his uncle was Monsignor Michael Cullen, who was secretary to the archbishop of Dublin at the time of the Easter Rising and there when Count Plunkett had come to tell the archbishop that he'd been to see the pope in Rome, to inform him the Irish were going to rebel against their English occupiers. Benedict XV had asked if there was any other way, but the count had told him there wasn't. The children hung on every word as Father Iggy explained how his uncle went up to deliver the count's message to the archbishop. He was ill in bed, only seeing his doctor, so the Monsignor had no choice but go down to the GPO where the rebellion had begun and hear the confessions of the Irish heroes of the revolution who wanted to die as good Catholics.

Sweet, kind Father Iggy was loved by the children before he told that story, but afterwards he took on hero status, to be so closely connected to such powerful princes of the Church and State.

Grace was still smiling as the Dingle bus passed her, Bobby the Bus being nearly on time for once. There must have been no funeral wakes being held in any of the houses he passed on the way for him to stop at to 'pay his respects' and finagle his usual glass of whiskey.

Chapter 2

Before Grace could push the pram the last few yards uphill to the bus stop, Tilly had already jumped down, as lithe and athletic as ever, her haversack slung across her back. Grace envied her friend her agility, feeling very slow and cumbersome by comparison.

'Hello, Aintín Grace, hello, Odile, *a chroí*,' cried Tilly as she strode towards them. She was dressed even more unusually than normal, with a beautiful wine-coloured fedora on her head and a black velvet jacket over her men's trousers and shirt. Her dark wavy hair had grown a little and was now at her jawline, and it shone like the conkers the children knocked out of the big horse chestnut tree.

'Well? How was Dublin?' Grace asked.

Tilly swept Odile up out of the pram and held her towards the sky as the baby squealed and kicked excitedly. 'Ara, grand altogether. They're sweet kids, but why anyone would want so many, I'll never know. Odile's quite enough work for me! Anyway, do you see this beautiful hat I'm wearing – wait till I tell you! An amazing thing happened on the train from Dublin to Dingle...'

'Do you want to come over to my place for a cuppa and a slice of Madeira cake while you tell me?' suggested Grace as Tilly paused to tuck the giggling baby back into her pram. 'Dymphna made some for the priests and brought a spare one up to me. She was giving out that she'd had to use lard and not butter because of the rationing, but you wouldn't know – you have to try it.'

'No, I'll come for it tomorrow. I'd better get home to Mam – she made me promise not to dally when I got back but bring Odile straight up to the farm. It makes me laugh how that child has Mam wrapped around her little finger. She dotes on her. I don't know what we'll do when her parents turn up.'

'I don't know what I'll do either,' said Grace wistfully. She really loved Odile and was delighted that Tilly had decided they were both the little baby's aunties. Though if Alfie did marry Constance, then Tilly really would be Odile's auntie while Grace would still be just an honorary one. It was hard to have no family of her own.

Well, she had her brother, Maurice, who was a priest in the Philippines, but she'd kind of given up on him. She'd been only a baby when he was last in Knocknashee, and all she'd heard from him during her life was his twice yearly Mass card saying he was praying for her, and what was the point of that when he didn't even know her.

She'd sent him a long telegram after Agnes died, asking him to write, but all that had come in the post was another Mass card.

'Ara, we'll jump off that bridge when we come to it, and by the looks of things, nobody will be going anywhere for the foreseeable if Herr

Hitler gets his way,' said Tilly, in her usual careless way. 'Will you walk with me as far as the turn up by the cemetery? Or is your leg tired after pushing the pram around? I can take Odile from here if you're wrecked?'

'No, it's grand. I'll come that far with you, and I'll push the pram if you don't mind – it actually helps to lean on the handle. And I want to hear the story of what happened on the train.'

But the story had to wait, because Father Iggy joined them again on the walk back down the hill, puffing and out of breath and wanting to know about Dublin, and Tilly had to tell him all about Marion's six stepchildren, and the baby girl of her own she'd had last Easter, and the new baby she was already expecting that was going to be called Alfie if it was a boy.

The Angelus bell rang out over the town and the bay, and they bowed their heads for a moment in prayer.

Father Iggy made the sign of the cross. 'Well, goodbye then, and see ye at Mass tomorrow,' he said cheerfully, then trotted off, rubbing his hands in expectation of a delicious dinner of three pork chops with apple sauce, followed by blackberry tart. It was a far cry from the days when Kit Gallagher fed him and Father Lehane on half a mackerel each and no dessert.

'So, Tilly, finally, what was this amazing thing that happened on the train?' Grace asked as they walked on.

'Well...' Her best friend's eyes sparkled. 'I was just sitting there reading that latest book by Radclyffe Hall, *The Unlit Lamp*, the one Jacob gave me from Sarah – he'd put his photograph of Alfie and Constance inside it, remember?'

'Of course I do.' Tilly and her mother had been delighted by the sight of the handsome Alfie sporting a week's worth of stubble, with his arm around his girlfriend, who had a wide, charming face, dark eyes and a small, pert mouth. The picture was framed now and sitting on the mantelpiece up at the farm.

'Well, this woman on the train saw me reading it and –'

'How're ya, Tilly?'

Tomás Kinneally, who had the farm beside the O'Hares', had been drawing seaweed from the shore with a donkey and cart as fertiliser for his land, but he had stopped at the turn to the cemetery and waited for them, staring at Tilly unashamedly as she and Grace approached with the pram. The silly little man was short and bald, but he had half a notion of Tilly, even though he was deluded if he thought she'd look sideways at him.

'Grand, Tomás. That's a fine haul you got there.' Tilly nodded at the piles of seaweed.

'I could spread a bit in your top field if you want?' he offered, eager as a puppy.

'If you've it going spare, I'd be delighted,' she said carelessly.

Tilly worked the farm singlehandedly and accepted help from her neighbours, and she in turn helped them; it was how it was done around here. But Grace was still surprised when she accepted Tomás's offer – the foolish farmer might read something into it. Sure enough he continued to hang around, favouring her with his goofy smile, which made him look even worse because it showed his two missing front teeth.

'Well, goodbye, Tomás,' Grace said firmly. 'I'm just having a chat with my friend Tilly here.'

'I can wait…'

'*Slán abhaile*, Tomás, we'll be ages yet.'

'Well, *slán*, Miss Fitz, Tilly.' The little man's shoulders slumped as he went reluctantly on his way, leading his old grey donkey up the stony lane. His and the O'Hare farms were beyond the cemetery, on the side of the rocky hill that gave Knocknashee its name, the hill of the fairies.

'You shouldn't encourage him,' she admonished Tilly as he passed out of sight.

'I'm not!' Tilly grinned.

'Well, letting him spread seaweed on your fields is…'

'A new form of flirting? God, Grace, you need a social life, girl.' Tilly gave her a friendly shove. 'What Bridie Keohane does with Declan, now *that's* flirting. I think you need to put poor Declan out of his misery. You know he'd drop Bridie like a hot spud if you gave him the slightest encouragement.'

She laughed. 'Oh, stop that, Tilly.'

Her best friend teased her all the time about being some kind of femme fatale and Declan being mad about her, but it was only old *rawmeis*. She and Declan were friends, nothing more. He'd had a whole trip to New York and back to say any different, and he never had.

'Now, go on and tell me, what happened with this woman?'

'So...' Tilly looked like she was going to burst with excitement. 'She started talking to me about the book – she knew it, and she'd read *The Well of Loneliness* as well – and asked me where I got it when it was banned, which I didn't even know it was, and I explained about Sarah Lewis. And then she introduced herself. Her name is Eloise, she's Swiss. She moved to Dublin at the start of the war and teaches German and French and Italian, because apparently the Swiss speak all three, imagine. And she's an amateur photographer as well – that's why she was on her way to Dingle, to take pictures of the coastline because she heard it was beautiful.'

'She sounds very interesting,' said Grace, thinking she'd never seen Tilly's eyes shine in quite that way before.

'Oh, Grace, she's not just interesting, she's so... She's not like anyone I've ever met. She was wearing trousers, and she admired my jacket – I bought it in Dublin. And this is her hat. She gave it to me as a present because she said it went with the jacket – wasn't that so generous of her? And it looked much better on her than it does on me. She's beautiful, tall, taller than me, and slim, with short wavy blond hair and the most amazing blue eyes. She grew up in the Alps, so misses the mountains. Her family were farmers, so she was really interested in our farm. And Grace, you won't believe this, but she wants to visit me. She has to go back to Dublin after Dingle, but she said she'd come back down here as soon as she can.'

'Well, that will give everyone something to talk about!' The arrival of a tall, multilingual Swiss woman would surely be a source of fascination to the people of the town. Richard and Jacob had only been here for three hours, and the place was still whispering about it. 'And if she does visit, maybe you could get her talking a few words of French to Odile?'

Tilly nodded eagerly. 'Good idea. And she will come, I'm sure she will, and I did warn her about everyone staring at her, but she didn't bat an eye. She said she's from the same kind of place, small and rural – people there are as curious about strangers as they are here. We talked about it for a long time, coming from places like this. We always think foreign places will be so much more...I don't know... advanced or something, but it's just the same. Now' – Tilly took the pram from Grace and pointed it up the hill – 'the sheep need tending and the spuds won't dig themselves, so me and my little apprentice here better get going. Are you sure you'll be all right walking home, Grace? I can bring the horse and trap back down to you, if you want to wait?'

'Not a bit of it. I'll see you tomorrow.'

'You will, and we'll have more time. God knows what state the place above will be in while I've been gone.' Tilly picked up the baby out of the pram again and waved her tiny hand, saying in a high voice, '*Slán*, Aintín Grace!'

Grace waved back. '*Slán*, Odile! *Slán*, Aintín Tilly!'

'*Slán*, Grace.' Her best friend settled the baby down again and raised her own hand in farewell as she pushed the sturdy pram up the steep rocky road.

As Grace went slowly home, she noticed that even after all the walking she'd been doing, she wasn't limping too badly. Not as badly as Bridie Keohane, anyway – that was, when the girl could decide which ankle she had twisted. And it wasn't just the new calliper. Her leg had been so much better since Declan had built her that little bath house with a tank and combustion chamber to heat up the water so that she could have warm baths to ease the pain from her polio. The contraption had been turf-fuelled at first but now ran on gas, and recently the local hotel had him install four of them for the guests, and a hotel in Dingle was interested now. Between his work at the school and making hot-water tanks and now Bridie, Grace hoped Declan would have enough time for the teacher training course once they got started.

She was really looking forward to having dinner with him and his father this evening, then unwrapping the big parcel of books that had arrived yesterday morning, tied up in brown paper and string, that they'd kept until today to open because she was busy minding Odile.

She thought the two of them studying together would be nice, and she hoped Declan would too. It was always more enjoyable to do that sort of thing with company.

Chapter 3

ST SIMONS ISLAND, GEORGIA, USA

THREE WEEKS EARLIER

Dear Grace,

I'm sorry it's taken so long to write; it's been a crazy time here. I have so much to say, so much to ask you, that I almost don't know where to begin. Sometimes I think us meeting in Knocknashee like that was a dream. Was I really there? Did that actually happen?

I want to say that you are even more beautiful than I imagined...

With a groan of frustration, Richard balled up the sheet of notepaper and fired it into the wastebasket near the foot of the wicker sofa in the conservatory.

This was not how it was with him and Grace, stuck for words, trying to find a way of saying what he meant. Usually he spoke openly, freely, from the heart. But the basket on the floor beside him full of crumpled paper told another story. He reached for the open bottle of beer on the table at his elbow and tilted it to his mouth.

What did he want? That was easy. He wanted to tell her how she was the most wonderful girl he'd ever known, how meeting her in person in Knocknashee a month ago was the best thing to ever happen to him. He desperately wanted to say that he loved her.

So just do it, he chided. *You call yourself a writer, so write down what you feel.* But instead he stumbled and stuttered over the words and tore up each effort in exasperation.

When he had first laid eyes on her, it had been like electricity. He was almost certain she had felt the same.

But what if he was wrong? On the beach he'd asked her about her time in New York with Declan McKenna, and her gorgeous face had lit up and she'd said in her soft voice, 'It was amazing.' Amazing. That word was burnt into his memory. Did she mean the city or the man? If it was the man…

No, don't risk it, better to remain friends, to be there for her always, not force her into a decision that can come to no good either way.

If he told her he loved her and she said she loved him too, she would have to abandon everything she knew to be with him – her home, her friends, her teaching career, everything she valued – for a life of danger. Because he couldn't give up his job as a war reporter. He and Jacob were heading to England as soon as Lucille, who ran the office at the *Capital*, could find them tickets.

And on the other side of it, if she didn't feel the same way about him but was in love with Declan, how could they keep writing to each other? Everything would change. They would never be able to be easy and open and honest with each other again.

With a heavy sigh, he put the beer down and pulled the notepad towards him once more, resting it on his thigh as he reclined on the conservatory sofa.

Dear Grace,

It was lovely to meet you in Knocknashee. I will treasure the memory always.

How is Odile? I'm sure she's thriving under the expert care of Tilly and her mama. How the poor kid survived my and Jacob's poor ministrations, I'll never know, but somehow she did.

I haven't received any communication from the Dreyfuses or from Alfie.

Please let me know if you hear anything. And write anyway, even if you don't.

As I telegrammed, Jacob and I got home safe, despite a couple of U-boat warnings.

The ship was hugely overcrowded with us Americans, cots placed up on deck, five and six people in two-bed cabins, people squashed in everywhere and almost everyone just grateful for the ticket home. One lady, a fur-clad, bejewelled old matron, demanded a better cabin and refused point-blank to share. She was given short shrift by the stewards, and three other girls were put in with her. Jacob and I had no cabin at all, but we took cots on the deck, and while it was cold at night, it was fine; we just muddled through.

Kirky, our editor at the Capital, was glad to see us—well, as glad as he is about anything—and he actually gave us a backhanded compliment about the articles and pictures we sent back. He said they connected well to the common American, so "we weren't as dumb as we looked" even though "you, Lewis, in your fancy clothes, clearly have no idea how the common man lives." And I thought I was dressed in ordinary clothes! Jacob says it's because I snuck off to spend the night in the St. Regis so I could get them ironed, while he insisted on sleeping with the bedbugs in some god-awful boarding house.

One thing we did agree on—we have asked Kirky to send us back, this time to England. We've suggested an illustrated weekly column about people trying to live their ordinary lives in wartime—schools, food, transport, hospitals, government, we'd cover everything. He knows from when we were in France that we have a knack for getting people to open up to us, and he knows readers like it, so in the end, it wasn't too hard a sell and eventually he agreed. Of course, he called us "dumb, foolhardy kids" and accused us of "tryin' to be heroes," among other things, but I think he's a little bit proud of us too.

Now deciding we want to go and actually getting there are two entirely different things. It's not easy, but Lucille, the scary woman in the office who sorts out everything, is working on it, so now we have to just wait. Germany has blockaded Britain completely, so getting in or out is very difficult. But Lucille knows the British ambassador and thinks she can persuade him to help us find a way. She says that anything that encourages American inter-

vention, like sympathetic reporting from the front lines, goes down well with the limeys.

Meanwhile I've been doing a piece on hurricanes—it's the season for them here. We had a pretty bad one just recently, fourteen-foot waves, millions of dollars of damage all the way from Florida up the coast to the Carolinas. Charleston and Savannah got the worst of it. I've been talking to the people whose property was damaged or destroyed, and they say they're sure the hurricanes are getting worse, though why that would be, I don't know.

But as interesting as hurricanes are, local reporting is not enough for me anymore. I feel like I got a chance at life in Europe, and it's whet my appetite.

Things are sure heating up over here on the subject of the war. A general of ours, Pershing, came on the radio to encourage people to support aid going to Britain. He said democracy and freedom were under threat worldwide, that Hitler and Mussolini had overthrown liberty, and that if America was to send help to Britain, as she stood alone, it was the best way of keeping the war on that side of the Atlantic. But then on the same day, Lindbergh, the famous aviator, spoke at a rally against getting involved, claiming we need to strengthen our military so nobody can invade us, and if we stay out of foreigners' business, nobody will have any need to come after us.

He's singing from the same hymn sheet as Ambassador Joseph Kennedy, who is always saying Britain doesn't have hope, which plays right into the isolationists' hands. I hear that Randolph Churchill, Winston Churchill's son, said, "I thought my daffodils were yellow until I met Joe Kennedy." Apparently Kennedy is very ambitious politically, but I can't see how he can recover from this, unless he sends his own sons to war or something.

Jacob hates people like Lindbergh and Kennedy. He almost got us black-listed by Gideon Clarendon last week, the editor of the Savannah Morning News, *and he'd commissioned a picture spread about the annual regatta of the Savannah Yacht Club. While we were there, Jacob said something along the lines of he thought the whole thing was stupid and self-indulgent and people should open their damned eyes and see what's going on in the world instead of dressing up like peacocks and swigging champagne. Well, the recipient of this speech was the commodore's wife, and she almost combusted in indignation. So you see, if we can't get him back to Europe, he'll have to find a different profession, 'cause he sure is burning bridges over here.*

I thought Sarah would be mad at him, but she wasn't. He's made her much more radical these days. She cares deeply about politics and far less about money. She has learned to drive—not very well, admittedly—and has taken a course in first aid. Like Jacob and me, having been over there and having seen the war with her own eyes, she says she can't just sit here in America doing nothing, she has plans of her own, she's itching to do something meaningful. Though I'm not sure she knows what exactly—she doesn't say...

He stopped and looked up in surprise at the roar of a car whose gears were being ground mercilessly. It accelerated up the solitary road to the house and skidded to a halt outside. Moments later someone's feet rattled up the front steps and around the side of the wooden wraparound porch, and Sarah stormed in through the double glass doors of the conservatory.

He could tell she was fuming as she threw herself into the wicker armchair near the foot of the couch and reached for the remains of his beer. Her brown eyes were dangerously bright, her mop of dark curls hanging unkempt to her jaw, her red long-sleeved dress rumpled from the long drive.

'What's up?' he asked mildly.

She exhaled through her nose and shook her head. 'Our mother is such a pill, Richard. Truly, how did we draw such a short straw? I swear I can't stand her, I can't.'

Richard waited patiently to find out what their mother had done now. Only Caroline Lewis possessed the skill to get under Sarah's skin like this. She'd hurt Richard too, deeply, but she didn't make him want to throttle her the way she did his sister. It was as if their mother knew the exact buttons to push to have Sarah explode, and then she would condescendingly demand that Sarah control herself.

'I was summoned there for lunch – you know how she does – and she launched right in. How irresponsible and childish we were running off to France, how you and I were raised in the lap of luxury and given every educational and financial and social advantage, and then for us to throw it all back in her face, so spoiled and ungrateful, you know, the usual.'

Richard did know. Their mother was like a broken record since they'd come back from Europe. She was mortified in front of her high-society friends that her children had lowered themselves to work for a Yankee newspaper and gone travelling around Europe with Jacob Nunez. She made no secret of the fact that she was appalled by their choice of companion. If she knew Sarah and Jacob were together, she'd blow a fuse.

She was still furious at Sarah for breaking her engagement to that chinless wonder Algernon Smythe, and at Richard for letting the beautiful heiress Miranda Logan slip through his fingers. The two most eligible young socialites in Savannah were married to each other now, and Caroline Lewis was always harping on about their 'perfect' marriage. Richard would never betray his ex-girlfriend by telling his mother this, but Miranda was already so bored with Algy, she had taken a lover to keep herself amused – a Costa Rican man who never talked about yachts.

Sarah lived in the family home when she wasn't with Richard in St Simons and so she was obliged to put up with their parents, but he often wondered why he continued to go back there whenever he was summoned for Sunday dinner. Maybe it was because of how his father had secretly followed him out of the house that day, after Richard had announced he was going to France, and had shaken his hand and wished him luck – all out of the hearing of his wife. Not that Arthur Lewis had shown him any open affection since; he just sat there eating moodily while their mother harped on.

'There's no point in reacting, Sarah. You know what Mother is like. She's trying to goad you.'

'No, this is different.' Having drained his beer, she leapt up and strode to the drinks cart, where she made herself an enormous gin and tonic. 'You?' she offered, waggling the Waterford Crystal glass at him, clinking with ice cubes.

He shook his head. 'How?'

Sarah took a wedge of lime from the bowl Esme had set out earlier beside the crystal decanters and glasses and took a long sip of her cocktail. 'She started saying awful things about Jews. You should have heard her – she'd make a good Nazi. She said how Jewish bankers were trying to drag us into this war for their own profit, and they wanted to impose socialism on everyone, and no wonder everyone hated them.'

'Really? That's a bit strong, even for her.' Richard could now see why Sarah was so upset. After all they'd heard for themselves in Paris about the way the Jews were being treated, it must have been very hard for her to hear this from her own mother.

'I mean, how can bankers be socialists? She doesn't even make *sense.*' Sarah fumed as she added more neat gin to her half-empty glass. 'Imagine what Jacob would think if he knew my mother was capable of coming out with stuff like that. I had to get out of there. You're sure you don't want one of these?'

'I think I probably do, after that. So you stood up and left? Good for you.' He usually deplored his sister's penchant for the dramatic, but in this case, he thought it fully justified.

Sarah fixed his drink, her back to him as she delivered the next bombshell. 'Yes, but not before I told her that Jacob and I are a couple.'

'You did *what?*' He sat bolt upright. 'A couple in what way?'

'I told her that we are in love. I'm sick of lying about it.' She handed him the drink and threw herself back into the wicker armchair with a triumphant smile.

'Oh, God… You didn't… But what did you say exactly?' He prayed she hadn't admitted to sleeping with Jacob. She'd never even admitted it to him, though it was obvious.

'The truth! That we were living as man and wife in Europe, and I love him, and that if she can't accept it, then that's unfortunate but it won't be changing.'

'Oh, God…' Their parents would be horrified to think their daughter was sleeping with anyone, let alone a Jew. No doubt this would be brought down on his head now too. There was nothing they could do to Richard – he had already been cut off by them financially following his refusal to follow his father into the bank – but he'd always felt a bit guilty about turning a blind eye to what Sarah was up to. It wasn't fair, but the rules for men and those for women when it came to sex outside of marriage were completely different. 'What did they say?'

'Mother went all quiet and her eyes went cold like an alligator in the swamps, and then she ordered me out of her house and told me never to set foot in it again, so basically I've been disinherited, disowned and banished.'

His heart sank. Sarah might be more serious about life these days, but she still had no idea what it was like to live without access to money. She had been raised a princess, in a gilded cage of privilege. In Paris she'd been strong and resilient and able to rough it, but that had been a one-off adventure, not a way of life.

'Did Mother really say she was cutting you off? In those words? What did Father say?'

'Nothing. Didn't need to.'

He thought rapidly. 'Maybe they'll come around if you got engaged at least.'

'Don't you get it?' Her eyes flashed furiously. 'I don't want to lie any more, and I don't want their money. I don't want *anything* from our parents, ever again.' In her temper she kicked off her handmade leather sandals so that they skittered across the floor, landing in two different corners of the conservatory. Tomorrow morning, Esme, the housekeeper who had minded them since birth, would pick the shoes up and leave them in Sarah's room, and Sarah wouldn't even notice that there were people around her paid to keep her life smooth and easy and clean.

He said, half to himself, 'Well, at least they can't touch your share in this house or your trust fund from Grandma.'

'Exactly. And you're managing just fine on your trust fund, aren't you?'

'Yes, though...' He winced and sipped at his drink.

His sister might have forgotten, but the sum in his and Nathan's trust funds from their grandmother was four times that in hers. As a privileged society girl, the assumption was that she would marry well and have no need to buy herself anything other than a few lunches out or trips to the theatre with friends. Plus both he and Nathan worked – and what could Sarah do?

'I know what you're thinking,' she said sharply, 'and I know it's a lot less, but I won't be crawling to you for a handout. I can earn my own money. I know you and Jacob are just itching to get back to Europe, and when you go, I'm going with you. I can afford the ticket from my fund, and I'm going to ask your editor to pay my expenses as a translator.'

He was taken aback. 'You want the *Capital* to pay your expenses?'

She bridled. 'And why not? Just because I'm a girl, is everything I do supposed to be for free? No, Richard, when we're in New York, I plan to meet your editor and I'm going to tell him face to face how much I contributed to your and Jacob's work because I can speak French and German and Italian.'

Richard winced at the idea of Sarah confronting the hard-bitten editor, who already thought Richard was too much of a 'posh boy'. What would he make of the entitled, demanding Sarah Lewis? 'I don't know, Sarah. Kirky's a tough nut to crack. He's a very cynical man...'

Sarah scoffed and tossed her dark curls. 'The point is, your "Kirky" is a man. No man is a tough nut to crack, not for me. And men aren't cynical around women – they're always trying to impress us on some level. Speaking of which...' She looked down into the wastebasket between her chair and the foot of the sofa, poked in her hand and stirred the crumpled papers. 'Dear Grace, Dear Grace...' she read, then tutted at him. 'So you still haven't gotten up the courage to tell that Irish girl you like her? Because I know you do. Jacob said you went all starry-eyed when you met her – he thought it was hilarious.'

Ruefully, Richard shook his head. 'Well, I'm not going to lie, I did like her, yes. But no, I think it's better to leave it. That McKenna fellow she went to New York with is much better suited for her.'

Her eyes flashed again. 'How do you know, for God's sake? And how dare you make that decision for her? Just write and tell her and let her make her own mind up between the two of you.'

'It's not that simple.' He already regretted talking to her about it.

Sarah was not like him. She charged into every situation all guns blazing and asked questions later.

'It *is*, though. Stop second-guessing her, stop taking her choices away. Tell her the truth. She'll either accept you or reject you, but whichever way, you'll know and you can get on with your life. And so can she.' She stood then and came over to him, placing her hand on his shoulder, speaking more gently. 'If this war is teaching us anything, it's that nobody is guaranteed a future, so if you love her, just be brave. You never know – it might just pay off.'

He sighed. 'I don't know.'

'It's good to be honest. You'll feel better. Now that it's all out in the open about Jacob with Mother and Father, I finally can breathe. By the way, I refuse to stay at the hovel' – it was what she called the apartment Jacob shared with a bunch of misfits – 'so I'm going to call him now to come here to live with me. Is that OK?'

'Of course it is, yes.' But his heart sank. If their parents turned up and Jacob was staying here...

'And then I'm going to find Esme and tell her he's moving in. And don't worry, I'll pretend to her he's staying in Nathan's room as usual, because while I don't care what our parents think, I do love Esme and I don't want to scandalise the poor woman. Now write your letter, and for God's sake, mail it right away. And use the public mailbox on the boardwalk so you can't change your mind and fish it out again.'

She dropped a kiss on his head and was gone, and moments later he could hear her on the phone in the hall, and after that greeting Esme in the kitchen.

Picking up his fountain pen, Richard began again.

Dear Grace,

I've written this and rewritten it around fifty times, so this time I'm just going to say what I feel and hope you don't run screaming.

Meeting you was wonderful. I loved it. You are everything I've dreamed and more, and I curse that bus for pulling me away so soon after I arrived in magical Knocknashee. I wish I'd had the guts to tell you that I love you and that meeting you in person was the best thing that ever happened to me.

I don't know how close you and Declan are—maybe you're only good

friends. Or maybe I have no right to say these things, but I have to. I love
you, Grace. I've never felt about anyone in my whole life the way I do about
you, and if you'd have me, I'd move heaven and earth for us to be together.

If you don't want that, I'll accept it and never mention it again, but please
don't cut off our friendship. Just write back something cheerful, like you
never got this letter at all.

Yours with all my love,

Richard

He folded the letter and stuffed it clumsily into an envelope – he
was all fingers and thumbs – smoothed it, addressed it, stuck stamps
to it and went out the double glass doors onto the wraparound porch,
then down the front steps into the garden. At the gate he walked
straight past their family mailbox, the one where you could put the
flag up to indicate outgoing mail and where he could easily take the
letter out again before the collection tomorrow – something he'd
done several times already. Instead, this time he took his brave, foolhardy sister's advice and walked down the boardwalk that overlooked
the Atlantic Ocean to where there was a public mailbox. Refusing to
allow himself time to ruminate and hesitate, he threw the letter in, his
heart pounding.

There. It was gone. She would get it, and his fate was in the lap of
the gods.

* * *

LATER THAT EVENING he sat in the large comfortable den, where the
wingback chairs were upholstered in light-blue silk that their mother
had had shipped from France especially to complement the pale-
green art-deco scroll sofa. 'Eau de Nil' she'd called it and he and Sarah
had sniggered at her trying to sound French. On the floor, covering
the walnut floorboards, was a Chinese silk rug in blues and aquas.
This house, like their family home in Savannah, had been decorated
with no expense spared.

Sitting in one of the armchairs, one socked foot tucked up beneath him, he tried to read a book, but nothing could keep his attention. The letter in the mailbox wouldn't be collected until tomorrow. In his mind it pulsated and glowed like a coal.

In the car that pulled up outside the house, its headlights sweeping past the curtains of the den, he assumed was Jacob. Like Sarah, the photographer had learnt how to drive on returning from Europe, because he never again wanted to do a bus journey like the four-day trip they had taken across Ireland to Knocknashee. He'd bought himself a very rusty second-hand Ford, nothing like Sarah's natty green two-seater, but he still had to keep it hidden down a side street from his roommates, who considered all property to be theft.

Above his head Richard could hear his sister's footsteps coming to the top of the stairs, and he decided to stay where he was, not to get in the way of their reunion. The person crossed the hall to the door of the den and opened it. Richard looked up in surprise to see his father standing there, the perfect Southern gentleman, in his cream linen suit, with a pocket watch and white fedora. For all that he was as rich as Croesus, Arthur Lewis had the common touch and could speak to a farmer in battered overalls as easily as a head of state. It belied his sharp mind the way he peppered his speech with Southern colloquialisms, and though she would never reprimand her husband, Richard remembered how he and his siblings would suppress a smile as their mother winced when their father said 'goshdurnit' or addressed them collectively as 'y'all'.

'Ah, Father, hello. I...I wasn't expecting you.'

His first thought was to reach for his shoes, embarrassed for his father to catch him lounging in his socks. His second thought was *Why is he here? Has he come to order Sarah home? This is going to be awful, and what if Jacob turns up in the middle of the fight?*

'Will you have a beer, Father?' he asked calmly.

'Thank you, Richard, I will.' Arthur Lewis took a seat on the art deco sofa.

Richard rang the bell and Esme appeared. 'Esme, can you get my father a beer please? And one for myself.'

'Right away, Mr Richard.'

'Thank you, Esme.'

'Thank you, Esme,' Arthur Lewis added warmly. He was always courteous when he addressed the help. His mother wasn't rude to them – that would be uncouth – but she was cold.

While the housekeeper fetched the beers, the two of them sat in awkward silence; the clock on the wall ticking loudly was the only sound. He and his father were not chatty at the best of times, but this felt excruciating. Upstairs all was silent. It seemed his sister had disappeared back into her bedroom and was keeping out of sight.

A minute later the housekeeper returned with a tray of glasses, ice and two bottles of beer already cold from the refrigerator, which she set down on the table between them before leaving the room.

Richard leant forward, stretching out his hand to the tray, glad of something to do. 'Shall I pour a glass for you, Father?'

'Not at all.' To Richard's astonishment, Arthur Lewis – a stickler for manners and doing things the right way – took one of the cold beers and swigged a mouthful straight from the neck. Setting the bottle back on the tray with a bang, he wiped his moustache with his silk handkerchief and asked, 'Well, Richard, can you call your sister now?'

Oh, God. 'Well, sir, I, er...'

'There's no reason to pretend she's not in this house. I saw her at the top of the stairs when I came in. Just call up to her, and let's get this over with.'

With a sinking heart, Richard stood up and crossed the room where he opened the door into the hall. Sarah was hovering at the top of the stairs, listening. Silently he beckoned to her. She scowled and looked nervous, and seemed about to retreat again, but then got up her courage, stuck out her chin and descended as proud as a painting he'd seen of Mary, Queen of Scots, on her way to execution.

As he turned to walk in front of her into the den, she swept past him. 'You wanted to see me?' she snapped at their father, with no trace of deference or respect.

Richard touched her arm from behind, murmuring softly, 'Sarah...'

She shook him off. 'There's no need to stay, Richard. I don't need my little brother to stick up for me or tell me how to speak to my own father.'

Arthur Lewis was on his feet. 'That's true, Sarah, but I still want to see both of you, if you don't mind, please. Richard, will you stay?'

'Ah, yes, sir, of course.' Was it his imagination, or was something different in his father's demeanour? Did he seem less forbidding somehow?

If so, Sarah hadn't noticed; she was as belligerent as ever. 'If this is to ask me to apologise to Mother, then you've had a wasted journey. The things she said were unforgivable –'

'I agree. I'm here on my own behalf, not your mother's.'

She stopped mid-flow, taken aback. Then jumped straight back on her high horse. 'Daddy, I know Jacob isn't what you had in mind for me, and Mother said the most appalling things, but I won't give him up.'

'Did I ask you to, Sarah?' He was using his mild, reasonable manner, the iron fist in the velvet glove that had gotten him so far in the cutthroat world of private banking.

'No, but I assume it's why you're here,' she retorted, but Richard could hear a softer note in her voice. Out of their parents, she liked their father better; they were the most similar, both extremely clever but also pig-headed and authoritative in the way they spoke.

'Shall we sit down?' Arthur Lewis indicated the wingback chairs. Sarah took one and Richard the other, while he resumed his seat on the sofa opposite.

'I know you're both wondering why I'm here…' He stopped, swallowed, cleared his throat, reached for the bottle on the tray and took another swig of beer. 'And no doubt you'd rather I wasn't.'

Sarah met Richard's gaze with raised eyebrows.

Richard, equally puzzled, had a thought – was their father nervous? Surely not. Arthur Lewis was normally as emotional as a clam; nervousness was just not part of his make-up. Sometimes Richard wondered what he felt about this man. He hadn't been a tactile or loving parent, he was always working, and besides, he was too well dressed to risk getting dirty playing games with his children when they were little. But he was reasonable and generous, they'd wanted for nothing, and he had never once beaten them or even raised his voice. Now that Richard thought about it, he'd never done much to interact with them either way, negatively or positively.

Noting that neither of them had contradicted his last statement, Richard's father allowed a small smile to play around his lips under his bushy moustache. 'So,' he went on, 'I'll get straight to the point. A lot of our boys, and maybe even our girls, are going to get caught up in this European business in the coming months, and maybe even years. Roosevelt is going to let us be dragged in one way or another.'

The siblings let their father speak, falling into the old habit of being passive listeners as he pontificated about the political situation, even though they were the ones who had been on the front line.

'And I fear you two are stuck in it already.'

Again a statement, not a question, so they stayed silent.

'And I just wanted to say' – he inhaled and fixed first Richard and then Sarah with a searching gaze – 'that I am very proud of you both. Your mother is upset. She thinks you are in danger, or were, and will soon be again, and that comes out as...well...madder than a wet hen.' He gave a little chuckle. 'But I think you are both brave young people, and I'm proud of you.'

Richard felt a rush of warmth for his father, the little boy in him so glad to be praised, and opened his mouth to say something. But the other man held up his hand.

'Not yet, Richard, I'm talking.' But he said it with another small smile, like he knew well what he was like. 'What I want to say is, I'm a self-made man, I didn't inherit anything.' He waved his hand around the opulent room to suggest his origins were humbler than this, that it was his wife's taste in this room. Arthur Lewis's background was not a topic ever discussed. Caroline Lewis came from old money and preferred to let it be thought her husband was the same. The Lewis grandparents were dead long before Arthur moved to Savannah, so there was nobody to refute the impression – except possibly Uncle

Harold, but he was *persona non grata* now that he lived with a married Catholic woman on Tybee Island.

'I arrived at Harvard, not broke but not far off it, I won a scholarship and because I was smart and I could hold my own in social situations, and I worked my way up as fast as I could, met your mother and married well.' He glanced again around the house, which their mother laughably called a summer cottage when it was in fact a very substantial home. 'Your grandmother on your mother's side left her wealth to you children, because I insisted on making my own money. Your mother trusted me. I built my way up to running my own bank. And though Caroline would like you to follow in my footsteps, Richard, and I would too, I admire you for taking a stand and doing what *you* want to do. You've both got more guts than you can hang on a fence. Sarah, you could never be stuck with that limp rag Algernon Smythe, and I'm glad you refused him.'

'You are? Really?' Sarah was incredulous.

'Yes really. Look, what I know about journalism doesn't amount to much more than a hill of beans, but I know grit when I see it, and you two have it in spades.'

'Thanks, Father, that means a lot.' Richard finally got a word in edgewise, but his voice was choked and came out almost inaudible.

'It means a lot to me as well,' said Sarah, more clearly, her cheeks pink with pleasure. 'I'm glad you see I've been working, Father, and not just being a parasite like I would be if I'd married Algernon Smythe or kept relying on you for money.'

'Sweetheart, you would never be a parasite, it's not in your nature.' Their father stroked his moustache solemnly as he regarded her. 'And I just want to say that your mother might well be talking about cutting you off and all of that – she's sure got her tail up now – but I won't be, and contrary to what she might think, I'm still wearing the pants in this family.'

'I don't need your money, Daddy. I'm going to get the *Capital* to pay my expenses this time around –'

He cut her off with another wave of his hand. 'You are my daughter, Sarah. Both of you are my children. And I am sure you will earn your own money doing whatever it is you do, but my resources, my connections and my support are always available, so never land yourselves in trouble or misery for lack of funds. My wallet is open to you both, always.'

'Oh, Daddy...' She stood and walked to him then, and he pulled her down beside him on the sofa and put his arm around her.

'I know you're fixing to get back there, so you two watch out for each other now, you hear me? And don't go doing anything downright stupid. There's no point to being all hat and no cattle, as they say in Texas. Just you watch yourselves over there, and that Jacob Nunez guy too.'

She moved out of his embrace to stare at him in amazement, and he placed both his hands on her shoulders, studying her face.

'I do understand about love, Sarah, believe it or not. When I first saw your mother, I knew she was the one for me, even though she was so far above me on the social scale, it felt impossible. I decided she would be mine, and I charmed her until she agreed, and I still feel the same way after all these years. If this man Jacob Nunez has wooed and won you, despite your differences and the snobbery of Savannah high society, if he truly is your choice, then he's got to be some man, because it's not every man who would have the courage to take you on.'

There were tears in her eyes. 'He is a good man, Daddy, I promise, and he wants to marry me. We're waiting until he can go into his uncle's business after the war.'

'I trust you to do what's best, sweetheart.' But he looked mightily relieved.

Richard wasn't sure he trusted Sarah to do what was best. He wasn't convinced of Jacob's attitude regarding the jewellery business, or of Sarah's attitude about marriage, but they'd cross that bridge when they came to it.

'Thank you, Daddy,' she said softly.

'So you both take good care, you hear me? I do not want to get a telegram saying some German put a bullet in my child, am I clear?'

'Clear.' She snuggled against him.

And then for the first time that Richard could ever remember, his father opened his arms to him as well, beckoning him over for a hug. Richard went to him, sat on his other side, and for a long few minutes, Arthur Lewis, the unemotional banker, embraced his son as well as his daughter.

To READ ON CLICK HERE: History's Pages - The Knocknashee Story Book 3

ABOUT THE AUTHOR

Jean Grainger is a USA Today bestselling Irish author. She writes historical and contemporary Irish fiction and her work has very flatteringly been compared to the late great Maeve Binchy.

She lives in a stone cottage in Cork with her lovely husband Diarmuid and the youngest two of her four children. The older two come home for a break when adulting gets too exhausting. There are a variety of animals there too, all led by two cute but clueless micro-dogs called Scrappy and Scoobi.

ALSO BY JEAN GRAINGER

Last Port of Call

The West's Awake

The Harp and the Rose

Roaring Liberty

Standalone Books

So Much Owed

Shadow of a Century

Under Heaven's Shining Stars

Catriona's War

Sisters of the Southern Cross

The Kilteegan Bridge Series

The Trouble with Secrets

What Divides Us

More Harm Than Good

When Irish Eyes Are Lying

A Silent Understanding

The Mags Munroe Story

The Existential Worries of Mags Munroe

Growing Wild in the Shade

Each to their Own

Closer Than You Think

Chance your Arm

The Aisling Series

For All The World

A Beautiful Ferocity

Rivers of Wrath

The Gem of Ireland's Crown

The Knocknashee Series

Lilac Ink

Yesterday's Paper

History's Pages

Made in United States
Troutdale, OR
02/11/2025